Praise for Denise Patrick's
Gypsy Legacy: The Duke

"This is a fabulous tale of true love, murder, betrayal, and mayhem in merry old England! What a treasure of a story! Plan on having enough time to finish because when you start reading, you will not want to stop!"

~ *Susiq2, Ecataromance Reviews*

Rating: 5 Cups "This is wonderful story that shows women where not the downtrodden creatures often portrayed. ...Ms Patrick's book is made realistic with not only the strength for the main characters. But the support and influence provided by the secondary characters bring the whole thing together."

~ *Hollie, Coffee Time Romance*

Look for these titles by
Denise Patrick

Now Available:

The Importance of Almack's

The Gypsy Legacy Series
Gypsy Legacy: The Marquis (Book 1)
Gypsy Legacy: The Duke (Book 2)

Gypsy Legacy: The Duke

Denise Patrick

A Samhain Publishing, Ltd. publication.

Samhain Publishing, Ltd.
577 Mulberry Street, Suite 1520
Macon, GA 31201
www.samhainpublishing.com

Gypsy Legacy: The Duke
Copyright © 2009 by Denise Patrick
Print ISBN: 978-1-60504-302-9
Digital ISBN: 1-60504-182-3

Editing by Lindsey McGurk
Cover by Natalie Winters

First Samhain Publishing, Ltd. electronic publication: August 2008
First Samhain Publishing, Ltd. print publication: June 2009

Dedication

For Tina, Amy and MaryAnn. You gals are the best. Without your comments this book might still be sitting on my computer where no one except myself might have ever read it.

To my children, Chelsea and Chuck, who survived the neglect and flourished without, or maybe in spite of, me. And, lastly, to my wonderful husband, Gary, who puts up with me and my obsession.

I love you all.

Prologue

June 1861

Thane Park, Devon

The interior of the gypsy *vardo* was dim—the aroma of herbs and wildflowers hung in the air. Sixteen-year-old Felicia Collings hesitated, allowing her vision to adjust, while taking in the familiar surroundings—the bench covered with a bright multi-colored cloth, the shelves crowded with gaily colored jars filled with potions and herbs, the small chest at the front, its intricately carved surface depicting a variety of animals and birds and the small open window allowing in the cool morning air. Nona, her great-grandmother, occupied the small bunk, propped up against a mound of brightly colored pillows.

Despite her age of eighty-plus years, three years ago Nona had still been a vibrant and commanding force among her small band of gypsies. All the same, time seemed to have caught up with her, reducing her to little more than a very old woman with thinning, snow white hair. The lines in her face were etched deeply, but her dark eyes, sunk deep into their sockets, were still sharp and alert, and her voice was strong as she beckoned Felicia forward.

"Come and sit, little one."

Heartened by the strength of her voice, Felicia sat on the low stool beside the bed. Next to Nona, on the faded blue coverlet, sat a small open chest.

"I do not have much time and I tire easily these days, but I have something for you," the gentle voice reached her.

"You should be resting and saving your strength. Should we summon a doctor for you?"

9

A ghost of a smile lightened Nona's features for a moment. "No, child. A doctor cannot cure age. But let's not speak of that. How are you faring, now that your brother has returned?"

"Tina did not tell you?"

The smile surfaced again momentarily. "I did not ask her. She would not have been an unbiased source."

"Why?"

"Because he is her destiny." Nona held up her hand as Felicia began to smile broadly. "But you are to say nothing. This is something she must discover on her own."

"Spoilsport." Felicia pouted good-naturedly. "Very well, no mention will cross my lips."

"Good." Nona's approval warmed her. "Now, I have something special for you."

Felicia watched as Nona lifted the small box and rummaged through it, coming up with a ring on a chain, then handing it to Felicia. "It is yours."

"Mine?" Felicia examined the ring. It was a slim gold band with an alternating pattern of sapphires and amethysts across the top. She slipped the ring off the chain and tried it on her ring finger. "It's too big," she complained.

Nona nodded, as if expecting it to be. "For now. But, someday it will fit. Until then, you will wear it with the chain."

"Someday?"

"Yes. Someday you will meet the one who can tell you the history of this ring. He is your destiny. You must not wed any other."

Shock kept Felicia still. "But how am I supposed to know him?"

"Your eyes will know."

"I will not even make my debut for another year and a half, and now you tell me I must wait for someone who will recognize this ring. I have already told my brother I want a duke."

Nona's smile brought a twinkle to her eyes. "And you shall have one. But you will need patience and it will be rewarded with sun-ripened wheat and highland heather."

Felicia shook her head, unwilling to tell Nona she'd only been jesting. Her great-grandmother often spoke in riddles when she gave advice. Why didn't she just come out and tell her what she wanted to know?

She sighed. "Very well, but I will come back and ask next year. Then you will have to tell me more."

Nona raised sorrow-filled eyes to hers. "I wish that I could, but it is not to be. I have given you this now, because I will not be here when you will need it."

Felicia was suddenly aware of the unhealthy pallor in Nona's wrinkled face and the thinness of her hands and arms.

"Death comes to us all," Nona said in understanding. "But it is not unwelcome. You will be happy and content. It is all that I would have wished for you."

"But, Nona..." Felicia's voice clogged with tears.

Nona sighed. "All will be well, although we will not meet again. You must be strong for others will depend on you. Now, I must rest. Do not forget what I have told you."

Felicia nodded, holding back the tears. Leaning over, she kissed the crinkled, paper-thin skin of Nona's cheek.

"I won't." She slipped the ring and chain into the pocket of her riding costume. "I love you, Nona."

"I know, little one. I love you too."

Chapter One

April 1864

London

"I'm sorry, my lord, but my answer is still no."

A light breeze moved across the terrace, disturbing the ebony curls resting against Lady Felicia Collings's temples. The cool night air, however, was not the reason she felt a small shiver go through her. No, that was caused by the intense, almost desperate look in Lord Caverdown's eyes as she turned down his third proposal of marriage.

"Why?" His voice was low, but the demand was obvious.

"Because I do not feel we would suit." She edged slightly away from him, toward the ballroom door.

"You should not dismiss me so cavalierly."

"I am not. I thought I made myself perfectly clear on the two previous occasions. Asking again will not change my mind." She half-turned toward the door. "I would like to return to the ballroom."

He said nothing, but merely continued to stare at her with a look she could only describe as distaste. She shivered lightly again. If he disliked her, why did he want to marry her?

The answer didn't matter, since she did not want to marry him, but she wondered at his tenacity nevertheless.

"Lord Edward is not likely to come up to scratch." His voice had a hard edge to it.

She faced Lord Caverdown again, exasperated. "I do not expect him to."

Disbelief was clearly written on his face.

"Everyone knows Lord Edward has only one ambition. A wife would only hamper him," she said.

"Ahh, but Parliament no longer allows the purchasing of commissions."

"That, my lord, is none of my concern, as I have no intention of marrying him."

"You will regret this."

Frustration welled up inside her. Why was it men reverted to spoiled little boys when something didn't go their way? She had nothing against Lord Caverdown. She just didn't want to marry him.

"Will you escort me back, or shall I return alone?"

The intensity in his golden eyes cleared and a moment later he gave her a short bow and offered his arm.

"I apologize if I have offended. I will trouble you no more on the subject."

Felicia couldn't believe he had become a different person right before her eyes. Gone was the rejected suitor who had nearly threatened her. In his place stood the handsome and charming dance partner she had accompanied around the floor many times. How *did* he do that? But, more to the point, why did his ability to do that make her uneasy?

Entering the brightly lit ballroom, they were met by a whirlwind in blue silk.

"There you are!" Lady Amanda Cookeson nearly pounced on her. "Come with me. I need your help."

She turned to smile at Lord Caverdown. "If you will excuse me, my lord."

"Of course." He gave her another short bow, then turned and walked away.

"Now, what is wrong?" Felicia asked Amanda as the two of them hurried in the other direction. "Has something happened?"

"Not really," Amanda answered, glancing back over her shoulder.

"Then why are we leaving? Edward will be looking for me for the next set."

Amanda shook her head, setting her golden curls to dancing. "No he won't. His mother arrived a few moments ago."

Felicia said no more as they strolled down a hallway lined with doors. Finding a sitting room unoccupied, they slipped inside. Felicia locked the door while Amanda lit a lamp.

Collapsing into one of the chairs by the fireplace, she let out a long breath. Amanda dropped into a chair opposite.

"Did Caverdown propose again?"

"How did you know?"

"You have a long-suffering look about you whenever one of your admirers proposes and you tell him no. Why do you think I came along when I did? Besides seeing the duchess arrive, I suspected when he asked you to walk with him that he was going to press his suit again. I'm glad you continue to refuse him. He's nice on the surface, but he makes me nervous."

"Did Edward send you to find me?"

"Not really. But, he did mention to me that you were his next partner. I think he assumed I'd tell you."

Felicia chewed her lower lip thoughtfully. Lord Edward's mother, Emily Waring, was the Duchess of Warringham. It was no secret she didn't like Felicia and had accused her of trying to trap Edward into marriage. Although friends, she and Edward agreed they needn't annoy his mother by being seen together. She knew he was protecting her against his mother's dislike, so at times like this, they kept their distance from one another.

"You're probably right," she said absently.

Amanda nodded. "And you should forget Lord Caverdown too. He's only after your dowry anyway. Eliza says he has connections in the French court, but there's some scandal in his background. It happened before she was born, so she doesn't know much about it, but she says the older people haven't forgotten because it involved an earl being convicted of treason by Parliament and stripped of his title."

Felicia laughed. Amanda's stepmother, the Countess of Barrington, seemed to know everyone, and Felicia wasn't surprised she knew about scandals that happened even before she was born.

"He's jealous of Edward."

Amanda's laughter echoed off the high, frescoed ceiling. "Edward? Why that's..."

"Preposterous? Of course, but he doesn't believe it. Like

everyone else, he thinks I'm out for a duke, and Edward's the closest there is."

Amanda's blue eyes sparkled. "Hmmm. That might be true if Grandpa would acknowledge him as such. But, since he won't, Edward's out of luck."

"Actually, he's in luck. We've been through this before. Edward does not want to be the next Duke of Warringham. I wish his mother would leave him be—and me too. I've never done anything to her."

"It's not your fault, you know. Edward knows he's to blame for her unrelenting hostility toward you. If he hadn't told her he was going to offer for you, she probably would have just ignored you." Amanda sighed. "Life would be so much easier if his brother would just show up."

Felicia agreed. Lord Edward Waring was the third, and youngest, son of the Duke of Warringham. The current Duchess of Warringham, Edward's mother, was the duke's second wife. His first wife had given him three children, of which Amanda's stepmother, Eliza, had been the youngest. The two oldest boys had vanished from the ducal seat over twenty years ago, and despite an exhaustive search, no trace of them was ever found.

A number of years after their disappearance, a gypsy purportedly told the duke his oldest son was still alive and would return someday. Since then the duke clung to the gypsy's words, steadfastly refusing to acknowledge Lord Edward as his heir. Even now, with his health failing, he was certain his oldest son was on his way home. And, although no one would express the opinion to her face, there were many who secretly thought the duchess had somehow been involved in the older boys' disappearance.

A rumor had surfaced not long ago which said the duke received a letter from his oldest son. The duchess, however, had confirmed the rumor about the letter by insisting it was a hoax. And a cruel one at that. Whenever it was mentioned in her hearing, she insisted someone was being deliberately callous by trying to keep a false hope alive.

Felicia didn't know whether it was true or not, but she had no interest in Lord Edward beyond the fact that he was Amanda's stepmother's brother. The problem was that the duchess, while insisting that Edward was his father's heir, was also very controlling. And Felicia, with her unusual background, was not considered suitable company for Edward, much less wife material. Of course, Edward had never followed through on his ridiculous comment, so she hadn't the chance to turn him down and thereby show the duchess she was not after him or his supposed title.

The truth was she didn't want to marry anyone. But she knew better than to let information like that out in public.

She'd never told anyone she didn't intend to marry. Her siblings all thought she was diligently searching for the person who could identify her ring. While she wouldn't discount the possibility such a person existed, the likelihood of her finding him, in her book, was slim to none. Which suited her plans nicely, because the ring was the perfect excuse to her brothers each time she refused an offer.

Two weeks later

The *Gypsy Star* pulled smoothly into the designated berth in the harbor. At the helm, Brand experienced a sense of satisfaction. He'd returned to England yet again, this time for good. This last voyage had spanned more than a year, and he'd sailed nearly around the world, buying and selling cargoes as he went. The ship's hold was filled with silks, spices, gold, silver, ivory, and jewels. There were also two horses—an Arabian stallion and mare purchased in a horse market in Egypt.

"McGregor!" He called to the flame-haired giant who stood on deck snapping out orders.

Casting one final look at the progress on deck, Sean McGregor turned to approach him. Bushy red hair and a full beard and mustache meant there was little to be seen of his face besides brown eyes and a small amount of sun-browned skin.

"Come with me." Brand turned to head down past the galley, to the captain's cabin.

His trunk and two smaller bags sat near the door of the large, comfortably appointed room. Sunlight streamed through the two portholes, and fell on the table bolted to the floor in the middle of the room. The captain's ledger sat open on the table, fitted into a specially carved indentation.

"You will probably be in dry dock for repairs for the next two months. I have created a list of repairs which need to be made, and some improvements that might be added. I will have Mr. Percival at the office make arrangements to have them carried out."

"Two months! I won't know what to do wi' meself on dry land for so long."

Brand laughed. "I'm sure you'll find something. In the meantime, I wanted you to know this was my last voyage. I need to return home and see to my father, so when it is time for the *Gypsy Star* to sail again, I have decided you will be her captain."

The statement rendered McGregor speechless, but only for a few moments. "Me? Captain?"

Brand smiled broadly. "I think you've earned it. You have been an admirable first mate, the men like you and will follow you, and I've no doubt as to your abilities."

Brand left the ship a short time later, McGregor's appreciation and gratitude ringing in his ears, and headed for the shipping offices. London's docks were crowded and noisy. The damp, fishy smell associated with a harbor assailed his senses as he strode purposefully toward the offices of Star Fleet Shipping. He wondered briefly where the rest of the fleet was, and did a quick accounting in his head. *Night Star* should be somewhere in America. *Diamond Star* might be in the Orient, but *Twin Star*, their newest ship, he had no idea.

The manager, Mr. Percival, greeted him warmly, showing him into an elegantly furnished office overlooking warehouses and a quieter part of the docks. They discussed the disposal of the cargo he brought back, the repairs needed to the *Gypsy Star*, and his selection of Sean McGregor to replace him as captain. Then he learned his partner and his wife were on holiday in Italy. "However, he did leave you this." The manager passed him an envelope. "And said I should tell you it was time for you to remain on dry land for a while."

Brand grinned. Just as his partner, the Marquis of Thanet, had returned home to an uncertain future three years before, so had he. He knew who he was, but he wasn't sure he could prove it.

He and his brother had been kidnapped as children. Small

and ailing, his brother died within days, but Brand was sent to a plantation in the Caribbean as a bondslave. He might not have endured, but just before he was put on the ship a gypsy approached him on the beach and told him he would someday return. His memory of his childhood, including his own name, was lost amid the work and abuse he suffered, but her words remained.

Someday you will return to your father's side.

Now, it was time. He'd briefly been in England three years ago and hired a detective to find out who he was. The knowledge stunned him, but the name had been the beginning of the return of his memory. Bit by bit over the last three years, pieces of memory returned and he now had a clearer picture of who he had been. And who he should be.

"Then I suppose I ought to take his advice and do just that."

A knock on the door interrupted the conversation. A clerk entered to inform them the Earl of Wynton was outside to see the captain. Surprised, Brand told the clerk to show him in.

Rising to his feet, Brand eagerly greeted his partner's brother-in-law. "Jon! It's good to see you again. How'd you know I was here?"

"I've had a man watching the docks for almost a month now. He was to inform me as soon as the *Gypsy Star* docked. I came straight here when I got the word this morning. Jay thought you might need help and I promised to lend whatever assistance was necessary once you returned."

Brand nodded. "Good. I could use a friend. I suppose I'm finished here for now, Percy. I will keep in touch."

Once in the Earl's coach, Brand looked down at his shirt, breeches and boots. "I suppose a new wardrobe will be in order." He stated the obvious. "But I've always hated dressing up."

The earl grinned, unrepentant. "If you plan to take your rightful place, you have little choice."

Brand stared out the small window, watching the traffic and buildings pass by. After a while, he spoke. "So, how's my father?"

"Not well, according to the rumors. Your stepmother has taken him back to the ducal seat. The word about town is the doctors have given him very little time, but he is stubbornly holding on in the hope you will return. If the gossip mill is to be believed, so are many others."

That surprised him. "Why would anyone care whether I returned or not?"

"Because your dear stepmother has declared the letter your father received three years ago was nothing more than a hoax— and a cruel one at that. She insists Edward should be the Marquess of Lofton, yet your father stubbornly refuses to allow him to use the title."

"I see. So, the gossip mill is anxiously awaiting my stepmother to be proved wrong and her darling Edward to become a mere second son?" The earl nodded. "And what does Edward think of all this?"

"Actually, Edward is anxiously waiting for you to return too."

Brand straightened, giving the earl his full attention. "Why?"

"So he can finally get out from under his mother's thumb. She has kept that poor boy on a short rein for most of his life and he is beginning to chomp at the bit. If you show up, he's off the hook."

"I would have thought being the heir to a dukedom would compensate for an overbearing mother."

The earl shook his head. "Edward's a good man, and he has stuck around because of your father, but I suspect if he inherited the title, he would be an absentee landholder. According to my sister, he would dearly love a commission."

"Your sister?"

"Felicia." The earl smiled. "She's in her second Season now. Jay and Tina brought her out last year, but this year I was left to watch over her. Thankfully the Duchess of Westover is officially sponsoring her, but I'm required to make an appearance now and again."

"You have my sympathy."

The earl's smile became a grin. "Save that sympathy for yourself. Felicia is stubborn, headstrong and has a mind of her own, but she makes the Season bearable—and she keeps the marriage-mart mamas and their daughters at bay for me."

Brand was curious. He'd met his partner's wife and she was a beauty. If her sister even remotely resembled her, she ought to be tripping over proposals right and left. "Hasn't she had any offers?"

"She's had her share of proposals, but none have appealed to her. And neither Jay nor I would force her to wed unless we felt it was in her best interests."

Reaching the earl's home, they retired to the library to discuss and create a plan of action. Brand needed not only a complete new wardrobe, but also to see his father without anyone else being aware of his presence. He might be the Marquess of Lofton, but without his father's acknowledgment, it was highly unlikely anyone would accept his word for it. As the earl noted, it was fortuitous the duchess had removed the duke from London. He could easily travel to the ducal seat for a reunion without the gossips intruding.

"I don't know how my stepmother did it, but I'm sure she was behind the kidnapping. It couldn't have been too hard to hire someone to do the job when she was conveniently away." They were settled in comfortable chairs, each sipping a drink. Light spilled into the room from two large windows behind Brand. "The trick was she had to arrange it so she had Edward with her when Michael and I disappeared."

The earl shook his head. "It doesn't make sense to me. If she wanted Edward to inherit, why didn't the men just kill both of you? Then she would have been sure of it."

Brand grimaced and shifted in his chair. "I've wondered about that too. Just last month another piece of my memory dropped into place." He took a large swallow of whiskey, feeling the liquid burn its way to his stomach. "When I was on the beach, just before they put Michael and me on the ship, I overheard some of the men laughing about being paid twice for one job."

The earl's eyebrows rose. "You don't think she paid them to kill you, but they decided on their own to sell you to slavers?"

Brand nodded. "I'm sure it's happened before. It's difficult to trust a job is done right unless you do it yourself." He drained the glass and set it down on the table beside him. "I'm sure they never expected I might return. I suppose I should be thankful for their greed. Without it, she would have succeeded."

"If there was a bright side to any of this—that may well be it."

"According to the letter Jay left me, she has apparently denied time and time again that I could possibly be alive. I would think unless she knew there was absolutely no possibility, she might have some hope—for my father's sake. The fact that she seems to continue to insist I'm not points to her guilt as far as I'm concerned, especially in light of the letter I sent three years ago."

"You may be right, but if I could make a suggestion. Be cautious. There are others involved who may be hurt by the revelations. This might be..."

The door to the library burst open and a woman breezed in. "Jon, I need your help."

Dressed in a daffodil-yellow walking dress adorned with blue ribbon, the vision brought with her sunshine and a breath of fresh air. Brand had no doubt this was the *stubborn, headstrong, with-a-mind-of-her-own* sister.

"Felicia!" Jon surged to his feet. "How many times must I tell you not to barge in without being announced?"

"Why should Higgins announce me? You're not doing anything I shouldn't see. At least, not in the library, I hope." Her smile was more potent than the whiskey he'd just finished.

Jon sighed, his frustration nearly tangible.

"Besides, I need your help. It's Davey."

Crossing the expanse of wine red carpet, she seated herself on one of the sofas and folded her hands primly in her lap.

"What about him?"

"He's been injured. I sent a footman with a message to Thane Park to find out what was wrong, but he brought Davey back to Town. I can't keep him at Westover House, so I need you to take him in until I decide what to do with him."

Either Jon had forgotten him, which Brand doubted, or he'd chosen not to make introductions. Brand suspected the latter, so he merely continued to observe the interaction between the siblings.

The Earl's eyebrows furrowed. "Injured? How?"

"At the moment, he has a broken arm. Some of the boys in the village set upon him. I know Ella would protect him if she could, but she and Daisy aren't enough and Ella's husband would be just as happy if he weren't there. I need to find someplace else for him to go."

Felicia was counting on her brother. He had always been there for her and she knew he'd know what to do.

She had been stunned when the footman, Henry, showed up at Westover House last evening with Davey in tow. She hadn't asked him to bring the boy to her—she just wanted to know how he fared. One look at Davey, however, and she knew sending him back to Thane Park was out of the question.

The inhabitants of Parkton, the village on the edge of Thane Park, never forgot that the cook's oldest granddaughter, Ella, had given birth to a bastard at age seventeen. Unfortunately, they didn't know that the child had been the product of a rape by Felicia's oldest brother, Aaron, then Viscount Collings. Aaron had been killed not long afterwards, but once Ella married the blacksmith's son and he refused to take Davey in, the boy became the target of all manner of taunts and cruelties. Left with Ella's mother, Daisy tried to protect him from the slurs and name-calling, but she was little protection.

Through correspondence with the housekeeper at Thane Park she learned Davey had been injured, and sent a footman down to find out what happened. When he showed up last night with Davey, she had been shocked. Although the bruises had begun to fade, she could tell there had been many over time. But, worst of all, his arm was horribly swollen and bruised.

Summoning a physician to attend him, she'd allowed Davey to stay the night with Henry in the Westover nursery, but she knew he couldn't stay there. Trying to decide what to do with him was difficult. She knew she couldn't send him back to Thane Park, but she also understood if she kept him with her and it got out many would speculate as to his identity and the speculation would drag her reputation through the mud. Something she could ill afford. Jon was her best hope for now.

Movement on the edge of her vision made her suddenly aware of another presence in the room. Turning, she found herself looking at the most handsome man she'd ever seen. Wide-spaced violet eyes under dark blond brows, high, defined cheekbones creating angles and planes, a sharp patrician nose over a full-lipped mobile mouth and a dimpled chin melded to create an arresting face. Skimming over his loose-fitting shirt, buff-colored thigh-hugging breeches and knee-high boots, she felt the blood rise in her cheeks as she realized he watched her with the same curiosity she extended to him. If he'd been sporting an eye patch, she would have thought him a pirate.

Jon made the introductions, and she was immediately aware of the differences between the two men. Jon's coal black hair was, like hers, inherited from their mother, his emerald green eyes from his father.

"Felicia, may I introduce Jay's partner, Brand. His ship just docked this morning."

Brand rose to his feet with an agility that belied his size. Felicia was used to looking up at Jon, but Brand seemed to tower over him. She rose to her feet as well, partly so as not to feel so small. There were times, like now, when she cursed her size. Her head just reached Brand's chin but she refused to be cowed. The dark blond hair hanging over his collar put her in mind of a lion's mane and she sensed the power he kept firmly leashed.

"I'm sorry, Jon," she said, still staring openly at Brand. Then, realizing she was being rude, smiled and held out her hand. "It's a pleasure to meet you, Mr. er..." she stumbled over his name.

Brand was instantly mesmerized by the blue-eyed, ebony-haired siren standing before him. All of his senses kicked in when she first entered the room and her soft yet husky voice drew him in. Then she smiled and held out her hand. For a moment, he forgot where he was. Taking the proffered hand, he bowed over it and raised it to his lips.

"Just Brand," he replied smoothly. "And the pleasure is all mine, my lady." Her hand was warm and soft, sending a spark right through him, and causing his heartbeat to double. It was suddenly warm in the room where a short time before he had been comfortable. His breeches were suddenly tighter and he could feel the blood rush into his nether regions as his body reacted to her touch.

"Brand." Hearing his name on her lips caused his blood to heat.

"Shall I order you some refreshment, Felicia?" The earl's voice brought Brand back to himself with a vengeance.

She turned to reply and the contact was broken. Brand let

out a breath he didn't realize he held and watched her move back to the sofa and seat herself. *Hell.* What was he doing staring at her like an untried schoolboy? What had come over him? He shook his head as he resumed his seat, moving the chair slightly so he could watch her better.

She turned suddenly as Jon moved to the door and pinned him with deep blue orbs.

"Did Jon tell you Jay and Tina are in Italy?"

"Yes, but it's unimportant, for now. So, who is Davey?"

A delicate shade of pink colored her cheeks and she dropped her eyes to her lap. "He's...uh...just one of the boys from the village near Thane Park."

Brand watched her twist her hands together in agitation. Obviously a family situation. Perhaps he should leave her and her brother to sort out Davey's fate. Because she came to the earl for help, he wondered if he wasn't eavesdropping on a private matter, but his curiosity was aroused. Having just made her acquaintance, he was intrigued enough to want to know more.

Jon returned and reclaimed his chair across from Brand.

"Perhaps we should forget the refreshments, and I should leave you two to continue whatever I interrupted," Felicia said to Jon with a glance in Brand's general direction.

"It's a little late for that. And what do you propose to do about Davey?"

"I will send him to you and you can decide. I would like, eventually, to send him to Journey's End."

This obviously surprised Jon. "Why would you do that? He's what? Eight, nine years old? Why would you want to send him there?"

Felicia's posture became rigid and Brand read defiance in every line as she answered her brother. "He's nine. And I won't send him alone, if that's what you think. But since I eventually plan to give him the property, I thought it might be nice for him to grow up there."

Jon looked at her closely for a few moments. "And when were you going to tell Jay about this decision?"

Felicia shrugged. "Someday, I suppose."

Jon grimaced as Higgins entered with a tray. Setting it on a low table beside Felicia, he inquired if Jon needed anything else.

"No, that will be all for now." Felicia also thanked the butler and helped herself to a small scone.

Brand watched Felicia nibble at the delicate pastry, his wayward thoughts imagining other uses for the enticing pink tongue he glimpsed. *Get a grip on yourself,* his conscience admonished. Perhaps now would be a good time to make his escape, but Jon's next words piqued his curiosity further.

"I suppose your future husband might have a say in the matter?"

She shrugged one slim shoulder, but did not answer him directly. Instead, she returned to her previous question.

"So, will you take Davey in until I make arrangements to travel to Journey's End?"

"Felicia, I'm a bachelor. What am I supposed to do with a nine-year-old boy?"

"It's only for a few days. I can make arrangements to leave by week's end."

"What?" Jon sat up straighter and turned narrowed eyes in her direction. "And just how do you think you'll get to this place?"

"I'll take Jay's traveling coach. It's here in London at Thane House." The glibness with which she answered seemed to indicate she'd thought about it for some time.

"I see. And were you planning on doing away with me before then?" Jon's voice had become hard.

Felicia laughed. "Don't be silly, Jon. Of course I wasn't planning on doing you in. What would make you think that?"

"It might have something to do with you taking Davey to visit a place you've never been, without a proper escort—or is there something else I don't know?"

For the first time, Brand noticed her smile falter. White teeth worried her bottom lip. The tension in the room increased. The silence stretched for a few moments, then her eyes lit up.

"You could come along too," she said brightly, rising to her feet. "Then you wouldn't have Amanda stalking your every move." Her attempt at lightening the tension only partially succeeded. "I'll send Davey over this afternoon." And with a brilliant smile which encompassed both Jon and Brand, she hurried out of the room.

Jon sat back in his chair with a groan.

Brand watched her sail out the door and knew he was grinning like a fool. She was incredible. Incredibly young and naive, that is. No woman dared to travel alone, especially one so young, and unmarried. She must have lost her mind. Still, he couldn't help but admire her aplomb, and found himself chuckling.

Jon glanced over at him and grimaced. "You're a fine one to be laughing. I should have told her who you were."

"Would it have mattered?" She hadn't seemed like a young woman who would fall over someone for a title and the earl's next words confirmed it.

"No," he sighed. "But she might have been more interested in you because she is well acquainted with the rest of your family. Amanda, her bosom bow, happens to be your niece of sorts."

"Niece of sorts? I can't imagine either of my siblings would have produced a girl old enough to be stalking you."

"She's your sister's stepdaughter, but since she considers Edward her uncle, you would probably be cast in the same role."

"And she's been stalking you?"

"Ever since she made her bow. She's a pretty little thing, but not my type. Unfortunately, she refuses to take no for an answer."

"I see."

The two sat in silence for a short while, then the earl got to his feet.

"I should inform Higgins young Davey will be arriving soon. Felicia rarely makes promises she doesn't keep. I suppose we can entertain a nine-year-old boy for a few days. I'll have to think about Journey's End."

"What and where is Journey's End?"

"It's a small property on the west coast in the Lake District. I understand she might not want the property—in fact, I don't remember her being pleased when Jay included it in her dowry. But to want to give it to Davey might be going a bit far."

"Why?" When the earl hesitated, Brand added hastily, "If this is family business, just tell me to mind my own."

Jon detoured to the sideboard and poured himself another whiskey, offering Brand a refill as he did so. Brand declined.

"It's not that—it's just...complicated." He resumed his seat across from Brand. "I'm pretty certain Jay has no idea why Felicia is so attached to Davey. Perhaps he'd agree if he knew, but with Felicia things are rarely so simple."

"I thought she was your sister. Why does it matter what Jay knows?"

"She is also his sister. My father died when I was six and my mother married Jay's father a year later. Felicia was their only child. I suppose she's closer to me than Jay, but Jay is her guardian, not I."

"And Davey?"

"Davey's story isn't pretty. I've never asked how she knew, but Felicia has told me that her oldest brother, Aaron—who is now deceased—forced himself on Ella. Davey was the result."

Brand wasn't surprised at Aaron's actions. Too often members of the nobility felt young women not of the nobility were fair game. What surprised him was that Felicia felt responsible for Davey for some reason. Although he hadn't been in England for most of his life, he knew many of the same rules applied in societies around the world and in most of them, someone in Felicia's position would have been expected to turn a blind eye—if they knew about it at all. That she hadn't ignored the situation brought forth his reluctant admiration.

Chapter Two

Felicia would have been heartened to know her brother was considering escorting her and Davey to Journey's End—if that had been uppermost in her mind as she sat across from her maid on her way back to Westover House. Instead, her thoughts were troubled by a pair of violet eyes under gold-tipped lashes.

Brand. Jay's partner. She'd heard Jay talk about him before, but never met him. Until today.

It had taken all of her willpower not to openly gawk at him as she tried to discuss Davey's fate with Jon. No man should be so beautiful, she thought with a sigh. It just wasn't fair. He'd watched her converse with Jon and she'd felt his eyes on her as if he had touched her the entire time. Just thinking of him now brought a warm flush to her cheeks and the interior of the coach seemed unaccountably close.

No man ever affected her like that. In the year since her debut, nearly every eligible male in England had crossed her path and no one affected her the way he had with just one glance.

She leaned her head back against the velvet squabs and sighed. There was something wrong with her. Perhaps she was just overwrought. Davey's appearance with a broken arm had shaken her more than she thought.

Years ago she'd promised herself she'd take care of him if Ella couldn't or wouldn't. Once she discerned his parentage, her duty was clear. She could not turn her back on her own nephew.

Her thoughts wandered back, before Davey was born. The day of his conception was etched deeply in her memory. She would never forget.

Her oldest brother, Aaron, always seemed larger than life to her. He had been betrothed to Tina, who was sixteen at the time and learning how to be a marchioness, and too busy to bother with a younger sister. With Jon away at school, she was at loose ends, and free to trail after Aaron and his friend, Rod. They didn't want a nine-year-old following them around, especially a girl, so she had become an expert at hiding herself. She wished now that she hadn't been such an expert—the day's events might never have happened if they'd known she was there.

Ella was Cook's oldest granddaughter. The same age as Tina, she was the prettiest girl in the village. Felicia spent a lot of her youth in the kitchen with Cook, and there was always something delicious for her to sample. Sometimes Cook let her knead the dough for bread, and she'd even taught her how to make scones.

Felicia never doubted her parents loved her, but with Cook and her family she felt as if she had a second family. Cook was there when she scraped her knees and didn't want her mother to know. The time she had gotten a splinter in her backside from playing in the stables, it had been Cook who had gently removed it, applied some salve and soothed the hurt. Beyond her parents and great-grandmother, Cook was the person she loved more than anyone. She wouldn't have done anything to hurt her or anyone in her family. Yet, she had and the guilt gnawed at her—rising to condemn her when she least expected it.

The sun was unseasonably bright, the day warm for late April. Felicia had spent the morning in the kitchen with Cook and Ella. They'd made scones and Cook was making a special cake for her father's birthday. It was the reason Aaron was home. Aaron and Rod usually stayed at Collingswood, the family's estate closer to London, but this week they were home to participate in the birthday celebrations. She had been glad to see him, but as usual he'd paid her little notice.

After the scones were finished, she went outside through the kitchen garden and slipped into the small stand of trees sitting just beyond the front drive. She was lounging on a large rock, enjoying the sun and reading one of her lesson books when Ella walked by on her way home. They waved at one another, then Ella disappeared into the trees. A few minutes later Aaron and Rod came by.

They seemed to be looking for something, but she pretended to ignore them.

"Carolyn," Aaron said. He always called her by her first name, even though everyone else, with the exception of her great-grandmother who used a shortened version of it, used her second name. It, therefore, took a moment for her to realize he spoke to her. When she looked up, he stood before her, haloed by the sun almost directly overhead. With golden blond hair and gold-flecked brown eyes, she imagined him as Adonis from her text on ancient Greece. Now he smiled at her and she was nearly giddy with the attention. "Did anyone come by here?"

"Just Ella."

"Which way did she go?"

"That way," and she pointed her brother in Ella's direction.

The coach swerved abruptly and threw her against the side, bringing her back to the present. She glanced out the small window and noticed the gates to Westover House. The three-story Georgian mansion built of gray stone was a welcome sight. Entering the cool, marble-tiled entry way, she inquired of the rest of the household.

The duchess was still in her rooms and Lady Weston was out, she learned from the butler. Glancing at the large clock in the foyer, she realized she had at least a half hour before luncheon.

"I'll be in the blue salon if anyone is looking for me," she said. "And would you have Henry attend me?"

Henry appeared quickly. He was one of the small staff left at Thane House while her brother and sister were away, but she kept in touch and sometimes had him run errands for her—such as with Davey.

"How is Davey today?"

"He be sleepin' right now," he answered. "He had a fever in the night, but the cook gave him somethin' an' it helped him to sleep."

Felicia nodded. There was nothing she could do for him at

this moment. Sleep was probably the best thing for him.

"Let me know when he awakens. I will be sending the two of you to stay with my brother until I make arrangements to leave the city."

"Owright, my lady."

"I may need you to go with us since I don't know to care for a nine-year-old boy."

"Tain't nothin' to it," Henry said. "Him's almost all growed up. He can do fer hisself."

After he left, Felicia took his words to heart. At nine, she had considered herself self-sufficient. A trip such as she was planning would have been an adventure. Perhaps Davey would look on it the same way.

At nine, she also learned life had an ugly side and men could be animals. Staring off across the small salon, she didn't dare close her eyes. She knew she'd once again be transported back to the stand of trees, hiding behind a large bush where she stopped after she ran toward Ella's scream.

The only person she'd ever told what she'd witnessed had been Mira, a woman in her great-grandmother's gypsy band who filled the void left by her mother's death. It had been Mira who explained to her about men and women and Mira who, after she blurted out she would never allow a man to do that to her, told her what she had seen wasn't normal; most men were gentle and the act could be pleasurable. Felicia hadn't believed her.

Years later she told her sister and brother she knew Aaron was Davey's father and Ella had been forced. She revealed nothing of her culpability, nor had she told anyone—until today—she meant to provide for Davey. It had been her way of keeping the guilt at bay. Someday she would provide Davey with the means to rise above his birth and Journey's End would do nicely.

Tina had inherited Journey's End from their great-grandfather—not directly, but through a series of coincidences. While she was undeniably happy married to Jay, Journey's End represented too much darkness and death for her. So, it had been added to Felicia's dowry.

If she married, she'd planned to insist her future husband allow her to dispose of the property as she saw fit. Since her decision never to marry, however, it no longer mattered. She would ensure that Davey eventually received it.

Geri, Lady Weston, returned from her calls shortly before luncheon. Felicia was glad of the respite from her thoughts. The morning had been all too disturbing for her, dredging up memories she only wanted to forget.

Brand spent part of the afternoon at the tailor's being measured and the rest lounging in the earl's library mulling over how he was going to travel to see his father. His stallion and mare arrived and he checked to see they were none the worse for wear.

Since he had no wish to reveal his presence yet, his self-imposed seclusion chafed at him. He did not want gossip regarding his presence to precede him to The Downs and tip off his stepmother. Tomorrow morning he had an appointment with Pymm, the detective who discovered his identity three years ago. Jay's letter informed him Pymm was making discreet inquiries about the twenty-year-old kidnapping. He hoped the detective had something to tell him.

It was more than likely Pymm would find nothing and he would have to let the whole matter drop. The perpetrators might be long dead with no one aware of the crime they committed or who hired them to do it. His best hope might be that whoever was behind it might try to eliminate him again. This time, however, he would be on his guard.

It occurred to him if, as he suspected, his stepmother was behind his disappearance, the best way to foil her plans would be to marry and beget an heir. It was a drastic step, but a plausible plan. He wasn't sure, however, about getting married so soon after his return. He had nothing against marriage, and knew he would have to marry eventually, but the timing was all wrong. The last thing he needed right now was a wife. Once he discovered what he wanted to know, and decided what to do with the knowledge, he might consider taking a wife. Until then, he planned to steer clear of marriageable misses.

A sudden vision of laughing blue eyes appeared before him and he was reminded of his reaction to the earl's sister just that morning. Shaking his head, he told himself sternly she would be the last person he'd want to tie himself to. She was far too independent, stubborn and used to getting her own way. They would never suit.

Mid-morning the next day found Felicia curled up on one of the embroidered cushioned window seats in the nursery at Kent House. Sunlight streamed through the large dormer windows, creating bright spots on the bare wood floor. Davey sat beside her, listening quietly as she read to him from one of the books they'd found. He was still subdued, as Henry told her the doctor had given him a small amount of laudanum for the pain in his arm. She wondered if Jon had looked in on him at all.

"Doc says the pain shouldn't be so bad in a couple o' days," Henry said, "but the arm would be a couple o' months mendin'. We's to keep it wrapped tight."

"Good." Then turning to Davey, she asked, "Does it hurt very much?"

Davey shook his head. He'd always been a child of few words, but now he seemed reluctant to talk at all. She had assured him he was safe, and she would not send him back to Thane Park. His solemn gray eyes sparked with interest when she suggested they explore his new quarters and she noted his obvious attraction to the stack of books they discovered in one of the cupboards.

Now she sat reading to him. The sun haloed his bright hair—the same guinea gold as Aaron's. He was quiet, though, so quiet she glanced over at him occasionally to make sure he was still awake. When she noticed his eyelids drooping, she found a convenient stopping place and closed the book.

"Perhaps you should rest for a little while. After lunch, I've told Henry to take you to see the park or the river. Which would you prefer?" Davey did not answer. "Would you like to see the horses in the stables? I know my brother has some fine ones."

She was relieved to get a response when his eyes lit up and he asked, "Really? I can see the horses?"

"I would imagine you could," she said as Henry came back into the room. She looked up and smiled. "I was just telling Davey maybe this afternoon you could take him down to the stables and see the horses."

"I'd be 'appy to, m'lady."

"Good, then it's all settled." Rising to her feet, she helped Davey up and gave him a hug. He didn't return it, but he didn't push her away either, she reasoned.

Henry took charge and she headed downstairs. As she reached the second floor landing a big, burly man with overly long dark hair came out of the library. Higgins hastened forward, handing the man a battered hat, and opened the door for him. As he turned to accept his hat, she noticed he had a patch over one eye and his clothing was slightly rumpled.

She completed her descent and acknowledged the butler with a nod. He stood impassively as she entered the library. Expecting to see Jon, she was surprised to find Brand alone, standing at one of the long windows.

For a few moments she studied him. Today he was dressed conservatively in a dark blue frock coat and gray trousers. Yet even that could not disguise the powerful set of his shoulders or the vitality he exuded. Standing with his back to her, she noted his golden locks had been neatly trimmed, but his shoulders were slumped. The air of despondency about him was nearly tangible.

Brand stood at the window, a glass of whiskey in his hand, blindly staring out over the street. Pymm had done what he could, but found little to go on. There were rumors, he'd told Brand, but none he could confirm. Most of the rumors led to men long dead. Those who were still alive remembered nothing or denied participation, and not even gold could jog their memories. In the end, he asked the detective to dig into his stepmother's background. There was probably nothing there either, but it made him feel like he was doing something.

He closed his eyes momentarily and his brother's face swam before him, forever frozen at age six. If not for the kidnapping, Michael might still be alive. His hand clenched the glass he held. Someone would pay for Michael's death. He would not give up his search for answers.

Turning from the window, he froze. Lady Felicia stood just inside the door, watching him. For a moment, they took each other's measure, then she closed the door and crossed the room toward him.

He watched her approach warily. The skirts of her light

blue morning gown swished around her legs as she walked and curiosity lurked in the blue depths. Her skin, fresh and unblemished, dared him to touch it, and he wondered if her lips were as soft and sweet as they looked. All sailors knew stories of the sirens of myth, but here was one on dry land and he was afraid drowning might be the least of his worries.

"Where's Jon?" she asked, coming to a stop in front of him.

It took a few moments for her question to register, but it shook him out of the daze he seemed to be in. Finishing off the contents of the tumbler, he put down the empty glass and moved further into the room, away from the window. It wouldn't do for either of them to be seen by a passerby.

"He's not here. He was called away this morning."

"Away?" She frowned. "Where?"

"To Wynton Abbey," he replied. "There was a groom waiting for him when he returned last evening with a report of a fire. The damage was apparently minimal, but he left early this morning to view it for himself. Said he'd be back in a week or so. He may have left a note for you with the housekeeper."

"Oh." Disappointment laced her words. She hesitated a moment, then followed him into the center of the room, where she seated herself on a settee as he took up a stance by the fireplace, one arm negligently resting on the mantle. He tried not to stare at her, but the puzzled expression on her face made him curious. He did not expect her next words. "And when do you leave for The Downs?"

The question hit him like a blow, but his reaction obviously surprised her because her own eyes widened in apprehension before she hurriedly continued.

"You and Eliza are obviously related. And since she has been hoping for the appearance of her brother for three years now, it did not take much to come to the conclusion you might be he. Of course—" she grinned impishly, "—you could tell me I haven't the faintest notion of what I'm talking about."

"I see," he said, his equilibrium restored somewhat by her grin. "And you reasoned it out for yourself?" His lips quirked and she responded with a bright smile, unaware of its effect on his temperature.

"Of course," she said. "It didn't come to me until the middle of the night when I finally realized where I'd seen eyes that unusual color before. No one who knows Lady Barrington and meets you would think anything except that you must be brother and sister. The resemblance is remarkable."

"Your brother warned me you might figure it out."

"Did he?" she asked. "Well, yes, I guess he would. No matter. Edward will be thrilled. I hope your father will let him purchase a commission now. It's all he really wants."

He stiffened and his smile vanished.

"And do my brother's wants mean so much to you?"

She frowned. "Well, yes. He'll be much happier once he has a chance to be himself."

"And where do you fit? Do you plan to help him be himself?" Why did he care?

"I don't suppose I'll be able to. I imagine he'll want to be posted somewhere outside of England and I don't think Jay or Jon would think it amusing if I tried to tag along."

"You wouldn't go along?" he probed. "Perhaps as his wife?"

Her laughter rang out in the room. It was a deep, throaty laugh, carefree and untrammeled. Its very lightness caused the tightness in his chest to loosen. "Now, why would I want to do that? Edward is like a brother to me. Besides, his mother hates me."

"Hates you?" He couldn't believe anyone could hate her. She seemed genuinely friendly.

"Well, it's Edward's fault, but she's made it clear that I'm not good enough for him. If it wasn't for the fact that I make an effort to stay out of her way, she probably would have ruined me by now."

"Edward's fault?"

"Yes, but it's not important. He's a good friend and he's my best friend's uncle." She stopped suddenly and tilted her head to the side, studying him anew. "I guess you are Amanda's uncle too. Of course, you aren't related by blood, so you could marry her. Oooh, that would be wonderful. Then she could stop chasing Jon."

He was having difficulty keeping track of her thoughts as she jumped from subject to subject, but he did catch the last thing she said.

"I'm not marrying my sister's stepdaughter," he blurted.

Felicia pursed her lips into a pout. "Pity. She's very pretty and would make a wonderful marchioness."

Brand wasn't sure he was hearing right. Here he was discussing marriage with a young, beautiful woman and she was pushing someone else at him. Why didn't she want him for herself? He understood enough of the ways of society to know any other young woman of marriageable age would, especially considering his title and prospects.

Vanity had never been an attribute Brand applied to himself, but he wondered what it would take for Felicia to consider herself a candidate for the position of his marchioness. His body was beginning to imagine what it might take to make those eyes glaze over with desire and what those lips would look like wet and kiss-swollen.

"And you wouldn't?" He didn't know why he asked, but he wanted to unbalance her on some level. Perhaps he wanted to know if his title really meant so little to her.

"Of course I would, *if* I was in the market for a husband. But I don't want one—and Amanda does."

Brand was stunned. What young woman didn't want a husband and a family? Even though he'd been raised outside England, he understood that for young women in civilized society freedom only came at the price of marriage.

Annoyance lit her eyes momentarily, then disappeared.

"So, when do you leave for The Downs?"

Brand recognized a red herring when he saw one.

"I think the day after tomorrow. I don't think your brother expects me to still be here when he returns and I understand my father is ill."

Felicia nodded solemnly. "Eliza, Amanda and Edward have all left the city already. The earl, Eliza's husband, is leaving today to join them. You could have gone with him."

"That might have been a plausible thought last night, but it is too late now."

Brand regarded her for a moment. It occurred to him she was alone with him in the house. He wondered if she was concerned about her reputation, but he wasn't about to allow the servants to speculate about her during her brother's absence.

"You should be leaving. No one else may know I am here, but the servants do. And, although they may not know who I am, they do know you are an unmarried female in a room alone and unchaperoned with an unrelated male."

Felicia shrugged her shoulders, then got to her feet and approached him.

"I don't care, you know, but I suppose Jon might. I'll be leaving in a few days with Davey, so it won't matter."

"Don't you think you ought to wait for your brother to return?"

"Why?"

"Because young women, especially young, unmarried, women, do not travel alone. I may have been out of England for twenty years, but even I know that."

She glanced away. "Yes, well," she licked her lips, "I don't want to wait. And I think the sooner I get Davey out of the city, the better."

"Why don't you want to wait? I think your brother is planning to return by early next week."

"I...I just don't," she replied evasively. "Davey and I will be fine."

"You can't possibly believe that," he said in a hard voice. "Only an idiot would consider such a trip."

Felicia put her hands on her hips and stared at him, fire in her eyes. "Are you saying I don't know what I'm doing? You don't even know me."

Brand was mesmerized by the change in her. He wondered if she blew hot and cold like this often. "Perhaps I don't," he answered. "But I do know no young woman in her right mind would do what you are considering without an escort."

Felicia's mouth dropped open. "Why...why you overbearing..." Biting off the last word with what sounded suspiciously like an oath, she stared at him mutinously before pivoting sharply on her heel, her skirts swinging wide with the suddenness of the movement.

Her anger touched off a similar emotion inside him and he reached out and caught her hand as she moved, spinning her back to face him. "I never thought Jay's family had madness in it, but it's the only explanation for such a ridiculous scheme."

His grip was firm as he pulled her toward him, grim determination in his face. "You must be mad to attempt such a thing."

The verbal attack astounded her and Felicia struggled against his grip, his words lighting a fuse on her anger. He was a perfect stranger—casting aspersions on her family. How dare he?

Crack! It sounded like an explosion in the room, but it was nothing compared to the sting she felt in her palm as it met that hardened jaw. Marble would have been softer. The tension in the room soared. Every instinct she possessed told her to break free and run, but she was rooted to the floor, fascinated by the stiffening of his facial muscles, especially the one that throbbed visibly as his jaw tightened. His eyes turned glacial and suddenly she was frozen in time, watching as he raised his hand and laid it gently against her cheek. She flinched anyway.

"I ought to make you pay for that." He leaned toward her. She could feel his breath on her face. He smelled of whiskey and sandalwood, the mingled aromas not unpleasant.

Nervously she licked her lips, not understanding the effect of the action on Brand's already tightly held control. She found out soon enough as his mouth covered hers.

The touch was so unexpected and soft she remained stock-still, unconsciously leaning forward to increase the pressure. The tension slipped from her body, her hands moved upward, gripping the lapels of his coat, and she sighed against his mouth.

She'd expected near violence after her attack on his person and was unprepared for the gentleness of his kiss and the way in which his tongue slipped between her lips to explore her mouth. He tasted of whiskey, the taste not at all repugnant. The heat from his body scorched her and there was suddenly not enough air in the room to fill her lungs. She gasped when he suddenly lifted his head.

Felicia opened eyes she hadn't realized she'd closed. Brand stared down at her and she wondered what he was thinking. Her lips tingled from the contact and she felt bereft now that it had been broken. She wanted to feel it again.

Brand's arms had slipped around her sometime during that brief kiss. Her hands rested against his chest and he was sure she could feel his heart beating. When they slid up and twined around his neck, a small voice in the back of his head told him to stop and let her go. But surprise left him like putty in her small hands. And when their lips met the second time, he could not have stopped if the room caught fire around them.

If the first kiss was chaste and soft, the second kiss was anything but. Brand slanted his mouth over hers fiercely, his tongue sweeping in, not just to taste, but to possess. The force of his kiss should have frightened her. He fully expected her to fight him, but she didn't. Instead, she took advantage, matching his ardor with her own.

Felicia had been the recipient of a few kisses over the last two Seasons, but none affected her as Brand's did. Her body was suddenly hot, her skin overly sensitive as his hands molded her figure to his hard frame. Her breasts were crushed against his chest, and she could feel her nipples tingling as they rubbed against the material of her chemise and gown. Blood pounded in her veins and she felt as if her heart was racing, even as her knees turned to water.

Brand's mouth moved from hers along her jaw as a whimper rose in the back of her throat, only to be muffled as his mouth moved back over hers. When he finally raised his head and looked down at her, her body stiffened at the firmly banked fire in his eyes.

Slowly her hands unlocked from behind his head and slid down the front of his jacket, resting momentarily over his rapidly beating heart. They stood in silence for several seconds until Felicia noticed a slight reddening of his jaw and remembered the slap. Reaching up, she touched it with her fingertips.

"I'm sorry," she said breathlessly. "I don't usually make a habit of assaulting people."

His lips lifted in a fleeting smile as his hands dropped to her waist. "Then that makes us even. I don't usually seduce young innocents."

Her eyes widened. "Oh." She moved slowly away from him, his arms dropping to free her. "It was only a kiss. And I've been kissed before."

"Not like that you haven't." His voice was smug.

She smiled. "True, and while I enjoyed it immensely, it

mustn't happen again."

Brand was startled by her candor. And while he privately agreed with her about repeating the kiss, the devil in him would not acknowledge it.

"Why?"

"Because I might enjoy it again, and..."

"I guarantee you would."

"...and I am waiting."

One blond eyebrow rose. "Waiting?"

"For the right person to come along and sweep me off my feet." She headed toward the door.

"I thought I'd just done that."

She laughed and the sound warmed him completely through. "You came close," she teased as she reached the door and turned to look back at him, "but not quite." Then she went through the door and shut it firmly behind her.

The room was suddenly empty without her presence and he stared at the door for a long time after she left.

Chapter Three

Felicia sat back in the carriage, her face burning with mortification. She had just told Brand the biggest lie of her life. That kiss had annihilated everything she thought she knew about kissing. Up till now, the few kisses she received had been soft, wet and sometimes sloppy. Never had they left her with the desire to repeat the experience. Never had they given her pause concerning her confirmed spinsterhood. Until now.

She had lost her mind. Somehow Brand had muddled her thoughts so completely she lost all sense of propriety. What if Higgins had come into the library while they were there? Brand was right. She should not have stayed in the library once she realized Jon was not even in the house, but her curiosity had gotten the best of her.

Speculation had kept her awake last night. Brand's resemblance to Eliza niggled at her until she put it together. What made both of them stand out was their violet-colored eyes. They were unusual—and another reason many supported the duke in his persistence Edward was not his heir. Edward had brown eyes like his mother.

It was amazing in this modern day that old superstitions could still persist, but they did. The inhabitants of Parkton had been easily convinced by an outsider she and her sister were not to be trusted because their great-grandmother was a gypsy. But among the upper classes another type of superstition reigned. That of family traits—and the violet-hued eyes which marked the Warings, especially each generation's heir, were legendary.

She closed her eyes and relived the kiss. Not only had it not been soft, wet or sloppy, but the feelings it evoked within her were troubling. Never had she felt so drawn to anyone outside her family. The kiss only confirmed the attraction.

"*I'm waiting for the right person to come along and sweep me off my feet,*" she'd told him. Well, someone had come along, but she didn't want him anymore than she wanted the person who would recognize her ring. And *why* had she told him she never planned to marry? She'd never told anyone else. Why him?

She wished she knew when and where Nona originally acquired the ring. Despite Nona's insistence, it wasn't hers—the engraving on the inside clearly indicated that. *My darling Caroline.* A name very close to her own, but still not hers. The ring was beautifully but simply crafted of the finest materials and she'd wondered if the stones had some significance.

Perhaps there was a matching ring, or a companion piece of jewelry. She'd questioned jewelers all over London, but none had seen anything like it before. Amethysts were not a popular jewel among the nobility, so she was sure anyone who recognized it would be a link to its owner. Originally disappointed to find no one, once she made the decision never to marry, she considered it fortunate. Until today.

What would it be like to have someone kiss her like that whenever she wished—or he wished? On the heels of the thought she was reminded of Mira's words; marital intimacy did not stop at just kisses. Kisses were the prelude and thinking of what was supposed to happen next only invited reminders of Aaron and Ella to intrude. She shuddered. Never! Not to her. Not ever.

The carriage drew up in front of Westover House and she entered to find the duchess and Geri about to go in to luncheon. Hurrying to join them, she cursed herself for being late, yet conversely realized she wouldn't have exchanged this morning for anything else.

Three days later Felicia watched Davey staring out the window of the Thanet traveling coach in wide-eyed wonder as the countryside north of London rolled by. Brand rode ahead on horseback and promised to meet up with them at the inn they had agreed upon for lunch. She wasn't sure he would forgive her, but for now she was content. Whether the duchess would understand was another question.

In the end she'd taken the coward's way out and left the duchess and Geri letters. They were to have attended a house party at the Hortensen's just outside of London for three days and, at the last minute, she asked to remain in London to wait for Jon. It had been easier than she thought to convince them Jon might return soon and she wanted to find out about the fire. Jon might only be her half-brother, but they understood their closeness.

She wouldn't dwell on the fact that she'd blackmailed Brand into escorting them as far as Wynton Abbey. She reasoned with him that as he was going in that direction it would not be out of his way to ensure she and Davey reached Jon before he continued on to The Downs. He had not been convinced until she threatened to let slip who he was. She'd only have to mention his title once in Higgins's hearing, she told him. The rest of the staff would know within the hour and the rest of London by nightfall.

She did feel guilty about delaying him, albeit probably only by a day. But if his father was as serious as everyone had been led to believe, it was possible he couldn't spare the day. When she mentioned it, thereby giving him an out as escort, he brushed it aside, confident the extra day would not cost him unduly.

The drive was tedious and long. It seemed to take an inordinate amount of time just to escape London, but the horses made up for the delay once they were on the open road. By the time they reached The Garter and met up with Brand, both she and Davey were in sore need of a break.

Handing Davey over to Henry, who was riding in the second coach with her maid, Lily, and the luggage, she went inside to find Brand had reserved a private parlor. Over a simple lunch of venison stew and fresh bread, she asked if he had planned out the trip and how long it would take.

"I sent my man, Hardwicke, ahead to bespeak rooms at inns along the way. You are fortunate your brother and I had already discussed the best route not only to the Abbey, but also to The Downs—and where to stay along the way—else you might be traveling with a little more uncertainty."

His voice held a touch of reproof in it.

She shrugged. "I'm not a hothouse flower. I spent much of my childhood with gypsies. A little inconvenience would not have hurt."

"I see." Brand was skeptical. "And have you had to fend off many unwanted advances in your travels?"

She blushed at his tone and implication. At nine she'd learned unwanted advances meant more than stealing a kiss or two.

"No, but I have a pistol and I'm not afraid to use it." Brand's golden brows raised in challenge. She raised her chin a notch in response. "The last person who didn't believe me when I was holding a pistol is now dead."

She knew that last statement got his attention when the look in his eyes bordered on approval. Why she interpreted his approval as admiration, however, troubled her. She should not want or need his approval.

"How is it—" he changed the subject, "—you don't know how far it is to your brother's home?"

She glanced away. "I've only been there once before. I've spent all of my life at Thane Park or Collingswood."

She rose to her feet and walked to the window. Staring out of the small grimy glass pane, she contemplated the patch of garden she could see.

"How well do you know my brother, Jay?"

"The marquis? Quite well, I would say."

"Do you know that his wife, Tina, is my sister as well as Jon's?" When he didn't respond, she continued. "It always seems strange to people who don't know, but Tina, Jon and I share a mother. And Jay and I share a father."

"Jon explained that your father married his mother when she was a widow with two young children."

"Jon and Tina," she concurred. "Their father died on the way home from India. What else do you know about Jay?" She was beginning to feel like a schoolmistress quizzing a student.

He chuckled, as if reading her thoughts. "I also know he and his father did not get along. That he left home at sixteen and never thought he'd return. He never expected to inherit."

"True. But, it's a blessing he did. Aaron would have

destroyed it all."

He was silent for a few moments, then asked in a gentle voice, "Does young Davey know of your relationship to him?"

She stiffened. Had Jon told him about Davey's background? The quiet in the room was unnerving and she could hear the muted noises of the patrons in the common room. Footsteps sounded outside the door, but continued past. Finally she turned and regarded him steadily. Her shoulders sagged and she let out a soft sigh. "No."

There was a wealth of sadness in that one word. She wanted Davey to know of their relationship, but how did one explain rape to a nine-year-old boy?

As they were leaving the inn, Davey raced up to her. "Can I ride up top?" he asked. "Wilkins said I could ride with him, but only if you said I could."

She looked up at the coachman. "Are you sure it's safe?"

"Of course, my lady," Wilkins assured her.

Davey's gray eyes pleaded with her as she looked up at the coachman's perch. It seemed so high above the ground.

"He'll be fine." Brand finally came to Davey's aid. "The fresh air will do him good."

She sighed. Outnumbered. "Very well. But you pay close attention to Wilkins."

Davey gave a whoop of joy and hugged her around the waist. Happiness washed through her as she recognized the cheerful little boy she'd left at Thane Park. Brand lifted him up as she climbed inside. Moments later, he joined her and took the seat across from her.

"Relax," he told her once they were on their way, his stallion tied to the back of the coach. "I'm not about to pounce."

"I didn't think you were," she replied defensively.

Stretching his long legs out as far as he could, he leaned his head back into the corner and closed his eyes. He was asleep in minutes.

The tension drained from her body as she watched him sleep. What had he been like as a boy, before he was stolen from his home and sent—where *had* he been sent? She wondered if he ever discussed his past.

He spoke as if he had been reared in the finest home in the

country. Few who met him would know he hadn't spent his entire life in England. She wondered if her brother had seen to his education somehow. He was a puzzle, but not hers to solve. She didn't need complications like him in her life. Jon was going to be angry enough with her as it was. The swaying of the coach soon caused her eyes to droop and, resting back against the comfortable cushions, before long she too was fast asleep.

Brand awoke sometime later. For a brief moment, he thought he was back on board the *Gypsy Star* until he spied Felicia across from him. She seemed uneasy in her sleep, shifting restlessly as if searching for comfort. He studied her as she slept. A slight flush had risen in her cheeks and he wondered if she was too warm. A soft whimper escaped and the long, dark lashes resting against her cheek fluttered, but she did not awaken. A lock of hair had slipped from the confines of her bonnet and now lay curled against her breast. His fingers itched to touch the dark curl, certain it would feel like spun silk.

Felicia shifted positions again, obviously uncomfortable. He sighed and switched seats to sit beside her, settling himself in the corner. The next time she moved, he slipped an arm around her and pulled her against his chest, where she relaxed and immediately fell into a more restful sleep.

He wondered why he was torturing himself. He told himself he was protecting his partner's little sister. He couldn't have let her go off on her own when he could prevent it. He'd want Jay or Jon to do the same if the tables were turned.

He smiled at her attempt at blackmail. It was advantageous she wasn't aware Higgins already knew who he was. Shortly after their arrival, Jon introduced him to the butler, then promptly swore the man to silence. That the rest of the household did not know proved the butler could be counted on to keep his word.

She cuddled closer and he was instantly aware of every inch of her pressed against his chest. A light, floral fragrance wafted around him. Now what had he gotten himself into? Why couldn't he have left her alone and uncomfortable? The little minx didn't want him. Hell, if she was to be believed, she didn't want anyone. And that was the problem, because he did want her. That kiss had fueled his imagination in more ways than he dreamed possible, and all of his imaginings ended the same way—with the two of them entwined, naked, in a very soft bed.

He glanced out the window—up at the sky to judge the time. They would be stopping soon to change horses and rest. Perhaps he should ride for the rest of today. Felicia shifted again and he bit back a groan. This was *not* a good idea, he thought as he rested his head back against the cushion and closed his eyes, trying to force his body to ignore the feminine curves draped over him.

Felicia awoke nestled against a warm, but hard, pillow. Beneath her ear she could hear the steady drum of a heartbeat. Her eyes flew open, going immediately to the seat opposite. It was empty. Her first thought was she had somehow moved into his seat, then she realized she was still facing the same way she'd started out.

Sitting up without disturbing him was out of the question, but she tried anyway. Lifting her head slowly and trying to put distance between them without otherwise touching him was impossible, but when she pressed her hands against his chest to push herself away, she found her wrists instantly captured by his hands. She looked up into his face and had to catch her breath.

An apology rose to her lips for disturbing him, but she quelled it. He had moved into her seat, not the other way around. As if he understood he was the trespasser, he spoke first.

"You looked like you needed a pillow." His voice was slightly strained and she noted something flicker deep in his eyes that she did not want to put a name to.

Pushing herself into an upright position, she watched uneasily as he levered himself up as well. The interior of the coach suddenly seemed smaller than it had earlier. He made no move, however, to reoccupy the seat across from her.

"Th-thank you, I think." Her pulse accelerated. She could hear her heartbeat loud in her ears. He completely flustered her in a way no one ever had before.

He smiled and the simple gesture caused her heartbeat to double. "Think nothing of it."

She suddenly wondered if convincing him to travel with her

and Davey had been a good idea. He seemed not quite civilized, but she sensed in him a rigid code of behavior that left her feeling safe in his company. On some level she understood if he ever felt he had compromised her, he would insist they marry, and she wished to avoid even the possibility.

Yet now, as she looked up into eyes darkening with appreciation, she began to feel a response. And it scared her.

The carriage started to slow and came to a stop. Brand turned to look out the window, breaking the contact. Felicia nervously straightened her bonnet, tucking a few stray curls back up inside. Brand opened the door and stepped out, turning to help her out after glancing around the small courtyard.

The inn yard was small, but clean, with none of the detritus sometimes found when no one cleaned up after a previous coach. The inn's interior was well kept and the small washroom she was shown to was spotless. Splashing cool water on her face gave her the chance to bring her racing pulse back under control and reorder her thoughts.

Davey provided a welcome distraction over a light tea with scones and jam. Chattering excitedly about the things he saw while riding with the coachman provided Felicia with a needed respite from the tension building between she and Brand.

The next three days were interminable. The weather was fine and the coaches made good time, but the inactivity wore on Felicia's nerves. After the first day, Brand only spent time in the coach when Davey was also present, so Felicia's afternoons were often spent alone as she allowed Davey to spend time up with the coachman during that time. A mixture of disappointment, apprehension and relief flooded her as her brother's home came into view on the evening of the third day.

Wynton Abbey was a large sprawling mansion built on the grounds of a former Cistercian Abbey. Once a thriving community, it had crumbled into ruin after the dissolution of the monasteries by Henry VIII and sat undisturbed for over fifty years before the Kentons were given the property by James I. Using stones from the original abbey, the newly titled Earl of Wynton built a veritable palace on the grounds.

The gray stone facade was stark against the verdant countryside as they bowled up the drive in the waning light. Felicia worried her bottom lip as Brand looked on. There was no obvious light in any of the windows, but she knew the library, where Jon was likely to be, was in the back of the house. At least he was still in residence—according to the pennant flying from one of the corner towers.

Jon's displeasure at her appearance was tangible. And he didn't seem to understand she felt Davey needed to leave the city.

She and Brand had been shown into the library where he was working. "The city is no place for a child used to running about in the country."

"That may be true, Felicia, but you still should not have come."

Felicia glared at him over the rim of her teacup.

"I could have gone to Journey's End without you," she challenged.

Jon's jaw hardened and she knew she'd scored a point. "You should have stayed at Westover House and waited for me to return."

"They were headed for a house party in the country. I couldn't possibly have left Davey alone with just the servants for company at Kent House for that long." She took a sip of tea, then put the cup down and tried another tack. "Besides, I'm tired of the endless round of mindless partying. There was no reason to stay."

"Your reputation was reason enough," he retorted, unconvinced. "And what do you expect me to do now you are here?"

Felicia perked up, seeing his comment as a victory of sorts. "You can take us to Journey's End. Brand, his lordship, or whatever he wishes to be called now we are out of London, needs to go on to The Downs. But you needn't return to London for us."

"I cannot take you someplace without knowing what we may find there. You have never been there—never wanted to go. We don't know if the manor is even habitable."

Felicia sat back in her chair. "Then Davey and I can wait here until you send someone to find out. There is nothing wrong with me staying with you." She picked up the delicate cup and saucer and took another sip.

Jon sat back in his chair. She'd exasperated him again, she thought. Why was it that her brothers and sister didn't seem to understand her?

"I ought to pack you back tomorrow."

Irritated, she dug her heels in. "I don't want to go back. If you try to send me back, I promise you, I won't arrive."

And on that note, she put down the cup and saucer, rose, and marched from the room.

Jon put his head back against the chair cushion and closed his eyes. Now what? Felicia had always been headstrong, but this new determination to remove herself from London was troubling. Had something happened?

"If it's any consolation," Brand spoke into the silence, "I knew the possibility existed I might have to offer for her if it got out or if anyone saw us together. In fact, I considered the possibility before we left."

Jon cracked open one eye and peered at Brand. Standing near a window with his back to the glass, he had not participated in the conversation between the siblings. "I didn't think madness ran in your family."

Brand laughed. The full-bodied sound filled the room. His hands shook as he laughed, so much so he had to put down the snifter of brandy he held for fear of spilling its contents.

Jon wondered if he was going to be let in on the joke. He would have thought after spending four days in Felicia's company in an enclosed carriage, the last thing Brand would find amusing would be the prospect of being married to her. But perhaps something occurred he was unaware of. If Brand knew when they left London the possibility existed he might have to marry her, but proceeded anyway, perhaps he wasn't so opposed to the idea. Of course, there was still Felicia's ring to consider, but she might have to abandon that search in the face of more practical matters.

Brand's laughter died down and he looked at Jon with watery eyes. "I suppose I should apologize for my laughter, but I will explain instead." Picking up his brandy, he crossed to the chair Felicia had vacated and lowered his large frame into it. He took a sip, then put the glass down beside the tea service.

"After you left, when Felicia told me she planned to leave London, I said nearly the same thing to her, asking her which side of her family had madness in it. She did not take it as humorously as I just did." He stroked his jaw. "She packs quite a punch."

Jon chuckled at Brand's words. "I see." Silence for a few moments, then he continued, "She hit you?" When Brand nodded, but offered no other comment, he added, "She takes offense easily at times. Sometimes unpredictably so. And yet, you brought her here anyway?"

"I didn't feel I had a choice." Brand's voice became serious. "She thought she blackmailed me into it by threatening to tell Higgins who I was. She assumed he would tell the rest of the household." When Jon merely nodded, he continued, "But, the real reason I agreed was she threatened to travel to Journey's End anyway—with or without an escort if I refused. Not knowing her well enough to call her bluff, I decided I was the lesser of two evils."

Jon agreed, then sighed. "She does tend to think she's invincible. She probably would have concocted some scheme whereby she would have posed as a widow with a young son or some such thing. And she's probably carrying her pistols."

Brand's eyebrows rose at the last statement, but Jon offered no further explanation. The two were silent for a time, the fire crackling in the grate the only sound in the room. Then Jon asked, "So, what are your plans now?"

Brand finished off his brandy, then set the glass down again. "I will leave in the morning for The Downs. I believe it is a day's ride from here."

"You may take my curricle if you wish. Although you'll make better time if you ride."

Brand considered the offer for a few moments. "Thank you, but I think riding will give me the option of crossing fields where I can and not necessarily sticking to the roads. I may be able to cut off some time by doing so. Arriving in a curricle might appear better, but I think time is of the essence right now, and I'm anxious to complete my journey now that I'm so close."

"Understandable. I wish you well and hope your find your father improving." Jon drained his own snifter and put it down. "I will send your man and luggage along."

"Thank you. I will try to return in a week or so to see if any repercussions have reached you from London."

"Don't hurry. You and your family have years to catch up on and I suspect it will take time to accustom yourself. Felicia and Davey will remain here until I determine whether it is safe to take them to Journey's End. If something happens which requires your attention, I will send a message."

Felicia waited in a shadowed alcove outside Brand's room. She knew if she was caught, there'd be hell to pay, but she needed to talk to him. Hearing footsteps coming down the hall, she slipped further behind the curtain in the alcove concealing her, nearly holding her breath as she heard the door open, Jon and Brand exchanging good nights, then the door close and Jon's footsteps continuing down the hall.

She waited until she could no longer hear the footsteps, then counted to one hundred before emerging from her hiding place. She approached the door stealthily on bare feet. Pressing her ear against it, she could hear nothing beyond the solid wood panel. A chill slithered down her spine and she pulled her blue velvet wrapper closer around her small frame.

Deciding against knocking, she turned the knob and opened the door on well-oiled, silent hinges. Slipping inside, she closed it as quietly as she could, but the catch clicked.

The room was dark except for a bedside lamp. Brand stood at the window beside the bed, staring out into the darkness. He was wearing a dark colored dressing gown that blended into the shadows, but his hair gleamed in the faint light.

"I have no further need of you tonight, Hardwicke," he said now. "You may seek your own bed. I will be leaving at first light."

"It's not Hardwicke." Her voice was loud in the silence.

Brand spun around, nearly knocking over the bedside lamp. "What are you doing here?" he demanded, his voice hoarse as he stalked toward her.

Felicia shrank back against the door. Perhaps she'd made a mistake. What made her think she could talk to him here? Now? She lifted her chin and stared up into eyes turned black in the dimness of the room.

"I wanted to talk to you, alone." She wet her suddenly dry lips. Her heart beat so loudly she barely heard her own voice.

"Talk? Alone?" His eyes narrowed. "What are you playing at?"

"Nothing." She shook her head. "I just wanted to thank you for bringing us here and...and to—" she licked her lips nervously again, "—to tell you...I won't allow my brother...to try to...force you into...a...a situation you may not...want."

He grinned, his amusement obvious. "You think to assure me you won't agree to a marriage if your brother insists?"

Felicia nodded.

He leaned closer and planted his hands against the wooden panel, trapping her head between them.

"And what makes you think I could be forced into such a...'situation'?" he whispered. She felt his breath on her face, her eyes going involuntarily to his mouth. His grin widened, white teeth gleaming in the dimness as his face inched closer. This was beginning to seriously resemble a mistake.

Her heartbeat doubled and her mouth went dry. She opened her mouth to reply, but the words never left her throat as his mouth covered hers.

There was nothing gentle about this kiss. The force of it slammed into her, her toes curling into the carpet beneath her feet, and her hands flattening themselves against the door. Brand's hands moved, one to behind her neck, cradling her head as his mouth ravished hers, the other to her waist, pulling her body flush against his.

Her hands went to his chest, ostensibly to push him away, but instead curled around the lapels of his dressing gown. She lifted her face higher, raising up on her toes, and made a soft sound when he raised his head. His eyes glittered in the gloom.

"Are you sure this isn't what you wanted instead?" he rasped before covering her mouth again.

She tried to tell him no, she hadn't come here to experience the wonder of his kiss again, but the words never emerged. She knew they were lies.

This time she sank against him, opening to his insistent tongue, and clinging to her wits by a mere thread. A distant cry echoed in her head but she ignored it as his mouth continued its plundering. Calloused fingers skimmed up her back, over her shoulder and slid into the vee of her dressing gown.

Brand knew if he didn't stop soon, he wouldn't be able to, but she was intoxicating. She tasted sweet, fresh, innocent, and his body demanded satisfaction. Awakening her untapped passion was slowly dissolving the thin veneer of gentility he'd cultivated, exposing the beast beneath. Her unbound hair invited his fingers to thread through the thick, silken curls, to bury his face in her neck and inhale its scent. The other hand pushed aside the robe, seeking and finding warm skin beneath.

She gasped against his mouth as his hand slipped inside her robe, the silk of her nightgown no barrier to his seeking caress. His hands cupped a rounded breast, savoring the texture and weight. When his thumb grazed the peak and it stiffened in response, he felt her shiver and a shout of triumph sounded in his head. His mouth trailed down over her jaw and neck, marveling at the softness beneath his lips, then sought that now stiff peak.

Her cry stopped him. For a moment, he forgot where he was, then just as quickly remembered. What in God's name was he doing? Lifting his head, he stared down into wide eyes, nearly black in the meager light. He couldn't have put a name to what he read there if his life depended upon it, but he felt the shudder that ran through her. He released her slowly, giving his head time to clear.

"You'd better leave now." He barely recognized the thick voice as his own.

Felicia pulled the velvet closed around her with shaking hands, fumbling with the tie. He almost reached to help, but knew he could not touch her again.

"I...I—" she began.

"Get out!"

She flinched.

"Now!"

She didn't hesitate a second time. Turning, she wrenched open the door and fled, leaving him to close it behind her.

Brand closed the door quietly and leaned his forehead against the smooth, cool wood. Taking deep breaths, he brought himself back under control. She was a menace. What did she think she was doing? Coming to his room in the middle of the night, in her nightclothes to tell him—what? That she wouldn't marry him if her brother forced the issue? It would be comical if he wasn't thinking about murder at the moment.

He blew out a frustrated breath. The next time he took that little bundle of femininity in his arms, he wouldn't stop at a few kisses. And if she wasn't already by their northward journey, she'd be well and truly compromised when he was done. Then he'd see whether she'd still refuse to marry him.

Chapter Four

Felicia entered her room in a panic. Stopping only long enough to close the door as quietly as she could, she threw herself across the room and onto the large four poster bed. Curling tightly into a ball, she squeezed her eyes shut, and tried to block out the sound of Brand's voice ordering her out of his room. Taking deep breaths to calm her racing heart, she could not stop trembling.

What had she done? How could she have let him take such liberties with her body? Her breast still tingled and her nipple throbbed, her body flushed from his touch. All conscious thought, her very sanity, had fled. She had gone where he led, willingly. What would have happened had he not stopped? She dared not think on it, but she knew.

It was irony of the worst sort. She'd gone to his room to reassure him she wouldn't marry him if Jon forced the issue. How could she have been so naïve?

Normally, she was proud of her ability not to be swept away by stolen kisses, but Brand's kisses were nothing like what she experienced before. Previous kisses had never muddled her thoughts. Nor had she ever wanted more once they were over. She never lost track of her surroundings, nor let a hand stray to forbidden parts of her person. But with Brand, the rules, if there ever were any, went straight out the window the moment he touched her.

At least he was leaving at first light. He would be out of her life forever. Once he was back in the bosom of his family, he had over twenty years to catch up on. It would be months, at least, before she saw him again. By then, she would be immune to him. She hoped.

She sat up and pushed her hair out of her face. The small bedside lamp cast shadows over the bed and reflected off the gleaming surface of the table. Sighing, she slipped off the bed, padded over to the washstand and splashed water on her face. Removing her robe, she slipped into the bed and turned down the lamp.

Staring up at the canopy above her, she resolved to put Brand out of her mind. There was no place in her life for Brand. Davey was her future, not a golden-haired, violet-eyed giant who reminded her of a lion she'd once seen in a menagerie. She'd forfeited her chance at a normal life—husband, children, and, someday, grandchildren—but Davey would not suffer for the circumstances of his birth. It was her fault he even existed. She would not desert him now.

The light was waning as Brand rode up the driveway to Waring Castle. Even so, he could see the pennant flying from the north tower, a sign his father was there, and lights in numerous windows.

He had worried throughout the day he might lose his way. He'd only been eight the last time he was here. Yet, as he rode through the surrounding countryside and approached the estate, memories returned. He knew which road to take when he came to a crossroads, and even recognized the small pony track leading to the gatehouse before he reached the main drive.

The massive front doors opened as he dismounted. A groom came hurriedly from somewhere and took his horse's reins.

"See that he gets an extra measure of oats," Brand threw over his shoulder as he ascended the steps. "It has been a long, hard day." Then he entered his home for the first time in twenty-three years, relieved at the absence of black crepe.

The butler closed the door behind him. "May I help you, sir?"

Brand stood in the cavernous, black-and-white tiled entryway. It rose a full three stories with an enormous chandelier hanging from a ceiling painted with scenes from Greek mythology. A massive marble staircase with highly polished oak banisters rose to his left. Closing his eyes, he was eight years old again and running up those stairs, headed for the nursery. At the top, turn left, to the end of the hall, and up another flight of stairs. The nursery sat above the ducal apartments.

"Shall I fetch Her Grace, sir?" The butler interrupted his reminiscences.

He blinked. "Oh, uh, no." The last person he wanted to see right now was his stepmother. "I'll see His Grace, for now." He started for the staircase, assuming his father would be in his suite.

"His Grace is not receiving, sir." The butler scrambled to move in front of him. "I shall inform Her Grace you are here."

Brand had spent most of the day creating and discarding numerous scenarios for what to say and do once he reached his boyhood home. Now the moment was upon him and he drew a blank. The butler was his first hurdle. Not a particularly difficult one—if he resorted to force. But he'd already rejected it as an option.

He could introduce himself. "*The Marquess of Lofton to see His Grace.*" Not only did he doubt the butler would believe him, but the man would still insist on fetching his stepmother. He didn't want his presence to reach too many in the household before he saw his father. His father was the only one who mattered at the moment. He sighed. No force—but intimidation would do. Pinning the butler with a hard look, he registered the widening of the man's eyes in silent recognition.

"I don't want to see my stepmother," he snapped. "I want to see my father!"

The butler's eyes grew round as saucers, but he gathered his composure, stepped to one side and said, "Of course, my lord. My apologies. I did not recognize you, at first "

Brand grinned, sending a short prayer of thanks skyward. The butler had last seen him as a boy of eight. How was he supposed to have known who Brand was?

"You could not have known," he replied graciously. "However, I will assume my father can be found in his rooms?"

The butler warmed to him instantly. "Yes, my lord."

"Thank you." Brand headed up the staircase. At the landing, the butler's voice stopped him.

"May I say, my lord, it is indeed good to see you returned?"

Brand turned and smiled down at the man. "That you may." Then he continued up to the second floor, striding down the hall towards the double doors at the end. With his way lit by wall sconces along the paneled hall, he noticed the stairway to his right leading to the nursery was dark. He wondered if it had continued to be used after his and Michael's abduction.

The ornately carved double doors opened soundlessly into a sitting room. There he stopped, unsure in which direction lay his father's room. Listening for a few moments, he heard voices coming from his right and crossed the room to another door which stood slightly ajar. He was relieved to hear a male voice inquire if His Grace required anything else? and an answering reply of "No". Waiting until he heard the quiet closing of another door, he approached the portal and pushed opened the door, freezing in the opening.

An enormous oak four-poster bed hung with gold-embroidered blue velvet dominated the room. The bed curtains were pulled back and he could see the bed was empty. Scanning the room, he noted mahogany paneling and dark blue silk covered the walls, broken only by a marble fireplace directly across the room. It was there, in front of the fireplace, he noticed the chair and the person occupying it.

Taking a deep breath, he started across the room, his eyes on the man in the chair, even as the man turned and noticed him. The moment of truth was upon him. How did one address a parent one hadn't seen in twenty-three years?

John William Sedgwick Waring, sixth Duke of Warringham, watched in fascination as someone who should have been a stranger crossed the room toward him. The young man was tall and lithe, moving with a grace and agility belied by his large frame, his eyes focused warily on him as he advanced. The man reached his chair and he looked up into eyes the mirror of his own.

Brand stopped beside his father's chair and dropped to one knee. "Hello, Father."

The duke lifted a thin, shaking hand and placed it on his shoulder. "Bertrand?" The voice was choked with emotion.

Brand nodded, unable to speak past the lump in his throat. He had very few memories of his father—and almost none of his mother—but those he had were of a warm, caring man who personally saw to his sons' riding lessons, approved all their tutor's lessons, and never sent them away when they wandered into his study—even if he was busy. And, because of these memories, he was not surprised when his father reached out and put his arms around him.

Sunlight poured through the windows of the long gallery. Along the walls, gilded frames held portraits of generation after generation of Warings, beginning with the first Baron, who fought beside William at Hastings. It was an impressive display of the history of one family, but Brand was interested in only one portrait near the end of the hall.

Standing before it in a pool of sunshine, he studied his mother's features. A perfect English rose. Blond hair lighter than his created a frame for petal-smooth skin and brilliant blue eyes framed by darker blond lashes. He stood beside her as a child of five while three-year-old Michael sat in her lap. Eliza as an infant slept in a cradle at her feet. Her smile, warm and inviting, enveloped him.

"She was beautiful, wasn't she?"

Brand spun around and came face to face with his half-brother. Edward stepped up beside him and looked at the picture again.

"I used to sneak in here when I was supposed to be napping and stare at her picture. She reminded me of an angel."

Brand turned and looked up at his mother's face. There *was* something ethereal about her smile, and he could understand how a child might think of her in otherworldly terms.

"I was sure she was watching over you and Michael wherever you were."

Surprised, Brand glanced over at Edward. He was smiling.

"Why?"

"At the time probably just out of spite to prove Mama wrong. Eliza missed the two of you dreadfully. To make up for it, she told me stories. They almost always ended with your mother returning the two of you safely home."

They stood in companionable silence for a moment, then Edward stepped forward and leaned in to study something in the painting.

"I don't think I've ever noticed that before. Interesting."

"Noticed what?"

"The ring your mother's wearing." He pointed to the jewelry in question on Brand's mother's right hand. "I've seen a ring just like that recently."

Brand's eyes snapped to the sapphire and amethyst ring his mother wore. Guilt assailed him as he remembered the last time he'd seen it.

"If I remember correctly, your partner's sister has it."

"My partner?" He stared, uncomprehending, at Edward. "What partner?"

Edward straightened and turned. "Didn't you tell us that you were in partnership with the Marquis of Thanet in a shipping company?"

"Oh. Uh, yes, I suppose I must have."

"Then I'm right. Lady Felicia Collings has a ring just like that one. Interesting."

Brand didn't respond to Edward's comment. Instead he asked, "Do you know where she got it from?" His voice emerged calmly enough, despite the buzzing in his brain.

"I think Amanda mentioned that her great-grandmother had given it to her. Or maybe she told me herself." Edward paused to stare off down the gallery, then shrugged. "Her great-grandmother was a gypsy, you know."

Brand forced himself to walk the few steps to the window seat across from the portrait. He needed to sit down before he fell. The air was suddenly thick and the buzzing turned to a dull roar as memories flooded his thoughts.

The night was cool and the small fire did little to keep the chill at bay. Huddled under a blanket, his small arms cradling his sleeping brother, Brand stared down the beach. A short distance away two men stood guard. Still further away, two more conversed in low tones, occasional words reaching his ears. Darkness threatened to overcome the meager light from the fire. One of the two guards turned and spoke to the other.

"They ain't goin' nowheres. Oi wants a drink." A few moments later, both men sauntered off.

He started to shake Michael awake, seeing it as an opportunity, but it only caused Michael to cough, bringing unwanted attention from one of the other men. Soothing him as best he could, Brand let Michael fall asleep again. Even if he had been able to run, he had no idea where he was. And he wouldn't get far with Michael so sick.

At least the men hadn't killed them. Visions of their tutor lying in a pool of blood still haunted him. He wondered again if the men had asked their father for money—and if he'd paid them.

A figure materialized out of the mist. Shawls, skirts and petticoats were all he was aware of before the woman sat down before him. Gold glinted in her ears and on her arms, but the jewelry made no sound. A gypsy. Automatically, he glanced at the men, but no one seemed to notice her.

When she reached out to touch a lock of his hair, he flinched.

"Do not be afraid," she said softly. Her voice, soft and slightly husky, soothed him and he sat still as she ran her fingers through his blond locks, humming to herself. Her hands dropped to his shoulders, startling him into looking into her face. Fathomless dark eyes looked deeply into his, compelling in their intensity, he could not look away. "You will experience much sorrow before you return to this land," she prophesied, "but return you will. And much stronger than when you left."

"Will Papa pay the money?" Hope filled his voice.

The gypsy shook her head. "I know nothing of any money. But these men will not harm you."

He was relieved to know they didn't plan on killing him, but he wondered how she knew. The men weren't gypsies. He recognized the broad Yorkshire accent spoken by the one he thought of as their leader. He'd heard them talking about being paid, so he was sure they were going to ask for money. "And Michael?"

"It is not to be." The sorrow in her voice caused him to clutch Michael closer. "But you will return. It is your destiny. And she will be waiting."

She was speaking in riddles. Bertrand merely wanted to

know whether his father would pay the ransom for them so they could go home. But she told him nothing. Instead she spoke of his destiny and some woman who would be waiting for him when he returned.

"I want to go home." He was trying his best to hold back the tears, but she seemed not to hear him, continuing to speak about a far distant future. When she reached out and lifted the chain from beneath the nightshirt he still wore, he grabbed at her hand.

"This is the symbol of your legacy," she crooned. "You must give it to me for safekeeping. If these men find it, you will never see it again."

Even at eight, he'd understood. His father had told him the ring was for his future wife and the gypsy promised to keep it safe for the unknown woman. "When you find it again, you will find your destiny. Do not let it slip from your grasp." Before she left him, she said, "Do not forget and all will be well. Someday you will return to your father's side."

Bertrand barely had time to reconcile these words before he and Michael were rousted from their place and put in a small boat. The air was cold and damp, raising goose bumps on his arms, and he shivered, pulling his brother closer. There was little time to dwell on the gypsy as Michael shuddered and began coughing violently.

Three days later Michael was dead and Bertrand was alone. Yet, in the dark, damp, and crowded hold of the ship, he remembered the gypsy's words. "*Someday you will return to your father's side,*" she had told him. He clung to those words. They would keep him going.

"Brand?" Edward's voice shook him from his memories.

When he looked up, Edward was watching him with concern. He gave himself a mental shake.

"You should meet Lady Felicia." Brand wondered if Edward knew how much his eyes lit up or excitement tinged his voice as he spoke of Lady Felicia. "I think the two of you would rub along wonderfully. She'd make a perfect marchioness." Edward grinned. "Just don't mention her in Mama's hearing."

Brand rose on steady feet. "Hmmm. I don't know that I need to be looking for a wife just yet, but why don't you tell me about this paragon, and why I shouldn't mention her in your mother's presence."

He glanced briefly at his mother's picture again. The sunlight streaming through the windows seemed to enhance her smile and light her eyes. He shook his head. He hadn't read approval in the blue depths. Had he?

Edward turned toward the door. "How about a ride—and I'll tell you anything you want to know."

As the two men left the gallery, Brand wondered if his gypsy and Felicia's great-grandmother were the same person. Or if Felicia had come by the ring, if it *was* his ring, another way.

Felicia stood at the fence surrounding the paddock, watching Davey receive his third riding lesson. Even with his arm securely bound and in a sling, he was able to hold on to the reins and follow the directions of the stable master. With his face alight, Felicia no longer doubted the impulse which led her to bring her nephew to Wynton Abbey. Here he could be himself, without the baggage of his parentage. She no longer worried for his safety when he was out of her sight. The local vicar had agreed to tutor him and Henry took him to the vicarage each morning for a couple of hours. For now, life was perfect for Davey. She wanted nothing more.

In the evenings, however, other thoughts intruded. Too often memories of Brand and his kisses invaded her thoughts and her dreams mocked her for trying to forget him. He'd left nearly a fortnight ago. She hadn't dared ask Jon if he had heard from him. She had written to Amanda, only to receive a return letter from London, where Amanda and the countess had returned shortly after Brand's arrival at Waring Castle. The duke, it appeared, had made a seemingly miraculous recovery after Brand's arrival.

"Did you see?" Davey's excited voice brought her out of her thoughts. "I was riding and Del said I was a natural."

Felicia smiled down at him. "Of course I saw. You looked like you were born riding." Felicia looked up and waved at Del, just as he was turning to lead the pony back into the stables. The stable master waved back.

"What's a natural?" Davey's face was glowing with happiness as they made their way to the house.

"It means you like horses and they like you."

Davey chattered about the horses, the stables, and Del all the way back, where Henry met them and took charge of him. Felicia smiled to herself as Davey regaled Henry with his pony ride as the two of them headed up to the nursery, while she headed for the library.

Knocking on the library door, Jon's voice bade her to enter.

"Felicia! What luck. I was going to send someone to find you shortly."

"Looking for me?" She regarded him suspiciously. "What for?"

She seated herself on a settee upholstered in leaf green damask under Jon's watchful gaze. He took a chair across from her. It was then that she noticed the paper in his hand.

"Has your man returned from Journey's End?"

"No, not yet. But, perhaps it's just as well. Davey seems to be settling in here and he's happy for now, so it might be best not to uproot him again for a while. In the meantime, we have another problem to deal with."

"Another problem?"

Jon sighed. "The Duchess of Westover has written to me. It seems you were seen leaving London in Brand's company. Of course, whoever saw you did not know who Brand was, but they knew enough to know he was not a relation."

Felicia was stunned.

"According to Her Grace, even the miraculous appearance of the Marquess of Lofton at The Downs has not distracted the gossip mill from your indiscretion."

Felicia remained silent. There was little she could say in her defense that he hadn't already heard. Davey's welfare had been uppermost in her mind and they'd departed early in the morning, assuming she ran little risk of being seen.

"Nothing to say?" Jon interrupted her thoughts.

"What is there to say? I've already given you my reasons for leaving London. I'm sorry word has gotten out."

A knock at the door interrupted them. The butler entered.

"Tea has been prepared, my lady," he addressed Felicia.

"Where would you like it served?"

"Here is fine, Milstead."

"Very well, my lady."

As the door closed behind the butler, Jon turned back to his sister.

"So what should I do about Her Grace's letter?" he asked. "I'm sure she expects a reply."

"I don't know. If it were anyone else, I would just ignore it. But the duchess has been good to me. And she has overlooked many of my idiosyncrasies over the past two Seasons."

"Something for which Jay, Tina and I have been extremely grateful."

Felicia's eyes registered surprise. "Have I been that much of a trial?"

"No, but orchestrating your come-out would not have been as smooth without the duchess. And having her support and my grandmother's as well has kept the gossipmongers at bay— until now."

Milstead entered with a maid and the tea trolley. Leaving it beside Felicia, the two servants left as quietly as they entered.

Jon watched as Felicia poured him a cup, passed it to him, then poured one for herself. He knew she was mulling over his last statement, but he wondered if she knew just how serious it was.

"I suppose everyone is convinced now my gypsy blood has reared its ugly head."

Jon did not need to respond. No one ever forgot they had gypsy blood running through their veins. Society might overlook it when all was sailing smoothly, but they were quick to condemn and ostracize when it suited their purpose. Until now, Felicia had done nothing too outrageous so, except for a few families and the Duchess of Warringham, they had withheld judgment.

He was accepted for his title and wealth. But for Felicia there were other obstacles to clear as she made her bow to society. He and Jay understood, and made sure her dowry would allow her to have her pick of anyone she wanted. Now, she had jeopardized it all over a nine-year-old boy.

"Did the duchess say precisely what the rumors were?"

Jon shook his head. "She didn't need to elaborate. I think you and I can imagine the possibilities."

"Oh."

Felicia spent the time between tea and dinner mulling over their conversation. She supposed Jon was thinking she'd ruined her chances for a decent marriage and she didn't have the heart to tell him she didn't care. She'd be happy raising Davey at Journey's End, and eventually leaving it to him.

She tried not to think of what it felt like when she held Tina's baby girl in her arms, how delighted she had been when the infant smiled and gurgled at her. She blocked out the thought of going through life not having children of her own. Perhaps it was to be her punishment for her part in Davey's conception ten years ago. She would just have to be content with Davey.

The gems in her ring mocked her. Nona told her she would have all she wanted. She would be happy. But Nona couldn't have foreseen the muddle she'd landed herself in. Reliving her last conversation with her great-grandmother brought a lump to her throat.

She closed her eyes and Brand's face swam before her. She wondered what he was doing now or if he ever thought about her.

Her body tingled as she remembered their last encounter. His kisses alone had the power to move her, and she wondered if he remembered her as anything other than an annoyance. She had pushed herself on him, forcing him to escort her and Davey here. He had been cordial, but avoided being alone with her. Looking back, she realized both times they had been alone and he had kissed her, she had sought him out. The last confrontation had been especially reckless on her part.

The door opened and Lily entered the room. "His lordship asks you to join him downstairs in the library."

Crossing the room to the dressing table, she sat and had Lily tidy her hair. She was still dressed in her afternoon gown of violet-blue sarcenet, but knew she needn't change. There was little use in dressing for dinner when it was just the two of them. A last glance in the mirror assured her she was presentable, then she was out the door and heading down the stairs.

Jon wasn't alone. Another figure rose from the depths of an overstuffed chair as she entered the room and her mouth suddenly went dry. Stopping in the center of the room, she was at a loss for words.

"Come and join us, Felicia." Jon motioned to her. "I'm sure you remember Brand, or should I formally introduce you now?"

"There is no need." Brand spoke before she could.

Approaching Brand, she dipped him a curtsy. "I hope you found your father well, my lord."

He bowed over her hand. "Not well, precisely, but recovering remarkably."

Had she noticed that mischievous twinkle in his eyes before? She seated herself on the same settee she had occupied earlier as Jon spoke.

"We have been discussing the duchess's letter."

"What! Why?" She wasn't sure whether she was surprised or outraged.

Jon peered at her over the rim of the glass of amber liquid he held. "I didn't think you were dense, Felicia."

"But..."

"No buts. You know there is only one solution."

Her heart rose into her throat. She had not expected Jon to take action this soon. Or perhaps he'd merely taken the opportunity Brand's return afforded. Either way, she'd promised Brand she would not allow it to happen. She couldn't. Fear slammed into her and suddenly she needed air. Jumping up, she began backing away from the grouping of chairs.

"No," she stammered. "I can't." She was aware of Brand watching her intently, but she couldn't bring herself to look at him.

Jon was unfazed by her actions. "Why?" His tone was sharp.

Searching wildly for any excuse, she used the first one to come to mind. "My ring," she blurted. "I still haven't found..."

"Have you shown it to him?"

She shook her head.

"Then do it now." Jon put down his glass and rose to his feet. Moving toward her, he said, "Here, give it to me and I'll do it."

She allowed her eyes to find and settle on Brand, as if seeing him for the first time, and stopped dead in her tracks as she remembered Nona's words. *You will be rewarded with sun-ripened wheat and highland heather.* Wide-eyed, she turned and watched as Jon approach her, hand outstretched.

"Jon?" She licked suddenly dry lips with an equally dry tongue. "What color is highland heather?"

"What?"

"What color?" Spots began to appear before her eyes. She couldn't breathe.

"Felicia, stop delaying and give me the ring."

Lifting her hand, she drew off the ring but held it tightly in her fist. "Not until you tell me," she insisted. "What color?"

Her heart started to pound, the throbbing developing into searing pain behind her eyes.

"Purple."

Oh God. The blood drained from her face and her knees gave way beneath her. The ring fell from nerveless fingers.

"Felicia!"

She heard Jon's voice cut through the darkness enveloping her as she was lifted and carried back to the settee. A glass was put to her lips and a fiery liquid burned its way down her throat. Gasping, she pushed the glass away and tried to sit up. Jon held her down.

"Stay there!"

She had no choice but to obey, eyeing Brand warily through watery eyes as he moved into her line of vision. He was holding her ring and the look of wonder on his face only caused her further dismay.

Sun-ripened wheat and highland heather. Nona's words pounded in her head. "*But I want a duke,*" she had said with all the naïveté of a spoiled sixteen-year-old. "*And you shall have one...*"

Sun-ripened wheat was the perfect description for his hair, she realized now. But it was because she was most familiar with white heather she hadn't given Nona's words much thought. Still, it remained to be seen whether he truly recognized the ring. His next words destroyed any hopes she had he might not.

"I don't think I really believed I would ever see it again."

She eyed Jon mutinously. "Let me up."

Jon looked at her closely, worry in the green depths.

"Oh, for heaven's sake," she exclaimed, "I'm fine. I was just surprised for a moment. Now, let me up!"

Jon relented and stood, allowing her to sit up. When he didn't move away, but continued to stand over her, she glared up at him.

"You may as well sit down. I'm not going anywhere." She regretted it moments later when Jon looked at Brand first, then back at her. Something passed between the two men, then Jon took himself off across the room and Brand sat beside her.

For a long moment, he merely turned the ring over and over in his fingers—as if examining it for damage. She was afraid to watch, but unable to look away as he closed his fingers over it as if he could imprint it on his palm, then raised the fist to his lips and closed his eyes. The moment was so poignant, she felt tears again.

The hand shook for a moment, then he opened his eyes and his hand and held the ring out to her. It looked so small in the palm of his hand, yet it sparkled as if it had been forged from the sun. She regarded it as a prisoner might regard the gallows. It represented the end of life as she knew it—the unknown stretching before her filling her with foreboding.

"Where did you get it?" His voice was hoarse with emotion.

"My great-grandmother gave it to me. She s-said that I should find the person who could t-tell me its history." She took a steadying breath. "Who is...was...Caroline?"

"Caroline was my mother. My father gave her the ring when I was born. When she died not long after Eliza was born, he put it on a chain and gave it to me with the admonishment that I was to keep it for my future wife."

She shook her head. "I don't understand. How did Nona get it?"

"Nona?"

"My great-grandmother. She gave it to me just before she died. She said the person who recognized it and could tell me its history was my destiny. It was a favorite litany of hers. She always said we should be searching for our destiny."

Chapter Five

"I see." Brand had been too worried about Michael that long ago night to listen to the gypsy closely, but he remembered her reminding him the ring belonged to his future wife and he would find her and his destiny when he found the ring again.

The irony was not lost on him. He was certain he would not have chosen Felicia had circumstances been different. He'd long since shoved the memory of the ring into the recesses of his brain. Had Edward not mentioned it, it would not have had any bearing on this situation.

He had known the risk when he agreed to escort Felicia to her brother; the possibility that she would be compromised. The only honorable way out was to marry her. He had taken risks for most of his life and this might be the biggest risk of all, but perhaps the old gypsy had known something. The coincidence of the ring certainly suggested it.

He was still holding the ring out to her and she was still regarding it as if it might bite. Sighing, he picked up her left hand and slid the ring on her third finger. It fit perfectly.

"I tried to find the jeweler that made it, but no one in London recognized it."

"It was made by a jeweler in York from my father's design."

"I suppose that explains why no one recognized it."

"Edward told me he had seen it."

Felicia looked up, clearly confused. "But, he-he's seen it many times before and said nothing to me."

What he did not tell her about was the conversation he had with his father about the ring. The irony of her possessing the ring was bad enough, but the improbabilities engendered by the conversation with his father would make a normal, rational person think twice about their ability to control anything in the universe. And, if that had not been enough to make him wonder, visiting his mother's grave only to discover her second name had been Felicia had nearly been enough to drive him back to the sea. He did not believe in omens, signs or fate, but even he could not escape all the coincidences. For better or for worse, she was, as apparently her great-grandmother would say, *destined* to be his wife.

Felicia was unconvinced. She had told herself she would never marry. The ring had been her best excuse to her brothers and sister for refusing every suitor. Now the improbable had happened.

She couldn't possibly trap him this way. She had promised. Besides, his stepmother hated her. He would have no peace in his own home if he married her. Glancing around the room, she noticed Jon standing at a window, his back to them.

"You can't do it," she hissed, drawing the ring off. "I won't allow it."

Brand put his hand over hers. "You do not have a choice." His voice was gruff.

"But, I can't let Jon force you to do this."

He grinned and amusement showed in his eyes. "There was no force involved. As I said, you do not have a choice, but I do."

"But..." He put two fingers up to her lips.

"No buts."

Milstead saved her from further protestations by announcing dinner.

She stumbled as Brand rose and pulled her to her feet, falling momentarily against his broad, solid warmth. Righting herself, she stepped away as Jon approached and felt the blood stealing into her face.

Dinner? She wouldn't be able to eat a thing. Jon looked thoroughly pleased with himself, and Brand... Well, he didn't look like he was *dis*pleased.

She was shepherded out of the library and down the hall toward the dining room. As they approached the main staircase she managed to steady her voice enough to say, "I'm not very hungry, nor am I likely to be good company tonight, so if you'll excuse me, I'll leave you two to enjoy your meal."

Then she fled up the stairs without waiting for either to react.

Felicia slipped into the stables early the next morning. It was still quiet and she waited for her eyes to adjust to the dimness before making her way down the row of stalls to the one at the end.

"It's been a long time, old boy," she whispered to the horse inside. Its ears pricked up at her voice and he nickered softly. "I know Jon has been very good to you, but today I need you."

Opening the stall door, she led the stallion out. He followed without a sound and stood still as she saddled him. It had been over a year and she'd forgotten just how big Midnight was, but she managed. He had been hers once. She'd raised him from a foal and trained him to do all manner of tricks. The one thing she had never been able to train him to do, however, was allow a ladies' saddle on his back. When the time came for her to make her come-out, she couldn't take him to London, but she hadn't wanted to leave him at Thane Park. Jay had kept him in London as a mount for a while, but when he and Tina went on their trip, Jon agreed to take the stallion.

Once the horse had been her salvation. Riding him, training him, grooming him, and riding him more had been her way of escaping from the conditions at Thane Park.

Leading Midnight out of the barn and over to the mounting block, she quickly mounted and the two headed out. "I've missed you," she told the stallion as she gave him his head over a long stretch of grass. Their destination was a copse of trees at the top of a distant ridge.

As they reached the end of the grass, she slowed Midnight to a canter. The cart tracks through the fields were filled with ruts and rocks and she didn't want to risk injuring him on land she was unfamiliar with. They wandered down one track after another, through planted fields and fields of sheep. There were even a few cows here and there. Finally climbing to the top of the ridge, she dismounted, looping Midnight's reins over the pommel, and let him graze as she dropped into the soft grass.

The ridge was the highest point for miles and she stared without really seeing out over undulating fields, pastures, and meadows as far as the eye could see. The one other time she'd visited, she had told herself she was sure she could see London from here. It had to be the black cloud near the horizon. Sighing, she took a deep breath of fresh, cool air and turned her eyes inward. It was the real reason she needed to come out this morning. She needed to think of a way out of her latest muddle.

She could just be stubborn and refuse. She was fairly certain Jon would not starve her into submission or force her if she absolutely, categorically, refused. What would it do to her family? How would it affect her other brother's partnership with Brand? What would he think of her refusal? And what might he do to force an agreement?

It wasn't that she didn't want to marry Brand, she didn't want to marry anyone. She was unfit to be anyone's wife. The fear, the terror, was too ingrained.

Although the day was warming up, she shivered lightly as she remembered their last encounter. She could not refute the way he made her feel, and she could not dispute no one had ever made her feel that way before. She was attracted to him. She was not repulsed by him or merely indifferent to him. But attraction would not change her mind. A few kisses were one thing, what was supposed to come after only made her heart race—in panic.

Brand was furious. Two maids were exiting from a room, their arms full of linens, when they noticed him stalking down the hall. Quickly scooting to the side, they watched him stride past, eyes full of frightened curiosity. Reaching Felicia's room, he threw open the door without knocking, surprising her maid in the act of straightening the bed.

"Where's your mistress?" he demanded of the terrified young woman.

"She-she's gone riding, my lord."

Brand nearly howled in frustration. Deprived of his prey, he turned and headed for the stables. Waiting while a horse was saddled would have been interminable had he not taken the time to question the stable hands to see if anyone had seen Felicia leave. As it turned out, someone had.

"She were a ridin' Midnight, milord," Jemmy told him. "She

headed off to'rd the ridge." Pointing Brand in the right direction when the horse was brought out, Jemmy went back to work—a shiny new guinea in his pocket.

Mounted on a strong, fresh, chestnut bay, he tore out of the stable yard and gave the horse its head across the same stretch of grass Felicia had traversed almost an hour before.

Brand's temper had cooled somewhat by the time he reached the ridge and began the short climb. He was still angry, but he'd had a chance to think along the way.

Approaching from the north, he noticed Felicia's small figure seated on a patch of grass at the south end of the small ridge. Her hair was pulled back with only a ribbon and he frowned at the sight. He didn't think ladies ever left home with their hair down.

Brand dismounted, looping the bay's reins loosely over a branch, and strode toward her. She turned and looked as he advanced toward her. Wariness widened her eyes.

Good, he thought. *She ought to wonder.* He wanted to shake her, kiss her, turn her over his knee, kiss her, scare some sense into her, kiss her...

She scrambled to her feet as he reached her, brushing the grass and dirt off of her legs and... Good God, what was she wearing now?

"Have you no sense of decency at all?" he blurted as he took in the loose-fitting shirt, breeches, and knee-high boots.

"No one will see me." She straightened defiantly. "And I wanted to ride Midnight."

"Midnight?"

"My horse. He won't allow a ladies' saddle on his back. Never has."

Brand glanced around the small area.

"I don't see a horse, although you obviously got here somehow."

She shrugged. "He's around. He won't go far."

"Hopefully not any farther than the stables."

She shrugged again, then turned to look out toward the horizon, presenting her back to him.

For long moments Brand merely stared at the view before he realized he was becoming uncomfortably warm. Shifting his eyes from her backside, enticingly outlined by the form-fitting breeches, and the wealth of raven curls caressing it, he cleared his throat.

She turned. "Did you come up here for a reason, or were you just out for a ride?"

"You lost something. I came to return it."

"Oh?"

Extracting something from his pocket, he picked up her hand and dropped into it the ring he'd found on his bedside table, forcefully folding her fingers over it when she tried to snatch her hand away.

"I didn't lose it. I merely returned it to its rightful owner."

"Then you lost it. Because *you* are its rightful owner."

"No, I'm not. Your father gave it to you."

"The ring belongs to my future wife. It was merely given to me for safekeeping until that person could be determined." Felicia's mouth fell open at the twisted logic. "Your great-grandmother told you it was yours, did she not?"

"Yes, but..."

"There you have it. It's yours, not mine. Your great-grandmother wouldn't have lied to you, would she?"

Felicia had nothing to say to that outrageous statement. Still futilely trying to free her hand, Brand noted she struggled for breath. Holding her wrist lightly, he was unperturbed by her pulling, yanking, and twisting. He merely stood there, looking down at her in mild amusement.

"Let me go!"

"Not until you promise not to lose it again."

That got her attention and she stopped fighting. "But...but why?"

"I think that should be fairly obvious."

"But why me? Why not Amanda? She'd make a much better marchioness than I."

"She's too tall." He watched her struggle to contain her outrage. "And her hair's the wrong color."

With his free hand, he reached up, took her chin between two fingers, gently closed her mouth, then covered her lips with his, taking the wind right out of her sails.

Felicia froze. Her heart stopped. Her brain went blank. Her lungs seized. Then Brand ran the tip of his tongue along the seam of her closed mouth, she gasped, and he made himself right at home. Her heart began to race. Her brain registered his presence. And her lungs drew air from him.

Time stood still. Brand's arms drew her firmly against his body and her own arms became trapped between them. The heat from his body scorched her, branding her skin through her shirt, and sending flames licking along her veins. Liquid warmth pooled low in her belly and a moan rose in her throat. His hand cradled the back of her head, holding it at an angle that allowed him free reign. Relinquishing her hold on reality, she gave herself up to the magic.

Felicia did not know how anyone could experience such ecstasy and not die from it. Yet she wanted more...and more...and more. A sigh escaped when he raised his head, only barely breaking contact.

"Promise me," he whispered against her mouth.

She lifted heavy lids to stare up into eyes darkened nearly to royal purple. What had he asked? Promise him what? At that moment she didn't care, she wanted him to kiss her again. Leaning towards him, she lifted her arms to wrap around his neck and tried to pull his head down to hers. Brand resisted.

"Promise me first."

She couldn't remember what he'd asked, but she'd promise him the moon if he'd just kiss her again.

"I promise." The breathy whisper was cut off when his mouth settled on hers again.

The flames turned to molten lava, incinerating everything in its path. Brand drank greedily from her lips, his mouth devouring hers as his tongue swept in to conquer, allowing his passion to engulf her. She had lost whatever battle they were fighting and she knew it. Brand's arms pinned her against his body and her feet left the ground. It wasn't until he straightened slightly and she felt the bulge at the juncture of her thighs that reality crashed in. Recognizing the significance of the hardness cradled there, she tore her mouth from his and fought herself free.

Surprise was on her side and she was free before Brand realized what happened. Stumbling backward, she backed up against the trunk of a tree, watching him through eyes wide with terror. Then she turned and ran.

Brand was slow to react, only galvanized into action when he heard a shrill whistle from the direction she had run. He went after her, only to stop and stare in stunned amazement as a huge black stallion came toward where she stood on a boulder.

"Down, boy," she ordered and the horse bent its front legs enough to allow her to leap into the saddle from where she stood. The horse straightened and she wheeled and galloped off as if the hounds of hell were after her.

By the time he recovered enough to retrieve his horse and follow her, he was sure she was nearly back at the stables.

Felicia did not emerge from her room for the rest of the day. Pleading an unspecified malady, she had Henry take Davey out for his afternoon riding lesson. True to her word, however, once she remembered what she promised, she put the ring in her jewelry box. She hadn't promised to wear it—only to keep it.

Jon watched Brand pace the length of the library like a caged lion. It was obvious to him Brand and Felicia had not come to a satisfactory agreement on the state of their engagement this morning. She had returned and retreated to her room; Brand returned dour-faced and uncommunicative, and spent the rest of the morning writing letters. Jon spent most of his morning closeted with his overseer and various tenants.

At lunch Felicia refused to leave her room and Brand wondered aloud whether he should force the issue. Jon realized he was going to have to provide Brand with ammunition for some strong-arm tactics and hope Felicia never discovered he was the culprit or at least eventually forgave him.

"Has she always been so headstrong?" Brand stopped and asked abruptly.

"Unfortunately, yes." Having Brand's attention, Jon invited him to sit. "Let me tell you a little about my baby sister."

Brand sat in a chair opposite Jon, then looked up. "Am I going to need a drink for this?"

Jon grinned. "It's possible."

Brand considered for a minute. "Go ahead. I'll consider it if I think I need it."

Jon chuckled. He hadn't seen anyone this out of sorts since his friend, Teddy Hartwell, fell for the Landaverde chit last year.

"Felicia, or should I say, Carolyn Felicia, was..."

"Carolyn!" Brand roared. "Her given name is Carolyn?"

"Yes, but no one, save Aaron, has ever called her by it. Our great-grandmother called her Caro, though. But there were reasons for that."

"Now, I need that drink." Once at the sideboard, he poured himself a liberal amount of whiskey under Jon's amused gaze. "Your great-grandmother wasn't a witch, was she?" he asked as he returned and settled himself back into his chair.

Jon laughed out loud this time. "I do remember telling Jay that two hundred years ago she probably would have been burned as one. She knew too much, and she lived by the predictions she wrung from her cards. Why do you ask?"

Brand hesitated. "How do I say this without sounding like I believe in signs and omens? You might decide I'd be better off in Bedlam rather than married to your sister, and I'm not sure I wouldn't agree with you."

"My great-grandmother was a gypsy. Signs, omens, witchcraft, magic, fate, destiny—it's all part and parcel of who they are. I doubt you could shock me. Coincidences happen and people see the mystical in them all the time."

"I know, but that doesn't make this one any less shocking. My mother's name was Caroline Felicia."

"You don't say!"

Brand took a drink from his glass.

"Perhaps I spoke too soon. With Nona anything was possible." Jon resettled himself in his chair. "Felicia was the baby in what should have been a family of five, but without Jay became four, and with Aaron being much older and distant, was in reality, a family of three. Tina and I spoiled her horribly—as did her parents. For my mother and Jay's father, she was their only child." The last was said as if it explained everything."

Jon sipped from his own glass, then continued. "And then there was Nona. We spent our summers being gypsies. Tina and

I, and Felicia from about the time she was five or so, spent months at a time with Nona's small band traversing various parts of England. Mira and Carlo were our surrogate parents, but Nona was the *shuvani*, the leader. I don't think either Tina or Felicia absorbed much of what she tried to instill in us, but I was fascinated by the herbs and healing methods. Jay's father gave me Culpeper's book on herbs one year for Christmas, but I digress."

Brand wondered if Jon knew how much his voice softened when he spoke of his sister.

"Felicia was eight when her father let her have her pick of some newborn foals."

"Midnight?"

"Midnight." Jon nodded. "She and her horse were inseparable until she went off to a Young Ladies' Academy. Before then she rode him almost daily. As she is fond of saying, 'He's very well trained', and Jay and I both have been victims of the training."

The mood in the room shifted, and Brand noticed Jon's grimace before he spoke again. "She was nine when Aaron was murdered, and ten when Davey was born. When Tina was thirteen, our stepfather became fascinated with small pistols being made in America called derringers. Having already taught both Tina and I to use his dueling pistols, he ordered two sets of derringers and gave one to our mother and one to Tina on her fourteenth birthday. When Mother died, we gave Felicia her set and taught her how to use them. Don't assume Felicia doesn't know what to do with a pistol. If she were a man, she'd be considered a crack shot."

He took a sip of his drink to cover his surprise. "She told me nearly as much on our trip here."

Jon paused to look at him, finished off his own drink, then continued, "Then there's Davey." Jon stretched his legs out in front of him, as if becoming more comfortable with his story. "If Felicia has an Achilles' heel, he's it. Although I don't know what, my instincts tell me there's more to Davey's story than Felicia has revealed which makes her feel responsible for him. I don't know what it is, but you might consider promising her she can give Journey's End to him if she consents. I'm not sure what Jay will do with the property if she doesn't marry, but I do know he and Tina don't want it."

"What makes you think I wouldn't want the property?"

"I don't," Jon admitted, "But it will add little to the dukedom you stand to inherit—and might make Felicia a more amenable bride."

Brand appreciated his candor.

"Then there's you and what you represent."

"Me?" Brand asked. "What do I represent that could be difficult?"

"Chagrin, embarrassment, consternation. Perhaps just an awkward feeling. Whatever it is, she's not feeling particularly comfortable with herself right now because you are exactly what she declared at sixteen she would not settle for less than. Fortunately, I think only the family, and the Westovers, know." Jon recounted the dinner conversation when Felicia, at sixteen, had stated she would marry a duke. "I remember nearly choking on my wine, but Jay simply asked her if the person had to be a duke or if an heir would do. Felicia answered an heir was acceptable. You might be interested in knowing you were the person Jay was thinking of at the time."

"I don't know if I should thank him for his confidence." He was smiling now, picturing Felicia at sixteen boldly announcing over the dinner table she would only marry a duke without batting an eyelash.

Jon fell silent and Brand sat, staring at his now empty glass. He had been right, but he wasn't sure the mix of adventurousness and innocence was a good one. He wondered how many scrapes she had been nearly involved in, or just extricated herself from in the nick of time.

"So she walks close to the line, but has managed never to cross it, until now?"

Jon nodded.

"And yet, despite that I've been told by both Felicia and my brother that my stepmother hates her, my sister, Eliza, whom I perceive as being very prim and proper, adores her."

"Amanda is your answer there."

"Amanda?"

"As I understand it, Amanda was eight when the mother she idolized died. She became withdrawn and the earl apparently didn't know what to do with her. Finally, when she was fifteen, she was sent to Miss Ridley's Academy for Genteel Young Ladies. There she met Felicia and the two became instant and close friends. What Felicia did, I don't know, but as far as Eliza is concerned, Felicia can do no wrong."

"That explains why Eliza, after hearing Edward mention Felicia in passing to me, spent most of the rest of the time she was at The Downs singing Felicia's praises and not trying to push Amanda at me."

Felicia sat in a window seat, staring out across the Abbey's extensive gardens. Why had she panicked? Hadn't Mira warned her men's bodies reacted like that? She had described what happened between men and women to Felicia years ago, and it wasn't until Mira had done so that Felicia linked Aaron's actions with Davey's birth nearly a year later. She knew Ella never again came up to the house when Aaron was there. That Aaron was dead only a few months later must have relieved her, but the steward, who had been Aaron's friend, remained. Ella avoided the estate altogether after Felicia's father died and the steward took up residence.

Resting her head on her folded arms, Felicia wondered what Brand thought of her actions. His surprise had allowed her to get away from him. How would he react if it happened again? It wouldn't, she decided. She could not allow him to kiss her again, especially if it affected him that way.

Which meant she couldn't marry him. If she married him, he would expect to share her bed. Something she knew she could never do. She would not suffer like Ella.

On some level, Felicia knew she was being unreasonable. Women gave birth every day—including her own sister—but the thought of allowing a man to do what Mira described to her filled her with fear. And each time the thought reared its head, she was once again nine years old, cowering behind a bush, watching Aaron, and hearing Ella cry and plead for him to stop.

Chapter Six

Felicia emerged from her room at midmorning the next day. Having spent most of the previous day thinking matters through, she felt confident she could discourage Brand in his pursuit.

She was disappointed not to find anyone in the library. Davey, she knew, was at the vicar's for his lessons, so she wandered into the drawing room. The piano in the corner of the room seemed to call to her and she drifted in that direction. Seating herself on the bench, she began to play and was soon oblivious to all but the music.

Losing herself in music was a favorite pastime. For her, music was a release from the rest of the world. Whether it was a sonata or concerto, a minuet or waltz, a country ditty or funeral dirge, she could close her eyes, play and leave her problems and cares behind.

She had no idea how long she played, moving through piece after piece, all memorized from years of playing. She was calm, nearly drowsy, when she finally opened her eyes sometime later to find Brand sitting in a chair not far away.

Neither seemed inclined to break the mood her playing had created, so they sat in silence. Eventually, however, Brand spoke.

"Jon said you played well. His praise did not do you justice." His low voice washed over her like a warm, spring rain.

"Thank you," she murmured in an equally soft, but slightly embarrassed, voice.

Glancing up at the clock on the fireplace mantle, she realized it was nearly time for luncheon. Brand rose as she did and the two left the room together.

The warm, comfortable feeling of the drawing room lingered over lunch, but only until Brand noticed she wasn't wearing her ring.

"Felicia?" Brand's voice was mildly curious, but the tone sent small shivers down her spine.

She looked up from her plate. "Hmmm?"

"Where is your ring today?"

"In my jewelry box." She resumed eating.

"I see." He took a bite of the poached salmon sitting before him. "And I suppose your promise of—"

"I promised," she interrupted, "to keep it, not wear it."

Felicia noticed Jon looking from one to the other. He smothered a grin, but Brand looked as if he could cheerfully strangle her right then and there.

Brand said no more, and Felicia felt his eyes on her throughout the rest of the meal. The silence was deafening and she was sure everyone in the room, including the footmen, could hear her heart beating. She managed to get through the rest of luncheon without her hands shaking or spilling anything, but as it took a monumental effort, she enjoyed little of Cook's excellent repast.

After lunch, Brand followed her from the room. Once in the hall, she hesitated. Brand did not. Taking her arm in a vise-like grip, he led her out into the gardens, away from the house. She was content to keep silent until they were far enough away from the house to be out of earshot.

"I think we should talk, my lord." She couldn't stop the nervous wobble in her voice.

Felicia stole a glance at him when he didn't answer. His face was carved in stone and the expression might have made a more timorous soul shake in their shoes. But she was made of sterner stuff, she told herself.

"I cannot..."

"Don't." Brand's voice was little more than a growl.

Felicia stopped and turned to look at him. He was still scowling, but his eyes softened as he looked down at her.

"We cannot continue on this way," she blurted out in a rush.

"On that we agree."

Heartened by his agreement, she dove in. "We just don't suit."

"What makes you think that?"

"I can't be what you want me to be."

"How do you know what I want you to be?"

Felicia turned to gaze out over the gardens. The early flowers were in bloom, turning some areas into a blaze of color. Folding her arms around her waist in a protective gesture, she told him what she'd never told another soul. "I cannot be your wife. I cannot be anyone's wife."

"Why?"

The question surprised her and she turned her head to look up at him again. "Why?"

"I don't think you misheard me."

"Because...because, I just can't." Felicia had never considered herself a coward, but for some reason she couldn't explain, she could not tell Brand she was afraid of the marriage bed.

"You'll have to provide more information if you hope to convince me to release you."

Brand felt a tiny twinge of guilt as he watched a small ray of hope dawn in her eyes. He had no intention of letting her go. She was his, and in a very short time he had grown used to the notion. Every possessive instinct he owned refused to see her any other way.

She lifted her chin defiantly. "I won't share your bed."

He managed not to let his astonishment show. "Why not?"

She looked away. "Because I won't."

He would not get any more information this way, he decided, so he tried another tack. Folding his arms across his chest, he asked, "So, if you don't plan to be anyone's wife, what do you plan to do?"

She began walking again and he followed. "I'll take Davey to Journey's End and raise him there. Then, when I'm gone, it will be his."

"I see you've figured it all out." He watched her head nod in agreement. "But there's something you should know."

She stopped and turned toward him again. "What is that?"

"Journey's End is not yours to give."

Felicia's mouth dropped open. "Wh-what?" Quickly closing her mouth, she looked up at him through narrowed eyes and demanded, "What do you mean it's not mine?"

Brand shrugged. "Jon and I have discussed the settlements. The property is only part of your dowry. No marriage, no dowry."

"But, but—" Felicia stammered, unable to create a coherent sentence.

"According to Jon, Jay does not want the property. If you don't marry, he will probably sell it. He has received offers from a number of landowners in the area around it."

Brand watched comprehension, then horror, dawn across her face. Something twisted inside him as he watched her realize all her planning was for naught. The property she so blithely assumed belonged to her didn't.

He was sure Felicia did not realize how suddenly lost and forlorn she looked. If she had, she might have done something rash. Instead she merely stood there and looked at Brand through wide, moisture-filled eyes. The pain in them was more than he could bear, despite that he had caused it.

Stepping toward her, he gathered her into his arms and held her gently. There was nothing he could say to make it better. He knew she would just resent him more if he offered now to let her give the property to Davey. He had told her she didn't have a choice. It was just taking her time to realize it.

She'd surprised him with her statement about not sharing his bed. But, he reasoned, all young brides held a fear of the marriage bed. He knew young girls often went into marriages knowing little about the physical side of it. There was no telling what mothers told their daughters, but what happened to daughters with no mothers, like Felicia? He sighed and looked down at the dark curls resting against his chest.

"Are you all right?"

Felicia had taken the time to regain her composure. "Yes."

"I'm sorry to be the bearer of unhappy news, but you must see there is no other way."

Felicia shook her head. "I shall just have to find another way." She spoke as if she hadn't heard him. "I know Papa settled some money on me, so I'll have to ask Jay about it.

Maybe I'll just convince Tina to give me the property anyway." Brand's arms dropped away and she stepped back from him. "Tina will understand," she said more to herself than him.

Brand ground his teeth in frustration. Would she never give up on this foolish idea of hers? What was it about Davey that required she waste her life for him?

"Felicia," he said patiently. "Felicia, I doubt you will sway your sister if her husband does not want her to be swayed."

She looked back up at him, before turning to walk away again. Once again, he followed. "Tina will understand," she threw over her shoulder. "Davey will need..."

He reached out and grabbed her arm, swinging her around to face him. "For God's sake, Felicia, why are you throwing your life away?"

Sparks flew from those blue orbs and she stared up at him as if he had two heads.

"You don't understand!" she nearly screamed at him. "I'm not throwing my life away. Davey needs me!"

"And what about you?" he demanded. "What do *you* need? Don't your needs matter?"

She shook her head and continued. "You just do not understand. Davey is the *only* thing that matters." Then she turned and hurried away, leaving him staring after her in consternation.

He followed at a slower pace, giving himself time to think. He knew where she was headed. It was time for Davey's daily riding lesson.

Davey is the only thing that matters. The words chased around in his head. Why? Why was Davey the only one who mattered? And why was she the only one who understood it? It was a puzzle and he was determined to solve it. In the meantime, however, it seemed the only way to get her to agree to marry him was to accept that Davey, for the moment, was more important than her own well-being.

Felicia stood by the fence watching Davey, the sun glinting off her dark hair. He'd hustled her out of the house so quickly after luncheon, she hadn't had the chance to put a bonnet on. While she stood there, a light breeze came up, lifting her curls off her neck, blowing her blush pink skirts about her ankles. For a moment, he had to catch his breath as he watched her profile. His gut tightened and the blood rushed from his head to a lower part of his anatomy. He groaned.

Reaching the fence, he stood beside her watching Davey take instruction from Del. Despite his tightly bound arm, Davey paid close attention and was able to follow the stable master's instructions easily. The boy seemed to be comfortable on horseback.

Glancing over at Felicia as she watched Davey, he wondered at the intense interest he saw there. She was so attached to him that, had Jon not told him of Davey's parentage and he didn't know her age, he might suspect her of being the boy's mother. That she had cast herself in that role, he did not doubt. The question to be asked, however, was why?

"He will be ready for more than a pony by the time his arm is healed."

She turned to look at him, pride in her eyes. "I think he might, but Jon doesn't really have anything in his stables he could advance to. All of his horses are too big. Davey will just have to be content with the pony for a while." Then she turned back to watch.

Brand watched Del put the boy and pony through a series of starts, stops, and turns, then turned to Felicia again.

"You'll forgive my curiosity I hope, but why is it you feel responsible for Davey?"

Felicia did not turn from watching Davey. "Because no one else does. His father is dead—not that Aaron would have acknowledged him anyway. And his mother doesn't want him. She's married now and has other children."

"I see."

"No, actually I don't think you do. Whether others want to acknowledge it or not, I *know* Davey is my nephew. There is no place for him in Parkton or at Thane Park. His only chance is to get away and have a chance at a new life where no one knows him. And I can give that to him. It's as simple as that."

"Wouldn't you like to have some help?"

"Help?" The puzzled note in her voice showed her confusion. "Help, how?"

"Having been a teenage boy once, I can tell you it will not be easy raising him alone." Leaning his forearms against the top rail of the fence, Brand slanted a glance in her direction.

She was chewing her bottom lip and Brand hoped she was considering the implications.

"Davey is obviously very important to you. As my wife, what's important to you would also be important to me."

She looked up at him in astonishment.

Davey was being helped down off the pony, his lesson over for today. Felicia took a step in his direction, but turned back to look up at Brand one last time.

"I will consider what you've said." With that she walked away and met Davey as he came through the gate, talking excitedly about his lesson. Watching her take his hand, Brand heard her say, "Let's go see if Cook has any treats for such an accomplished little boy." Then they headed up the path toward the back of the house.

Brand watched her go. She was too stubborn for her own good, but at least he had her attention. She hadn't missed his meaning. He needed to thank Jon for that bit of advice.

His last thought as he turned to retrace his steps toward the house was that she'd be good with children. Davey obviously adored her. That boded well for the future.

Felicia mulled over Brand's words throughout the afternoon. Going back and forth between thinking she should agree and telling herself absolutely not, she was still not sure of herself by the time tea rolled around. Of one thing she was certain. None of her other suitors would have agreed to raise Davey—especially not Lord Caverdown.

She didn't dwell on the fact that neither Jon nor Brand joined her in the large drawing room to partake of Cook's excellent tarts. They were probably out doing something—or planning something. She didn't waste time wondering. The solitude, however, gave her more time to think.

She hoped it hadn't been so obvious to Brand that she hadn't known what to say when he revealed the fallacy behind her expectations. She'd assumed if she didn't marry, the dowry would become hers. So, now what? What would she do about Davey now? She felt as if the ground beneath her feet had turned to quicksand.

Trying to be honest with herself, she admitted she liked Brand. He was gentle and considerate. He would never hit her, she was sure. Intuition and a healthy helping of gossip told her

Lord Caverdown wouldn't hesitate to use violence to achieve his own ends, hence another reason she would never have married him.

Of course Brand's stepmother hated her, but something told her that that would mean little to him. It was likely the duchess hadn't welcomed him with open arms, either.

Then there was Davey. Brand's ready acceptance was encouraging.

She sighed. Could she do it? Could she marry Brand knowing she couldn't, maybe wouldn't, give him children? She wasn't sure. And, she wasn't sure how far Jon was prepared to go to make it happen. Perhaps she could put it off.

The thought was instantaneous. Put it off! Of course, yes, that was it! She nearly clapped her hands with glee. How could she postpone the possibility until...until when? Until he gave up and found someone else? No, she wasn't sure that would work. Until the gossip blew over. Not likely. Until Jay and Tina returned? Possibly. She could say she couldn't be married without her sister present.

She didn't have anything to wear. That would work to start. She'd have to go to London—no, Paris—to have a trousseau made up. Yes! That was the answer. It could take weeks, maybe even months, to get it all ordered, made, and return to England. She'd have her wedding dress made there as well. By then the little Season will have started, Jay and Tina would be back, and she could talk to Jay about Journey's End.

Felicia left the drawing room in a happier frame of mind. She would insist she had to have a trousseau created by Worth himself, which meant a trip to Paris. She smiled to herself. She'd love to see Paris.

"Are you out of your mind?" Jon nearly shouted at her over dinner. Brand, for once, kept silent although she could tell he heartily agreed with Jon.

Used to Jon's blustering, she merely stared at him in consternation.

"Of course not. If I'm to marry, I need a trousseau. And since there's no reason to have a hasty wedding, I don't see why I can't take the time to have the wedding the way I want it."

"Absolutely not!" Jon's tone was hard, and, for once, she worried that he meant it.

"I suppose I don't deserve to have my wedding the way I want it?"

Jon shook his head. "That's not what I mean, and you know it. But, I am not taking you to Paris just to have some dresses made up."

"You had one made for Tina. Why can't I have one—or two? Jay can afford it." She knew she sounded spoiled, selfish, petty and a host of other not-too-complimentary descriptions, but at the moment she didn't care.

"That was different. And, as you point out, it was only one."

"And I can't even have that?"

"I didn't say that. But it takes time, something you don't have much of at the moment."

"Why not? There's no hurry. If I'm already ruined, what will an extra few weeks do?"

He muttered something under his breath and Brand smiled.

"What?" Turning narrowed eyes on Brand, she looked from one to the other. "Well?"

Jon looked up at Brand. Something passed between them, an acknowledgment, and she felt her blood turn to ice water. Then Jon turned to her. "The answer is no." The look in his eyes chilled her to the bone. "You will marry his lordship in a fortnight. End of discussion." Then he went back to his meal.

I will not! The words rose to her lips, but were never uttered. The tone of Jon's voice brooked no argument. She was losing ground fast.

"And if I refuse?"

Jon did not look up from his plate, but answered her between bites. "Then I will send Davey back to Thane Park."

Felicia reacted as if she'd been slapped. "You wouldn't." The words emerged from a suddenly dry throat. "Would you?"

Jon did not look up.

"You have a fortnight to find out."

The rest of dinner was accomplished in strained silence. As soon as the last plates were cleared away, Felicia rose from her chair and glared daggers at the two men. "I'll just leave you two gentlemen to your port," she announced in a voice which should have drawn blood. Then she left the room, closing the door none too gently behind her.

Jon sat back in his chair, leaned his head back and closed his eyes. Blowing out a strained breath, he cracked open one eye and looked at Brand.

"At least you're not bleeding."

Brand grinned. "Who says I'm not?"

"Why don't you look like you're in pain?"

Brand merely took a sip from his glass.

Jon straightened and looked at Brand soberly. "I'll call it off if you just say the word. I would hate to see her ruined, but I can't seriously see myself forcing her to wed you if you had doubts."

Brand understood. Jon was torn between Felicia's obvious reluctance which seemed to go far beyond general obstinacy. Yet, he wanted what was best for his beloved sister—and felt it necessary to save her from herself. Because she didn't realize how unrealistic her plans were she only reinforced his opinion that he was acting in her best interests.

"I can take care of myself. And Felicia. And Davey too. You needn't worry." Brand took another drink. "But I did think I might head back to The Downs tomorrow. I would like to bring my father back with me. I've already written to Eliza and Edward."

Jon groaned. "You don't suppose Eliza might leave Amanda in town?"

"Not if Amanda is truly Felicia's best friend." Brand knew he sounded entirely too cheerful considering the circumstances.

"You needn't sound so blasted happy about it."

Brand leaned back in his chair, his eyes glinting with amusement. "Misery loves company, you know. I don't want to be the only one off-balance." Jon's expression caused Brand to laugh.

"Are you sure it's Felicia you want?"

Brand nodded. "Surprisingly, yes. Your great-grandmother went through a lot of trouble to match us up. Don't you think we ought to give her the benefit of the doubt?"

At the moment, Jon was beginning to question Nona's sanity. If it was causing this much trouble to marry Felicia off according to Nona's mandate, he refused to contemplate what might happen when he found the woman with his item.

Felicia was still fuming over Jon's ultimatum the next morning. Having spent the previous evening heaping epithets and curses upon both his and Brand's heads, she finally settled down to think about her predicament in the early hours of the morning.

Brand had listened to the entire exchange and said nothing, so he must have agreed with Jon. Whatever happened, she now knew Jon would see her married to Brand regardless of her wishes in the matter. The unfairness of it all rankled, but fighting against something she now understood she couldn't change was an exercise in futility. She was stubborn, not stupid.

So be it, she decided. She had already told him she wouldn't share his bed. If he wanted her despite that, he would suffer the consequences. His brother Edward might marry someday and provide an heir.

That decision made, she finally went to sleep, awaking shortly before noon. Taking a tray in her room, she finally emerged in time to watch Davey's daily riding lesson.

It wasn't until dinner she learned Brand had left.

"Why?"

"He felt he was needed back at The Downs. It's only a day's ride away."

"I see. So, he'll be back in a fortnight?"

"I think that's what he was planning. There was certainly no reason to stay. You have made it clear you are not happy with the way things have been concluded. There was no reason to stay and continue to argue with you over something that was already decided."

"So he ran away."

"I don't think he was running from anything. After you left us last night, I gave him the opportunity to cry off. He refused." Jon pinned her with his emerald gaze. "He *wants* to marry you. Although why, after your actions over the last few days, I'll never know. You might do well to remember that."

"I don't know why either," she grumbled. "I've made it clear

I don't want to marry him."

"Even though he correctly identified your ring?" Amazement colored his words. "Is there someone else you'd prefer?"

"No."

"Then, why...?"

"I don't want to talk about it."

"Very well, then we won't." Jon waited while their plates were cleared away and an assortment of pastries and fruit was left on the table before them. The butler and footmen withdrew, then he asked, "So, shall we plan a small wedding?"

"No." She reached for a peach.

Jon watched her peel and slice the juicy fruit before taking a bite. He shouldn't be surprised she refused to plan her own wedding. He wondered if he should tell her Brand would return with his father and stepmother. Or if he should tell her Brand had written to his sister and brother? Maybe. But, maybe not. He'd wait a few more days and see what happened. In the meantime, he'd let her temper cool. Despite her calm facade, he knew she was still simmering over the previous night's dinner conversation.

"I see. So, nothing special?"

"I don't see any reason for it," she replied defensively. "It's not my choice. I'm not even going to get a new dress out of it."

He sighed. Back to speaking around the issue. "Why should you?" he asked. "You have plenty of suitable gowns, some of which you probably haven't even worn."

"Because a wedding gown ought to be special, that's why."

"Then you should have stayed in London, where you could have ordered one made in time and not be in this predicament at all. Although, I'm glad Brand was the one who recognized your ring. I was afraid circumstances would have required us to let Nona down."

Felicia had no response to that sally, so she finished her peach and rose from the table.

"I'm going up to say good night to Davey. I'll see you in the morning." Then she left Jon to stare at the closed door behind her.

Two days later, three carriages came up the drive and deposited their passengers at the Abbey. Felicia was in the drawing room reading when she was informed guests had arrived and, upon reaching the front hall, was not pleased to see the Duchess of Westover, Jon's grandmother and Geri being admitted. And, when the duchess and Geri admitted their husbands were following on horseback, she nearly screamed in frustration.

Jon's grandmother immediately took charge and the staff, used to taking orders from her, jumped to do her bidding. Soon all three ladies and their belongings were on their way to their rooms. Felicia was instructed to order tea in the drawing room, and they would be down shortly.

Felicia wished she could excuse herself from their company, but she knew they were only here because of her. Well, she thought, at least she had some answers for them, even if they weren't what she would have wanted to tell them.

"Well," the duchess demanded after Milstead and the footmen left the drawing room and closed the door, "I'm waiting for an explanation."

"There isn't one." Felicia remained calm, although she'd never experienced the duchess when she was angry. "I wanted out of London." She paused to pour the duchess a cup of tea. "I'm sorry for the fabrication. I knew Jon wasn't due back yet, but I just couldn't stomach another house party."

"And the young man you were seen leaving with?" This from Geri.

Felicia gave them a brittle smile. "It was only Brand, but you are just in time to plan my wedding. I'm sure Jon will be pleased to see you, especially since I refuse to take part."

"Brand?" Geri again.

"Otherwise known as Bertrand Waring, Marquess of Lofton."

It was gratifying, in a way, to watch the looks of pure amazement cross all three faces. It really should have heartened her to know she could still surprise the duchess and dowager countess, but she was still smarting over Jon and Brand's heavy-handedness to take much joy from the situation.

"No one else has laid eyes on him yet—and you're about to marry him?" the duchess's anger had become wonder.

Geri began to laugh. The other three looked at her as if she belonged in Bedlam, but she continued to laugh until the tears began rolling down her face. She put down her cup to keep from spilling her tea, then produced a scrap of lace to dab at her face.

"I'm sorry, Felicia, but this is all too much," she said between giggles. "I can't believe you actually did it. What about your ring? Was he the one?"

Felicia gritted her teeth. Of course Geri would see the humor in the situation—and remember the ring, too. "As it turned out, yes, he was." She wanted to scream in frustration. "But I still don't want to marry him."

That got all three ladies' attention.

"Why?" the dowager snapped. "What's wrong with him?"

"Nothing," she replied.

"Is he too short? Missing his teeth?" The dowager's sharp questions shook her for a moment.

"Does he look like Edward or Eliza?" the duchess asked.

Felicia sighed. "He's not too short. In fact, he's taller than Jon. As far as I can tell he's got all his teeth. And he resembles Eliza, not Edward. He rather reminds me of a lion. And, yes, he's handsome. He could have his pick of anyone, but now he's stuck with me."

"By that you mean he could have his pick of any of the currently reigning beauties of the Season—of which you don't consider yourself one?" Geri asked.

Felicia shrugged, but didn't reply.

"And why," the duchess snorted, "would she want to be lumped in with that empty-headed lot? At least you won't bore him to death."

Felicia considered this for a moment. No, she wouldn't bore him to death. She might drive him mad eventually, but she'd never bore him. For a heartbeat, she actually saw her present situation in an amusing light.

"So, where did you meet him?" Geri again.

"At Jon's. He's Jay's partner in his shipping business. With Jay and Tina in Italy, Jon was watching out for him to return."

"You mean the Marquis has known his whereabouts all these years?" The dowager asked the question all three ladies were thinking.

"Yes, I suppose he has."

After tea, Felicia and Geri left the drawing room together. "Have you decided what to wear?" Geri asked as the two climbed the staircase.

Felicia shrugged. "No. And, I don't particularly care. I don't have a wedding dress, although Jon insists I should have something suitable in my wardrobe."

Geri looked at her closely. Felicia knew she must look like a petty, spoiled child. "I suppose he wouldn't postpone it long enough for you to have a trousseau made up?"

"No. He insists I'm ruined, so it needs to happen quickly."

"Then perhaps it's just as well. I think we brought something suitable with us."

Felicia stopped and turned to look at her. "You think? Why would you think you have it—don't you know? And where did it come from, anyway. I certainly didn't order it."

"When my mama-in-law and I returned from the Hortensen's, there was a package waiting for you. It's from Jay and Tina."

They approached her room. The door stood open and two footmen were exiting, each carrying a trunk. "We brought it with us with the rest of your things."

Geri followed her in. Lily was just coming out of the dressing room. Another footman stood beside a smaller trunk sitting closer to the foot of the bed.

"An' waddaya want done wid dis one?" he was asking Lily.

"Leave that," Lily told him. "Her Grace's maid said my lady was to open it herself."

As he turned to leave, they both looked up and noticed Geri and Felicia. The footman continued out the door as Lily said to Felicia, "I finished unpacking the rest of your trunks, my lady. But Her Grace's maid said not to open this small one. Although I don't remember seeing it before, she insisted it was yours."

Geri came to her rescue. "This is what came for you from Jay and Tina. The man who delivered it said it came from Paris. The card delivered with it merely said "The House of Worth" on it.

Felicia nearly groaned aloud. After the scene she made

about wanting a new dress and a Worth trousseau, she wasn't sure she wanted to open it. But Geri was waiting, eyeing the small trunk with undisguised curiosity.

"Thank you, Lily," Felicia dismissed the maid, then turned to the small trunk on the floor. It was bound by a strong leather strap which had already been loosened. Pulling it off, she lifted the lid. Inside she found a sealed missive, her name written on the front in Tina's careful hand. Turning to Geri, she tried for cheerfulness as she invited, "Why don't you see what's in it while I read Tina's note?"

Geri didn't wait to be asked twice. Reaching into the trunk, she removed a parcel wrapped in tissue and began to unwrap it.

Felicia settled on the window seat to read the letter from Tina. After describing their crossing and travel to Paris, Tina turned to the contents of the trunk.

Jay and I are sending you what we hope will be your wedding gown. At Maison Worth, we were treated to a wonderful display of stunning gowns and patterns, from which I picked this one for you. Jay agreed you would look exceptionally beautiful in it and even though I may not see you married in it, I hope it will meet with your approval. There is also a necklace, bracelet, earbobs, and a small tiara to match. (I thought the tiara was necessary for a duchess even though Jay still finds it amusing.) Consider the jewelry our wedding present to you. If, by chance, you have not found the person who recognizes your ring, do not feel you have to marry because we sent you the dress—wear it to the next ball instead.

Finishing the letter with news of their daughter, Tina sent her love and wished her well before closing the letter by saying they did not plan to return before August.

Setting the letter down in her lap, Felicia looked up without really seeing. She supposed it served her right that she would get what she wished for. The tirade about the gown and trousseau had been a stalling tactic, but it had fallen on deaf ears. So, now what?

Destiny, the fates, the powers that be, God himself—whoever was orchestrating her life wanted this wedding to take place. Perhaps it was time to accept the direction her life was going and make the best of it. But, she hated to settle for less than what she wanted.

Then make it what you want. The words floated through her head. Could she? Could she learn to love Brand and he learn to love her? Could she eventually accept him into her bed? A shudder ran through her at the thought. Would she ever be able to set aside her fear?

The rustle of tissue paper brought her out of her dour thoughts.

"Felicia, look!" Geri's excited voice carried her way. "It's beautiful. Just perfect for a wedding."

Felicia rose, leaving Tina's letter on the seat, and approached the bed where Geri had laid out her finds. The gown was indeed the most beautiful thing she'd ever seen.

The bodice, a simple off-the-shoulder garment of fitted white silk, was overlaid with a very fine white lace. The underskirt was of the same soft, white silk of the bodice, then came two layers of white gauze which provided fullness without weight, overlaid by a matching layer of fine white lace. Although the style of wide hoop skirts were slowly diminishing in size, this one employed the style to advantage without making use of so many petticoats that the dress became heavy or uncomfortable. It looked like a fairy creation, fragile and insubstantial, with a sprinkling of tiny sapphires across the front of the skirt giving one the impression of blue stars twinkling in a white sky.

From the bottom of the trunk, Geri brought out a jewel case which held a single strand necklace and matching bracelet of sapphires, single sapphire earbobs and a small silver tiara also set with sapphires.

There were also all the accessories; shoes, stockings, a lace handkerchief, a veil of matching lace, silk gloves, and even a small reticule. Tina had thought of everything. And had chosen well.

Felicia sat on the bed and fingered the delicate creation. It was the most beautiful gown she'd ever seen—and it was hers. So why did she not feel fortunate? Why did she wish she had never laid eyes on it? Why did she feel as if she had been solidly backed into a corner with no way out except down the aisle?

Because she had. She had lost control. Since her mother

died when she was thirteen, she had considered herself in control of her life. But now she had lost control. Jon decided she was ruined. Brand decided he had ruined her. So, Jon and Brand decided she was to marry. She might want to deny it, but the sequence of events had left her control the moment she left London in Brand's company. Perhaps even the moment he had given in to her request to bring her and Davey along.

She should have known better. She did know better. But she didn't think far enough ahead to realize she might not get out of the tangle if word got out. She had blithely decided she didn't care, but hadn't reckoned on the fact that Jon—and Brand—would.

Felicia didn't realize she was crying until Geri sat beside her, a worried look in her dark eyes. "Felicia? Do you want to talk about it?" She handed Felicia the still damp handkerchief she had used earlier to dry her own eyes.

Felicia accepted the bit of lace, but shook her head. She couldn't explain to Geri her trepidation at entering into a marriage with Brand. Geri wouldn't understand. For her, as for Jon, if Brand recognized the ring, he was the right one. After Jay and Tina, Geri would never understand why Felicia wasn't thrilled to have found him.

Pulling herself together, she gave Geri a wan smile. "I think I'm just overwhelmed," she prevaricated. "The dress is just what I have always wanted."

She knew Geri was not convinced, but she said nothing more.

Chapter Seven

"Violets," Geri said the next day as she and Felicia strolled in the gardens after luncheon. "They will look wonderful with your dress."

Felicia shrugged. She didn't particularly care what kind of flowers she had and stubbornly refused to be drawn into the planning which she knew had begun. Jon's grandmother had informed her that the wedding would take place at eleven o'clock, followed by luncheon.

Geri looked worriedly at her. The day was warm, unseasonably so with a clear sky and a light breeze. Flowery scents filled the air.

"Felicia?"

"Hmmm?"

"Why the sadness? And don't tell me that you're overwhelmed. That was yesterday's excuse."

Felicia gave her a colorless smile. "I don't know," she answered truthfully. "I suppose I've been fighting this wedding for so long, it's become second nature to continue to do so."

"And you don't want to give up being contrary?"

Felicia sighed. "I suspect the problem is I'm too stubborn for my own good and I hate to let Jon think he might be right." The admission felt better said out loud.

Geri giggled. "There is that, isn't there? If you let the men think they are right once, they will think they are right all the time."

They walked in silence for a time, through the hedgerows and into the rose garden. Then Geri asked, "How did he find out about the ring?"

Felicia let out a half-hearted groan. "Oh, Geri, you wouldn't have believed it. I nearly swooned."

Geri laughed when Felicia finished recounting the scene in the library. "I suppose it could be worse. His mother's second name could have been close to mine too."

Geri laughed outright then. "Maybe we should ask."

"Maybe we shouldn't."

"Coward."

Felicia looked at her friend askance. She knew Geri was teasing, so hadn't taken offense. "Perhaps. My great-grandmother seemed so other worldly in her knowledge sometimes it was frightening. She knew too much, and there was no explanation of how she gained her knowledge. She couldn't even read or write."

Geri considered this information for a moment. "Then you own there might be something to your match with Brand?"

"Possibly." The admission emerged grudgingly.

"And if it turns out his mother was also Felicia—or even a Felice, or some other version of your name—then what?"

"What do you think I should do?"

Geri considered the question as they continued walking. Leaving the rose garden behind, they followed the path headed for the stables.

"Maybe you should stop fighting and try to make the best of it."

Felicia threw her a speaking glance. "Somehow, I thought that's what you'd say."

It was Geri's turn to shrug. "There's no use fighting fate."

They reached the fence around the enclosure just as Davey was being helped onto the pony he was learning to ride.

"So, will you?"

Felicia turned. "Will I what?"

"Stop fighting if it turns out Brand's mother's name was very close to yours?"

Felicia narrowed her eyes suspiciously. "Do you already know what her second name was?"

"No, I just think all the coincidences are so peculiar there ought to be something to it." Geri turned to watch Davey ride around the enclosure for a few minutes, then glanced over at Felicia again. "I'll ask my mama-in-law. Maybe she knows. Or better yet, the dowager countess might know."

"It would be interesting to know."

"Well?"

"Why do I think I'm being hoodwinked into agreeing to something I don't like?"

Geri laughed. "Because you think the same thing I do. The possibility exists it's true. And your curiosity is getting the better of you."

Felicia smiled genuinely for the first time in days. "Very well. You win. If it turns out Brand's mother's name is close enough to mine to cause comment, then I will give in and try to make the best of it."

Geri nearly crowed in triumph, but Felicia had the last word.

"But I'll bet her name was something like Elizabeth, which is how Eliza got her name. After all, I was named for my mother." Then she turned to watch Davey and no more was said on the subject.

Over tea, Geri asked the duchess and dowager if either of them knew the previous Duchess of Warringham's given names. Neither did.

When Geri and Felicia left the drawing room afterwards, Felicia nearly laughed at Geri's sigh of disappointment.

"I was sure one of them would know—and I would be right," she complained. "What's the use of knowing everything about everyone if you don't know the truly useful information?" she said, speaking of her mother-in-law.

"I'm not sure knowing everyone's given and second or third names is considered useful information." Felicia was smug in her enjoyment.

"That's easy for you to say," Geri groused. "I was sure you'd be well on your way to accepting your lot in life by now."

"Instead, I can continue to be obstinate and stubborn."

The next morning, Felicia and Geri were just finishing breakfast when she was summoned to the dowager's room.

"Now what?" She looked at Geri as if expecting her to know why.

"I don't know. But I wouldn't keep her waiting."

"She probably wants to ring a peal over my head about something else to do with this wedding. I've already promised not to interfere—what else could she want?"

Geri laughed and Felicia threw her a speaking look. "Felicia, only you would consider helping to plan your own wedding to be interfering."

Leaving the breakfast room, the two women headed for the staircase. "You ought to be glad I am not insisting on my own way in all this."

Just before they reached the top of the stairs and parted ways, Geri said to her, "Be wary of the dowager. I suspect she knows more ways to intimidate a person than anyone else. She's had years of practice."

Felicia shrugged. "I'm not worried."

As she walked down the corridor then up another flight of stairs, she reminded herself she wasn't concerned about the dowager countess. It was Jon she was worried about. His threat to send Davey back to Thane Park still hung over her head. She wasn't sure whether he really would do it, but she wasn't about to jeopardize Davey's well-being over it.

The dowager countess occupied the only easily accessible tower room. Originally built with steep stone steps leading to it, when an addition was built on to the Abbey, a four-story section was added in such a way that the top floor was level with the entrance to the tower room. The other tower room still required a very steep climb to get to it, and Felicia was surprised the dowager preferred a room requiring such a climb to get to.

Knocking lightly at the door, she was admitted by the dowager's maid into a room filled with sunshine. Two large windows took up most of the wall space, the heavy burgundy drapes pulled back to allow the day in. A large oak four-poster bed sat on one side of the room, its coverings of burgundy velvet neatly in place. On the other side of the room, near one of the windows, sat the dowager on a chaise. Two comfortable chairs, upholstered also in burgundy, were arranged nearby with a small table between them. In her gray-silk-covered lap, she held a sheaf of papers. She looked up as Felicia entered.

"It's about time."

Felicia approached and curtseyed. "You sent for me, ma'am?"

The dowager waved an emerald- and diamond-bedecked hand at one of the two chairs. "Sit!"

Felicia sat. And waited.

The dowager finished perusing the papers in her hand, occasionally making a mark on one with the pencil stub she held.

Felicia watched her for a while, then allowed her gaze to wander. The brick walls were quite thick, but Felicia was sure that, if not for the heavy drapes at the windows, this room would be cold in the winter. The fireplace was on the opposite wall from the bed, nearly behind where she sat, with the dressing table the maid was now straightening situated beside it.

Finishing her work, the maid turned to ask the dowager if she needed her any longer.

"No, not for the moment. Take these with you when you go." She handed the maid the sheaf of papers, now divided in two. "This bunch goes to the cook, and these to the housekeeper. See you don't mix them up."

The maid nodded and, taking the papers, quickly left the room. The dowager then turned her sharp green gaze on Felicia. "Well," she barked. "What have you to say for yourself?"

"Nothing, ma'am. You sent for me."

The dowager stared at her for so long Felicia began to grow uneasy, but she refused to show it. Sitting without squirming under the older woman's regard took all of her willpower.

"Where's your ring?" The question was like a pistol shot in the room.

Instinctively, Felicia clasped her hands together. "My ring?"

"Yes. His lordship's mother's ring, I understand. Why aren't you wearing it?"

"I—I choose not to."

"Why?"

Felicia blinked. "Why? Oh, uh, I—because I choose not to," she finished lamely.

"Are you trying to embarrass your brother in front of his

guests or your betrothed in front of his family?"

Felicia was taken back. "Embarrass Jon? How?"

"By continuing to be pigheaded."

Unable to respond, Felicia waited for the explanation she was sure was forthcoming.

"When his lordship returns, he will be accompanied by his father and stepmother." Felicia caught herself before she groaned in dismay. "In addition, he has requested the presence of his sister and brother at this wedding. Do you intend to continue this childish display of behavior in front of them?"

It took all of the discipline she possessed to not allow her astonishment to show. The effort was for naught, however, as she knew the dowager could tell she was taken aback by the revelation.

"Did you think he was just going to marry you, take you off somewhere and hide you away?"

"N—no, I—I didn't..." she began haltingly, only to be cut off again by the dowager.

"Then what did you expect to happen?"

That was a loaded question, for Felicia suddenly admitted to herself she hadn't thought of anything past the wedding. Somehow, she had thought of the wedding as the end. Yet, now it occurred to her she should be thinking of it as a beginning of sorts. But what kind of beginning?

"I—I hadn't thought about it," she replied. "Truthfully, I've tried to think of it as little as possible."

"That's obvious." The dowager shook her finger at Felicia as she spoke. "Now, you listen to me, missy. In less than a fortnight, you will marry the Marquess of Lofton. There is nothing you can do to stop it, and acting like a spoiled infant will not change anyone's mind. In fact, your actions have convinced me what you need is a strong husband to keep you in line. You have made your bed, so to speak, now you will have to lie in it. So, buck up and make the best of it or you will be miserable for many a long year."

The dowager's eyes narrowed as they pinned her to her seat.

"Someday you will be the Duchess of Warringham and a leader in society. And, despite Emily's thoughts on the matter, you'll likely make a good one. But, you'd better start learning now how to live with adversity and accept the distasteful things life will throw your way, or you will end up a bitter old woman."

Felicia knew the dowager was speaking of herself. It was no secret the dowager sorely regretted the "wasted years", as she was known to call them, she'd allowed to pass while refusing to acknowledge her only living grandchildren.

"Did you truly hate Mama so much?" Felicia abruptly changed the subject.

The dowager's face softened as she looked at Felicia. "I suppose I did at one time," she sighed, "but it was so long ago, I have no real recollection of why except I knew her mother was half-gypsy."

It sounded too close to home for her, for Felicia knew that that was exactly why Brand's stepmother disliked her. Her gypsy blood was tainted—not fit to be mingled with the blood of purebred Englishmen.

"But it didn't matter that she could make Jon and Tina's father happy."

"Not at the time." The dowager smiled sadly and Felicia glimpsed a little of the woman she must have been when she was younger. "But I learned over the next few years just how important it was. Jonathan's letters home were so full of life I knew she had to be the cause. I might have eventually accepted it if I hadn't lost my husband and remaining sons so quickly, leaving Jonathan as the next earl, and making your mother his countess.

"I may regret I was unwilling to accept her, but I don't regret your father, old reprobate that he was, raised Jon and Tina. He did a fine job—much better than with his own sons. And probably much better than if I had taken them in."

"I suspect Mama was the reason. Sometimes when Jay talks about our father, I have to wonder if they were the same person, and I know he feels the same when Tina speaks of him as well."

Felicia left the dowager's room in a better frame of mind. She supposed she always knew she had to accept the marriage. Fighting it was making her crazy. If she kept it up, she would be a candidate for Bedlam.

Unable to explain her fears to the dowager or Geri, she had

no real excuse for why she didn't want to marry Brand.

Entering her room, she went over to her dressing table and lifted the lid to her jewel case. The ring sat on top, winking at her in the light. Picking it up, she slipped it on her left hand, sighed, then closed the case and left the room. There was no turning back now. She would make the best of it, but she still would not share his bed.

Felicia was up in the nursery with Davey when Brand's sister, Eliza, and her husband, the Earl of Barrington, arrived shortly before luncheon near the end of the week. It was another bright, sunny day, but Davey had been feeling a bit under the weather, so the two of them had spent most of the morning playing indoors. He looked so tired by the time she left that she suggested he forego his riding lesson today and rest.

Entering the drawing room just before luncheon, she was therefore, surprised to find the Earl and Countess of Barrington, with Amanda, there.

"Felicia!" Amanda greeted her warmly. "What a surprise."

"Surprise?" Felicia asked. "Didn't you know I was here?"

"Your engagement, silly."

"Oh, that."

Eliza greeted her warmly. "I was so glad to hear from Brand. I just know you will be perfect for him."

Felicia smiled weakly. She had always liked Eliza, but now she felt like a fraud. Jon joined them and she watched Amanda surreptitiously watch him, and smiled. At least some things never changed. If only Brand had been interested in Amanda. But Jon had given him the chance to cry off and he had refused. Why? There was no time to ponder the question as Milstead announced lunch.

After lunch, Felicia and Amanda wandered the house and grounds, talking and catching up. Although Amanda tried to ask Felicia about Brand, after Felicia refused to talk about it more than once, Amanda recognized the subject as being off limits for the time being and the two spent a comfortable afternoon.

"Edward was laughing," Amanda told her.

"About what?"

"Your engagement to Brand." Amanda grinned. "Think about it. His mother didn't want you to trap Edward because she said you weren't good enough to be the next Duchess of Warringham, so what happens?"

Felicia could see how Edward would be amused at thwarting his mother.

"That witch, Lady Craley, asked Edward if you'd dumped him once his brother showed up."

Shock caused Felicia to nearly scream. "What?"

Amanda giggled. "Edward just laughed at her and said, 'better him than me'." Amanda's laughter petered out as she continued. "Unfortunately, Lady Craley took it in exactly the wrong way, and asked Edward if his mother would approve."

Felicia stopped and turned to look at Amanda. They were standing near a fountain in the middle of the rose garden, the scent of budding roses faint in the air. The sky was mirrored in Amanda's eyes, especially with the light of amusement shining in them, while a warm breeze teased the ribbons on both their bonnets.

"And what did Edward say to that?"

"He laughed even more so and told her bluntly that his mother had no control over his brother."

Felicia didn't know if she was relieved or disappointed. It might have been easier to still derail the wedding if Brand was willing to take his stepmother's advice, but since she, and many others, thought the duchess might have been behind Brand's disappearance in the first place, the likelihood of that happening was not at all.

"I bet she doesn't dare cut you in public," Amanda mused.

"Who?"

"The duchess, of course. She might have been able to make your life miserable had you married Edward, but now..." Amanda let the statement trail off and Felicia did not bother to answer. She knew what her friend meant.

It was over tea that Felicia received another shock. The ladies had all congregated in the drawing room, the men had yet to join them, when Geri asked Eliza why her brother was referred to as Brand, rather than Bertrand.

"I asked Brand when we were at The Downs and he said he didn't know. He'd just always been referred to by that name. But Papa overheard me and told us that I had given him the nickname when I was about two. He said I had a hard time learning to pronounce Bertrand and often slurred over the first syllable. What I did manage to say was Brand, and it stuck."

"Oh." Geri sounded disappointed. "I was hoping it came about because he was such a firebrand, or some such."

Eliza shook her head. "I'm afraid not. In fact, he was apparently very somber as a child and very protective of Michael and me."

Felicia had a difficult time seeing Brand as a somber or serious child. He exuded a restless energy she would have thought hard to contain. She thought brand, as an explosive reference, fit him well. Eliza's next words, however, brought her out of her thoughts with a vengeance.

"Oh, Felicia, I have to tell you of the most astounding coincidence. I suppose I had forgotten over the years, but I was reminded when Brand and I went out to visit our mother's grave." Felicia felt a chill slither down her spine. "Our mother's second name was Felicia," she announced blithely. "Isn't that amazing?"

Felicia stopped breathing. Her, thankfully empty, teacup fell to the thick carpet at her feet. She was sure her mouth had dropped open and tried to close it. The strangled gasp she emitted, however, was drowned out by Geri's unladylike shout of laughter.

The men chose that moment to join them. Jon took in Geri, doubled over in laughter, and Felicia's shocked face and wondered what had happened now.

The Westovers had become the best of friends where their family was concerned. First appearing at Tina and Jay's wedding, then helping to select a young ladies' academy for Felicia, and helping with Felicia's debut and presentation. Over the years, they had provided much moral support to all of them, but Jon was beginning to worry Geri was enjoying Felicia's discomfort a little too much in all of this.

Seating himself beside his sister, he retrieved her cup from the floor and took the saucer from her nerveless fingers before setting them both on the small table before her.

Amanda saved him from asking what was wrong. "You have to admit, Felicia, it *is* funny," she said with a giggle, but her eyes held a hint of worry. Felicia's reaction was obviously not what she expected.

"It's not!" Felicia snapped. "It's not funny at all. It's sick!" Then she jumped to her feet and ran from the room.

Her outburst stunned everyone into silence and sobered Geri in a way nothing else could have.

"Oh, dear," Geri was the first one to break the silence. "I've put my foot in it this time," she said, raising worried eyes to her husband. "I don't think even I thought such a coincidence was truly likely."

Chapter Eight

Felicia sat on a bale of hay in a corner of Midnight's stall, her legs drawn up, arms folded and resting on her knees. With her head resting on her arms, she didn't hear Jon approach. Not that it would have mattered. She was too deep in her own misery to care.

She had made a fool of herself and probably embarrassed Eliza too. Why couldn't she have seen it as funny the way everyone else did? Because there were too many unnerving coincidences to this whole situation.

Trying to be honest with herself, she acknowledged if it weren't for what happened when she was nine, she might be looking forward to marrying Brand. He was everything she'd ever dreamed about in a husband. The quip about only marrying a duke notwithstanding, she found him handsome, gentle, caring and intelligent. So, why couldn't she set aside her fears and look forward to becoming his wife? Because her fear overrode all else.

It seemed no matter what happened when they were together, he only had to touch her and she fell apart. His kisses transported her to another world. A world of magic and beauty, where nothing dark or corrupt ever intruded. Yet the moment she registered desire on his part, she froze completely. What would happen on their wedding night? How would she explain herself? Could she tell him—and would he understand? She shuddered at the thought.

How do you tell someone you witnessed something so perverted and so vile even thinking about it made you shudder with revulsion and fear? How would she explain to him that too many times she had put herself in Ella's place and had nearly made herself sick with terror? That the nightmares never stopped? That the guilt and pain never went away? That every time she looked at Davey all she saw was a nine-year-old girl pointing her brother in Ella's direction?

Midnight nickered and she raised her head, freezing at the sight of Jon standing by the stall door. For long moments, she watched him, expecting him to say something. When he didn't, she sighed, rose to her feet and walked toward him. Leaving the stall, she stood before him, chin up, and waited.

"I was beginning to worry about you." His voice was gentle.

"I'm sorry. I just panicked." Her voice was equally low and soft.

He put an arm around her shoulders and led her toward the doors. "Why?"

"I don't know. I suppose it was just one more thing. One more coincidence to add to all the others."

Jon did not respond, but she knew he agreed. As they reached the gardens behind the house, she said, "I will apologize to Eliza. I'm sure what I said must have sounded like an insult, but I was just too upset to curb my tongue."

"You may need to talk to Geri, too. She was truly worried she had caused you hurt."

"She ought to be. It's all her fault. My reaction, that is."

"Why?"

"Because we were talking about the ring and its inscription at one time and she brought up the notion that it would be peculiar if it turned out Brand's mother's second name was close to mine, like the first name had been. I, of course, scoffed at the possibility, saying I thought it might be Elizabeth. It would have been a good explanation for Eliza's name."

"I see."

She looked up at him, raising her hand to shade her face from the sun, and smiled. "No, you don't. But, thank you for trying."

They walked further into the garden, heading toward the house.

"So, where do we stand now?"

She blew out a long breath. "I have decided to accept my fate. As you, Brand and your grandmother have told me, I have no choice. I just hope Brand doesn't regret it."

"Why Brand? Why not you?"

"Because he was truly the innocent party here. He tried to save a spoiled, self-centered twit from herself and ended up having to marry her. It doesn't sound particularly fair to him. As for me, I knew better, but as with too many other things, I considered myself above it all. The truth is I deserve to be ruined. And I wouldn't have minded the status, as long as I could have held on to my dowry."

"I'm sorry."

She shot him a look of patent disbelief. "No you aren't. If it wasn't for that, I would still be fighting. Trying to stall long enough for Tina and Jay to return so I could talk him into letting me have it my way."

She heard him chuckle over her last admission. "Very well, you are right. I happen to think Brand will make you a very good husband. If I have to let you go, at least he's someone I know and trust. And, let's not forget Nona in all of this. I was quite gratified to tell some of the others 'no' who have courted you over the past months."

She slanted a glance his way. "Any in particular?"

"Lord Caverdown, for one. He was quite aggressive and refused to believe you would deny him. He, by the way, is part of the reason you are marrying Brand."

That revelation made her stop in her tracks and turn to face him. "Lord Caverdown? How?"

"According to Gerald, he's the one who saw you leaving town and spread the rumor. He was probably hoping if you returned ruined, you'd have no choice but to accept him."

"He doesn't strike me as quite stable."

"If some of the rumors I've heard about him and his family are true, he's probably not. Which is why he probably thought starting a rumor might garner your acceptance."

Felicia felt an instant's irritation. Remembering her last exchange with Lord Caverdown, mild apprehension fluttered her pulse. She took a deep breath. Lord Caverdown was no longer important. Marriage to Brand would, she hoped, remove her from Lord Caverdown's orbit. She could add that to the list of benefits of this marriage.

She shrugged. "I wouldn't have." They resumed walking. "There was something about him that made me wary. I'd prefer to remain ruined and unmarried rather than marry him."

Jon fell into step beside her. "I don't think I would have forced the issue. I don't trust him enough to want him as a brother-in-law."

She laughed this time. "You've never forced me to do anything before. It's probably why I was so surprised when you did this time."

"Perhaps."

"You don't need to patronize me. I know I'm spoiled, but I have tried not to become selfish in the process. Mama and Papa, and you and Tina, and more recently, Jay, have all done nothing but indulge me as best you could. But, I have to grow up sometime. So now, I suppose, is as good as any.

"After all, marriage is forever."

Brand reigned in his mount and looked up at Wynton Abbey in the distance. His third visit in as many weeks. Only this time when he left, he'd be taking a wife with him.

The mid-afternoon sun was warm and he reached up with his free hand to wipe the sweat from his brow. Glancing behind him, the road was clear. He sighed. He'd just have to wait.

Moving into the shade of a nearby tree, he hoped he hadn't ridden too far ahead of the traveling coach carrying his father and stepmother. He dismounted and looped the horse's reins over a low-hanging tree branch. As he leaned back against the tree trunk, he was glad he'd chosen to ride. It would not have been comfortable cooped up in a traveling coach—no matter how luxurious—with his stepmother for hours on end.

He closed his eyes and relived the scene of a week ago. Edward and Eliza had already left by the time he decided to return to the Abbey to speak to Jon. A whim, or perhaps a premonition, had prompted him to go. His father had improved remarkably, so he felt comfortable leaving for a few days and headed back to Wynton Abbey. He'd told his father it was to discuss business.

The day after his return home, over luncheon, his father had asked him how things went. There had been no good way to drop what he knew would be a bombshell. Luckily, his father and stepmother were the only ones present.

"I'm getting married in a fortnight," he'd stated.

His father had merely looked up suddenly from his plate and set down his fork, waiting for more. His stepmother, however, was less controlled.

"What? To whom?" she'd demanded.

"Lady Felicia Collings."

The fury that darkened the duchess's eyes was nothing short of hatred.

"That—"

She was cut off with a sharp word from his father. "Emily!"

He was surprised she obeyed the unspoken command. After the ride with Edward, he was sure she'd try to forbade him from the marriage. Of course, she didn't know him. She might have raised Eliza and earned his sister's devotion, but he was an outsider to the family circle. And, he suspected her of masterminding his kidnapping all those years ago. Her wishes meant little to him.

"How did you meet her?" his father asked.

"When my ship docked, I was met by the Earl of Wynton. Not only is he the Marquis's brother-in-law, but he is also Lady Felicia's brother. We met at his home in London."

The duke nodded. His stepmother seemed about to say something, but Brand knew there was nothing wrong with how he and Felicia had met.

He was thankful neither asked about Felicia's reaction. He would have had to lie, of course. It would not do to have his father know he was forcing Felicia down the aisle.

The duchess was seething. He was pretty sure he knew what was going through her head. Edward had made it plain that his mother thought Felicia nothing more than a light-skirt out to trap the highest title she could find. It didn't seem to matter that she was the daughter of a Marquis. Her great-grandmother had been a gypsy and that was enough to taint her in the duchess's eyes.

The sound of a horse cantering down the road reached his ears and he opened his eyes to see a rider approaching. For a moment, he wondered if something had happened to the coach and someone had been sent for help. As the rider drew closer, Brand gathered his own horse's reins and stepped into the road.

"Well, well, fancy meeting you here," Edward grinned down at him from the back of a chestnut bay. "Are you headed to the Abbey?"

"Yes, but I'm waiting for the coach to catch up."

"Coach?" Edward slipped from his saddle and joined him.

"Father and your mother are following me. Did you get my letter?"

"Of course. I can only imagine what my mother thought of your sudden engagement. How'd she take it?"

Brand grinned. "She was furious, but said little. I'm sure she doesn't believe that Felicia and I met by pure coincidence."

Edward nodded, his coffee colored hair glinting in the sunlight. "I'm sure she's decided that Felicia must have orchestrated it somehow. You do know that once people discover that you and her brother are in business together, they will assume it was all arranged."

Brand shrugged. "I'm fine with how anyone wants to view it, as long as it doesn't destroy Felicia's reputation."

"So, are you the unknown person she left town with?"

"Yes. It was more chance than anything else, but I couldn't let her follow her brother alone. That might have been worse than the loss of her reputation."

Edward glanced down the road from where the sounds of an approaching carriage came. "No, I don't suppose you could have. And even though it seems in indecent haste, I wish both of you the best in the future."

The ducal traveling coach came into view. Both men mounted and waited for it to catch up.

Felicia was standing at the fence watching Davey when she felt a presence behind her. For a moment, the hair on the back of her neck rose, then as recognition washed over her, she relaxed. Moments later, two large hands appeared outside of hers on the rail and warmth engulfed her.

"You're back." She hoped she didn't sound as breathless as she suddenly felt.

"Were you hoping I wouldn't return?" The honey-and-gravel

of his voice blanketed her, yet she felt him tense behind her, the warmth receding.

"No, it never occurred to me you wouldn't return. I just didn't know when."

He relaxed and the warmth returned. He leaned closer to her and she felt his chest against her back.

"I brought my father and stepmother back with me. Edward came too, although he doesn't have much time."

"Eliza is already here. And the Westovers: the duke and duchess, and Gerald and Geri. And, of course, Jon's grandmother."

"Of course." She heard the smile in his voice and smiled herself.

"I think Jon was actually glad to see her this time. Which is more than I can say for Amanda. She's completely smitten, but Jon is just barely civil."

She felt the rumble of laughter against her back before she heard it. Releasing her hands from the railing, she leaned back into him, trying not to tense as she felt his arms encircle her waist.

To say Brand was surprised at her actions would have been a colossal understatement. He could feel the tension thrumming through her body as she forced herself to relax, yet he could only hope she wouldn't bolt at his next action. Sliding his arms around her waist, he pulled her body flush against his and savored the feel of her against him, inhaling the scent of lavender she wore. And nearly shouted in triumph when she stayed put.

"Why doesn't Edward have much time?"

"Because he is on his way to India. My dear stepmother is very unhappy with my father at the moment."

She turned around within his arms, placed her hands on his chest, and looked up at him. Her eyes seemed to glow in the sun, and he caught his breath.

"He got his commission?" At his nod, a brilliant smile blossomed on her face. "How? I thought Parliament outlawed the purchasing of commissions years ago."

"They did, but my father, shall we say, reserved one for him. He was merely awaiting my return before allowing the War

119

Office to act on it."

"Wonderful. He must be excited."

Brand felt a spurt of irritation. He didn't want her to be so excited for Edward. He wanted her to be happy to see him. Yet, after the way they parted, he should be content she was speaking to him at all.

He bent close. "I believe he is." Then his lips touched hers.

Felicia would have never admitted to herself she wanted him to kiss her. Would not have thought she would encourage him to do so. But from the moment she had turned in his arms and looked up into those violet depths, she had been lost. Unable to stop him as his head descended, heat exploded in her body the moment his lips touched hers. The touch was firm, yet tender, and over all too quickly for her peace of mind, as Brand raised his head almost as quickly as he had lowered it.

"I missed you," he murmured thickly, his eyes on hers. "Dare I ask if you missed me at all?"

"Not until three days ago," she answered truthfully. Sliding her hands upward around his neck, and lifting herself up on her toes, she pulled his head down and pressed her lips to his.

Brand took immediate advantage, pressing her closer against the length of his hard frame, his tongue dueled with hers as he drank in her essence. Her body melted against his and he groaned in reaction. He could feel his body tightening with desire and on its heels rose an image of Felicia's reaction the last time he allowed his passion full reign.

The terror he had glimpsed in her eyes effectively doused his ardor, allowing him to pull back and check his runaway emotions. He did not want that to happen again.

"Felicia!" The childish voice was accompanied by the sound of running feet. "Can I go see the puppies now?"

Brand lifted his head as Davey approached and Felicia dropped her arms and turned her face into his chest, her cheeks burning with mortification. Looking at the golden-haired child over Felicia's head, he asked, "What puppies?" to give her time to recover.

"The new ones. They're in the barn," Davey responded. "Do you want to see them?"

Brand looked down at the dark curls. He was still lightly holding her, his hand splayed on her back, but she made no move to break free. "Felicia?"

"I-I'm fine." She raised her head to turn and look down at Davey. "Of course you can go see the puppies, but remember what Del said last time. They are still too young to play with yet."

"I know, but I was going to ask if I could have one, so I want to watch them to decide which one I want."

Felicia smiled. "Very well, but be careful. Remember their mama doesn't know you don't mean to hurt them."

Davey's gray eyes lit up. "I will." He turned and sprinted for the barn.

"Don't run!" Felicia called after him, but he was out of earshot by then. She sighed.

"He's a boy, Felicia. Boys never walk anywhere."

"Not even with broken arms?"

Brand laughed. "Especially not then."

Nonplussed, she threw him a look of frustration as she broke away and headed for the barn. Brand followed at a leisurely pace and waited outside until she returned. He did not want to intrude on her relationship with Davey at this point. He had yet to ask Jon what he wanted done about the boy. Until then, he would remain a bystander.

Their arrival late for tea caused intense speculation in a number of the pairs of eyes watching them enter the drawing room. Felicia did her best to quell the blush she knew was rising into her cheeks as she and Brand approached the group gathered around the dowager and the tea trolley.

Introductions were made all around and Felicia noted the light of approval in Brand's father's eyes as she curtsied before him. His stepmother, however, was a different story. Her eyes narrowed as Felicia greeted her and her lips thinned in disapproval. As she looked into the duchess's dark, emotionless eyes, the trickle of uneasiness Felicia felt at thoughts of Lord Caverdown turned to foreboding.

The men left the room not long after, their perfunctory duty done, and the women fell to discussing wedding plans. Brand's stepmother also excused herself, indicating her intention to rest before dinner after the long day of travel. As soon as the door closed behind the duchess, Geri turned to her.

"Whew!" she exclaimed, fanning herself dramatically with her hands. "Felicia, you have some explaining to do!"

Felicia smiled. Her short interlude with Brand before tea had mellowed her, and she just couldn't find any offense to take at Geri for the moment. She knew what Geri was thinking. "*And, yes, he's handsome...*" she had told the ladies. The understatement of the week, perhaps the month, she guessed Geri was thinking.

"You're just lucky I'm already married," Geri teased her now.

Felicia allowed her laughter to surface. "I'm afraid you have the wrong color eyes and hair," she told Geri.

"You don't think I could have changed his mind?"

Felicia shook her head. "No. I don't think you could." She turned and winked at Amanda, then said, "I even offered to step aside for Amanda and he didn't even blink before he said no."

"Stop it, you two," the dowager's amused voice interrupted their sparring. "There are still young ears here."

It was Amanda's turn to laugh. "Don't stop on my account. This is the most fascinating conversation I've heard in ages."

"Besides," Felicia continued as if the dowager and Amanda hadn't spoken, "what would you do with a lion?"

"The same as you. Tame him."

Felicia shook her head even as she laughed. "I'm not sure it's possible, but I most assuredly intend to try."

Geri reached over and gave her friend a hug. "Oh, Felicia, I'm so glad you're back."

Felicia grinned. "Believe it or not, so am I."

The rest of the afternoon passed uneventfully. Felicia was surprised to learn the dowager had told Amanda she could be Felicia's bridesmaid, provided she had something suitable in her wardrobe in light blue.

Felicia was returning from the stables the next morning when she came upon Brand. Standing at the edge of the rose garden, he seemed to be searching for something—or someone. He was dressed for riding, but she knew he hadn't been at the stables. He turned suddenly as she approached him, a scowl marring his handsome features until he noticed her. The scowl disappeared and his face relaxed into an affably neutral expression.

"Good morning. Looking for something?"

"No, someone. You." Taking in her royal blue riding habit, he frowned. "I thought Midnight wouldn't allow a ladies' saddle on his back?"

"He won't. But since I didn't want to scandalize your stepmother, I rode one of the mares this morning."

"Scandalize my stepmother?"

She nodded. "Geri and the duchess are used to my hoydenish ways, but I think Eliza and your esteemed stepmother would be horrified if they saw me in breeches."

She knew she'd surprised him. But, having made her decision to accept her lot in life, she determined to become a paragon of propriety—at least while there was company to impress. If there ever came a time when it was just the two of them in the country, she'd be back to riding Midnight, breeches and all.

"Have you had breakfast yet?" She turned toward the house.

Brand moved to her side. "Not yet."

Slipping her arm in his, she smiled up at him. "Good. Then we can do so together."

Brand looked down at her, his eyes suspicious. She tried to keep her gaze guileless, but knew he was not convinced. She had been fighting for or against one thing or another since the first day they had been introduced. He had no particular reason to trust the new, congenial I-will-accept-my-lot-in-life Felicia. Except for yesterday afternoon by the stables, they had not spent more than five minutes in each other's company without arguing about something. She wondered what he would say if she just came out and told him. He might laugh at her, she concluded—and she didn't want or need that right now.

They reached the house and Brand ushered her through the door into the dim hallway. Passing the library, Brand suddenly stopped, turned and backed her up against the wall beneath the stairs. Taking advantage of her surprise, he took her mouth in a long, leisurely kiss. When he raised his head, she was disconcerted to realize her arms had wound themselves around his neck, yet she needed the support because her legs had turned to water.

Slowly, unwinding her arms, she ducked her head as she felt the blood suffuse her cheeks. So much for being a paragon of propriety. All he had to do was kiss her and all inhibitions disappeared.

Brand straightened and as she looked up, she saw a flash of white teeth in the dimness. "Now that we have already had dessert, it's time for breakfast." Then he slipped her arm through his once again and they entered the breakfast parlor overlooking the front drive.

Felicia had never been so thankful to see an empty room than this moment. She knew her cheeks were still warm and her lips had that just-kissed look about them.

Filling her plate from the array of dishes on the sideboard, she took a seat and waited for Brand to join her.

"So, tell me about this wedding." Brand tucked into his heaping plate.

Felicia shrugged, a piece of toast dripping with honey in her hand. "I don't know anything other than it's supposed to take place in, what is it, three days, at eleven o'clock in the morning. Amanda has been appointed as my bridesmaid, and luncheon will be served immediately after." She took a bite of her toast and chewed thoughtfully. "Oh, and Jon is giving me away, I suppose."

"I see. Anything else?"

"If you want to know anything else, I'm afraid you'll have to ask Jon's grandmother, the duchess or Geri. They have done all the planning."

"And you? What have you done?"

"Stayed out of their way."

Edward entered the room, saving her from having to explain.

"Good morning." Her smile was warm. She noticed he was also dressed for riding. "Have you been out? I'm surprised I didn't see you."

"No, not yet. I think all the men, except perhaps Papa, are riding out with your brother to view some improvements he is making to the north end of the estate." He finished filling his plate and sat across from Brand and Felicia at the table.

"I see." She was unconvinced. "I think it's called escaping."

Brand chuckled beside her and she felt warmed by the sound. Edward looked up at her.

"You might be right," he agreed. "No reason to hang around and listen to wedding plans."

"Brand tells me you received your commission. Allow me to extend my congratulations and wish you Godspeed on your upcoming journey."

Edward's ears turned an endearing shade of red, something which happened when he was embarrassed.

"Thank you," he mumbled around a mouthful of eggs.

"So, what are you going to be doing? Do you know?"

"Not at the moment," he answered. "For the time being, I'm being posted as an aide to the Governor in Bombay, but hopefully once I'm there, something else will come up."

"It sounds exciting. Be sure to write often."

Brand, who had remained quiet during this exchange, found himself unaccountably annoyed over her easy camaraderie with his brother. Why, he wasn't sure. Hadn't she told him she viewed Edward as a brother? Yet he still wondered if she might not have eventually accepted Edward as a husband if he hadn't arrived.

He joined the conversation. "I didn't ask before, but when do you leave?"

"In a week," Edward replied. "I'm afraid I'm here only long enough to dance at your wedding, then I have to head out. I plan to stop to see an old friend along the way, then I am to report to Lord Helmsley as soon as I arrive back in London."

"Oh." This from Felicia.

"Sorry to be popping out and leaving you to clean up the mess," he said to Brand, "but I'm sure you'll handle things better than I would have. I do, however, hope you find your answers."

Brand sobered, then replied, "So do I."

Jon entered the room on the heels of Brand's comment. Immediately behind Jon, Amanda entered. Brand smothered a grin as Jon was forced into being the host, seating Amanda beside Edward, and then asking whether he could fill a plate for

125

her.

Edward and Brand greeted both Jon and Amanda, then Amanda turned to Felicia. "You were out riding this morning?"

"Of course," Felicia answered. "If you'll recall, I invited you to join me."

"Perhaps tomorrow," Amanda replied. "I was up late going through my wardrobe with Eliza. We have narrowed the choices to three."

Felicia smiled, and said nothing, but Edward asked the question everyone else was thinking.

"Three what?"

"Dresses," Amanda answered. "I'm to be Felicia's bridesmaid, but the countess said the dress had to be light blue. So, Eliza and I went through everything I brought with me to see if there was anything suitable. Thankfully a majority of my wardrobe is in blue and green, so I have any number of possibilities."

Felicia finished her breakfast and excused herself. Brand rose with her and escorted her out of the room.

"Are you going out with everyone else this morning?" she asked as they climbed the main staircase.

"Yes," he responded, "And you?"

"I'll walk Davey into the village for his lesson with the vicar." Brand stopped as they reached the second floor and turned to her. Realizing he had stopped, Felicia turned to look at him.

"You are truly not involved with the planning of your own wedding?" he asked incredulously.

"No, I'm not," she replied a little defensively. "If Jon's grandmother hadn't arrived, there wouldn't have been any planning at all."

"Why?"

She shrugged. Brand was beginning to hate that gesture, so often did she employ it. "I have accepted I have no choice in this. I have agreed not to fight any longer and agreed not to embarrass you or Jon in front of your family. I have agreed I will try to make the best of this and accept my destiny or fate, or whatever you want to call it. I have even agreed to wear the ring. But, I draw the line at planning something I did not want in the first place."

Her eyes had darkened with her explanation and he watched her struggle to contain her anger. Yet, now he understood her actions of yesterday and this morning. She was making an effort to accept what she couldn't change—and do so without causing discomfort to those around her, but deep down she was still fuming over what she considered to be the injustice of it all.

For now, it was enough. He would not push her further.

"Very well. A truce it is. We will fight our battles in private, but present a united front to the rest of the world."

Dropping her eyes to his chest, she said nothing more. Brand placed two fingers under her chin and tipped her head back to look into her face. Her lashes shielded her eyes from him, but it mattered not.

Bending his head, he set his lips gently to hers. The kiss was brief, featherlight. Enough. He raised his head.

She stepped back. "You've already had dessert," she reminded him, then turned and walked down the hall.

Brand's shout of laughter followed her.

Light and fluffy clouds were helping the sun to play hide and seek as Felicia returned from the village with Davey. Henry followed a respectful distance behind. As they reached the edge of the front drive, they encountered the Duchess of Warringham. A tall, thin woman, her dark brown tresses sparsely streaked with gray, she was an imposing figure in a burgundy morning gown. Felicia felt small and somewhat insignificant beside her. There was no way to avoid her without being obvious, especially once she had seen them. Introducing Davey briefly with as little information as possible, she sent him on his way with Henry. It was a good move, for they were barely out of earshot before the duchess attacked.

"I'm on to you," she stated flatly. "I should have known you'd be in the middle of this farce."

"This farce?"

"This so-called wedding. You were just leading Edward on. It's unfortunate no one warned his brother before he returned what kind of family he was involved with."

"Pardon?" Felicia was taken aback by the suddenness of the strike. "I'm not sure I understand you."

"You were leading Edward on just in case his brother never returned," the duchess spat. "But you knew all along he was your brother's partner."

Felicia was stunned. It never occurred to her someone might come to that conclusion. "You are mistaken. I never even met his lordship until three weeks ago." The duchess started to speak, but Felicia forestalled her. "Oh, I knew my brother had a partner and his name was Brand, but how I could have connected him with Edward I fail to perceive."

"You expect me to believe you had never been introduced before three weeks ago? Yet here you are now about to become his wife."

"That's exactly what I expect. I don't know what Brand may have told you about how we met, but I met him for the first time at my brother's home in London."

The duchess made a very unladylike noise. "You didn't waste any time snapping him up."

Felicia laughed. She wasn't sure she'd snapped anyone up. If she'd had her way, she wouldn't be marrying Brand at all. It was only Jon's and Brand's code of honor which required her to do so. But, she wouldn't tell the duchess. What had Brand said this morning? They would present a united front to the world. So be it. She turned wide eyes on the duchess.

"I'm afraid events just conspired against us," she told her. "What precipitated matters, however, was we were seen leaving London together—" Everyone knew that, she thought, so it made no difference if she told the duchess,"—when he agreed to escort Davey and I to the Abbey. Davey was not well, and my brother had to leave London quickly before he could make arrangements. Since Brand was headed to The Downs it was only a small detour to ensure Davey and I arrived safely before continuing on his way."

The duchess's lips thinned as she pressed them together, disapproval in every line. Under normal circumstances Felicia might not know whether the duchess was relegating her to the category of mindless innocent or shameless schemer. But, she already knew what this duchess thought of her and her background.

"He thought it best to wait until he discovered how his father fared before saying anything," it was just a small lie, she rationalized, "but when he returned, Jon had already received a letter from the Duchess of Westover about the rumors circulating in town. We had no choice but to move ahead."

"Yet you refuse to take part in the planning?"

Felicia was startled she knew that small bit of information. There was nothing to do except brazen it out.

"I planned and executed my sister and brother's wedding, but I am unfamiliar with the Abbey and its environs. My brother's grandmother is his hostess, and most familiar with the area. She is, obviously, the best person to plan such an event. I have my dress, and have been consulted on flowers. She hasn't needed my input for the rest." The bit about the flowers was a stretch, but Geri *had* mentioned them.

The duchess' brown eyes narrowed. "Your dress? You couldn't possibly have had the time to have a proper wedding gown made."

Felicia's smiled as she looked up at the duchess. "I did not need to. My sister sent it from Paris." For the first time, she was pleased to have the fairy-like creation hanging in her wardrobe. At least she would not disgrace Jon or herself. And, it might be worth all the trouble to discomfit this particular duchess a little bit.

"Although why I should bother to explain myself to you escapes me." She nearly clapped her hand over her mouth at that bold statement.

"How dare you." Felicia was nearly knocked over by the blast of hatred in the woman's eyes. "You are nothing more than—"

"I know what I am," Felicia snapped. If the gloves were coming off, so be it. "I also know that you have no reason to hate me except that you are a narrow-minded bigot who relies on gossip to form opinions. I do not wish to cause discord in your household, but I do not think Brand cares whether you approve of me or not." She sank into a perfect curtsy. "Good day, Your Grace."

Then she turned and walked away.

Chapter Nine

The men hadn't returned by luncheon, but Brand's father joined the ladies in the dining room. Afterwards, he asked her to walk with him in the garden. Like the duchess, he didn't waste words getting to the point.

"I must say I was delighted to hear Bertrand was to marry. And you, my dear, are just perfect for him."

They were strolling in the rose garden, the pace sedate out of deference to the duke's health. Although still tall and commanding, his heart was uncertain. Felicia didn't want to disappoint him by wondering out loud how he could know she was perfect for a son he had only met again three weeks ago, yet wonder she did.

"I do not expect to be here long enough to greet my grandchildren, but at least I know I am leaving my son in good hands." He patted the hand resting on his arm.

"And Lord Edward?" she asked. She wasn't even sure why she asked, but something compelled her to.

"It is good he is leaving. He will be better off in India when I go," the duke told her. "There are things he will be better off eventually learning from his brother."

Felicia was puzzled by this train of thought. Did he expect to die tomorrow? Why was he telling her? Did he think she knew something he did not?

"I know Brand hopes you are recovering and expects you to be around for many years yet," she said carefully, unsure of herself. How did one tell someone they weren't going to die when one didn't know?

She knew little about the duke's condition save he had a

heart ailment which often left him weak and near death, only to seem to recover within days. She glanced in his direction. He seemed well enough today. His color seemed healthy enough, although there were circles about his eyes, and he did walk slowly.

They came upon a small bench and Felicia suggested they sit and enjoy the late spring sunshine. The duke smiled at her subterfuge, but did not refuse. The air was warm, but not overly hot, the chill of the morning having given way to a near summer-like afternoon.

They sat in silence for some time before the duke spoke again. His voice was wistful. "You remind me of my Caroline."

Felicia turned to him. "Brand's mother?"

"Yes." There was a sadness in his voice that spoke volumes. "You still miss her?"

"Very much," he replied. "She had boundless energy, but a calm spirit, and I sense the same in you. You will balance Bertrand's restlessness. A restlessness I suspect he developed during his years at sea."

Felicia wasn't sure she had ever been calm in her entire life, except perhaps when she played music, but she wasn't about to contradict Brand's father. Restless energy she understood—there were times when she felt as if she would go mad if she didn't do something.

"Perhaps he will settle down," she offered. "My brother did."

"Thanet?" he asked, then continued as if not expecting an answer. "I understand I owe him a debt of considerable magnitude."

"How so?"

"According to Bertrand, Thanet saved his life, then took him under his wing. Bertrand is convinced he would not be here if it wasn't for your brother."

"What did Jay do?"

The duke was silent, staring off into the distance. Then he replied, "I do not know the whole of it, but he apparently rescued Bertrand from a band of pirates."

"Pirates? In this day and age?"

"Hard to believe, is it not? But apparently so."

Davey's arm was healing nicely and his skills were developing apace on his pony. As she watched him gently handle the small wiggly puppy Del put into his arms, her heart swelled with pride. He had emerged from his shell and was back to being the happy little boy she'd left behind at Thane Park nearly three years ago.

She still worried for his future, but for now, she was content that his present was a secure one.

"What will you name him?" she asked Davey now.

He cradled the brown-and-white speckled spaniel, giggling when the animal licked his face. In the quiet of the stable, the sound carried.

"Jack."

"Jack?" she asked him then looked over at Del. "Is it a boy?"

"Yep. There was only one bitch in the litter." He reached down and picked up an all brown puppy with white paws. "This one here."

"Maybe you should have one of each," she said to Davey.

The boy shook his head emphatically. "No. Girl dogs have puppies and I don't want any puppies."

Felicia laughed. "Jack will keep you company when I'm gone."

Davey nodded. "His lordship said I can let my puppy sleep in the nursery with me."

"He did?"

Davey nodded again. "He said as soon as Del says I can take him from his Mama, he can stay with me all the time—even in the house."

Felicia hadn't realized that Jon had interacted with Davey at all. Although, she supposed he had seen him sometime. She wondered when Jon had made the time.

"He looked at my arm, too, and said it would be good as new when it was time to take the bandage off for good."

"Does it still hurt?"

Davey shook his head. "But his lordship says that even though it doesn't hurt doesn't mean it isn't still broken. He says it takes a long time for it to mend just right."

She didn't let her surprise show, but she was glad Jon had taken the time to see Davey too. With no other children around, she wondered if he was lonely. But, she could see now that a puppy would be the perfect companion for him.

Someday she would tell Davey about their relationship, but for now, he would be just fine as Jon's ward. She still needed to talk to Brand about Journey's End, but now she had some time.

"Aren't you even curious?" Brand asked her as they strolled on the terrace leading down into the gardens after dinner that evening.

"Not unless I have a choice in the matter," she answered, her voice tart.

"I suppose it would depend on what you might choose?"

Felicia stopped and turned to look up at him. The moon, nearly full and high in the sky, silvered his hair and sharpened his features. It was difficult to see his eyes in the dark, so she couldn't tell what he was thinking.

"I haven't completely discarded the notion of going to Journey's End."

"I see. And when did you want to make that trip?"

Felicia turned to look into the darkness beyond the terrace, placing her hands on the waist-high carved stone balustrade.

"I don't know. I haven't asked Jon whether his man has returned from there yet. I suppose it would depend on what he found."

Brand moved behind her and she felt herself enveloped by his warmth.

"Jon has mentioned to me he is willing to keep Davey until we decide what to do with him."

"And what does that mean?" Her voice betrayed her irritation that he and Jon had discussed Davey's future without her input.

Brand sighed and she felt his breath stir the hair at the back of her neck.

"That he will stay here through the summer until we decide where we will settle. Then we can either send for him, or Jon will deliver him to us."

"Oh." She was a little disappointed she had no argument

with those plans.

Brand's knuckles trailed up one bare arm, his hand stopping to rest on her shoulder.

"I thought we could go to St. Ayers from here. Although, the duchesses both want to hold a fete in our honor at the end of the Season in mid-to-late May. I suggested they tax you with the particulars."

"That's not very far away." Felicia was having difficulty thinking with Brand's thumb moving lightly over her collarbone, heat in its wake. His other hand moved to her waist and she suddenly felt as if she were standing in a furnace. "I would rather they...wait." She sucked in a sharp breath as his lips replaced his thumb. "I...would like my sister and...brother to be there. Perhaps during...the little Season...in September."

Brand raised his head a fraction. "Then tell them no," he murmured in her ear. "And we will spend the summer at St. Ayers."

Fire coursed through her body, melting everything in its path, yet somehow her legs managed to continue to hold her up. His lips touched the spot where her neck and shoulder met and she felt him taste her skin.

"St. Ayers?" She knew her voice was trembling.

"Our estate in Cornwall."

Unconsciously she tipped her head back, resting it against his shoulder. Her hands gripped the stone beneath them so hard it should have been painful. But she was oblivious to all except Brand and the spell he was weaving around her as he placed a trail of tiny kisses along her shoulder.

"You should like it there." His voice was like molasses, thick, dark, and sweet. "The landscape in Cornwall is wild, untamed." His hands moved then and suddenly she was facing him, his head descending, blotting out the moon. "Just like you," he whispered against her lips before he crushed them beneath his.

Felicia went up in flames. Her hands moved to his shoulders, fingers digging into the dark blue superfine covering them. His mouth possessed completely, tongue delving deeply, rubbing and teasing her own as he slipped past her defenses before she had a chance to erect them.

Nothing in her young life prepared Felicia for the effect

Brand had upon her. She had never felt as if she could be absorbed by another person, but if it was possible she knew it would be happening now. Brand enveloped her in a way no one else ever had, yet it did not frighten her. Deep within herself, she knew she would always be safe with him, and no harm would be allowed to come to her. Being surrounded by him meant safety in a way she had never been safe before.

Brand drew her against his body, her breasts pillowed against his chest. One hand moved upward, dislodging hairpins and displacing curls until they spilled from her carefully arranged coiffeur, tumbling over his hand where it cradled her neck in a shower of ebony silk.

Felicia barely noticed the destruction of her maid's hard work, the pins dropping to the stone terrace scarcely registering within the sensual haze in which she floated. Brand had effectively removed all but himself from her thoughts and when he raised his head, she was disappointed at the loss of contact, rising up on her toes to prolong it if she could.

Felicia drifted back to earth slowly. Unable to persuade Brand to kiss her again, she opted to rest her head against his chest. The rapid thudding beneath her ear told her he was not unaffected by her nearness, and that comforted her on a level she did not yet understand. The fingers sifting through her hair were soothing, lulling her into a peaceful state. She sighed. For the time being, she was content where she was.

Approaching voices brought them back to the present. Felicia's head snapped up at the same time Brand seemed to register the pending intrusion. Swiftly, he took her hand and led her down the steps and into the darkness beyond. Skirting around the back of the house, they reached the door to the back hall and slipped inside.

Felicia started up the back stairs as Brand closed the door, stopping a few steps up to turn and look down at him. With her hair swirling about her and eyes bright in the lamplight, she reminded him of a gypsy and he wondered if her great-grandmother had looked much the same at a young age.

"Good night, my lord." She spoke softly into the silence, then whirled and fled up the stairs.

Two mornings later Felicia stood in front of the mirror in her room exchanging wary glances with herself in the mirror. The person looking back at her resembled the fairy princess of her childhood dreams. The only thing missing was her crown as Felicia declined to wear the tiara. The sapphires around her throat and in her ears, however, competed in brilliance with her eyes, which shone with an excited anticipation she hadn't expected to feel on this, the morning of her wedding.

A knock at the door was answered by Lily, who admitted Amanda and Geri.

"Oh, my!" Geri's exclamation spoke volumes and Felicia, who hadn't realized she was nervous, smiled.

"What a beautiful dress," Amanda blurted.

"And yours too," Felicia replied. "That particular one is one of my favorites."

Silk in a shade slightly darker than her sky blue eyes draped Amanda's tall, shapely form. The narrower crinolines which were fast becoming the fashion suited her, emphasizing her narrow waist and ample bust. Decorated along the scalloped hemline and low neckline with white rosettes, it was the perfect foil for Felicia's dress. Amanda's maid had gathered her golden tresses up at the crown, tied them with a ribbon, then left the curls to artlessly spill down about her shoulders.

Felicia's hair had been dressed in much the same fashion, except Felicia's veil covered most of her curls. The delicate lace fell in soft folds beside her face, over her shoulders and arms, ending nearly at her knees. She refused to allow it over her face and the effect was to highlight her smooth, creamy skin, touched by just a hint of color offset by the deep blue of her eyes under ebony brows.

Jon waited for her at the bottom of the stairs. His gaze briefly rested on Amanda before turning to her. Felicia felt Amanda tense, then relax, beside her as they descended the stairs and she briefly wondered if Amanda would ever give up.

Amanda dipped Jon a graceful curtsy, then turned to Felicia, "I will meet you at the chapel." Then, with a last brilliant, but patently false, smile for Jon, she turned and headed toward the back of the house.

Jon watched Amanda go, a frown between his eyes, then turned to greet her. She nearly smiled at the interchange between the two.

"Once again, I feel as if I have usurped Jay's place," he said as he offered her his arm, "but I wouldn't have it any other way."

Felicia laid her hand upon his arm and they turned to follow Amanda.

"Although I would have wished to have Tina here, I am relieved not to have had to choose between you and Jay. Society would have dictated he be the one to give me away, but I'm glad you are the one here."

He glanced in her direction as they passed the doors to the ballroom. "Why?"

She was silent for a moment, then replied, "I have grown to love Jay, it's true, but he has only been part of my life for the past three years, whereas you have always been there. You were there when I was born, when I learned to ride; you taught me to shoot, to fish, to swim, to climb trees, and so many other things that are a part of growing up I've forgotten them all. And, despite the fact we have not always agreed on everything—this wedding, for instance—I know beneath the sophisticated exterior you present to everyone else beats a heart of gold and you would never do anything you didn't truly feel was in my best interest."

"Thank you."

The simple acknowledgment touched Felicia as nothing else had in a very long time. They turned down the corridor leading to the chapel. Amanda waited at the end, two footmen standing at attention before the large double doors. Felicia stopped and turned to look up at him.

"Actually, I suspect it is I who should be thanking you," she told him. Then she lifted up on her toes and kissed him on the cheek.

Jon smiled down at her and, as they turned to walk the remaining distance, he said, "You will—by making your marriage work."

Amanda handed her a bouquet of violets, white and purple heather, and orange blossoms tied with blue, violet, and white silk ribbon. She smiled, seeing Geri's hand in the arrangement.

"Ready?"

Felicia looked up at her best friend who was trying not to

stare at Jon, smiled even brighter, and nodded. Amanda turned to the footmen and nodded. The doors swung wide and the music began.

Nervousness set in halfway down the aisle. Taking in the abundance of flowers and ribbon adorning the chapel, Felicia drank in the flowery fragrance and the subtle scent of the beeswax used to polish the pews to a bright shine. Sunlight streamed through the high windows, casting bright patterns over the stone floor, one shaft in particular falling on the large flower arrangement on the altar behind the vicar.

Her eyes skimmed over the guests—Brand's father and stepmother with Eliza and her husband on one side of the aisle; the Westovers and Jon's grandmother on the other side. The rest of the small chapel was filled with as many of the staff as could be squeezed in. Davey sat beside Henry near the back.

It was when she finally allowed her gaze to rest on Brand standing beside the vicar, and Edward standing beside him the reality of what she was doing sunk in. And with it, momentarily, came troubled thoughts which were ruthlessly squelched. Today she would enjoy herself. She would not allow doubts or insecurities to intrude. There would be plenty of time for those later, but she would try today to put them behind her and appreciate the celebration the duchess and dowager countess had planned for her.

Regardless of her determination to enjoy herself, she was still nervous. Her voice shook when she repeated her vows and she had forgotten to transfer her ring to her right hand. Brand merely removed it before sliding a slim gold band onto her finger. She felt the blood rising in her cheeks over that, but knew her cheeks were burning with mortification when Brand raised his head and smiled triumphantly after the brief, passionately intimate kiss that followed the vicar pronouncing them man and wife.

"When I come back, you'll be so big I won't even recognize you," she told Davey as they left the house by a rear door.

"An' I won't have my arm all wrapped up anymore," he piped in. "His lordship says I'll be able to ride much better when I'm allowed to use both hands."

"That will be wonderful."

Having changed from her wedding gown into a traveling dress of deep violet, she was walking with him to the stables for his daily riding lesson before she and Brand left. It was her last opportunity to speak to him and reassure him she was not deserting him again.

"You do not mind staying here with my brother?"

"Oh, no. His lordship's promised to teach me to swim and to fish. An' he says we might go to the coast to look at some property there."

Felicia nodded. Brand had told her he had left the decision to Jon as to whether Journey's End was suitable for Davey and Jon had agreed to take Davey there during the summer to see it. If she couldn't be there to see to Davey herself, at least she knew he was in good hands.

"Now you are learning to read and write, I will write to you. Perhaps the vicar can help you write back."

"I'll ask him," Davey promised as they reached the stable yard. Del was waiting with the pony already saddled.

Felicia gave Davey a hug, which he returned enthusiastically, before opening the gate to let him through. Once mounted, he waved at her. Waving back, she turned to make her way back to the house and found Brand standing only a few feet behind her.

For a few moments, they looked at each other, then he held out his hand and she moved to take it.

"I hate to think it, but I don't think he will miss me at all," she said of Davey as they entered the house.

"I doubt he'll completely forget you," was Brand's only comment.

Felicia sat back against the luxurious cushions of the traveling coach, sneaking glances at Brand from under her lashes. Seated beside him, she could feel the warmth radiating from him, enveloping her as it always did. Yet it did not relax or comfort her as usual. Instead she was tense and a bit out of sorts.

It wasn't difficult to discern the reason for her mood. The evening loomed ahead, her imagination making it larger than life. Regardless of her attempt to think about something, anything else, her mind would not let her. And as each hour passed since the ceremony, her fear escalated proportionally.

Brand sat beside her, staring out at the passing countryside, seemingly oblivious to her discomfort. Casting about for something to say to dispel the tension she was feeling, she came up blank. She refused to ask where they were going—she had already told him she didn't care, and nothing else seemed appropriate.

"Relax." He turned to her, and she was reminded of the trip to the Abbey.

This time, however, there was no particular urgency concerning their destination. Wherever they were going, they would get there in due time. The only timetable she was aware of concerned the duchesses' plans.

Despite Felicia's wishes to the contrary, they had agreed she and Brand should be in London in a fortnight and make an appearance at the Westover Ball. Even Brand's father had agreed to the plan, indicating he expected them to put in an appearance. Having just been reunited with his father, Brand was reluctant to refuse.

She looked up at him and felt some of the tension leave her body as his eyes caught and held hers. Reaching up, he untied the ribbons and removed her bonnet, laying it on the opposite seat.

"There's no need to be afraid. I don't bite."

"I'm not." She was lying and they both knew it.

He smiled benignly, but did not, to her relief, pursue it. Instead he removed something from his pocket and held it out to her.

"I forgot to return this." Her ring sat in the palm of his hand.

Refusing to take it this time would have been churlish and rude. Besides, it really did belong to her now.

"Thank you." She slipped it on and tried not to view it in conjunction with her wedding ring, like a pair of handcuffs.

Brand slipped his arm around her, pulling her up against his side.

"Relax," he told her again. "Rest for now. It has already been a long day." And promised to be longer still. The unspoken words hovered between them.

Felicia leaned her head against him and closed her eyes. Very slowly the tension drained from her body, leaving her boneless against his side. Minutes later she was asleep.

Brand looked down at her and sighed. Frightened was too tame a word to explain the emotions he sensed in her. She was terrified, pure and simple, and he wondered what do to about it. She'd told him she wouldn't share his bed, but he had merely attributed the statement to fear of the unknown. Now he wasn't so sure.

Over the last few days, he knew she'd tried her best to mask her fear, but now that they were actually married, it had arisen again and he wasn't sure she could continue to suppress it. The question he asked himself was why? Why was she so afraid?

He'd never forced a woman in his life and he didn't plan to start with his wife. They would have to conquer this fear together, but would she let him help her, or would she continue to suffer alone? He would find out this evening.

Clouds had been building all afternoon as the coach progressed, but the storm held off until they were safely inside the manor where they were to spend the next few days. Night had fallen by then and the addition of the clouds made it darker still.

The housekeeper greeted them warmly and showed Felicia to a beautifully appointed suite decorated in peach and blue, where she found Lily had already unpacked and laid out a gown for her to wear to dinner. It wasn't until after she was dressed and Lily was putting up her hair that she realized that she was wearing a gown she hadn't worn before.

Of midnight blue velvet, it threw into prominence her white skin and made her hair appear to have blue highlights. Low cut and off-the-shoulder, she had always considered it daring for her as a mere Miss, which was why she had yet to wear it. Obviously Lily thought it the perfect gown for an intimate supper with her new husband. She considered wearing her sapphires to break up the large expanse of bare skin above her bosom, but decided it was too much blue. Sending Lily off to find her own supper, she left the room to head downstairs.

Brand stood at the window, drink in hand, staring out at the raging storm. For a moment, she allowed herself to gaze at him unobserved. Black superfine stretched across broad shoulders; his golden hair gleamed in the lamplight. She was attracted to him in a way she had never been to any of her other suitors and it both worried and heartened her.

She was still trying to quell her fear of the night to come, knowing if she wasn't able to, he would demand an explanation. Could she tell him? Would he understand? She was sure he wouldn't force her, but could he seduce her? Could he make her forget? She almost hoped he could.

As if realizing she was there, Brand abruptly turned his head and their eyes met. Even across the room she could see the desire flare up in his eyes and she shivered slightly. She could do this, she told herself. He wouldn't hurt her.

She'd known when she told him she wouldn't share his bed she was talking to air. She might have told herself she was warning him, but she knew better. She was his wife and it was her duty to submit. But could she?

As if drawn, she moved across the room to his side.

Brand watched her approach, noting the wariness in her eyes. He wondered if he would be able to erase the fear he read there. He also wondered if she knew how desirable she was. Her eyes reflected the deep blue of her dress as the lamplight cast a warm glow over her skin. His fingers fairly itched to touch her and he put down his glass to keep from crushing it.

Over dinner he drew her out, asking her about growing up and spending her summers with her great-grandmother's gypsy band. He watched in fascination as, with eyes alight, she told him about the places she'd traveled, people she'd talked with—mostly children—and places they camped. With Jon and Tina, eight and six years older respectively, she was often left to her own devices from the time she was about seven. Mira and Carlo watched over them, but with very few other children as part of the band, she had trailed around after either Jon and the other boys, or gone off on her own. Tina was usually occupied with Nona. There were occasionally village children, and one summer for about three weeks there was a little girl about her age who came nearly every day to the camp with her mother.

"It wasn't until I was older that I realized her mother had been having an affair with Gregor, who was one of the other members of the group."

"Do you ever wonder what happened to her after you moved on? It sounds as if you two became close."

Felicia paused for a moment to sip her wine. The ruby liquid stained her lips a deep red and he nearly groaned when she licked the moisture from them.

"Actually I know what happened to her. That little girl was Amanda."

Brand's eyebrows rose. "Does Jon know?"

"I don't know. I haven't said anything to him, so unless he has figured it out for himself, I would say no."

"Is that why you and Amanda have become such close friends?"

"No, that happened at Miss Ridley's Academy. Actually, I think Amanda needed a friend and I was in the right place at the right time. It wasn't until we began talking we realized that we shared a past." She took another sip of her wine. "Jon taught her to swim. He was sixteen."

"And he doesn't remember her at all? Interesting."

Felicia laughed. "It is, isn't it? Especially since she never forgot him."

Leaving the dining room, Brand sensed the amiable mood from dinner fade and he could think of no way to retrieve it without further postponing the inevitable. Felicia's fingers trembled on his arm as they walked toward the stairs, but she did not pull them away when he covered them with his own. Reaching the foot of the staircase, he stopped and turned toward her. The eyes she raised to his were luminous in the dim light of the entry hall, yet he could read the trepidation she tried to hide.

"I suggest it is time to retire. Would you like me to escort you up, or would you like some time to prepare?"

She nibbled her bottom lip. "I would...I would...like some time, if you...don't mind."

He stepped back. "Very well. I will join you shortly."

Felicia inclined her head in acknowledgment, then turned to ascend the stairs. Brand watched her until she disappeared, then turned and went back into the parlor. Pouring himself a drink from the sideboard, he settled into a chair to contain his impatience.

Felicia managed to maintain her calm exterior while Lily helped her out of her gown and into a thin silk nightgown laced up the front and tied with a bow. Taking down her hair, she waved Lily away when she approached with a brush. She knew Lily mistook her nervousness for impatience when Felicia ushered her from the room as soon as the dress had been safely hung in the dressing room. She might have thought it amusing if she hadn't been on the verge of panic. Brushing her own hip-length tresses often helped to calm her when she was out of sorts, but tonight the exercise did nothing for her and she dropped the brush on her dressing table in frustration.

She should have told him. She shouldn't have let it get this far. But now she had, what should she do?

Instinct told her to hide, but common sense asked her where. She didn't know the house. She didn't even know where they were. Besides, she had never been a coward. Hiding was not an option.

She wished she could fall into bed and go to sleep, but she knew that was impossible the moment she thought of it. Brand would just awaken her anyway. It was their wedding night. She knew what he expected; the role she was expected to play.

So, what now? Could she do it? Could she lie impassively and allow Brand to exercise his husbandly rights? Mira had told her there was pain and blood the first time, but the pain was negligible and the blood minimal. But Aaron had hurt Ella and she had not stopped crying.

Felicia paced to the window and stood at the casement, staring at her reflection, trying not to see the scenes flashing before her eyes. She had saved Davey, but at what price? Goose bumps rose on her arms and crossing her arms beneath her breasts, she rubbed her hands up and down her arms to dispel the chill.

Turning, she crossed to the fireplace and held icy hands out to the blaze. She didn't know when she began to shiver. Eventually she collapsed into a chair in front of the fire, arms wrapped around knees drawn up tight against her chest, staring with unseeing eyes into the depths of the flames.

Chapter Ten

Brand entered from the sitting room a short time later. He hadn't expected her to be waiting for him in the bed, he knew her to be too nervous, but he did not expect to find her in a chair nearly paralyzed with fear.

"Felicia?"

He dropped to one knee before the chair as he called her name. When he received no response, he cupped her face, turning her eyes up to his. The blank stare chilled him clear to his bones. He had never before seen such naked fear in anyone's eyes.

"Felicia?"

Raising his other hand, he cradled her face and stared into her eyes. Brushing his thumbs over her eyelids caused her to blink and seemed to bring her out of her daze.

She stared at him for a moment, taking in the dark purple dressing gown and the sprinkling of blond hair on his chest exposed by the deep vee. Shaking her head, a rich, thick fall of ebony silk fell over his hand, nearly hiding her face. He pushed it back.

He bent closer and noted the flash of fear in her eyes before it was shielded by her eyelids as they fell over the dark blue circles. Her lips trembled beneath his, yet she did not pull away as he expected. Encouraged, he pressed deeper and her lips parted beneath his.

His hands moved then, one to the back of her neck, the other to her back, bringing her closer. When her hands crept up around his neck, he slipped his arm beneath her and rose to his feet in one fluid motion. He broke the kiss as he reached the bed, but gave her little time to react as he lowered the two of them to the sheets and took her mouth again.

Careful not to crush her beneath him in his eagerness, he nevertheless found himself nearly on top of her, his hand sliding under the thin silk to explore the warm skin beneath. When she stiffened, he dragged himself back and removed his hand, settling it on her hip instead.

When he raised his head, her eyes were closed, dark lashes resting on her cheeks. Dropping light kisses on her nose, eyes and cheeks, he returned to her mouth.

"Open your eyes," he murmured against her lips. "Look at me, Felicia." His tongue brushed lightly against her lower lip, eliciting a gasp from her in response.

Felicia slowly lifted her lashes. It took an extreme effort not to shudder at the look in his eyes. She could not, however, conceal the dread she knew was blooming in hers. Tightening her arms around his neck, she drew his head down to hers, hoping to stem the panic before it reached unmanageable proportions.

Brand obliged by taking complete possession, his tongue sweeping in to seize absolute control. A whimper rose in her throat and was smothered as his mouth slanted over hers to explore deeper. His hand stroked her hip and thigh, then rose higher to her ribcage. Heat roared through her, igniting fires beneath her skin everywhere he touched.

His mouth left hers to move lower, down over her jaw, to the hollow at the base of her throat. When his hand moved to cup her breast and his thumb brushed over the peak, she moaned, and arched into his hand.

Brand's mouth on her skin was gentle, yet hot, the hand that cupped her breast firm. Keeping her eyes closed, she concentrated on him alone. From the moment he'd touched her, drawing her out of the dark place to which she had retreated, she'd centered her thoughts solely on him. She would survive if she could keep herself focused.

But it was difficult. Brand's caresses evoked responses which threatened to undermine the control she sought. She lost track of everything else. Slowly, he enveloped her in his desire, igniting a fire within her in answer to the blaze she sensed in him. The purely emotional responses he drew from her urged her to let go, to feel, to experience the passion he wrapped her in. Instinctively she knew that way led to disaster, and fought to keep control of her wits.

It was all for naught. The bow on the front of her gown came untied and Brand's hand slipped inside, separating the material and exposing her breasts to his hot eyes. She was no longer cold. The storm outside was nothing compared to the storm raging within. Bending his head, Brand took a nipple into his mouth. Her moan emboldened him further and, nudging her legs apart, he settled himself between them.

Her reaction was instantaneous. A terrified scream tore from her throat, her hands unclasped themselves from behind his head and began to push frantically at his shoulders, her head flailed from side to side, eyes squeezed tightly shut, and her legs thrashed wildly in an effort to escape him. The tearing sound barely registered as her nightgown ripped in her efforts to get away from him.

Astounded by her near-desperate actions, Brand raised up to look down at her.

"Felicia?" His voice was sharp, but it did not seem to register. Moisture began to seep from beneath her lashes, and she burst into tears.

She did not scream again, but sobs wracked her body and he heard the anguish in her voice when she cried out. "Noooooo, no. Stop it, don't please, no, oh no! Please stop." He moved off of her as she went limp, then watched her curl into a tight ball, crying as if her heart were breaking.

Brand watched her for a few moments, thoughts racing wildly through his head. What in the hell had happened? One moment he was making love to his wife, the next he had a terrified child on his hands. He had known she was afraid, but had not realized the depth of that fear. Now, confronted with it, he was unsure of what to do next.

The question uppermost in his mind, however, was why? Why did she have such an overwhelming, unreasonable fear? The answers that came to mind were disturbing. He did not want to think she might have been misused before. Nor did he want to think of what his reaction might be if he found out she had.

Her sobs had quieted, but now she was shaking. He could

not see her face, but he could hear her gulping in huge amounts of air, trying to calm her breathing. Reaching to the end of the bed, he pulled up the coverlet and wrapped it around her. Getting off the bed, he readjusted his dressing gown, retied the sash, then picked her up, coverlet and all, and sat back down on the bed, his back resting against the headboard, to wait out the storm.

It was sometime later Felicia raised her head to look up at him. The tempest had passed, leaving her drained and exhausted in its wake. Utterly weary, but still a little afraid, she was unprepared for the gentle compassion she read in his expression.

"I..." she faltered. "I'm...sorry."

"For what?"

"For...for...I don't...know."

"Perhaps, for doubting me? For not thinking I might understand? Or perhaps for thinking I might force you?"

Felicia dropped her eyes. She hadn't considered it from his point of view.

"Do you know what happens between a married couple?"

She nodded. "Mira told me when I was fourteen."

"I see. And what did she tell you?"

She began to squirm uncomfortably. "She...she explained how...our bodies are different...and how people mate. And...and she explained that...that was where babies...came from."

Brand didn't see how any of this information could have engendered the kind of fear she displayed, until her next statement.

"That was when...when I realized..."

"Realized what?"

She dragged in a breath. "When...I realized Aaron was...was Davey's father."

Aaron? Davey? For a long, puzzled moment Brand didn't see how or where the conversation had diverged to Davey's parentage. He was tempted to dismiss it as Felicia always thinking about Davey when the significance of it hit him and the realization nearly undid him.

Oh, my God! Remembering what Jon had told him of Davey's conception, he couldn't believe what he was thinking, but he had to know.

"How did you know?"

Felicia took so long to answer he wasn't sure she was going to. He could feel her hands moving restlessly beneath the coverlet she was wrapped in. Her whole body tensed and she squeezed her eyes shut. The tears began to fall again.

"It was my fault." The agonized whisper pierced him. "I shouldn't have told them."

"Them?"

"Aaron, and his friend Rod." She fought her hands free of the coverlet, raised and covered her face with them. "They asked me which way Ella had gone—and I told them. I shouldn't have told them." Her sobs increased.

Slowly he drew the story out of her. At nine, she had witnessed a horrible act and it had scarred her deeply. Not only had she been an unwitting accomplice, but it had happened to someone she loved and she had watched it in terrified horror. Even he was shocked by the brutal indifference displayed by the brother she idolized—Aaron had hit Ella because she wouldn't stop crying, knocking her unconscious, and when he was done had merely offered her to his friend.

"No thanks," Rod had declined, "I like them conscious enough to put up a fight. Maybe next time." Then the two had turned and casually walked away.

He didn't ask why she hadn't run for help. Nor did he ask why she hadn't helped Ella after the two men left. There were probably many reasons why she hadn't—all of which would have made sense to a terrified nine-year-old child. What happened was in the past, and she would never get over it if she dwelled on it. Ella had obviously been able to get beyond it—having married and had more children—but Felicia remained that frightened nine-year-old girl.

The tears finally stopped and Brand used a corner of the coverlet to dry her face. Lowering her to the bed, he stretched out beside her and immediately felt her tense.

"Sleep." He arranged the coverlet around the both of them.

She raised tear filled eyes to him, a question in their depths. "But..."

"Shhhh," he admonished softly. "You have had a rough night. Go to sleep."

"But...what about you?"

"What about me?"

"We didn't...I mean, you didn't... Will you leave...?" Her voice trailed off.

"No." He infused his voice with tenderness. "I won't leave. My place is beside you. I can't keep the nightmares at bay in another room."

"Oh." At that moment, Brand could see the lost, forlorn child she hid from everyone else.

She asked no more questions and allowed him to settle her back to his chest within the curve of his body. With his arm resting across her waist, anchoring her close, he felt her body relax and she drifted off to sleep.

It was much later before he followed her.

The sound of a distant door closing awakened Felicia the next morning. Turning onto her back, she opened her eyes and surveyed the room. No one was about, but Brand entered from the sitting room carrying a tray as she sat up and pushed her hair out of her face.

"Ah, awake at last," he grinned at her. He put the tray down on her dressing table, then approached the bed. "Did you sleep well?"

She nodded, even as she watched him with unsure eyes. He was still wearing the purple dressing gown, but now also had on a pair of what looked to be black silk loose-fitting trousers. He looked to be freshly shaven and his hair was neatly combed. Beside him, she felt decidedly disheveled.

Brand didn't seem to notice. Instead, he stacked some pillows behind her, straightened the coverlet, then retrieved the tray, which he set on her lap. He even retrieved a ribbon from the dressing table, tied back her hair, and re-tied the ribbon on the front of her nightgown.

"Why...?" she began, but he cut her off with a swift kiss.

"'Lead me not into temptation'," he quoted with a grin, then sat beside her on the bed. Hearing him quote from the Bible might have been humorous if she hadn't still been thinking about the events of the night before.

Felicia looked down at the tray. On it an array of meat, cheeses, scones, jam, and honey tempted her. There was also a pot of chocolate and two cups. Her mouth watered at the aromas and she realized she had eaten very little last night. Brand picked up a scone, spread it liberally with jam and presented it her. She took a bite.

"Mmmm." She washed it down with a sip of chocolate. "How did you know?"

"Actually, I can't take the credit. I asked your maid to make up a tray for you. She was ecstatic to find Mrs. Reeves had some apricot jam. She said it was your favorite."

Breakfast was accomplished congenially. Felicia experienced a side to Brand she would not have guessed existed. He fed her choice bits of the meats and cheeses, spread copious amounts of jam on scones for her, and kept her cup filled with chocolate. And when she finally said she'd had enough, he whisked the tray away and took it back into the connecting sitting room to leave for one of the maids to clear away.

While he was gone, Lily arrived, helped her into a fresh gown and robe, and brushed her hair. It was Lily who informed her his lordship had said she need not get dressed. Felicia could feel her cheeks pinkening, but noting it was still raining outside, she was not adverse to remaining *en déshabillé* for the day.

Leaving Lily to straighten the bedroom, she wandered into the sitting room and found Brand there already. He was standing at the window, staring out at the dreary day beyond. Unnoticed, she took the opportunity to study him with new eyes. He was still wearing the black silk trousers, but a different dressing gown, this one of burgundy velvet, now covered his broad shoulders, reaching nearly to the floor. She smiled, remembering the chocolate he'd spilled on the purple gown. She hoped the laundress could get it out—the purple intensified his eyes and she could look at them forever.

Drifting into the room, she moved to his side, and was surprised when he turned just as she reached him and drew her into his arms. Perhaps, she thought, there was hope for their marriage. Last night and this morning had proven Brand was not cut from the same cloth she suspected many other men were. Remembering Mira's words about men often being irrational when frustrated, she marveled Brand had maintained his control last night, yet worried over the results should he ever lose it.

She had briefly wondered whether he would set her aside after last night, but this morning had shown her he harbored no thoughts in that direction. So, now what? Would she ever get over her fear? Could she eventually accept him as a lover as well as a husband?

She wished she knew what he was thinking. Not knowing how he planned to proceed worried her. Maybe she should just ask? After last night, she probably could not shock him further. Looking up at his profile, she gathered her courage.

"Now what?"

Brand dragged his gaze from the tiny rivulets of water running down the glass to look down at her. "Hmmm?"

"What do we do now?"

He did not pretend to misunderstand. "That depends upon you." He leaned down to brush his lips across her forehead.

"Me?" She leaned further back, resting her hands on his chest as she looked up into his eyes. "How?"

Brand stroked her cheek with one long finger, his gaze lingering on her lips. The touch warmed her and heat spread through her body. Bending his head again, he briefly touched his lips to hers before he answered.

"One day soon we will indeed make our marriage a true one." She tensed. "But not today, nor probably tomorrow. First, you must learn to trust me."

That got her attention. "Trust you? But, I trust you." Confusion colored her words. "I wouldn't have married you if I didn't."

"I believe you, but it will still take time. You have never had the chance to talk about what happened to your friend; never had the opportunity to come to terms with the fact that it really wasn't your fault. Instead you have tortured yourself with it over the years and that will take time to overcome."

He pulled her closer, one hand sifting through her dark curls.

"But it was my fault," she insisted. "If I hadn't told them..."

"They would have found her some other time, or it would

have been someone else. Or you could have told them and it might have happened further away and you would never have known."

Felicia digested this information in silence, her face buried in the softness of his dressing gown. She had never considered it might have happened and she might not have known. What would have happened to Davey, then? Would she have known that Aaron was his father? She sighed and raised her face to his again.

"Now I think about it, I think I was the only one who seemed happy at Davey's arrival—but it was probably because I didn't understand."

She broke away and drifted toward the couch near the fireplace. Brand followed.

"What do you mean?"

"Aaron died nearly three months later. By the time Davey was born, Aaron had been dead more than half a year. It was a long time." She stared into the flames, remembering.

He came around the front of the couch and dropped onto the cushions beside her. Stretching out his long legs and crossing them at the ankles, he leaned against the back cushions.

"I cried when Aaron died," she admitted, "but it was because I was happy. I must have felt guilty, but all I knew was he wouldn't hurt anyone anymore. Papa was never the same afterwards."

She curled her feet up under her and turned to face him. Her hair, a cascade of black silk, pooled on the cushions behind her.

Brand stared down into clear blue pools and wondered if he had set himself an impossible task. He had all but promised they would not consummate their marriage until she was ready. And he knew it would take time before it would happen. She needed assurance and he planned to do whatever was necessary to ensure she received it. He just hoped it didn't kill him in the meantime.

They left for London two days later.

Brand wasn't in any particular hurry to reach London, but traveling afforded him the opportunity to spend more time in her company without the servants casting knowing smiles their way every time they emerged from their rooms. He did not like being the subject of curious speculation among the servants, and he was sure Felicia did not appreciate it either.

"That will be all, Lily," Felicia said as Brand entered the room.

Casting furtive glances at Brand, Lily scurried out, leaving Felicia to face her husband across the small space. Brand watched her go, then turned back once the door was closed.

"I hope she doesn't think I bite."

Felicia grinned as she picked up her brush. "I don't think so. She's just not sure what to do when you walk in and I'm not completely ready."

"You look ready to me."

His wolfish grin caused her skin to prickle and she blushed as he began to unbutton his shirt. Turning away from the sight, she moved to the window as she brushed her hair. Darkness had fallen, so there was nothing to see, but she continued to stand at the casement. Moments later, Brand came up behind her and slid his arms around her waist.

"Mmmm. You smell good," he murmured into her hair.

She trembled, her brush arrested in mid-stroke. When they left the manor yesterday morning, she'd not considered that traveling to London meant stopping at inns for the night. Last night Brand seemed to sense her anxiousness, sending her upstairs after their meal alone. He hadn't joined her until she was nearly asleep—and he was gone when she woke up.

Fear tried to make its presence known as he held her now, but she ruthlessly pushed it away. He would not hurt her. He would not bed her. He'd said so and she believed him. If only her body would.

Brand released her and took the brush out of her hand. Stepping back, he swept her hair behind her and began to pull the brush through it. Surprise kept her still, then the soothing motion of the brush invaded her senses. Brand's fingers were gentle as they sifted through the strands in the wake of the brush. Its gentle stroke, the soft tug on her scalp, and the smoothing trail of his hand lulled her into near drowsiness. She sighed in pleasure and closed her eyes. Never had having her hair brushed felt so good.

How long they stood like that, she wasn't sure. Eventually, however, her legs began to tire and she yawned.

"Tired?" he asked.

She nodded. "A little. Although I will never understand why. I've done absolutely nothing all day except sit."

Brand put down the brush and began braiding her hair.

"Where did you learn to do that?"

"On board ship. Braiding hair isn't any different than braiding rope, although I'm sure you don't want me to knot it at the end."

A playful giggle emerged. "No. I have a ribbon to tie at the end." When he finished and handed her the end of the braid, she turned to look up at him. "Thank you. I didn't know having my hair brushed could be so relaxing. You have a soft touch."

The dimness in the room cast his features in shadow, but she saw clearly that he was smiling.

"You are welcome, my lady. My services, such as they are, are yours to command."

His all-knowing gaze looked deeply into her own, searching, weighing. She didn't know what he saw, but it must have amused him because a teasing light entered his. Reaching up, he cupped her chin in his hand and bent his head.

The kiss was brief and non-threatening. Her lips tingled when he raised his head, but the passion and desire she expected to see in his expression wasn't there. Had he truly suppressed that side of his nature for her?

They had been married less than a week. She knew she was becoming more comfortable with him each day and since her revelations on their wedding night and the morning after, his touches had become almost impersonal. He was treating her like a china doll; as if she might break should he demand more of her. It was difficult, but she admitted to herself she missed the more passionate kisses they had shared before they were married. Unfortunately, she also remembered the physical effects of those more heated embraces and she wasn't sure she was ready to go beyond the kisses.

Someday she hoped she would. For now, however, she accepted that Brand was wooing her gently, trying not to resurrect her fears. And, for that, she was grateful.

The day before they arrived in London, she asked him about the years before he met her brother.

"Like you and the incident with Aaron and Ella, I have tried to forget those years," he told her. "Unlike you, however, I have been mostly successful." He turned from his contemplation of the passing scenery to look at her.

"Were they so terrible, then?"

"Yes, they were. There are times when I wonder I survived. As I told Jon, I forgot nearly everything about my life before my brother and I were kidnapped. When Jay and I finally returned because of your father's death, he suggested we try to find out more about me."

"I don't understand. You mean you didn't know anything about yourself?"

"Only I had been stolen from my home and my name was Brand. I wasn't even sure Brand was my real name."

"But the investigator was able to find out?"

"Actually, he took one look at me and knew, but he did some checking to make sure he was right. I don't know who was more surprised, Pymm, Jay or I. But, it was precisely because Pymm was able to discern my identity on sight that I left England again. I needed time for the information to sink in—time to get used to the idea, without the possibility someone else might recognize me."

"But how did you remember everything else?"

"I think Pymm's revelations jarred my memories because over the last three years I have slowly remembered bits and pieces of my life before Michael and I disappeared. As those pieces have fallen into place, they have also given me a clearer idea of who might have been behind it all in the first place."

Felicia thought about this for a moment, then said, "I suppose your stepmother is the prime suspect."

Brand was not surprised she got right to the crux of the matter, but he wanted to hear her opinion, so he asked, "Why?"

"Because, besides Edward, who couldn't have been more than two when it happened, she had the most to gain—through

Edward, of course. And, by the way, I'm not the only one who thinks that way. I would guess most everyone else thinks she probably had something to do with it, too. She's not very well liked."

"Why?"

"She has not been very welcoming. She tends to put herself above everyone else."

"Isn't that what duchesses do?" The cynicism in his voice made her think.

"I suppose, to some extent, that's true. But, for instance, when you and your brother disappeared, I've heard that many people tried to extend their sympathies, but she rebuffed them all."

Curiosity surfaced in Brand's eyes. "Does anyone know why?"

"No. Your father and the Duke of Westover had been friends for many years, but your stepmother apparently cut your father off even from his friends, insisting he be allowed to grieve in peace."

"Did anyone ever ask if there was a ransom demand?"

"I don't know. Maybe His Grace knows more. Of course, most of what I know is gossip, so it may or may not be true."

"What about Edward?"

"What about him?"

"Jon told me she has kept him on a short leash for most of his life. Is that true?"

"I would guess so. She is very controlling. I'm glad he got the chance to get his commission. He told me once it was all he ever wanted, but his mother insisted he was to be the next duke and couldn't have one."

"She was quite displeased when she discovered my father had made arrangements for Edward to have a commission—despite Parliament's ban on their purchase."

Felicia giggled. "She thought I had known you for at least three years."

"Why would she think that?"

"Because Jay is my brother. She assumed I had been leading Edward along all this time, but knew you would return."

"Did she enlighten you as to why she thought that?"

"Not really. She was surprised when I told her I had only met you three weeks prior. I'm afraid I had to lead her to believe we fell in love at first sight, but decided to wait until you were reunited with your father. Unforeseen events, however, forced us into a hasty marriage."

"And did she believe you?"

She shrugged. "I think so, but I don't particularly care. Once Edward and I discovered our feelings went no deeper than friendship, he and I became close friends. It was the best thing for him as she regularly scared off anyone he might have been interested in." She grinned at him conspiratorially. "Amanda and I often ran interference for him."

"And she didn't consider you an eligible *parti*?"

Felicia burst into laughter. "Oh, no. Not me—not with my tainted gypsy blood. I could never aspire to become the next Duchess of Warringham." She gasped for breath. "Despite my brothers, I was beyond the pale."

"Yet, now here you are, just as you said."

Felicia sobered instantly, her head swiveling to look up at him. She supposed her sister and brothers now had leave to tease her forever about that impulsive boast.

Brand leaned closer, tipping her head back. "Perhaps there is hope for us yet." His breath moved softly across her cheek just before he kissed her.

Felicia expected it. Even before he touched her, her skin began to heat up and her blood began to race. Warmth seeped through her, melting her bones and turning her insides to mush. His arms tightened around her and she was lifted higher against his chest. Gripping his shoulders, she held fast, sighing in frustration when he raised his head.

Dipping slightly, Brand brushed his lips over hers. Trying to pull him closer, she was disappointed when he held fast. She wanted to feel his mouth on hers again, wanted to experience the exhilaration only he could create within, but he held back. Lifting heavy lids, she stared up into eyes dark with carefully controlled desire.

"Someday soon, sweetheart," he said in a low, deep voice, "but not today." Then he lifted her to a sitting position and reached behind her to open the door of the now still coach.

Felicia knew her cheeks were burning as he helped her out

of the coach. And she was extremely thankful the coachman hadn't opened the door when they stopped. As Brand ushered her inside the inn where they were to spend this night, she wondered what he was thinking.

He had been thoroughly solicitous throughout their journey, ensuring her comfort before his own, holding her gently, and kissing her often. It was the latter she enjoyed most, but was loath to admit.

Yet, she understood he still held himself back. He denied himself so as not to frighten her into reliving the fear she experienced on their wedding night. Instead he touched her often and kissed her frequently—all actions designed, she knew, to put her at ease with his presence and his touch. She slept in his arms each night, and occasionally during the day as they traveled.

She wondered how long his patience would continue. Mira had told her men needed the intimacy occasionally. It was why, she had explained, there were always loose women who would allow men the use of their bodies for coins. Some men, she said, felt by using these women, they were actually being good husbands because some women—especially women in the upper classes—did not enjoy such attentions.

"It is not true," Mira said. "Women enjoy mating as much as men. And you will too, when you find your true mate."

Felicia hadn't believed her. She would never enjoy what she had witnessed as a child. Recently, however, she had begun to wonder if Mira hadn't been right. If she might indeed enjoy it with Brand, if he were gentle with her and made her feel as he had before the past reached out to grab her. Perhaps, as Brand had said, she needed to get beyond her past and stop torturing herself with it. He was helping her the best he could, but she knew she would have to participate as well, or she would never get over the incident. Besides, the thought of Brand in another woman's arms disturbed her for reasons she didn't want to examine too closely.

Chapter Eleven

They arrived at Waring House the next afternoon. Felicia wasn't sure she wanted to spend a week or more under the same roof as Brand's stepmother, but kept her doubts to herself as the coach rolled through the gates and to a stop in front of the large edifice.

An imposing mansion built of gray stone when it was fashionable to have access to the river, Waring House was set in a miniature park with the gardens ending at a private pier. The house itself was much older than it looked because it had been completely redesigned and refurbished by Robert Adam in the mid-seventeen hundreds. The inside had been redecorated many times over the years, yet as each previous duchess left her imprint on it, they had managed not to allow the changes to clash, leaving a quiet, stately grace to the entire house.

The apartments Felicia was shown to were nothing less than opulent. Walls covered in lavender and white striped silk; ornately carved white marble fireplaces with gold accents; thick Turkish carpets in brilliant hues of reds, blues, and greens only slightly faded; heavy mahogany furniture covered in lavender and mauve damask, and windows hung with plush royal purple velvet drapes.

The housekeeper informed her she and Brand had been given the Royal Suite. Brand's parents had been close friends with George IV, both during his Regency and his ten-year reign as sovereign. He had taken to spending so many nights in their company that Brand's mother had completely decorated an entire suite of rooms, consisting of a bedroom, sitting room, dressing room, and bathing chamber, just for him. She then ordered them to be permanently kept in readiness for him. This suite was one of the few which had not been changed since the previous duchess' death. The duke had not allowed it, the housekeeper confided.

The rooms reminded him not only of his first wife, but also his friend and king. It had been George IV who had given the duke St. Ayers—the estate in Cornwall—when the former Earl St. Ayers had been stripped of his title and lands for treason. There were few people still alive who remembered that sad episode as it happened before Brand was born, but the housekeeper did. She had been a new housemaid all those years ago and would have been happy to continue to regale Felicia with all the parties and goings on that transpired when the Prince Regent and, later, His Majesty, happened to drop in for a visit, but Brand chose then to wander in.

Felicia was glad to see him. Not averse to conversing with the servants she, nevertheless, wasn't ready to become the housekeeper's confidant. He glanced around the sitting room as the housekeeper left. "A bit overdone, but it will do," he commented, and Felicia burst into laughter.

"I'll have you know your mother decorated this suite."

"I wouldn't have thought she had such lavish tastes."

"Well, she did have it done for the king. Apparently your parents were friends and confidants of the Prince Regent in his time."

"Hmmm."

Felicia wandered over to a set of double glass doors to peer out and discovered they led to a small balcony overlooking the garden. Opening one of the doors, she was greeted by a gust of cool air and a sprinkling of raindrops. She had noted the clouds as they entered the city, but was surprised to find it was now raining. She closed the door as Brand came up behind her, slipping his arms around her from behind.

"You can see the Thames from here—just barely beyond the trees," she remarked.

"Let's just hope you can't smell it."

She giggled and leaned back against him. "I suspect you can when the wind is coming from the right direction." Still staring out the glass doors, however, she sighed and said, "But the gardens look lovely from here. I can almost imagine them in full bloom."

Settling her hands over his at her waist, they stood in companionable silence for a long time, Brand's chin resting on her head.

Felicia couldn't explain to herself the utter contentment she felt in Brand's arms. Cares, worries, fears—they all seemed to fade away when Brand held her. Perhaps it was his presence that made her feel protected. She'd never dwelled on it before, but she knew she never really felt safe with any man outside her own family. Until Brand. Instinctively she knew she was safe with him, that he would, as he termed it, "keep the nightmares at bay".

She'd spent most of the day thinking about their marriage. "Someday soon," he'd told her yesterday. "You will tell me when you are ready." She now knew she wanted that day to come, but each time she thought she could do it, the fear returned. It was the discovery the fear dissipated when Brand held her that gave her some hope. Perhaps she had already learned to trust him. The thought gave her the courage to think it was possible. She trusted few in her lifetime and old habits were hard to break. Perhaps it was time. It was not an easy decision to make. But, for Brand, she was willing to try.

Brand stood staring into the dusk gathering beyond the doors, his wife tucked securely in his arms, and wondered how he'd come to this. The frightened boy of eight he had been on a long ago beach had endured much, been stolen a second time by pirates, then rescued by another "lost soul", as he and her brother had labeled themselves. He'd helped to build a thriving shipping concern, then returned home to discover a life of wealth and privilege, and end up married to a slip of a girl he would not have consciously singled out in a ballroom. And, if that wasn't enough, he had proceeded to fall in love with her.

If anyone had asked him a mere month ago what love was, he might have told them it didn't exist. That it was a fairy tale created to make young girls gullible and men weak and controllable. It would never have occurred to him he could feel protective of a woman, yet admire her courage. He could feel he was acting in her best interests when he made a decision, yet still applaud her principles which seemed contrary to the decision. That he could put her needs ahead of his even though it resulted in untold frustration for him. But with Felicia, he would happily remain celibate if it meant he never saw the terror in her eyes ever again.

"He's staring at you again."

Felicia grimaced at Amanda, forcing herself not to turn and look across Lady Darden's drawing room to where she knew Lord Caverdown stood. Since her return to the capital three days ago, she had joined Amanda in making calls. With Brand spending much of the day closeted with his father learning about the various responsibilities which were now his, she was left at loose ends.

After the first day, when the duchess made it clear she did not want or need Felicia's assistance with the household, she did not try again. Amanda turned out to be a godsend and escaping each day with her friend to attend various at homes and make calls allowed her to spend as little time as possible with the duchess.

"Who is he pretending to talk to now?" She didn't turn. She didn't need Lord Caverdown to think she might encourage his attentions.

Amanda giggled. "It looks like Alicia Landen."

"Poor girl. If he makes an offer, her mama might force her to accept."

"Let's hope he doesn't. She'd be no match for him."

"True."

Lady Darden sailed up with a young man in tow. Of medium height, thin, and with dark red hair and dark eyes, although fashionably dressed, he seemed uncomfortable in the assembled company.

"Lady Lofton, Lady Amanda, may I present my nephew, Lord Patten," she said in a loud voice. Thankfully they were standing far enough away from the rest of the room's inhabitants that only a few who stood the closest turned briefly to investigate.

Felicia was still getting used to hearing her newly acquired title. She managed to present a steady hand and mumble something acceptable as the young man bowed over it.

"My nephew just returned from two years on the continent," Lady Darden informed them as he turned to greet

Amanda.

"Oh?" Amanda replied politely, addressing the young man. "That must have been fascinating. What were you doing there and where did you go?"

"I was in Italy most of the time, studying some of the ancient ruins. Pompeii, in particular."

"I'd love to hear all about it."

Felicia found herself being led away by Lady Darden as the matron said, "I have yet to see the marquess. Does he plan to appear sometime soon?"

Felicia nearly smiled at the veiled attempt to uncover information. With Brand closeted with his father for most of the day, and she and Amanda making the rounds alone, people were beginning to suspect he did not exist, despite the announcement in the papers and other evidence to the contrary. She and Brand attended no evening entertainments leaving the gossips with no details except what they could glean from the small circle who had actually met him. And that circle was being uncharacteristically tight-lipped.

"We are planning to attend the Westover ball tomorrow night," she told her hostess. "But, we will be leaving for the south not too long afterwards."

"I see."

Felicia smothered a giggle. "We are still newly married."

Lady Darden turned to look at her. "And newly met as well, I understand."

Felicia turned guileless eyes on her. "That too," she agreed, and said nothing else.

The speculation in town had been much worse than the Duchess of Westover had led Jon to believe, and once here, Felicia had heard so many outrageous stories she bounced between hilarity and indignation. At least one rumor had her kidnapped and married by force, but most seemed inordinately interested in Brand's appearance. She knew some wondered if he was disfigured or misshapen, and she had not bothered to correct the sly innuendos floated her way. They would just have to judge for themselves tomorrow night. Until then, she planned to keep her lion all to herself.

She looked up from her thoughts to find Lady Darden had stopped in front of Lord Caverdown. He bowed over her hand, holding it a bit too long as he said, "I have not had the opportunity to extend my congratulations, my lady. May I do so now?"

Felicia inclined her head. "Thank you."

Lady Darden wandered off, leaving her alone with him. It was the last place she wanted to be, but short of rudely walking away, something she was tempted to do, she could do nothing except exchange pleasantries with him. He ignored the pleasantries with his first comment.

"Forgive my inquisitiveness, but I recall you telling me there was no one you fancied at the last ball we attended."

Felicia felt her temper rise. How dare he call her a liar! Well, if the shoe fit, she didn't mind wearing it. Raising her chin a notch, she looked into his eyes and admitted, "I hadn't met him yet."

It disconcerted him, just as she expected it would. His eyes narrowed and a flash of something dark flickered in the golden depths. She suppressed the tremor that threatened her composure.

"I had planned to wait and approach the marquis on his return."

No doubt, she thought, by then she'd be suitably grateful to be saved from disgrace.

"I do hope I haven't broken your heart." *That's assuming you have one.* "But I knew he was the one the moment I met him." It was possible she was overdoing it a bit, but perhaps that was the best revenge—that she was happy with someone other than him.

"Did you break his heart?" Amanda teased in the carriage on the way back to Barrington House.

"Lord Caverdown? No, of course not. I've decided he doesn't have one."

Amanda laughed outright. "I suppose that's possible but I'll never find out. He's a fine enough dance partner, but he's not for me."

"And Lady Darden's nephew?"

"Lord Patten? Oh, he's nice, but he's not for me either. Besides, he confided in me he's only here to please his aunt for what's left of the Season. Then he will return to his estate near

Brighton. He's apparently quite taken with one of his neighbor's daughters and hopes to make an offer now he has come into his title and his mourning period is over."

"Too bad. He seemed quite nice. There are not enough nice ones out there."

"I suspect you got the last one, before he was even available."

Felicia groaned. "Not you too?"

"Of course, *I* don't think he was the last one. But that's because not only would I not have wanted him anyway, I still think there's one more out there. He just won't admit it. On the other hand, the Lady Dardens of the world with marriageable daughters will want to scratch your eyes out once they get a look at Brand."

Felicia said nothing. She wasn't worried about the Lady Dardens of the world. It was those who only paid lip service to marriage that bothered her. With their marriage still unconsummated, she was concerned one of them might lure Brand into their bed. Then what would she do?

Brand entered the room just as Lily was anchoring the tiara in Felicia's hair. Dressed once again in her wedding finery, this time wearing all the jewelry but minus the veil, he caught his breath at the vision she made. As she rose from the seat and turned toward him, he was struck by a primitive urge to keep her all to himself, to keep her home, here in this room, and continue to chip away at her fear. He reminded himself he was a very lucky man, but it did not mean he wanted to share his good fortune.

Reaching her side as the door closed behind Lily, she looked up at him anxiously. "How do I look?"

He wondered why she was nervous. She was in her second Season. She had attended so many balls, parties, routs, masquerades and other entertainment she moved easily in society.

"Beautiful, of course, but not finished dressing." Pulling her into his arms, he took her mouth in a hungry kiss. She smiled when he raised his head and he was nearly blinded by its brilliance.

"Am I properly dressed now?" she teased.

Reaching into the pocket of his dove gray waistcoat, he drew out a large square cut sapphire ring. Slipping it on beside the plain gold band, he admired it on her hand for a moment, then said, "Now you are."

Eyes the same deep color as the stone roved over his face. "It's beautiful. Thank you." Lifting herself up on her toes, she brushed her lips against his cheek, then pouted. "I hate being so short!"

"Why?"

Lifting herself back up on her toes, she looped her arms around his neck and said, "Because I can't reach to thank you properly." He resisted the urge to laugh at the color that painted her cheeks.

Wrapping his arms around her, he lifted her and took her mouth in a deep, drugging kiss, barely catching himself before he let it go too far and frightened her.

"You are perfect as you are, sweetheart." His tongue seemed thick in his mouth and his voice didn't sound like his at all. "And someday soon, I will prove it to you."

Felicia knew her eyes were over-bright, her cheeks pink, as they descended the stairs. The duke and duchess were already there, being helped into cloaks and coats. Brand took her cloak from the butler, draping it around her shoulders himself, before accepting his own coat.

The duchess watched them intently through narrowed eyes and Felicia could feel her hostility. She wondered if Brand sensed it as well.

The Westovers had planned a small dinner party to precede the ball. Unfortunately, small meant at least fifty to sit down, and more than three hundred had been invited to the ball afterwards. It would be the crush of the Season. It was rare that the Westovers threw dinner parties, so an invitation was not to be taken lightly, especially when the guests of honor were another ducal family.

Entering the large foyer of Westover House, Felicia was reminded she had been living here a mere month ago. So much had happened since then. Geri met them as they entered the drawing room.

"Are you ready for this?" she asked in greeting.

"No," Felicia answered bluntly. "You know how much I hate being on display. Tonight promises to be worse than my come-out ball last year."

Geri turned to Brand for support and received only pink cheeks for her effort when he merely said, "We would have enjoyed ourselves much more thoroughly had we stayed home and we wouldn't have had to get dressed for it."

"Brand!" Felicia's cheeks turned bright scarlet at the comment.

Geri's mother-in-law joined the conversation at that moment, looking from Geri to Felicia, then to Brand who stood between the two women watching innocently.

"What have you done now, you naughty boy?" she demanded.

"Don't encourage him, Your Grace," Felicia said. "Geri and I will survive."

The duchess looked mildly amused, but said nothing.

Felicia knew Brand would not remember everyone he met tonight, but she was acquainted with most. Many were surprised to see Brand's father and stepmother, especially the duchess, but Felicia had to admire the way she fended off the gossips. Brand's stepmother might not appreciate him turning up the way he did, nor did she appreciate him marrying the one person she deemed unsuitable to be the next Duchess of Warringham, but she knew how to keep up appearances, so despite her hostility at home, no one else was any the wiser.

Felicia did notice the duchess later in the evening speaking with Lord Caverdown. She seemed to speak with him more familiarly than with any other person in attendance. And when, at one point, the two had turned and looked at her, she'd felt a chill snake down her spine.

Jon arrived for dinner, escorting his grandmother. Seeing her safely ensconced on a chaise under their hostess's eye, he turned to find Felicia waiting for him.

She greeted the dowager countess and answered a number of questions before she and Jon moved into the crowd. "When did you get back in town?"

"Yesterday. Needless to say, I was practically under orders not to miss tonight. And grandmother wouldn't have missed this for anything."

"How is Davey?"

"He is doing very well. I'm not sure he will even miss me for the short while I'm gone."

"You wouldn't have actually sent him back to Thane Park, would you?" The question was moot for now, but she wondered, nevertheless.

Jon shook his head. "No, I would not have sent him back. I was fortunate you did not realize it. Your father taught me never to make threats I wasn't prepared to carry out, but I didn't feel I had a choice."

Felicia smiled at him. "I forgive you."

Brand approached and she had no idea her brother noted the softness in her eyes as she looked up at her husband of barely a fortnight. Brand and Jon exchanged greetings, then Brand excused them by explaining he had been sent to find her by Lady Anniston-Smythe.

"I shouldn't be surprised," Jon said to himself as he watched Brand steer her away into the crowd.

Geri joined him. "You may stop worrying now." She, too, watched Felicia and Brand navigate through the crowd. "You've done well. Tina and Jay will be pleased."

He laughed. "Of course Jay will be pleased. He has wanted the two of them to make a match of it all along. When she made that outrageous boast at sixteen he already had Brand in mind. He's just lucky Brand turned out to be the one to identify the ring." He glanced in the direction the pair had gone. "I will admit I had my doubts. She can be stubborn when she wants to. Before you arrived at the Abbey, she had dug her heels in."

"I know, which is why I reserved judgment until I met him."

"And now?"

"He is perfect for her. You may not realize this, but she has some real deep fears and I sense he will help her overcome them."

"Fears? Of what?"

"I don't know what they are, but I know they are there. I have also noticed she has changed quite a bit just since they were married. They may not realize it yet, but they are very much in love."

Jon shook his head and looked down at Geri in wonder.

The women he had known at different times in his life never ceased to amaze him. Thinking of the watch fob Nona had given him, he wondered if the biggest surprise of all didn't still await him.

Felicia melted blissfully into the circle of her husband's arms the moment the carriage door closed behind them. Despite her misgivings, the evening had turned out to be nearly perfect.

With the exception of two encounters, one with Lord Caverdown and one with Lord Marsh, she had thoroughly enjoyed herself. Lord Caverdown had only proved himself a nuisance during their one foray around the dance floor, asking veiled questions she merely turned aside. Lord Marsh, however, had openly propositioned her.

She had not let her outrage show but the incident had opened her eyes to undercurrents she would rather have remained innocent of. She knew many engaged in liaisons outside of marriage, but she had not realized it was assumed once married, a person was then free not only to seek out others, but to also be approached. That said, she had valiantly stifled her gleeful satisfaction at his hasty departure once their dance had finished and he returned her to Brand's side. Brand, noting his hasty departure, asked her about it, but she had disclaimed any knowledge of the reason. Seeking Geri out in the crowd, the two had escaped together. They retreated to Geri's personal sitting room for some privacy.

"He said what?" Geri had nearly screamed, affronted.

"He merely asked if I would be interested in viewing a private art collection he owned he thought I might like. Of course, he thought I would like it because it contained some scenes of gypsy camps."

"Oh, Felicia, I suppose I should have warned you about the predators out there. Marsh is one of the worst." Geri looked worried, but she needn't have been concerned that Lord Marsh had frightened her.

"I wouldn't have had this much fun if you had." Felicia giggled. "You should have seen his face when I told him I would have to ask Brand first. Then I suggested maybe Brand could come along too. I thought he was going to faint."

Geri collapsed on a chair, doubled over with laughter. "Oh, Felicia, you didn't? I'll bet he was mortified."

Unable to control herself any longer, Felicia joined her, falling into a matching chair opposite a small tea table.

When they had regained control of themselves, Geri said, "I wouldn't advise mentioning this to Brand. I'm afraid Lord Marsh will be looking over his shoulder from now on every time you and Brand appear at any function, wondering if you've said anything."

"It would serve him right. He very nearly ruined my evening, until I decided to ruin his. He left shortly afterwards."

Now, as the carriage made its way through the streets, she turned to look up at Brand and sighed. The soft sound made him turn and look at her.

"Did you enjoy yourself tonight?" she asked him.

"I suppose 'enjoy' is relative," he answered evasively. "I enjoyed watching you, but I did not enjoy watching every other man in the room watching you as well."

His arms tightened around her as he spoke, and she wondered if he was jealous.

"And you?" he asked. "I remember you distinctly saying you disliked being the center of attention."

"I do. But despite my reservations, I did enjoy myself tonight. Perhaps it was because I was free to be myself."

"How so?"

"I didn't feel the need to watch every word. Or worry about offending someone. Or wonder whether speaking to someone else might ruin my reputation. Or if I am consorting with the right people. And all the other myriad rules young, unmarried women have to follow. If you step out of line just once, you could be ostracized—which would destroy any hopes of a good marriage." She snuggled closer to him. "I enjoyed the Season, to a point, but it always seemed so unfair."

"And now you needn't worry about all the rules?"

"Well, I can't just ignore them all, but I don't have to worry about so many of them."

Brand leaned back against the cushions and closed his eyes, content to hold her and breathe in her freshness. For him, the evening had been startling. Even with the primer he had received on behavior from his father, the Duke of Westover and the Earl of Weston, he had been surprised at the immorality lurking just beneath the polished veneer of the polite world. More than once, he found himself staring daggers at some young man who remarked on Felicia within his hearing.

It was the Earl of Weston who pointed out he had the advantage because no one knew him—but they knew what he represented—and no one wanted to offend a future duke of the realm.

And then there were the ladies, those who truly were, and those who were not. It was the latter who tried to capture his attention most often. More than one had hinted at their availability when married life grew tedious, and he found it increasingly difficult to hide his aversion.

Felicia had fallen asleep by the time the carriage stopped in front of Waring House. Waking her just long enough to help her from the conveyance, Brand lifted her in his arms and strode up the steps.

"My parents have returned?" he asked Wharton, the butler.

"Yes, my lord. And retired immediately."

Brand nodded and turned toward the stairs, when Wharton stopped him. "A Mr. Pymm delivered a packet for you earlier this evening, my lord. I instructed Jamison to leave it in the library."

"Thank you, Wharton." And wishing the butler and footmen good night, he proceeded up the staircase with his precious burden.

Felicia stirred as he laid her upon the bed, then struggled to sit up. Lily hurried in moments later, hesitating when she found Brand there. He looked up, noticed her, and beckoned her to Felicia's side. Leaving Felicia in Lily's care, he headed back downstairs to retrieve whatever Pymm had delivered.

Felicia stood staring out the window beside the bed. The stars seemed especially bright tonight, but perhaps it was just that her senses were more acute than usual. She was on edge. She could hear and feel her heart beating within her chest, almost feel her blood's rhythmic surging through her veins in time with the beat. Despite the almost giddy feeling she experienced, her mouth was dry and her palms sweaty. She had never been so nervous in her entire life.

There had been that moment at the end of the first waltz of the evening when Brand had, for a split-second, allowed his control to slip. She had glimpsed a hunger in his eyes which called to her. Her body had responded and the shiver that rolled through her had not been from dread—rather she experienced an anticipation so keen she had nearly suggested they leave right then.

Sighing, she turned away from the window and approached the bed. It beckoned like a warm, dark cave. The heavy velvet curtains had been pulled partially back on each side, the ones at the foot of the bed entirely closed. Lifting the heavy coverlet, she slipped between silk sheets and let out a long, deep sigh. She would wait. The clock in the sitting room chimed the hour of three. He could not be much longer. She would tell him then.

Brand entered the bedroom from the dressing room just as the clock in the sitting room struck the quarter hour. Rubbing his hand over his eyes, he blew out a breath. He was tired, but wondered if he would be able to sleep. Tonight had severely tried his patience. Being on display had never been his forte, and feeling the need to keep a constant eye on Felicia had been taxing.

But, he had never seen her more beautiful or desirable. She sparkled like the crystal chandeliers hanging from the ceiling, bringing with her a scintillating presence he longed to capture completely. "Someday soon," he had told her often, but would he still be sane when the day came?

His body stirred at the memory of waltzing with her. The sensuous movement of the dance teased and tantalized him and, at the end of the dance, he had nearly forgotten where they were and kissed her. He had, however, allowed her for a moment to see the barely leashed passion raging inside him before carefully bringing himself back under control. Her eyes had widened, and he felt her shiver, but he hadn't been able to tell whether it was from fear or something else.

Extinguishing the lamp left burning for him, he shrugged out of the dressing gown then slipped into the bed and reached for her.

He did not expect her to reach up and wind her arms around his neck. The movement caught him off guard and before he knew it she pulled his head down to hers and pressed her lips against his. For a fleeting moment, he wondered if she knew she was playing with fire, but moments later he didn't care as her tongue slipped into his mouth.

Chapter Twelve

Felicia knew she had completely thrown him off balance, and she was thankful for the darkness that hid her burning cheeks from his gaze when he finally gained control and broke the kiss. Yet she was not prepared for the shuddering groan that escaped him as he gathered her close and nuzzled the skin where her neck and shoulder met.

"Felicia," he breathed raggedly against her skin. "A man can only stand so much temptation."

"I know," she purred. When he said no more and she felt his body begin to relax, she knew it was time. "Brand?"

"Mmmm?" She wondered if he was falling asleep.

"I—I'm ready."

His body stiffened and he raised his head slowly, staring down at her in the gloom. She could barely make out the outline of his head in the darkness of the nearly enclosed bed and he was still so long she wondered if he could see her better than she could see him. She could almost feel his eyes on her face, searching, probing, considering, wondering. It took all of her willpower not to turn away from him.

"Are you sure?" His voice was full of cautious wonder.

She dropped her eyes from his penetrating stare, even though she was convinced he couldn't see her.

"Yes," was all she was able to whisper before Brand lowered his lips to hers.

The kiss was light—just a brush of his lips against hers. Once, twice, and a third time. She tried to pull him closer, but he would not allow it.

"Easy sweetheart," he murmured gently. "We have the rest

of the night."

His lips moved to her temple, then to one eyelid, then the other. His aim was so sure, so true, she wondered anew whether he could actually see her or not. She was trembling and once again she was struck by an acute sense of expectation.

Despite his words, Brand knew he did not have all night. Since their aborted wedding night, he had lived in a semi-aroused state, but he wanted to ensure that, for Felicia, the experience would completely erase the devastating memories she carried.

His hand moved up to cup her breast, his thumb moving lightly over the nipple. Even through the material he felt the tip pebble and heard her gasp. When his mouth replaced his hand, she moaned. Laving the sensitive tip through the material, he could feel the tremors coursing through her body.

"Brand." His name escaped at the end of a sharply exhaled breath.

"It's all right," he soothed, "relax, sweetheart, and let me love you."

And she did. Brand quickly stripped her of her nightrail, then his hands stroked and caressed every inch of skin. His mouth teased and tasted, his tongue creating erotic patterns on her skin. And all the while Felicia tried to follow his lead, her hands moving over his skin, her mouth attempting to follow. Her eyes closed, wrapped in the warm darkness of the bed, Brand kindled a flame deep within her that answered his own. And when she was shaking with need, her body demanding he quench the fire he had built to a fever pitch, then, and only then, did he allow himself to satisfy his own hunger.

Felicia barely registered the quick, sharp pain which accompanied Brand's possession of her body. It was over so quickly, the sensations running riot through her body overwhelming her so completely, she could not even cry out. Myriad emotions roared through her, like water tumbling over a waterfall to crash onto the rocks below. She did not know she cried out Brand's name before oblivion overtook her, nor was she aware of the intensity of Brand's own release before he followed her.

Brand stood beside the bed and watched Felicia sleep. She looked like little more than a child within the massive bed, but he knew he had not held a child in his arms in the early hours of the morning. She burrowed deeper into the spot he'd recently vacated and let out a long sigh. Reaching out, he adjusted the bedclothes to cover the bare shoulder that peeked out, and smoothed an ebony curl back from her forehead. His body reacted instantly. Resolutely, he stepped back. He had one thing to do, then he would rejoin her. He smiled at the possibility, then turned and left the room. Despite having only had a few hours sleep, he felt more refreshed than he had in days.

In the sitting room, he summoned a maid, who brought him a breakfast tray, then settled down to read and study the documents Pymm had left for him.

An hour later, he put back his head and sighed. Pymm had been profusely apologetic for not finding out more about his stepmother. Unfortunately, what he did find only created more questions.

A small sound had him looking toward the door. Felicia stood there. Attired in her nightgown and robe, her hair trailing down her arms and back, large blue eyes the only color in her face, she looked lost and unsure, until Brand smiled at her and held out his hand.

Felicia found comfort and reassurance in that smile and walked toward him. She noticed the papers in his hand as she reached him. "Bad news?"

Brand drew her down on to his lap, watching for any sign of hesitancy. There was none and he relaxed as she settled her head against his shoulder.

"Not particularly. Just not good. Or, more to the point, not useful."

"Oh. Useful for what?"

"For proving my stepmother was behind mine and Michael's kidnapping." Brand put the papers he had been studying down on the small table beside the chair before wrapping both arms around her. "I know anything I discover would be hard to prove, but despite that, I'm convinced she was behind it and, if nothing else, I would know why."

"But isn't that obvious?"

"I suppose it appears that way. With me and Michael out of the way, Edward was in line to inherit. But there is something more here, I can feel it."

"What did Mr. Pymm find out?"

"Very little. She apparently appeared in London the year before Eliza was born. She was a widow, having been married to the younger son of a French Comte. No one seems to know anything more about her. Society accepted her, so that was the end of it. After my mother died, she became my father's mistress, and he married her when she became pregnant."

"She doesn't seem French to me."

"No, she doesn't to me, either. Perhaps that's what's bothering me. If she's English, what was she doing in France? And why hasn't she claimed any connection to any English family?"

"So, what will you do now?"

"I'm tempted to let it go, but something keeps bothering me. Something tells me I shouldn't. Now that I'm back, I have displaced Edward, so the likelihood of him inheriting is nearly nonexistent. And, I think my father suspects as well, which is why he not only made sure Edward received his commission, but also that he was posted away from England."

Felicia was reminded of her conversation with Brand's father at Jon's estate. "There are things he will be better off eventually learning from his brother," the duke had said of Edward.

"Your father said as much." Felicia related the short conversation she'd with the duke at the Abbey.

"It pains me to think of it, but I can feel he is not long for this world. He seems weaker every day."

"But it doesn't show. He did not look weak or infirm last evening."

"No, he didn't, but he needed to leave early. Despite appearances, last night in all likelihood drained him. I shall ensure we take it easy today."

"Do you have much to do?"

"No. I have an appointment at the shipping offices this afternoon and I planned to take my father with me. With your brother out of the country, it is left to me to ensure we remain afloat. Mr. Percival is an astute and able manager, but there are some decisions which require my attention."

"Oh."

"What about you?"

Felicia felt the tenor of the conversation change instantly. Their relationship had changed dramatically this morning and the seemingly innocent question now held a deeper meaning.

"I don't have any plans if that's what you mean. But it's likely Amanda may call, or Geri."

"And if they don't?"

"Then I will stay here and read—or something. I do not need constant entertaining and your stepmother does not want my help running the household." She raised her head to look up into his face. "You needn't worry about me, I know there is much for you and your father to do still. And I'm sure you will want to contact Mr. Pymm again too. I will be fine."

Brand shifted uncomfortably at the reference to his father's mortality, but knew she was right. In recent days he had watched his father grow increasingly weak. Although originally against stopping in London for any length of time, he had come to acknowledge this might be the only time he had with his father, whereas he expected to spend a lifetime with Felicia.

"Pymm suggested he might be able to contact a French counterpart to do some digging. I think I will instruct him to do so," he said now. "There is more to this episode than we are seeing. Perhaps someone in France can shed some light on it."

Brand and his father left for his shipping offices right after luncheon. Felicia overheard the duchess tell Wharton she would be out for most of the afternoon making calls and when she did not invite Felicia to go with her, Felicia wandered into the library to find a book to read.

She should not be surprised the duchess would make calls without her, Felicia thought as she scanned the tightly packed bookshelves. The duchess made no secret of her disapproval of Felicia and Brand, but after last night, she knew the gossips would find it strange they never saw them together. At the very least, they would have been expected to make a few calls for

Denise Patrick

appearance's sake. Finding a volume of Shakespeare's sonnets, she extracted it from the shelf.

An hour later, she was settled against a mound of pillows, comfortably blanketed, a pot of tea beside her, reading the volume of sonnets. Ensconced in a window seat overlooking the garden as weak sunlight filtered through high clouds, she discovered she was still tired from the previous night's activities, and, setting her book aside, allowed herself to doze off.

She didn't know what woke her sometime later. She wasn't even sure how long she had been asleep. The high clouds had moved away and now she was overly warm, bathed in the sunlight streaming through the window. Throwing off the blanket, a movement in the garden below caught her eye and she turned to see the duchess standing on one of the paths.

Felicia would not have thought the duchess one for strolling in a garden. She seemed too severe, too aloof, to get much pleasure from simple flowers. *But there are obviously things about her I don't know.* She was about to turn and pick up her book again when the duchess moved. Curiosity compelled her to watch as the duchess glanced to her left, right, and behind her—almost as if checking to see if anyone was about.

Moving into the garden, she was nearly beyond Felicia's sight when she stopped at a patch of what looked to be stalks of purple and white flowers, once again checked to see no one was around, then reached down and pulled a few of the stalks. Felicia chuckled to herself. The duchess's gardener must be a terror if she had to steal flowers from her own garden.

The duchess stood and glanced up at the house. Felicia ducked instinctively. If the duchess didn't want anyone to know she had to sneak flowers from her own garden, Felicia wouldn't compound the problem by being caught spying on her. Waiting a few minutes, she lifted up, peeked down and noticed the duchess had stopped almost directly below the window. Felicia could see clearly the flowers she carried. They were familiar, but Felicia couldn't remember where she had seen them before.

Slipping off the seat, she discovered she was still feeling a little groggy. *No sleep will do that to you,* she told herself. It was strange how only a month ago she could have stayed up dancing into the wee hours of the morning and still make calls

180

the next afternoon. The clock on the mantel chimed the hour of three. It was still early yet. Yawning, she crossed the room and entered the bedchamber.

She was glad she had decided to change after lunch into a much more comfortable day dress, dispensing with her corset for the afternoon, and fortunate the bodice buttoned up the front. Slipping out of the dress, she slipped between the cool sheets of the bed, garbed only in her chemise.

The softness of the sheets against her arms and legs reminded her of how they had felt against her entire body earlier, and she was reminded of the feelings Brand had generated. Mira's descriptions, while preparing her on one level, could never have prepared her for the depth of feeling she experienced in Brand's arms.

She remembered telling Mira she would never want a man to do that to her, but as she drifted into sleep, she couldn't help wondering when Brand would make love to her again. And, she admitted to herself, she wanted him to.

Brand entered the sitting room, expecting to find Felicia curled up on the sofa reading since Wharton had informed him Felicia was still home. As he headed up the stairs, his mind imagined how they might occupy the rest of the day.

The late afternoon sun streamed through the window and balcony doors, picking out the reds, blues and greens in the carpet. Glancing around the sitting room, he noted the empty sofa in front of the fireplace, and the mound of pillows in the window seat, but the room was empty.

Moving into the bedroom, he was tempted to call Felicia's name, but stopped instead to scan the room. Reaching the bed, his lips lifted in a smile at the picture she made. Wearing only her chemise that he could see, her hair fanned out against the pillows, she looked young and innocent. He could see the deep, even breathing of sleep in the steady rise and fall of her chest, and memories of the early morning hours came to mind, stirring his body.

He had been falling asleep when she said his name, having just barely regained control of himself. That she hadn't been asleep when he entered the bed surprised him less than the fact that she had obviously been waiting up for him. The kiss had nearly been his undoing, but her next statement had nearly caused him to stop breathing. What followed had been an experience so incredible it defied description.

Never before had a woman moved him the way she had with her innocent, eager response. He told himself because he loved her, he wanted to make it perfect for her. That he wanted to give her a taste of the passion he knew she harbored deep inside. But he also wanted to purge the memories she carried and replace them with something which would eradicate the terror. Something to bind her completely to him and him alone.

She stirred in her sleep, shifting positions, but did not awaken. Brand turned and quietly left the room. Summoning a servant, he gave a series of instructions for the rest of the evening, then returned, closing the door behind him. Undressing, he joined her in the big bed, gathering her into his arms. He half-expected her to awaken with the movement, but she merely snuggled close, let out a deep sigh, and continued to slumber.

Staring at the canopy of purple velvet, he allowed his thoughts to drift back to the morning. He wondered what prompted her decision. Had something happened at the ball last evening? She had not seemed particularly upset or shaken over it. Her earlier comment that she didn't like being on display might have concerned him if she hadn't told him later she had enjoyed herself. Perhaps enjoying herself had brought down the last of the barriers. Whatever it was, he wasn't about to start complaining now. If she wanted him to know, she'd tell him—of that he had no doubt.

Felicia gradually came awake sometime later. For an endless moment, she lay in Brand's arms, her head resting on his bare chest—and savored his warmth. She wondered briefly when he had joined her, but realized she didn't care when, only that he had. Raising her head, she looked up into his face. In sleep, his features relaxed, he looked younger, more carefree and she glimpsed the boy who had become the man. For several minutes, she watched him sleep, wondering if he dreamed and of what.

He was so unlike the rest of the men she knew, yet he blended in so well he continually surprised her. No one meeting him last night would have thought he hadn't been brought up like any other young man of noble lineage. His manners and speech were impeccable, his knowledge of the rules and dictates commendable. She worried he might slip, say something out of place, or take offense at some thinly veiled barb, but he had weathered it easily, as if he had never been brutally torn from his home and exiled for twenty years.

She moved slightly and let her gaze rove over his chest. Sprinkled liberally with golden hair, defined by ridges of muscle and sinew, he was a magnificent specimen and he was all hers. She smiled at the thought. It never occurred to her she would feel so possessive about anyone, but the thought of another woman experiencing what she had with Brand tied her stomach in knots and bothered her for reasons she did not care to explore too deeply.

Reaching up, she ran a hand lightly over his chest, delighting in the feel of warm skin stretched over corded muscle. Her hand skimmed a flat male nipple and she felt his whole body tense and heard a strangled gasp above her head. Eyes wide, her gaze flew to his only to find him watching her intently.

She could feel the blood rising in her cheeks and she dropped her eyes to the cleft in his chin. Worried about what he might think of her bold exploration, she almost didn't hear his low gasp. "Don't stop now. You've barely begun."

She looked up sharply as he shifted them both to their sides to lay face to face. One large hand, threaded itself through her thick tresses as he continued. "I want you to touch me," he rasped. "I've dreamed of you touching me, exploring every inch of my body just as I've longed to explore yours."

Felicia could only stare in mute fascination as his head moved closer to hers with each word. Licking suddenly dry lips, she nevertheless met his kiss with a hunger as deep as his own, fueling the fire she had unknowingly ignited with her initial touch. When he broke the kiss, she was already trembling.

"This morning," he murmured, dropping kisses on her shoulder to punctuate each word, "I didn't take the time to fully appreciate you." His voice deepened and she felt it settle in her bones. "But now," he nudged her onto her back, "we have all night."

It wasn't until he pushed back the covers and stripped her

of her chemise that she realized he was already nude. She steeled herself not to turn away in embarrassment and curl into a ball, instead allowing his gaze to roam over her. His eyes were hot and ravenous and she felt as if she was being devoured inch by inch, yet she experienced no fear of him, only an answering longing within herself.

Shyly she let her eyes wander, but she could not bring herself to look any further than his navel. Someday, maybe, but not today. Intimacy was still new to her, but she instinctively understood that, with time, she would learn to view his body as easily as he did hers.

Brand watched the uncertainty chase across her face, watched her eyes drop, then lift again, and smiled. They had plenty of time for her to become as comfortable with him as he already felt with her. But, for now, he wanted to reacquaint himself with the ecstasy he'd found in her arms just that morning.

Dipping his head, he kissed the tip of first one breast, then the other and heard her catch her breath. Trailing his lips over her skin up her chest and neck, he finally settled on her mouth. Her tongue slid into his mouth, questing on its own and her hands slid around his back, one sliding up into his hair as she kissed him back enthusiastically.

Brand knew he was drowning. He planned to take it slowly this time, to give her time to enjoy, and himself time to savor, but she was clearly not going to allow that to happen. Her body rubbed against his, arousing him with her innocent passion. For a moment, he wasn't sure who was seducing whom, but moments later didn't care as she welcomed him into the wet heat of her body.

Outside, night fell on the city, enveloping London in a cocoon of darkness. Tradesmen closed up shop, workers trudged home, the lamplighters began their rounds and Society prepared for yet another evening of glittering entertainment. But inside the Royal Suite of Waring House, in a room once occupied by a king, two people learned the inexplicable joy of giving and receiving, of sharing and loving.

For Felicia, the night was one she would never forget. For Brand, it teased him with the knowledge that maybe there was something to signs and omens. Traveling in the Far East, he had encountered many things which could not be explained, except in those terms, and had absorbed much of the culture and customs. He had worshiped in mist-shrouded temples, mastered a form of fighting utilizing only his hands and feet, and learned discipline, tolerance and understanding that stood him well over the years.

He understood now the reason he hadn't been ready to remain in London three years ago was because Felicia hadn't been ready yet. His memories might have come back earlier had he returned to the place of his birth earlier, but the events would have played out entirely differently. Whether he would have consciously looked for his mother's ring as he remembered the gypsy's words, he would never know. And he would never know whether he would have been drawn enough to Felicia that she might have considered him a suitor and, therefore, shown it to him.

What he did know now was that she was his other half. They complemented each other in ways that were more than just physical. Soon, he hoped, she would realize it as well.

"I sent Pymm off to Paris." They were eating the cold collation he ordered left for them in the sitting room.

Felicia looked up from the roast chicken she had been dismembering. "Did he say when he thought he might be back?"

"He thought perhaps three weeks or a month."

"I hope he brings back some answers for you." She popped a piece of meat into her mouth.

"Me too."

"But..." she began and he looked up sharply as she stopped.

"But what?"

"What will you do if you are able to prove it was your stepmother behind your disappearance?"

Brand knew what she was asking and he had no answer for her. He wasn't sure. There were too many others involved. The scandal would not bother him, but he now had Felicia to consider. And how would it affect his sister and her family, not to mention Edward?

"I don't know. If it was just me to think of, I would hand her over to the authorities and insist they prosecute. As far as I'm concerned, she murdered my brother. But, the scandal would be enormous. I'm not sure my father would survive it.

"And despite my wish for vengeance, it would hurt Eliza deeply. Regardless of how I feel, she is the only mother Eliza has ever known. Eliza was too young to have formed much of an attachment to Michael." The tenor of his voice changed. "But I...it was my responsibility to protect him." She heard the anguish in his voice. "And I failed."

"Oh, Brand." She got up from her seat and rushed to his chair, dropping to her knees and wrapping her arms around his waist. "I'm sorry." Her soft voice clogged with tears. "I'm so sorry."

Brand lifted her to his lap and tipped her face up to his. She did not try to hide the tears and he was touched by her empathy. Brushing away a tear, he looked down into pools as deep and clear as an Egyptian oasis. And just like an oasis, he found comfort and rest in her arms. And so much more.

"Don't cry for me, love."

"I can't help it." She sniffed. "You were so young, and Michael even younger. I could not imagine, but it hurts to think of what you must have suffered." She reached up and laid her hand against his cheek. "What happened to Michael? Can you talk about it?"

He closed his eyes and savored her touch as he relived Michael's last days.

"Michael had always been small and a little sickly. He seemed to have a permanent cough and sometimes he struggled to breathe. After we were taken, the men took us to a beach somewhere. It was cold and damp most of the time and even though they gave us blankets, they weren't warm enough and eventually, they too became damp. Michael was coughing badly. Then your great-grandmother came along."

Felicia looked up, surprise in her eyes. "Nona?"

He nodded. "I assume it was she. She spoke to me. I didn't realize at the time, but she told me in her own way Michael wouldn't make it." He smiled briefly. "She talked me out of my mother's ring by simply saying she would keep it safe for me until I returned."

"I wish she had helped you instead."

"Even if she'd wanted to, she couldn't have. She only spoke to me for a few minutes before one of the men noticed her and ran her off. A rowboat arrived shortly after that and Michael and I were bundled on and rowed out to a waiting ship. Michael died two days later." His voice hitched as he continued. "They just threw his body overboard."

She gasped in horror. "Oh, Brand!"

"They had to knock me unconscious, then tie me down to prevent me from going over after him."

"How can you stand to be in the same house with the person you consider responsible for it all?"

Brand smiled sadly down into her tear-filled eyes. A deep sigh rumbled through his chest and was expelled. She had surprised him yet again with her understanding. He too had debated the wisdom of staying at Waring House, but knew not to do so would provide too much fodder for the gossip mill, and for the time being, his father was more important than his own personal notions of revenge. He would bide his time. Sooner or later, something would happen and force him to act. And when it did, he would not hesitate.

He took a deep breath and gave himself a mental shake. He hated talking about the past. He could think of better things to do. "We should not be dwelling in the past. Tonight is our beginning." His hand slipped inside the wrapper she wore, moving lightly over her stomach and ribs.

She leaned against him, tucking her head beneath his chin and mirrored his actions with her own hand. "Very well," she murmured, her voice catching as his hand moved downward. "We will let tomorrow bring what it will, but the rest of tonight..." She gasped as his hand moved between her legs and touched her intimately.

"Is ours," he finished. Then he stood and carried her back into the bedroom, firmly kicking the door shut behind them.

The insistent knocking on the door a week later tugged Brand slowly into wakefulness. Felicia lay curled asleep beside him, her hair a tangled skein of silk spread across his chest. A door opened and he swore under his breath, promising dire retribution for whomever intruded on their privacy. Felicia stirred as he moved.

"What is it?" she asked in a drowsy voice, just as he heard Hardwicke's tentative voice.

"My lord. Beggin' your pardon, but you must come quickly." It was the tone of his voice that snapped Brand into instant alertness at the same time a sliver of dread pierced him.

"Go back to sleep," he said softly to Felicia, pulling the covers up over her nakedness. Picking up his dressing gown from the floor, he shrugged into it and followed Hardwicke from the room.

Hardwicke stood near the door of the sitting room, wringing his hands, his face as stricken as Brand had ever seen. "I'm sorry to disturb you, my lord," he began, "but Stearns insisted I bring you to His Grace's apartments immediately."

"Why?" The question was sharp, and the valet flinched, even as Brand headed for the door.

He did not wait to hear his man's answer, which was just as well because Hardwicke had not given him one. Striding down the corridor toward the ducal apartments, the dread surfaced again, this time full blown and impossible to ignore.

His worst fears were confirmed when he entered his father's bedchamber to find the doctor there speaking quietly to a stoic duchess. He looked up as Brand entered, his eyes solemn.

"What the hell is going on?" He kept his voice low, but his mouth had gone dry. He had not since he was eight years old felt so helpless in the face of such quiet.

The doctor approached shaking his head. "I'm sorry, my lord," he said gravely, glancing toward the bed. "His heart just gave out."

Brand approached the bed. His father looked to be asleep, yet the pallor of his skin and the stillness of his face told him otherwise. Rage poured through him like acid and Brand looked around for a target to vent it on.

The duchess now sat in a chair, head erect, shoulders back—as if facing a firing squad. When his eyes landed on her, she blanched, but otherwise did not move or speak. She seemed to be in shock, her dark eyes blank and unfocused.

He brought his emotions under control and tipped his head toward her as he spoke to the doctor at his side. "Shouldn't someone be taking care of her?"

"I think it would be best if someone sent for her maid. She is undoubtedly in shock."

Brand glanced at the door where Stearns, his father's man,

stood unobtrusively. Beckoning him, Brand instructed him to find his stepmother's maid and send her up to see to her. Turning back to the doctor, he drew a deep breath and asked, "What are you doing here? Why wasn't I summoned before?"

"When he is in London, it has become my practice to check on His Grace regularly. When I arrived this morning, Stearns had not yet checked on him."

"Why not?"

"Lately His Grace had instructed Stearns not to awaken him in the mornings, but to await his summons. It is not so very late as yet. I'm somewhat of an early riser. Stearns was merely doing as instructed. However, I have been known to awaken His Grace before, so I was allowed in."

Brand nodded, then took a deep breath and let it out slowly. "I need to get dressed—and inform my wife. I will meet you downstairs in the library."

There was nothing else for him to do here. The duchess's maid entered as Brand was leaving, her eyes casting a nervous glance in Brand's direction before she hurried over to her mistress. The doctor was talking to the maid as he left.

Felicia stood at the balcony doors as he entered their suite through the sitting room. Dressed only in her robe, she took one look at him and flew toward him. Catching her in his arms, he crushed her against him and buried his face in her hair. He was shaking and she slipped her arms around his waist, holding him as close as she could. Even when her own father died, she had not felt the loss as keenly as she sensed Brand did now.

"I'm sorry," she whispered tearfully. "Oh, Brand, I'm so sorry."

Felicia looked up at her husband, now the seventh Duke of Warringham, and watched him pull himself together. The next few weeks would be painful, but they would get through it. They had no choice.

"I must get dressed," he said in a surprisingly steady voice. "The doctor is awaiting me in the library. You will need to take over the household, I don't think my stepmother is in any condition to do anything right now."

She nodded gravely, feeling the sudden weight of responsibility settle on their collective shoulders. He turned to leave, but hesitated, looking down at her.

"I will send for Eliza," she told him, and, turning him toward the bedchamber and dressing room beyond, gave him a little push. "Go, the doctor is waiting. I will be fine."

He turned back for an instant, kissed her gently, then headed for the door.

Chapter Thirteen

Felicia escaped the house with Jon for a brief walk in the gardens at The Downs. The funeral service was tomorrow and family and friends were still arriving. Eliza had been indispensable, helping her to situate people and introducing her and Brand to distant family members.

The duchess, now the dowager duchess, remained in seclusion. The arrival of Lord Caverdown had surprised Felicia until he admitted he was a distant cousin of the dowager duchess. He did not, however, remain at the house, but took rooms in a local inn and only requested the dowager duchess be informed he had called.

"How are you holding up?" Jon asked her now. He didn't really need to ask the question. The reason he insisted she accompany him outside for a few moments was that he could see for himself she was barely keeping herself together. Her face was drawn, dark shadows lurked beneath her eyes, and he was sure she was not eating properly.

However, she looked the picture of health compared to her husband. Brand looked haggard. His self-assurance and vitality were lost beneath the pain and grief he did not try to hide. That Felicia tried to absorb some of the Brand's pain was obvious to Jon.

She gave him a wan smile. "Better than yesterday. But I'm worried about Brand."

"I know." He smiled when she turned to look up at him, a question in her eyes. "It is probably only obvious to me because I know you so well."

"He's always known this was a possibility, but I think he's

feeling guilty now."

"Guilty? For what?"

Felicia shrugged. "For everything. For not spending more time with his father. For not staying in England three years ago. For not being with him when he died. For not helping him more. You name it—and he has a reason for why he's responsible. It's destroying him." Her voice clogged with tears. "I can't help him, and I'm afraid he will begin to blame me."

Jon put his arms around her and gave her a hug. "Why do you think he will blame you?"

"Because if it weren't for our marriage, he would have spent more time with his father."

"Yet your marriage pleased his father."

"I know." Felicia moved away and wandered down the path.

She knew the duke had been delighted with their marriage, but she couldn't help but wonder if Brand begrudged the days he had been away from his father after their initial reunion.

On one level, she understood Brand's father had wanted him to marry. He wanted to ensure the succession. But she also knew Brand needn't have married so soon. He could have spent more time with his father if it hadn't been for her insistence on having everything her way.

She had been through it many times over the last week while they traveled, and settled in. If she hadn't coerced Brand into escorting her to Jon's estate, he wouldn't have had to marry her. If he hadn't had to marry her, he could have spent more time with his father. Maybe he would have stayed at The Downs instead of going to London. If his father hadn't insisted he be present when she and Brand appeared, he might not have taxed his strength and further drained an already weak heart. Her head ached with the possibilities, but it all pointed back to her forcing Brand's hand in the first place.

If Brand loved her, she might not be thinking this way, but she had no idea how he felt about her except for the normal attentiveness due her as his wife. They were well matched in bed, but beyond that, she knew and understood him little. Excluding the revelation concerning his brother's death, he'd never opened up to her.

She sat down on a bench under the branches of a large oak. Jon ambled leisurely behind her, looking over the flowers and plants as he came. Reaching her perch, he started to join her when something caught his eye and he stepped around the bench instead. Turning to see what caught his attention, she froze as she watched him examine a small patch of purple, white, and yellow flowers.

Clustered in the shade of a small hedge, the tall stalks held bunches of slightly elongated bell-shaped flowers. Small and delicate, she watched them sway slightly in the light breeze.

"What kind of flowers are those? I think I've seen them before, but I'm afraid you were the only one Nona convinced flowers and herbs were worth knowing about."

"Foxglove." He joined her on the bench. "They are pretty, but poisonous. You'd do well to tell your gardener to keep an eye on them."

"Poisonous?" A cold feeling began in the pit of her stomach.

"Mmmhmm. Medical science has only just recently begun to use it under the name of digitalis to treat a variety of illnesses, but the dosages are not precise and too much can kill with little or no warning."

Felicia said no more on the subject, but in her mind's eye she saw the dowager duchess surreptitiously picking those very same flowers in the garden at Waring House.

They sat quietly for a brief time, Felicia trying unsuccessfully not to dwell on the implications of what she had seen. Had the dowager duchess poisoned her husband? If so, why? Edward was on his way to India, Brand was his heir. What would she gain by doing away with him now? And, why now and not before?

"You should tell him." Jon broke into her thoughts, startling her back to the present.

"Tell who?" And, about what?

"Brand," he answered. "You should tell him how you feel. He may not realize it because he has so many other things on his plate right now."

She was relieved he hadn't meant the flowers. "I don't want to bother him right now. We can talk later."

Jon slanted a cynical glance in her direction. "Putting it off won't make it any easier."

"Perhaps. But right now, I do not want to be added to his

list of worries."

Jon let out a frustrated breath. "Very well, I won't push, but I won't allow you to drive yourself too hard. You may now be a duchess, but you are still my baby sister."

"And you will never let me forget it, will you?"

"No, and neither, I suspect, will Jay or Tina."

Felicia sighed. She'd warred with herself over whether to write and interrupt their holiday. They had waited nearly three years to have a proper honeymoon. Waiting first to have the yacht built, then their first child came along, and then her own come-out. The decision to go had finally been made this year after Tina miscarried their second child early on and Jay felt the change in climate would help her recovery. Jon agreed to stand in Jay's stead for her Season this year, but Felicia secretly wondered how much of a honeymoon they could possibly have with a child and Nurse along.

"I haven't written to them yet. I haven't wanted to interrupt their time together."

Jon harrumphed. "I, of course, had no such reservations."

"Jon! There was no need. They didn't need to cut their time short for this."

"I didn't ask them to do so. I merely informed them of Brand's father's death. I did not expect they would hurry home. In fact, I distinctly told Jay they needn't do so."

"Oh."

Felicia felt marginally better as they strolled up the path toward the house. Although she would not admit it, Jon had been right about her need to escape, if only for a few minutes. The oppressive atmosphere in the house was, at times, more than she could bear. In addition, she knew she was being watched, assessed, and judged by those present as to whether she was duchess material.

Of course, she already knew what the dowager duchess thought of her. Perhaps she ought to be thankful the dowager remained out of sight. If she thought her come-out was difficult, and her appearance with Brand had promised to be worse, but an occasion such as this far exceeded her worst nightmares. Trying to be perfect was exhausting.

The small parlor they entered, one of many that faced the gardens behind the house, was empty. She wondered where

Eliza was, and whether she should be helping her. As if on cue, Eliza appeared as they entered the hall, Amanda beside her.

"Ah, Your Grace," she addressed Felicia. "There is another carriage approaching, and I am hoping it is the Westovers. At least we have already set aside rooms for them."

"Please, Eliza, not so formal when there is only family to hear. I feel enough like a fraud as it is."

"You shouldn't," the countess responded. "You will make a wonderful duchess." Then turning to Jon, addressed him. "Might I ask a favor, my lord?"

"Of course."

"It is Amanda's turn to play in the drawing room, but I cannot locate cousin Derrick, who I enlisted to turn pages for her. Would you mind stepping in until I find him?"

Felicia smothered her grin as Jon found himself neatly trapped into not only squiring Amanda to the drawing room, but remaining with her. Glancing at him once she was sure her eyes held no trace of amusement, she added, "You might as well contribute too, Jon." Then, turning to Amanda, she said, "Chopin is his favorite. Let him play any pieces you come across by him." Amanda did not respond, but Felicia detected a hesitancy she found odd.

She thought she could hear Jon grinding his teeth as he offered his arm stiffly to Amanda and the two of them headed for the drawing room, while she and Eliza headed for the front door.

She only managed to suppress her giggles until Jon and Amanda were out of sight. "I know I shouldn't have," she began, and was interrupted by her companion.

"No, you shouldn't have," Eliza agreed, "but I'm glad you did."

The Westovers, entering the foyer at that moment, were confronted by the realm's newest duchess and her sister-in-law giggling like two naughty schoolgirls. The two sobered instantly at the sight of the Duchess of Westover's frown. Sighing, Felicia moved forward to greet them.

Geri dipped into a graceful curtsy, and Felicia greeted her by saying, "I hope we are friends enough you only did that for the sake of appearances."

Geri did not answer except to hug her friend upon

straightening and ask, "How are you and Brand holding up?"

"As well as can be expected." Ascending the stairs with the ladies, the men having been directed to the billiard room where most of the other men in attendance seemed to congregate, she added, "My great-grandmother was fond of saying death is a natural part of life, but it is difficult to accept something that causes so much pain as natural."

The duchess chuckled as, first glancing at Geri, then Eliza, and lastly Felicia, she commented, "Wait until you have your first child."

Much later, Brand climbed the same staircase, fatigue in every step. He tried not to think of how much he needed to see Felicia. How much he needed to hold her. For the moment, she was his safe harbor, the only place he could find rest and rejuvenation.

By this time tomorrow the worst would be over. His father would be laid to rest beside his mother, and the solicitor would have finished with the obligatory reading of the will. Hopefully the majority of their houseguests would be preparing to leave the next day, giving Felicia and him breathing space, and time to grieve in peace.

Entering the suite through the bedroom, he found Felicia already there, standing at the window. She turned as he closed the door, and moved toward him. As she stepped into his arms, he felt some of the weariness drain away. This was the only place he wanted to be—forever.

They stood together for a few minutes, until Felicia stepped back and took his arm, leading him to one of the chairs in front of the fire. Helping him out of his jacket, she tossed it into one of the other chairs.

"Sit." He sat. She pushed a footstool underneath his feet, then reached down to loosen and remove his cravat. "I told Hardwicke to prepare you a bath in a half hour. Until then—" she handed him a glass of wine, "—rest."

"And you?" He watched her pick up his jacket from the other chair and lay it across the foot of the bed, dropping his neckwear on top.

She turned to regard him. "What about me?"

He held out his free hand. "Come here." She walked toward him, stopping before his chair. "Join me."

"Only if you promise to rest. There will be time enough for other...um...activities later tonight." She tried to deliver the statement impassively, but the reddening of her cheeks told him she was anything but.

"Very well, I promise." He pulled her down into the chair, arranging her comfortably across his lap. Sipping his wine, he could feel the tiredness pulling at him and he wanted nothing more than to succumb to it. Despite her obvious concern, she was safe from him for the moment. He was just too tired.

As if sensing his thoughts, she said, "You are working too hard." He looked down into worried blue eyes. "Will you at least slow down some after tomorrow?"

Brand wasn't sure it was wise to make such a promise, but he couldn't resist the appeal in her eyes. The worry he read there was real—and he knew it was only for him.

"I will if you will."

"But I'm doing so little now if I cut back I would be doing nothing at all. Trent is never going to let Eliza come visit us again. She has been the real hostess, I have only been her shadow."

"Then why do you look as though you haven't slept in a week?" His thumb brushed softly over the smudges beneath her eyes.

"It's possible I haven't, but not from lack of trying."

"I see."

She wished he did. Fretting over him had become her main occupation during the last few days, but she was hopeful that after tomorrow they would gain a measure of peace. And enough breathing room to help them put their lives back on an even keel.

Brand sat behind the massive oak desk dispassionately surveying the members of his family gathered in the library. There were only a few, as the solicitor had informed him his father had given specific instructions on who was to be present when his will was read, despite the tradition of having everyone present who was mentioned in the document.

Eliza sat closest to the desk, and therefore, him. He knew

she had taken the seat deliberately to provide him with unspoken support. He'd discovered a backbone of steel in his little sister over the last few days and was immensely thankful for it.

The dowager duchess sat on a sofa situated beside Eliza's chair as Eliza was the only person in the room who seemed to be willing or able to speak to her without reservation. It had been Eliza who braved the dowager duchess's chambers and insisted she attend the funeral. Likewise, it had been Eliza who she leaned on during the service.

On the sofa beside the dowager duchess sat his father's sister, Annabelle. An aunt he hadn't known existed until this week. At five years younger than his father, she was still very active. He wondered why he hadn't met her in London, until he learned she lived in Scotland.

Derrick Waring lounged indolently in a chair beside Aunt Annabelle. The only child of his father's and Annabelle's younger brother, he was close in age to Eliza and might have been considered handsome but for the permanent sneer which seemed to mark his features. In the short time he'd been at The Downs, Brand found him lazy, undependable and selfish. His one redeeming feature seemed to be his devotion to their aunt. If it weren't for Edward, Derrick would currently be his heir. Brand shuddered inwardly at the thought.

The only person Brand considered missing was Edward, however, the solicitor had informed him his father had known Edward would not be present, leaving Brand to speculate on his father's intuition concerning his own death.

The solicitor sat on the opposite side of the desk from Eliza. A tall, thin, spindly-legged man with thick red hair and sideburns, he commanded the assembled group's attention simply by clearing his throat.

Introducing himself as Mr. Charles Coleridge, he stated he had been handling the affairs of the dukedom for a number of years, having inherited it, as it were, from his father. He then informed them the will he was about to read had been prepared a mere two weeks before the duke's death—and signed and witnessed only the day before.

Brand's eyebrows rose at that. The day before his father's death had only been a few days after their trip to his shipping offices. He'd said nothing about meeting with his solicitor then.

Mr. Coleridge began reading and Brand listened with only half an ear to most of the bequests. To Eliza, certain pieces of their mother's jewelry; to Edward, fifteen thousand pounds per year for life and one of the non-ancestral estates—the decision of which estate to be left to Brand's discretion; to Aunt Annabelle, the sum of ten thousand pounds and a direction to Brand to continue the amount left her by their father for the remainder of her life; and to Derrick, the sum of ten thousand pounds with the admonishment that he invest it wisely and continue to care for Aunt Annabelle.

To my wife, Emily, I leave the sum of two hundred pounds per month, to be paid in quarterly installments, until such time as Bertrand's wife is safely delivered of a son who survives until his second birthday. Upon the child's second birthday, the amount shall be increased to two thousand pounds per month for the remainder of her lifetime.

Eliza gasped, her eyes going to Brand as the solicitor continued, listing minor bequests to other members of the family, servants, and other retainers, including Stearns. Brand did not indicate outwardly his surprise, yet his mind did not miss the implication. Whatever happened, Edward was not to inherit under any circumstances, and conditioning his mother's inheritance on Felicia giving Brand an heir who survived an appreciable amount of time was meant to keep her from trying to secure just that.

To Brand it also indisputably indicated his father, too, thought she was behind his and Michael's disappearance. That he'd said nothing to Brand during the time they had spent together left Brand wondering whether his father had ever meant to do anything about his suspicions. Certainly, Brand never said anything to his father about finding the person or persons responsible. Perhaps his father had decided to let sleeping dogs lie, as it were.

The dowager duchess said nothing and, beyond a slight flaring of her nostrils, revealing her understanding of the insult she had been dealt, did not move. When the solicitor was finished, he handed Brand the document for his review. Scanning the closely written lines, Brand flipped to the end noting his father's signature and the date, followed by those of the witnesses. All was in order.

A short time after the others left, the solicitor remaining to confer with Brand on the best method for handling the disbursement of the remaining bequests, a knock came at the door. When Brand called for the person to enter, it was none other than his brother-in-law, the Earl of Barrington. Brand was mildly surprised—he had expected Eliza herself.

"Am I interrupting?" the earl asked.

"No," Brand answered. "I believe Mr. Coleridge and I are finished."

"That we are," the solicitor confirmed, picking up his case from the floor and stuffing a sheaf of papers inside. "I will see those distributions are made as soon as I return to London, Your Grace."

"And when will that be?" Brand asked as the solicitor rose to his feet.

"By the end of next week."

Brand nodded and rose also. "Fine."

"Good day, Your Grace. My lord," he included the earl in his farewell and left.

Brand turned to his brother-in-law. "What can I do for you, Barrington?"

Trent Cookeson, the Earl of Barrington, was one of those people who aged well. Approaching forty, he still maintained his nearly six-foot frame in excellent condition, needing no padding for any of his coats. With light golden-brown hair over steely gray eyes, he was known to pontificate at times, but he loved Eliza and, for Brand, it was enough.

Eliza had been upset over the slight to their stepmother in their father's will. Brand had expected her to come back and speak with him over it, but perhaps it was better if he spoke to her husband instead.

The earl settled himself in a chair facing the desk and Brand resumed his seat. He got right to the point. "Eliza is quite upset over your father's will."

"I had guessed as much. She was clearly appalled at the slight to our stepmother."

"You may tell me to mind my own business if you wish, but I find it difficult to believe your father would do something so obvious without a reason."

"And what does Eliza think?"

The earl shifted in his chair and steepled his fingers beneath his chin. "She thinks, as I do, that your father believed your stepmother responsible for your disappearance and is punishing her by insuring Edward will never inherit." Brand sat back in his chair and regarded his brother-in-law intently. He wondered how much he should divulge and whether the earl could be trusted to keep the knowledge to himself.

"True. I don't yet know all the details of why my father did what he did, but for all intents and purposes, what he did do is leave his wife in my care. Obviously my father suspected she was involved in my disappearance—or perhaps he had more information which confirmed it, but whatever information it was he kept to himself."

"I see."

"One of the things I discovered about my father during the short time I knew him was that appearances were important to him. In his own way, he was trying to avoid a possible scandal. It would hurt Eliza and Edward and, despite his mother, my father loved Edward every bit as much as he did Eliza and myself."

"So, now what?"

Brand understood what he was asking. "Nothing. For now, she is safe." The earl's eyebrows raised a fraction. "Make no mistake about it, I hold her responsible for my brother's death, but at my father's request I will do nothing about it."

"His request?"

Brand leaned forward and extracted a sheet of paper from the pile of papers left by Mr. Coleridge. He stared at it for a moment, then looked at the earl. "My father left me a separate set of instructions concerning his wife. In it he requests I ensure she wants for nothing and is allowed to live wherever she pleases, with the exception of St. Ayers. Once the succession is assured, she will be able to do that for herself. Until then, I will not dishonor my father's last wishes by doing anything against her."

"Very well. I will tell Eliza, without going into too much detail, she has nothing to fear."

Brand stood. "Thank you."

They left the library together and parted ways in the main

hall, each heading in a different direction, but both seeking their wives.

Brand found his in the drawing room playing the piano. Crossing the room in her direction, he was compelled to stop and speak to each person who greeted him along the way. When he finally reached the sofa on which the Earl and Countess of Weston sat, he dropped into a vacant chair nearby with a sigh.

The earl looked over at him. "We have been enjoying listening to her play for some time now. This is a rare opportunity and few people in the room know it."

Brand looked over at him. "How so?"

Geri answered for her husband. "Because she doesn't like to play for crowds."

"Why?" he queried. "You know as well as I do that she plays like an angel."

Geri nodded. "I don't know why—she just doesn't."

She turned her attention back to Felicia playing at the piano, obviously lost in her own little world. Brand was reminded of the day at the Abbey when he had wandered into the drawing room while she was playing. He had never heard anyone put such emotion into their playing, nor lose themselves so completely in the music.

"She usually refuses to play when requested. Until today."

"Why today?"

"Mama requested she play," the earl answered.

Geri smothered a laugh, but Brand heard.

"Actually, she informed Felicia it was her duty to do so. And Felicia, who considers my mother-in-law the perfect duchess, accepted it along the lines of a decree." Geri apparently noticed Brand's frown and, sobering, reached over to touch his sleeve. "She, Tina, and Jon have lasting scars when it comes to their heritage. Society only tolerates them as long as nothing too outrageous happens. Tina's marriage has made her acceptable, Jon's acceptance by his grandmother secured his acceptance, but Felicia is still trying to be perfect in order to garner that acceptance," she said to him, but her eyes begged him to understand. "Once we are all gone, it will be up to you to prove to her she needn't be."

He understood. Felicia was still insecure in many ways. No

one else saw it, but they did not really know her. They didn't understand her need to prove she could be a duchess, her gypsy background notwithstanding. All they saw was the façade she allowed them to see. Instinctively he knew becoming more comfortable with herself and their relationship would give her the confidence she needed and he intended to bolster that confidence every chance he got.

Felicia was entranced by the extensive gardens at Waring Castle. Unable to investigate while the castle was filled with family and friends for the funeral, she now spent much of her days exploring them. They were beautiful and peaceful, soothing and comforting when she needed it most. She discovered a large lake, complete with a boathouse and several rowboats, a maze, a formal rose garden with a gazebo at its center, a statuary and a greenhouse full of flowers and various fruit trees.

One of her first instructions upon making the head gardener's acquaintance was to direct him to find, dig up, and dispose of all the foxglove in the garden. She didn't want to believe the dowager duchess would poison her own husband, but then again, she could believe she might have ordered the murder of two young boys. Felicia wasn't sure there was much of a difference.

At least the dowager no longer resided at the castle. Eliza had, before she left, helped the dowager duchess move to the Dower House, a twenty-five room house which sat across the lake. Brand had given her permission to move after what must have been a horribly painful interview. Felicia had not been present, but Brand had been extremely tense and uncommunicative for hours after the dowager left the library.

Following Eliza's advice, and taking advantage of the seclusion afforded by being in mourning, Felicia began to discuss redecorating some of the rooms with the housekeeper. The first set of rooms on the list were the ducal apartments. For that reason, she and Brand still occupied the suite they had taken upon their arrival. For the time being it suited them, but she knew eventually they would need to move into the master suite.

She did not dwell much on the fact that she had accomplished that long ago sixteen-year-old's dream of becoming a duchess. Instead she spent many hours contemplating and wondering when and how she had fallen in love with her husband. It wasn't that she didn't want to love him, but not knowing how he felt left her at sea. And, for the first time in her life, she was afraid to ask.

She had come to accept his protectiveness and possessiveness as a constant in her life in the short time they had been married. She had even begun to understand the high-handedness he had exhibited before they were married, accepting it as part of his nature. But she wondered whether the tenderness he often displayed was merely designed to continue to allay her fears, or an indication of deeper feelings.

She did know one thing, however. He had accomplished something she had not thought possible. Aaron and Ella no longer haunted her. She no longer heard Ella's screams when she thought of Davey, no longer experienced the terror of remembering, and no longer feared the same thing would happen to her. Brand had, indeed, kept the nightmares at bay. In fact, he had banished them altogether.

Not since she was nine years old had she been able to look at men outside her family without feeling off balance. It was a liberating feeling to realize she was no longer afraid. To know she was free to live her life without fear. Free to love Brand and someday bear his children. Nona had promised her happiness and Felicia no longer doubted all would be as she said. She just wondered when Brand would fall in love with her as she had with him.

She felt his pain so keenly at times, but how he bore up under the strain was a mystery to her. Too often she found herself wondering what he had been through, her imagination conjuring up beatings, deprivation, starvation, and worse—and every time it happened, the tears would flow. She had sympathized with others in the past, but this went beyond sympathy and she questioned whether she'd traded one nightmare for another—and someone else's at that.

Now, walking along the edge of the lake, she turned and looked back at the castle. The massive edifice had five separate sections to it and she was becoming familiar with it slowly. Knowing she was going to be here for an extended stay, she'd decided to take it on a section at a time.

She had already begun with the family wing. That section included the main portions of the castle, consisting of the drawing rooms, parlors, library, office and music room—all found on the main floor—the ducal apartments, and approximately twenty rooms of various sizes and configurations, and the nursery.

She toyed with asking Brand to tour the section with her, but decided against it when she realized she would be inspecting the nursery. She wasn't sure he was ready to face those rooms yet and she wasn't sure it was necessary for him to do so. The rooms, however, had been a delightful surprise.

Large, bright and airy, the nursery was a child's dream. Toys and books, some in perfect condition, sat on shelves built into the walls, and scattered about the room she found two rocking horses, a doll cradle, a small table set with a miniature porcelain tea set, an enormous dollhouse complete with furniture, another table set with toy soldiers in formation, and more. The housekeeper opened large dormer windows covered by blue chintz curtains, allowing in sunlight and a warm breeze.

Felicia found it hard to believe the room had borne witness to death and darkness. The housekeeper, Mrs. Gibbons, however, seemed to know what she was thinking and filled her in.

"It was completely redone after the two young masters disappeared. His Grace even had the floorboards torn up and replaced as they was stained with blood and he didn't want Master Edward and Lady Eliza to see any of it."

Felicia was still looking around in wonder at a room she knew couldn't have sat empty for as many years as Edward had been gone. Voicing her question, she learned the room was always kept ready for when Lady Eliza came to visit and brought her children, causing Felicia to wonder how much noise could be heard in the ducal apartments, which were situated beneath.

Reaching the boathouse, she sat down on a bench beneath a large oak tree beside it. The day was becoming warm and she was glad for the shade and light breeze that caressed her face. Her gaze roamed over the calm, expansive surface of the lake, skimmed over the area beyond, and rested briefly on the Dower House.

Brand had told her of his father's will and separate instructions and while she thought she understood his father's motivation, she could see it troubled Brand to be forced to support and care for someone he considered a murderer. Yet his code of honor would not allow him to do anything less.

A movement near the Dower House caught her eye and she watched curiously as a figure, a man, exited from a side door, walked quickly to a stand of trees nearby, and disappeared into it. For a moment, she thought she recognized him, but couldn't be sure. A moment later, she forgot all about him as she heard footsteps behind her and turned to find Brand approaching.

"I have been looking all over for you," he growled.

She got to her feet. "I'm sorry, did you want me for something?"

He stopped in front of her and looked down at her. For a moment, she thought she saw worry and fear in his eyes before he shuttered them.

"I just didn't know where you were—and neither did anyone else."

Felicia felt a spurt of irritation. "I didn't realize I had to leave an itinerary whenever I left the house."

Brand sighed. "No, don't get angry. I didn't mean it that way."

"Then what did you mean?" she asked suspiciously, hands on her hips.

He ran his fingers through his hair in a gesture of frustration.

"Felicia." She bristled at the blatantly patronizing tone. "Waring Castle and Park are extremely large and wide open, and only a portion of the entire estate. There are portions of the The Downs crossed by public roads. It is impossible to keep people out—in fact the Warings have never done so. And while the gardens and lake up to and just beyond the Dower House are considered private, for family only, others can and do ignore that."

He stepped forward and pulled her into his arms.

"I do not want you to feel afraid in your own home, but I

would like you to take care, and always tell someone where you are going when you leave the castle or the immediate garden."

Felicia felt her blooming indignation deflate quickly. It hadn't occurred to her he might be worried someone might come on the estate and do her harm. It hadn't occurred to her it was a possibility. Remembering that he and his brother had been stolen from this beautiful, peaceful place, she understood his anxiety.

"I'm sorry. It just hadn't occurred to me. I will take care from now on."

Brand raised his hand and tipped her face up to his. "And you will let someone know where you are going when you leave? Or better yet, take a footman with you?"

"I will let someone know, but I cannot promise always to take a footman."

"Very well." Brand accepted the concession.

Sealing their agreement with a kiss led to other things, which meant they did not return to the castle until more than an hour later. By then Felicia's hair was hanging loose down her back and her dress looked a little more the worse for wear. Brand's cravat had been loosened, then carelessly retied, and his clothing was rumpled. The staff was too well trained to do anything other than pretend it was normal for the duke and duchess to appear so disheveled after a walk, but would discover in the ensuing months no pretense was needed.

Chapter Fourteen

Felicia took Brand's words to heart, but in a different manner than he expected. Returning to their suite, she sent for Lily, then went into the dressing room. Standing amidst rows of brightly colored muslins, silks and satins, Felicia grimaced as she looked down at the plain, unrelieved black she wore. Its dull color seemed to sap her energy as well. Nearly a month since Brand's father's death, and many more to go. At least she would be in half-mourning by the time the Season was underway next year.

Lily entered the dressing room and Felicia turned toward her. "Where did you put my pistol case?"

The maid slipped by her and knelt down to rummage beneath a row of ballgowns, coming up with the plain wooden case and handing it to her. Leaving the room, Felicia sat at the dressing table and opened the case. If Brand was worried about her safety, at least she could provide herself with some degree of protection.

Lily redid her hair as she removed each of the small, mother-of-pearl-handled pistols, checked them over, then loaded each one in turn. Each had only one shot, but if someone accosted her, it should be all she needed. Nevertheless, she had preferred some of her father's pistols precisely because they held more than one.

As she went through the motions, she wondered if her mother had ever used them. Her father had originally ordered two sets of the small pistols, giving one set to Tina and one set to her mother. After her mother's death, Jon had given her mother's set to her and taught her to use and care for them. She hadn't been satisfied, though, and had slipped into the main house at Thane Park once when the steward was out and taken a set of her father's pistols from the study. She taught herself to use them, relying on the coachman to occasionally resupply her with ammunition.

Finished with her hair, Lily asked if there was anything else she needed.

"Do I have any sets of drawers with no pocket on them?"

"I will check, Your Grace." Lily returned to the dressing room.

It had been her idea to come up with a way for she and Tina to carry both of the small pistols at once. It was too easy to carry one in a reticule, only to have someone who meant them harm to immediately take it away. An assailant wouldn't expect them to be carrying another one and so an idea had been born. They had thought long and hard before she had come up with the idea of sewing a small pocket on the outside of the drawers they wore under their petticoats.

It had been a while since she required Lily to sew the first pockets on and she knew she had new pairs that had not been altered. She had not insisted on it lately, but now she knew she needed it done again.

Lily entered with a number of pairs draped over her arm. "These do not have pockets. Would you like me to add them?"

"Yes. I do not necessarily feel I am in danger, but until I learn my way around and meet the people in the area and get to know them, I will feel better carrying something." As Lily headed for the door, she added, "I don't think I need to remind you no one else is to know of this."

Lily nodded. "No, ma'am. And I will use the usual excuse if the laundress asks about the pockets."

Felicia smiled as the door closed behind the maid. Lily knew what the pockets were for, but she had created her own excuse for any others that might spy them, the usual one being Felicia often needed more than one handkerchief.

As she went downstairs to join Brand in the library, she was reminded there were a few things about mourning she didn't mind. One was that most mourning clothes were made with small pockets, usually designed to carry a handkerchief, and another was many of the usual rituals, such as tea, were severely scaled back. Having tea served in the cozy comfort of the library while Brand worked suited her just fine.

Brand glanced up as she entered the library. He looked very much like the lion she had labeled him seated behind the massive desk, surveying all before him. Yet, in his shirtsleeves, with his shirt opened at the neck, he brought back glimpses of her father as she remembered him doing the same thing.

Seating herself on a blue damask upholstered sofa, she watched him sign and sand a letter, then set it aside and pick up another document.

The butler entered, accompanied by a maid pushing the tea trolley. At his direction, she parked it next to Felicia's perch and, with a respectful dip in Felicia's direction, left. The butler remained momentarily to ask if Her Grace required anything else.

"No, thank you, Matthews. I'm sure I have all I need for the moment," she assured him, eyeing the pile of little sandwiches, tarts and cakes on the plate.

Brand rose from the desk and sauntered over as Matthews closed the doors. "Looks to me like you have more than you need. Does Cook know something I don't?"

"Such as?" Felicia reached for the teapot as Brand dropped down beside her.

Handing a cup of the fragrant brew to her husband, she then turned to pour herself a cup.

"I thought perhaps she knew we'd worked up an appetite earlier."

Felicia turned shocked eyes upon him. "Brand!"

He chuckled. "You are too easy to tease."

Felicia let out a *humph* and went back to her tea. Brand picked up a tart and popped it into his mouth. For a time there was only the clinking sounds of cups and saucers as they sipped their tea in silence. Felicia rested against the back of the sofa, chewing thoughtfully on a piece of lemon cake.

This was an odd honeymoon to have, but it was definitely turning into theirs, with interludes like this afternoon happening often. Mourning certainly made it easy to ignore the rest of the world and focus solely on each other. Brand was still occupied sorting through the affairs of the estate, but he always managed to find her sometime during each day and spend time with her. She was touched by his attentiveness and thoughtfulness.

A knock on the door brought her out of her musings. It was Matthews with the post. Leaving it with Brand, he retreated again.

She glanced over at Brand as he flipped through the stack of cards and letters. "Any more Royal missives?"

Brand grinned at her. "Thankfully, no." She had been surprised when he told her he had received a handwritten letter from Her Royal Majesty. But what surprised both of them was its contents. The queen had apparently been aware of his story as the letter began by welcoming him back to his family with condolences for Michael's death and hopes he would recover from his ordeal.

"Does she think you've been chained in a dungeon somewhere for the past twenty-three years?"

"Who knows?"

The letter had then expressed her condolences on his father's death, and ended with an admonition that he was now expected to take his seat in the House of Lords.

"I suspect she covered everything in the first one." Brand extracted a letter from the pile and handed it to her.

"It's from Jon!"

Brand rose to his feet and crossed the room to deposit the rest of the stack on his desk while she read.

"Anything interesting?"

"Not much except he's leaving the country—and taking Davey with him." She put the letter down in her lap and turned to look at him, exasperation in her eyes. "He says it's time for him to spread his wings, so he has hired a tutor for Davey and the three of them are headed for the continent. He doesn't know when they'll be back. Oh, and he's sending me back Midnight."

Brand said nothing. Her disappointment was palpable, but Jon had hinted to him of his plans when he'd been here for the funeral. He'd told Brand now that he no longer needed to watch over his sisters, it was time for him to go on a grand adventure. He had not decided whether to take Davey along when they had talked, but apparently made the decision to do so. It was for the best. Felicia would have smothered the boy.

"He's running away." Felicia laced her statement with a

laugh. "Perhaps it's for the best. Amanda will find someone else while he's gone."

Brand chuckled at her logic, but did not disagree with her. He would tell her later he had known about Jon's plans and had even provided him a letter of entree to the captain of any ship in the fleet to provide him and any companions he might have passage to wherever they wanted to go. It was the least he and Jay could do.

Brand knew without Jon he would not now be married to Felicia. She would have stubbornly dug in her heels and refused to budge without her brother's prodding. He'd revealed to Brand his great-grandmother's admonitions regarding his sisters. If Brand hadn't recognized Felicia's ring, he would not have forced her to marry him. After Tina, what had put Jon staunchly on Brand's side in the whole affair had been the ring—and only the ring.

Brand sat atop his horse and surveyed the devastation before him. The Tuckers were lucky to have escaped alive. In the torchlight, he could see the charred beams and blackened thatch which littered the spot where a cottage once stood. The men helping to clear the mess were moving around him, but his gaze focused on Nat Tucker, his head wrapped in a bandage, and his wife, huddled with their four children around a small wagon. Swinging down from the horse's back, he approached the family.

"Do you know of anyone who might have taken a dislike to you for some reason?"

"No, Your Grace, none. Me an' my Mary, we gets along with ever'one."

"Hmmm." Brand glanced around, locating the person he sought. "Mervis?"

"Yes, Your Grace?" John Mervis hurried to his side. The steward was short and rotund, with a shock of thinning brown hair.

"How soon can we rebuild?"

The steward stroked his chin for a moment. "The supplies can be ordered tomorrow. They would be here by the end of the week. It shouldn't take more than a week to put it up, especially if we hire some men from the village."

Brand nodded. "See it done."

"Thank you, Your Grace." Nat nearly fell to his knees.

"Oh, and Mervis," Brand stopped the steward as he turned away, "make this one larger than the last one."

Mervis nodded. "I will bring by plans for your approval tomorrow, Your Grace." Then he went back to helping the men to clear and make sure the fire was completely out.

Brand turned back to the displaced family. "Have you somewhere to stay?"

"Me sister and her husband will take us in. They live just over the way on the next farm." This from Mary.

"Very well." Brand turned to go, but was approached by one of the other men.

"We'll be keepin' our eyes and ears open, Your Grace, to find out who did this. Nat an' Mary are well liked. I don't rightly know why anyone would want to harm them."

"See that you do. I want whoever did this found."

The light from the moon was obscured as Brand rode back toward the castle deep in thought. He couldn't believe the attack on the Tuckers was just a random attack. It was possible it could have been a robbery gone awry, but, it just didn't feel right. Mervis told him Nat awakened to find two men ransacking the small cottage. They could have been looking for something to steal and when confronted by Nat, hit him and deliberately set a torch to the cottage on their way out. But Nat and Mary obviously had very little, if anything, to steal. So why had they been the target?

He was still some distance from the castle, picking his way through a small wood when the hairs on the back of his neck stood up, alerting him that he was no longer alone. Then he heard the unmistakable click of a pistol being cocked.

"Well, whaddaya know," a rough voice came out of the gloom. "That there fella was right."

Brand looked around, but could see no one in the darkness.

"I be thinkin', Yer Grace, ye'd better be gettin' offa that there horse," another, different, voice said.

"Show yourself," Brand demanded.

"I be thinkin' yer not the one's givin' the orders here. But, it makes me no difference where I shoot ye."

Brand debated whether he should just spring the bay into a gallop, and ride away, but he wasn't sure whoever was holding the pistol might not just shoot him before he moved. Deciding he had better odds against his assailants on the ground rather than from the top of a horse, he slid out of the saddle.

"Move away from the horse," the first voice demanded.

Brand complied, taking the time to loop the reins around a tree branch, and moved into a small clearing. Deep darkness had fallen but the high clouds obscuring the moon were thinning overhead.

"Stop right there!"

Brand stopped and turned in the direction of the voice. A man stood not ten feet away, a pistol trained on him. Out of the corner of his eye to the right, he saw another man step into the clearing as well. Turning his head, he noted that the second man was not armed. *Good,* he thought. The odds just got better. Turning back to the man with the pistol, all he could make out was that he was of medium height and build. The man to his right was slightly smaller.

"What do you want?" he demanded. "I haven't got all night."

The man with the pistol snickered and stepped closer just as the moon emerged from behind its cloudy curtain. The other man moved to his side and said, "Go on, tell 'im, then git it over wid."

The moon silvered the clearing, throwing the faces of his adversaries into shadow but clearly outlining where they stood. Brand relaxed his stance, appearing bored. "Tell me what?"

"We're s'posed t' tell yer that ye have insulted the house of Villiers an' must die." And with that, the one holding the pistol leveled it and squeezed the trigger.

Brand moved first. Lashing out with his foot, he connected with the hand holding the pistol, sending the shot wide and the pistol into the grass. Leaping toward the second man, his foot connected with the man's head, snapping it backward and sending him flying into the dirt at the base of a tree. The first one recovered and rushed him, fists outstretched. Catching the leading fist, Brand pivoted, bent and flipped the assailant over his back, sending him flying into the trunk of a nearby tree with a sickening thud.

There was complete silence while Brand waited to see if there were any more men and, once he was convinced there weren't, he approached the two figures on the ground.

"Damn!" He'd let his temper get the best of him. They were both dead. Part of the training involved when he'd learned the art of Oriental fighting was discipline and control, but tonight he had not exercised either. He had already been angry at the attack on the Tuckers, and then to be accosted himself, he had allowed his rage to take over. His master in China would have reminded him that had he remained in control, he would not have killed both men and might have learned more about whoever sent them.

Searching until he found the pistol, he dragged the bodies to the edge of the clearing, searched them, then went to find his horse. Thankfully, he was still where Brand had left him. Pocketing the pistol, and the two pouches of coins he found, he remounted and headed for home. He would have Mervis dispose of the bodies tomorrow.

Giving orders to have a bath prepared as he entered the house, he went in search of Felicia and found her in the library. He gave her a cursory report on what happened at the Tuckers, omitting the incident in the woods, then headed upstairs.

Stopping only long enough to order a tray be prepared for him, Felicia followed.

As he soaked in the large tub, Brand wondered who Villiers was. And how had he insulted him. *You have insulted the house of Villiers...* The name sounded French, but that was not dispositive. There were any number of families of French background in England, many having fled France before and during the Reign of Terror and settled. Enough generations had passed that, despite the surname, the family would be wholly English now. He would ask Mervis if there were any families in the area by that name.

Quitting the tub, he dried himself and shrugged into the robe Hardwicke had left for him.

Felicia sat curled in a chair in front of the fire in the sitting room. On a table in front of her sat a tray of food. She looked up as he entered, indicating the tray. "You missed supper."

Brand barely glanced at the tray. He was not hungry. Instead, he reached down and scooped her out of the chair.

"Not supper." Burying his face in her neck, he inhaled her freshness. "You. I missed you."

Felicia didn't question his obvious need as she put her arms around his neck, and for that he was thankful. Brand knew he was reacting to nearly being killed earlier, and losing himself in Felicia was the only place he wanted to be at the moment. The attack had shaken him more than he would admit, hence his unwillingness to tell Felicia about it. Before Felicia, confronting his own mortality would not have bothered him unduly. It had happened too many times before to concern him too much, but now the thought of leaving her behind, alone and unprotected, wreaked havoc with his emotions.

"Was the situation bad?" she asked as he carried her into the bedroom.

"No. Not really. The Tuckers were all fine, except Nat, who had a nasty gash on his head."

"Will you help them rebuild?"

"Of course. I've already instructed Mervis to order the necessary materials."

"Good."

He put her down on the bed, then shucked his robe and joined her.

"You have too many clothes on." He nuzzled her neck.

She giggled at him. "According to you, I always have too many clothes on."

"You do, most of the time."

She sat up and untied the sash on her robe as he watched. The robe was quickly discarded, then she turned to him, a teasing light in her eyes. "Now?"

He eyed the thin lawn nightgown she wore. "You still have too many clothes on. You'll suffocate in this heat."

She gave him a sultry smile. "What heat? It's not hot in here."

"Yet," he growled and reached for her. Grabbing her by the waist, he lifted her over him until she straddled him. The nightgown hiked nearly up to her waist, and he seized the hem and quickly drew it over her head, watching as she shook out her hair behind her, the ends pooling over the tops of his thighs.

Felicia took advantage of her position and leaned down to tease a flat nipple with her tongue. Brand groaned and felt his body stiffen beneath her. His hands gripped her thighs gently then began moving upward slowly, stroking her skin softly.

"You are so beautiful," he rasped. "I never tire of looking at you, touching you—" he pulled her up the length of his body, cupping the back of her neck as he drew her head down to his, "—tasting you," he murmured against her lips.

Felicia sank into the kiss. Her tongue dueled with his, her hands moving up, threading through his hair. His hands slid up her back, then back down, cupping her derriere, pulling her tight against his groin. She moaned into his mouth.

Shifting to the side, Brand moved his mouth from hers to taste the skin on one creamy shoulder. She shivered. "Are you hot yet?" His voice was thick with need, yet he held back.

"Yes," she gasped, feeling his mouth move over her skin toward a breast. One hand stroked lightly over her hip, then traced the crease at the top of the leg. She trembled as his hand slid between her legs, gasping when he did not touch her as she suddenly, desperately, wanted. Gripping his shoulders, she arched against him as he took a nipple into his mouth.

The room spun dizzily around her and she closed her eyes, reveling in the sensations running rampant through her body. Brand's heat engulfed her, her own emotions swamped her with feelings that were out of control. And finally when she was beyond wanting, and shaking with the need he built to a fever pitch, his body joined with hers and she shattered in his arms.

Mervis sat in shock as Brand informed him of the previous evening's attack.

"I'm sure I was the target," he told the steward. "There were two of them, and they weren't from around here."

"But why attack the Tuckers if they wanted you?"

"They needed to draw me out—away from the castle. Since my father's death, I have not ventured out much, so lying in wait might have taken a long time. Instead, they created a diversion they guessed would bring me out to inspect the damage."

There were other things Brand did not tell him, however. He wondered how they knew the direction by which he would return to the castle. It could have just been the most direct way back and, because it was at night, they had surmised he would be in a hurry and choose that route. But, he hadn't forgotten one of them had indicated someone told them he would return via the forest.

"I want to know everything you can find out about those two men. Anything anyone may have seen or heard regarding them. I want to know the first time anyone noticed them, when they might have come into the area, if anyone noticed them talking to someone else, local or not. I want to know if they hired rooms and where. And—" he fixed Mervis with a hard stare, "—I want no one to know why. Ask around by telling people you are looking for whoever attacked the Tuckers."

After the man left, Brand leaned back in his chair and let out a deep breath. His thoughts immediately laid the attack at his stepmother's feet. He knew she was involved somehow, but couldn't yet see it clearly. Absently he wondered if the Comte's family name had been Villiers.

According to Pymm's report, the word around town was that the Comte's family had washed their hands of her when her first husband died, which is why she appeared in London. If she was English, which Felicia had confirmed she must be if she was distantly related to Lord Caverdown, then why might a French family who turned their back on her be insulted by anything that happened to her?

He was tempted to ride over to the Dower House and demand an explanation, but after his last interview with her, he was afraid he might be tempted to do something he had never done before in his life—strike a defenseless woman. It was probably dangerous to leave her alone because he couldn't keep tabs on her activities, but for now he had no choice.

Instead he would concentrate on more pleasurable activities—such as getting his wife pregnant. And, once he accomplished that, he would take Felicia to one of the other estates until she delivered safely. He smiled as he remembered the night before. Nearly getting himself killed had honed his senses beyond their normal levels. He wouldn't have recommended facing his own mortality as an aphrodisiac, but last night their lovemaking had taken them both to previously undiscovered heights.

A knock on the library door interrupted his musings. It was Mervis again, with the plans for the Tucker's new cottage. Beckoning the man in, he set aside the pleasant ruminations in favor of more sobering pursuits, like running a dukedom.

Chapter Fifteen

Felicia stared in awe around the vast ballroom. Silk wall coverings, three huge crystal chandeliers, a second floor gallery which encircled the entire room, gold mouldings around the windows, a wooden parquet floor with the ducal coat of arms worked into it and a plastered ceiling painted with scenes of mythological revelry all combined to create what once must have been a stunning room.

"His Grace's mother held the most wonderful parties," Mrs. Gibbons explained, "often attended by the Prince Regent. But after she died, the ballroom was closed off and never used again."

Felicia listened to the housekeeper's accounts of balls, local assemblies, and country dances alike—all held in this magnificent room. Now dust coated the floor, the silk covering the walls had faded and was peeling in places, and cobwebs laced the chandeliers. It would take a small army at least a month to restore this room to its former glory. She intended to do it, eventually.

Making notes on the pad she carried, she turned to her companion. "It will take some time to restore, and it need not be done until next year, so we will wait on it for now."

Mrs. Gibbons nodded her approval. "Just what I was thinkin'," she said. "Perhaps in the spring when we hire on a few extra maids for some heavy cleaning, we'll tackle it then."

"Excellent."

Leaving the ballroom behind, Felicia climbed the stairs to one of the guest wings. They were in the oldest part of the castle and she noticed some of the stairs needed repair. The ballroom had once been a massive great hall, converted and refurbished almost a hundred years ago when the castle was expanded.

"Tis said this old section is haunted," Mrs. Gibbons told her, "but I've never seen nor heard anything strange in all my years here."

Felicia smiled. "I believe most country houses are said to be haunted. What self-respecting English castle wouldn't have a ghost or two? The question, however, is whether they are friendly or not."

The rest of the morning was spent wandering through rooms, apartments, and suites, some of which had not been ventured into for many years. The castle itself was structurally sound enough, but Felicia was sure some of the fireplaces were probably blocked, a few windows were broken and she could see where rain had been blown in and water had damaged some of the floors and ceilings, and much of the furniture would have to be replaced. It would be a multi-year project to do all that was needed, but she looked forward to the challenge.

She wondered as she entered yet another dusty bedchamber, if there were any secret passages in this section of the castle. She knew many older castles and keeps often had built-in secret passages designed to get the lord's family to safety during an attack. Turning to ask the housekeeper, a noise at the window caught her attention instead and she went to investigate.

The small casement window had been nailed shut, and the grime covering the window blocked her view of the outside. Using the apron she wore over her gown, she wiped a circle in the glass, allowing her to look out. The noise she heard turned out to be none other than a trellis against the wall that had come loose, and was tapping against the side in the breeze.

She was about to turn away when movement below caught her eye. Someone seemed to emerge from the castle directly below where she stood. The person, a woman, moved quickly to a small thicket of trees, where a man emerged. The two embraced and Felicia smiled, thinking one of the maids had a suitor. The two stood together for a few minutes talking, then the woman gave the man a large bundle and the man gave her something in return. They stood speaking for a few moments, then parted.

Frowning, Felicia turned from the window and spoke to the housekeeper. "What is directly beneath these rooms?"

"The old kitchen is on the first floor. Years ago, when these rooms were used regularly, the old kitchen was used to heat water for baths, so the footmen didn't have to carry it so far."

"I see. I would like to see it." She headed for the door.

The housekeeper led the way down a set of narrow, winding stairs, then down a small hall past the ballroom, where they emerged into a spacious room. An old scarred worktable sat in the middle of the room. Large enough, she was sure, to gut and dress a wild boar, it showed evidence of much use. Two huge fireplaces faced each other across the room, both large enough to roast a whole deer. Shelves still held crockery and utensils, pots, kettles, basins, and even some long forgotten dried herbs.

Felicia moved to the door at the end of the room that led outside, noting it opened easily, almost soundlessly. Faint footprints could be seen in the dust covering the floor, but it looked as if there were more than one set. Closing the door, she threw the bolt on the inside, then tested it again. As she left the room, she told herself she would check tomorrow and see if the door had been opened again.

Brand reread the letter from Pymm before putting it down on the desk in front of him. It didn't say much—only that Pymm had the information he had asked for and would be in London by the fourteenth either to meet with him or receive further instructions. Brand grimaced. He'd heard London in July was miserable. It was the reason everyone who could deserted the capital for their country estates during the summer.

He supposed he could send back instructions to Pymm to come to The Downs, but that would be another three or four days. On the other hand, Felicia had been talking about sending to London for some fabric samples and colors to continue the decorating she had already begun. Perhaps they could do both and get away for a bit at the same time. With no one in London they wouldn't have to worry about callers intruding. They could accomplish their business together, and return, or continue on to St. Ayers.

And, it would be unlikely that his stepmother would find

out what he was doing. He might now be the master of all he surveyed, and Felicia its mistress, but he was not so naïve he didn't understand his stepmother probably knew nearly everything that happened on the estate. Even if the servants were completely loyal to he and Felicia, there would be talk between the servants in both residences, and information would pass, albeit innocently. Alerting his stepmother that he was investigating her background was something he wanted to avoid.

After his brush with death a week ago, Brand had been on constant alert every time he left the castle and it was beginning to wear on his nerves. Getting away would help to relax him and possibly provide him the information he needed to put his stepmother out of his life forever.

The decision made, he broached the subject with Felicia over tea.

"We wouldn't be gone long," he explained. "But it would give me a chance to look in at the shipping offices, and you the opportunity for some shopping. With all the redecorating you are planning, I'm sure you could use some time to do that."

She smiled up at him. "That's true. I'd love to have a chance to pick out some fabrics and colors. Maybe even talk to some designers. And, our suite should be ready by the time we return. The local shops have been wonderful and they have excellent wares, but they will not be able to completely supply everything I will eventually need."

Brand watched her nibble on a cucumber sandwich. Even dressed in dreadful black, she was beautiful. The color should have made her skin look sallow and her hair dull, but she had a glow all her own that outshone the lifeless color. She looked up and noticed him watching her.

"So, when do we leave?"

"Three days."

True to his word, three mornings later they were on their way.

The day promised to grow warm and Felicia was grateful for the light breeze blowing in the small windows of the traveling coach. Brand toyed with bringing his stallion along, but decided not to at the last moment. She didn't mind, knowing it meant he would be closeted with her for the whole three or four days it would take to get to London, although he was preoccupied for most of the journey with papers he brought with him to work on. She was content to sit beside him and read or doze.

Three afternoons later, as they neared London, disaster struck. On a particularly desolate stretch of road the coach suddenly began to slow. They were both asleep, not coming fully awake until it was too late.

The coach had come to a complete stop before Brand awakened enough to realize they had not stopped in an inn yard as he had supposed. The door opened and he found himself staring down the barrel of a pistol, the person holding it dressed in Warringham livery.

"Ye will step down, if ye please, Yer Grace." Please or not, it was unmistakably an order.

"No." Brand turned to shield Felicia with his body.

The man grinned, showing broken, yellowed teeth in blackened gums. "Then I'll jest have to shoot ye where ye sit."

"No!" Felicia's scream and frantic movement distracted him. He swung around to find the door on the other side of the coach had been opened and another villain was dragging her out. He lunged just as the man dragged her free, but was stopped with the report of a pistol and a searing pain in his shoulder. He fell from the coach, landing in the dirt on his injured shoulder.

The pain nearly caused him to black out, but Felicia's scream of terror brought him back.

"Brand!"

Looking up, he regained his feet quickly and headed toward them when suddenly the man holding her produced a pistol and put it to her head.

"Stop right there, or she dies now."

Brand stopped cold. Impervious to the pain in his shoulder, he concentrated all his energy on the villain holding Felicia in a vise grip. She had gone completely still at the touch of the barrel against her temple, eyes widening in fear.

"Now, that's better," the man holding Felicia smirked. "See, Charlie, ye jest have to know how to talk to the toffs."

The man named Charlie joined his companion, a second pistol in his hand and pointed at Brand's chest.

"What do you want?" Brand demanded.

"Nuthin' from ye," Charlie answered. "I'll be gettin' me fee from someone else."

Felicia began struggling against her captor, who responded by merely tightening a big beefy arm around her, cutting off her air.

"He's hurt," she gasped. "Let me…"

"It won't make no never mind where he's goin'," her captor responded. He began backing up, dragging her with him as she began to fight. It was all for naught as he merely hauled her up by the waist, raising her feet up off the ground, and carried her toward the side of the road.

It was then Brand noticed there were four of them altogether, two of them dressed in Warringham livery. He wondered if they had been with them all along, or if his coachman and footman had met with an accident on the way.

"I wouldn't if I were you," Charlie warned as Brand moved. "Cat ain't gonna 'urt her unless'n ye try somethin'."

Brand turned back to his assailant. For the moment, he could do nothing to help Felicia.

"If he does…" Brand did not need to finish the sentence. Charlie looked up into his eyes, blanched and backed up a step. Brand judged the distance between them and knew he would have to talk his way out. It was his only hope. His shoulder throbbed and he could feel the blood running down his back, soaking his shirt. "What do you want?" he demanded again.

"I tol' ye. Nuthin' from ye."

"Then why are we standing here?"

The man spat on the ground and yelled, "Nat!"

One of the other men, this one small and wiry with beady eyes in a thin face, came forward.

"'Urry up, an' git goin'." Charlie was obviously the one in charge. "I ain't got all day. An' remember, not one mark."

The man turned and ran back to where Brand could see that Cat had tied Felicia up by wrapping a rope around her waist, pinning her arms to her side. Felicia continued to struggle, even when it was obvious it was futile. He nearly smiled at her stubborn streak.

It suddenly occurred to him they were going to take Felicia and leave him here with Charlie.

"Where are they taking her?" he asked, striving for calm. His anger was beginning to surface and he knew it wouldn't take much for it to overpower him.

"Ye needn't worry 'bout that, Yer Grace. They'll be real good to 'er. Won't put nary a mark on 'er. Them's their orders."

Brand's frustration nearly erupted. "They'd better not harm a hair on her head," he said grimly.

"Or what?" Charlie sneered. "They ain't afraid o' a dead man."

Brand leaned against the back of the coach. His head was beginning to swim. The loss of blood was beginning to make him lightheaded.

"Am I allowed to know who wants me dead?" he asked.

"I'm jest s'posed to tell ye the 'ouse of Villiers is avenged."

"Ah, yes," Brand bluffed. "My dear stepmother."

Charlie started. Eyes narrowing, he blurted, "The old duchess said ye wouldn't know."

"Know what?" Brand asked nonchalantly. "That she was the one?" He shrugged his good shoulder. "She's the only one who wants me dead."

Charlie eyed him speculatively and Brand wondered if he could strike a bargain. The other two had already taken off with Felicia and he could no longer see them. He wondered why his stepmother might want Felicia—instead of killing them both, but for the time being, he was grateful Felicia was unharmed.

"I hope she paid you in advance," he said, returning his attention to Charlie.

"Wot?"

"I said I hope she paid you in advance," he repeated. "Once you kill me, she won't have a penny to her name."

The second man, also dressed in Warringham livery, came forward.

"Wot d'ya mean by that?"

"Shut up!" Charlie snapped at him. "He's jest tryin' to talk 'is way outta gettin' shot."

"Of course, I don't want to be shot," Brand agreed, "But I'm telling you the truth."

"She said once you were dead, 'er son would be the new duke and we'd get our blunt." This from the second man. He looked at Brand suspiciously.

Brand shook his head. "Sorry to disappoint you, old chaps. But, once I'm dead, my cousin becomes the new duke and she and her son don't get a penny."

"Yer lyin'," Charlie spat.

"Perhaps," Brand conceded, "but do you want to take the chance? Especially if you haven't been paid yet."

"'Ow we know ye ain't feedin' us a line?" the other asked.

"Shut up, Tick," Charlie snarled. "'e's jest tryin' t' worm 'is way out."

"My father left me a letter telling me what he'd done. The duchess doesn't know anything about it." Tick watched him closely. "She didn't pay you anything up front, did she?"

Neither men spoke, but they exchanged glances, telling Brand what he needed to know.

"It's because she only gets paid a small amount per quarter—and only if I sign the authorization. No signature, no money. No money for her, no money for you. It's that simple."

Brand could see Tick was thinking seriously about what he said. It was obvious his stepmother had only promised them payment. It was a good thing his father had left him a letter detailing the arrangements he had made in case she tried to do away with him again.

It must have hurt his father deeply to disinherit his own son in favor of a cousin Brand saw nothing commendable in. But he had. His letter informed Brand that, in case of his death without an heir and under suspicious circumstances, the solicitor had been instructed to deliver to the Crown a letter in which his father detailed circumstances which would preclude Edward from ever inheriting. The title would, therefore, pass to Derrick. Brand shuddered at the thought.

Bringing himself back to the matter at hand, he now contemplated the men before him. He had no quarrel with them, provided they had done no harm to his men. They'd already told him the other two wouldn't hurt Felicia and he had no choice but to believe them.

"What did you do with my coachman?" he asked.

"Nuthin'," Charlie cackled. "We been with ye the 'ole way."

Brand relaxed. "Then, gentlemen, I have a bargain to strike with you."

"An' wot makes ye think we'd be interested?" Tick asked.

"I'll double whatever you're being paid if you let me go."

"Don't ye be listenin' to 'im," Charlie interrupted. "She said 'e would try somethin'."

"Why should we believe ye?" Tick ignored Charlie to ask.

"Because I'm a man of my word." Brand could still feel liquid running down his back, but now he wasn't sure whether it was blood or sweat. "You could kill me—and no one would be the wiser, except my wife. And, there's something you ought to know about her."

The two men watched him warily, but said nothing.

"My wife has two brothers—an earl and a marquis. She is also part gypsy. Even if you elude her brothers, her gypsy cousins will find you."

He watched their eyes widen in fear at the mention of the gypsies. Among the lower classes, the fear of gypsies was still strong. Too many of them thought gypsies were little more than witches, all-knowing and all-powerful.

"You could save yourselves a horrible death and make more money to boot."

"An' 'ow would we git this blunt?" Charlie seemed suddenly interested.

"You'd have to take me the rest of the way to London." He looked up at the sky. "We won't get there until after dark as it is, but tomorrow morning first thing I'll have my man take you to the bank and give you your money on the spot."

"Why can't ye give it t' us when we git there?" the other man asked.

"Because I don't keep that kind of money laying around. I'm guessing she promised you a lot of money."

Charlie nodded. "One 'undred a piece."

Brand grimaced in pain. "I'll pay you five hundred a piece."

"That's more'n double," Charlie said suspiciously. "Wot 're ye tryin' t' pull?"

"Nothing. I just think my life is worth more than what you've been promised."

"'E's right, Charlie." The other man grinned, rubbing his hands together.

Charlie didn't seem quite convinced, and Brand wondered whether he was going to have to try to fight his way out of this after all. Stepping away from the back of the coach, he approached the two men as they discussed his proposition.

"I don' know," Charlie was saying. "S'pose the ol' lady finds out an' comes back for us?"

"She won't," Tick insisted.

"An' wot 'bout the other two?"

"What other two?" Brand asked, suddenly alert.

"The other two sent t' do ye in," Charlie answered. "They botched it, an' she made 'em pay. Ain't no one seen 'em since."

Brand grinned. She was cleverer than he gave her credit for, taking credit for the disappearance of the other two by claiming she'd done away with them for not finishing the job. He toyed with telling them he had been the one to eliminate the others, but couldn't be sure of their reaction.

"Very well," he said. "Then hurry up and get it over with, or I'll bleed to death before you get a chance anyway. But with the money I could give you, you could go far enough away and she'd never find you. And, at least you will get your money. Suppose she decides to do away with you instead of pay you? You know she's the one behind everything. You could identify her. She might worry you'd blackmail her and it would be easier to just kill you instead."

The two men shot startled looks at each other and Brand's hopes rose.

Felicia struggled futilely against the rope that bound her, sitting stiffly in front of the man named Cat, his arm wrapped around her as they rode through the forest. Her mouth was dry from the rag stuffed into it and she nearly gagged at the taste. After a while they stopped, as if waiting.

"Stop yer wigglin'," Cat growled, "Or'n I'll tie ye down."

"Remember," the other man said, coming up beside him.

"Not a mark, or'n we don't git paid."

She turned to look at the other man, a question in her eyes.

"She wants to know wot we're waitin' fer," he said to Cat.

"Ye tell her," Cat said. "She'll figger it out soon anyways."

Felicia was sure she didn't want to know. A feeling of dread snaked up her spine, leaving a cold chill in its wake, despite the heat of the sun. She closed her eyes and turned away from the sneer on the man's face.

Just then a shot rang out from the direction they had come. A scream echoed in her head, "No!" Frantically she tried to push herself off the horse, but Cat's arm wouldn't budge.

The two men looked at each other and smiled. "Done. Charlie an' Tick will be on their way t' collect. Now it's time for us, too." This from Cat.

The second man looked into her tear-filled eyes and confirmed her worst nightmare. "I 'opes ye 'as lots o' memories o' yer man, 'cause at's all at's left."

Then he turned his horse and they moved deeper into the forest as the tears fell unheeded from her eyes.

She wondered why they hadn't killed her as well. If the dowager duchess wanted to be sure Edward would inherit, she had to be sure Felicia was out of the way, too. Fear rose like bile in her throat at what they might do to her when they stopped. Trying to keep her thoughts from straying in that direction, she thought of Brand.

He couldn't possibly be dead. Her mind steadfastly refused to believe it was true. He was her destiny. Nona promised. *I intend to hold you to that promise, Nona. It's all I have.*

Even as she thought it, though, she was certain she had more. She suspected she was pregnant. Waiting to be completely sure, she'd said nothing to Brand. She knew he had been counting on it, knowing it would possibly mean the end of his stepmother's machinations. But he hadn't known.

Nor, she thought sadly, had she ever told him of her love. He had been gentle and caring with her. He'd helped her over her nightmares. They were finally building a rapport between them, but she'd never told him. Why had she resisted? Now, she might never have the chance.

She shook her head violently. *No!* He couldn't be dead. She just wouldn't believe it—ever. But, she would be strong for the child she carried. Even if she didn't believe Brand was dead, a small part of her acknowledged her child might be all she had left of him.

They stopped at a ramshackle hut on the edge of a field as darkness fell. Barely able to stay upright, she shrank from her captors as they pulled her into the dark interior. Visions of Ella and Aaron rose before her as they pushed her down on a pallet inside, but were unnecessary, as they turned and left her inside, in the dark, alone.

Cat and Nat, she learned her captors were called, while not especially gentle, didn't hurt her. She learned only that they had been hired by a "toff" to deliver her to him unharmed. Pleading with them to let her go, even promising them more money than they had been promised, fell on deaf ears.

Whoever hired them had garnered their loyalty for the duration of the job, and she found herself speculating on the person's identity. Who would want her, knowing she would fight no matter what? And, what were they going to do with her once she was delivered to them?

It was heartening to know she could have escaped if she wanted to. She had both her pistols, and both were loaded, but chose to confront her true abductor instead of his hirelings. If she escaped from these two, she reasoned with herself, he might just send more after her and she still would not know who he was.

A fresh stab of pain streaked through her at the thought of Brand. As before, she refused to believe he could possibly be dead. Yet, if he was, who would miss her? Both Jon and Jay were not even currently in the country. By the time Jay returned sometime next month, what might have happened to her?

They reached a small manor house late the second afternoon. Set back in a grove of trees, it was invisible from any road that might have been near. Of red and brown brick, the three story house blended well with its surroundings.

After dismounting, she was taken inside, up three flights of stairs, and locked in a room at the top. As soon as she heard the men leave, she flew to the window, only to be confronted by an iron grill. Disappointment crashed in on her like a toppled brick wall and she turned to survey the room through frustrated eyes.

It might have been pretty under normal circumstances. The walls were painted white, as was the furniture. A light blue lace-edged coverlet and a mound of pillows covered the large four-poster bed dominating the room. It looked comfortable and inviting.

Starting at the door, she allowed her eyes to wander over the room. To the right of the door stood a dressing table, complete with mirror. Rounding the corner, against the far wall, was a fireplace with two overstuffed chairs and a small table sitting before it. In the corner between the fireplace and the wall with the window in it stood a small writing desk and chair. On the right of the window stood the bed, with two small tables situated on either side of it. Against the wall opposite the fireplace was a washstand with a rose-patterned porcelain pitcher and basin. A screen stood in the corner, behind which she discovered a large tub and chamber pot, and finally against the wall beside the door, a large armoire.

Footsteps approached and her hand automatically went to her pocket, gripping the pistol concealed within. Standing across the room with her back to the window, she watched as the knob turned and the door swung slowly inward to reveal a maid carrying a tray. Behind the maid, she noted Cat standing there, beefy arms folded across his massive chest.

Relaxing her grip on the pistol, she watched as the maid glanced nervously in her direction, set the tray on the small table before the fireplace, then scurried out, closing the door behind her. Felicia heard the key turn in the lock and their footsteps recede. Hurrying to the door, she put her eye to the keyhole, disheartened to find that she could see the opposite wall. They had taken the key with them.

Approaching the table, her stomach growled and her mouth watered at the delicious aromas wafting up from the tray. At least they didn't plan to starve her. And, she had to keep her strength up. For now, she had no choice but to accept her captivity, but she would watch and wait. Soon she was sure she would have a chance to escape, and when it happened, she would make her move.

After a filling meal, during which she devoured every morsel on the tray, she wandered over to the armoire. Opening it, she found an array of brightly colored dresses and other articles of feminine apparel. It wasn't until she began looking closely at the clothing that a stab of apprehension pierced her. The dresses all looked vaguely familiar, but her astonishment knew no bounds when she found a small stack of drawers—all with pockets sewn on the outside of the right leg. These were her own clothes!

Closing the doors on the sight, she backed away from the armoire. Her knees hit the edge of the bed and she sat down heavily. Her head swam with the implications. Whoever had planned this, had been doing so for some time. A scene flashed through her head of a maid exiting Waring Castle while she and the housekeeper were inspecting the rooms in the old wing. Of that same maid passing a bundle to a man and he passing something to her. Putting her head in her hands, she wondered how many times the scene had been played out.

It didn't matter, however, because she knew she wouldn't have noticed a few missing gowns. Being in mourning meant she no longer paid attention to what she wore. Lily wouldn't have noticed either. Jon was right. She had more gowns and dresses than she ever needed. If a few went missing, she wouldn't notice—in fact, she hadn't.

Tiredness washed over her suddenly. She did not want to fall asleep, but Morpheus tugged relentlessly. Trying valiantly to smother a yawn, she failed miserably. Getting to her feet, she walked to the window to stare out at the gathering darkness, and wonder when her captor might make an appearance. Her head dropped forward and she jerked upright, realizing she was falling asleep on her feet. Glancing over at the bed, she tried not to wonder if it was as comfortable as it looked.

She couldn't go to sleep now. She was convinced her captor would introduce himself soon. *Maybe he'll wait until tomorrow,* a little voice said. *Or perhaps he's not even here.*

It hadn't occurred to her he might not be in residence yet. That she might have been brought here to wait for him to arrive. If Cat and Nat were still here, maybe they were waiting to be paid. Maybe, then there was no harm in getting some rest. She might need it when he did finally appear.

On that thought, and yawning hugely, she shed her dress, leaving on her chemise and drawers. At least she hadn't worn a corset, she thought as she slid beneath the coverlet and between cool sheets. Having the presence of mind to retrieve her pistol from the pocket of her dress, she put it under her pillow. *At least I will be able to protect myself,* was her last thought before sleep claimed her.

Chapter Sixteen

Felicia paced the length of the room restlessly. It had been five days since she had been brought to this place and still no sign of her abductor. The skirts of the mint green dress swirled around her ankles as she turned to pace back across the room, reminding her of her close call.

The morning after she had been left here, she had awakened to find the same timid maid leaving her another tray while retrieving the previous one. A glance at the doorway revealed Cat standing guard, watching her. Once the pair left, she had slipped from the bed and gone to investigate the tray. The smells, however, caused her stomach to lurch sickeningly and she ran for the corner behind the screen.

After emptying her stomach and bladder, she emerged on trembling legs and crawled weakly back into bed, leaving the tray untouched.

She was awakened an hour later by the door opening again. This time it turned out to be a large woman directing Cat and another man carrying buckets of steaming water. They filled the tub behind the screen, then left her alone with the woman.

"C'mon now," the woman said sharply. "Up with ye and into yer bath afore it gets cold."

Felicia nearly panicked. How was she to get up and undress without the woman finding her pistols? Shaking hands reached down to untie the ribbon on the pocket of her drawers, retrieving the pistol still hidden there. Slipping it under the pillow with the other one, she sat up.

The woman approached the table, glanced down, and

picked up the tray. "Not 'ungry this mornin', eh?" Then she went to the door, turning back to Felicia before she left. "Ye git up now an' take yer bath, an' I'll be back," she promised, then went out the door.

Felicia waited until she heard the key in the lock before she breathed a sigh of relief. Glancing around the room, she evaluated possible hiding places for her pistols. Not the armoire. Not the dressing table, nor the dresser. Her eye fell on the writing desk. Perfect.

Hurrying over to it, she searched it carefully, noting that it was stocked with writing supplies, including paper, quills, and ink. Finding a small space at the back of a drawer, she concealed both pistols there, then hurried to undress and slipped behind the screen.

Just in time. She had no sooner settled in the warm water when she heard the door open again. Using the soap left for her, she washed herself absently while listening intently to the movement on the other side of the screen. She hadn't realized how tense she was until she heard the door close and lock again, and silence fell in the room.

Emerging from the bath a short time later she found the bed had been made and fresh clothes laid out for her. There was no sign of the clothes she'd arrived in. She shivered at the close call. If she hadn't removed her pistols from her dress and drawers, they'd now be gone. Likewise, if she had left them under the pillow, they might have been found. She'd have to be more careful in the future.

Now she waited. Five days. Five mornings of not being able to face food. She was sure now that she carried Brand's child. By the time she was brought a tray for lunch, she had learned she could stomach small amounts—but only the blandest of offerings. By tea time each day she was ravenous.

The matronly woman was still the only person who ever spoke to her, the maid who often brought her trays still silent and wary. Felicia spoke to her anyway. Yesterday she had written a short note and left it on the tray, hoping the maid would find it and deliver it to someone in the area—preferably the sheriff.

She had also learned something else. Her abductor was in residence. Just this morning, she asked the matron where were the clothes she arrived in and was told "the master 'ad 'em burned". When she had asked who the master was, the woman had only smirked. "Ye'll find out soon enough."

A different, but no less timid, maid brought her afternoon tray and she wondered if the other maid had slipped away to deliver her note. Perhaps there was hope.

Going to the window, she stared out at the forest surrounding the house. She knew how many trees she could see from her window—had even been able to identify which were oak and which were maple. She had noticed squirrels and bird's nests, many of which seemed to be empty, and small game. Last night, she had heard a shot and wondered if someone was hunting, but there had only been one.

Turning away from the window, she moved to the fireplace and dropped into one of the chairs, staring into the empty grate. As usual, her thoughts wandered to the child she carried. If Brand were truly dead, she prayed she carried a son. Yet, her mind would not let her go there. She would not believe it unless she saw his body, she told herself. Until then, her heart told her he was still alive. And, she hoped, searching for her.

Footsteps approached her door and she heard the key turn in the lock. Raising her head listlessly, she watched the door begin to swing open, then heard a male voice. "Wait here."

Suddenly alert, her stomach clenched, and she froze. A figure entered, closed the door, and leaned back against it, watching her as intently as she watched him.

"Well, well," drawled Lord Caverdown. "As lovely as ever, I see."

Felicia knew her face showed her complete astonishment at his identity. Yet, as she searched blindly for a possible reason, scenes flashed before her eyes. Lord Caverdown's expression when she told him her answer to his offer would remain no, he and the dowager duchess speaking together and watching her in London, his pointed questions about meeting Brand, and him showing up at The Downs for the duke's funeral. And now she knew why the person she had seen slip from the Dower House seemed familiar, as well as the person who met the maid from the castle.

Feeling at a disadvantage, she scrambled out of the chair and backed up against the wall between the writing desk and the window.

"What? No greeting for the person who saved your life?"

"Saved my life?" she asked in bewilderment. "How?"

He moved away from the door and approached her. He paused to put something down on the small table before the hearth, then continued toward her, stopping only a few feet in front of her. "Emily would have had both of you killed. I convinced her to spare you."

Felicia would have backed away if she could. Instead she could only stare helplessly into his golden eyes. She knew now how a mouse felt when cornered by a cat—a feral cat.

"Wh—why?"

"I should think it would be obvious. But, it will do nicely for our purposes." He moved to the chair she had just vacated. "Come, sit. We have much to discuss before we leave."

"Leave?" Her mind wouldn't work. "Why are we leaving? Where are you taking me?"

"Come, sit," he invited again, but this time there was an implacable note in his voice which warned her of consequences. Remembering her thoughts before about him turning violent if thwarted, she moved to the other chair and sat.

"You realize, of course, you are now a widow," he said casually, smiling at the flash of panic she couldn't conceal.

"How do you know that?"

"Because that was the plan, of course. Didn't you hear the shot when my men took you away?"

Felicia refused to give in to the tears that threatened. She would not give him the satisfaction.

"It doesn't matter now. Once we appear together, people will understand."

"Understand what?"

"That you could no longer live with such a brute when you preferred me. They will believe the story Emily will put about that he found us together and instead of shooting me, was shot himself. Such a tragic ending."

"No one will believe that nonsense. I won't support it."

He shrugged one elegantly clad shoulder. "You won't need to as you won't be here to refute it."

Felicia regarded him warily for a moment. "And where will I

be?"

"In Paris, of course. You'll love Paris. It's beautiful this time of year. Once we take up residence there, it will not take long for word to get back." He glanced at her as she shifted nervously in her chair. "Of course, you won't ever be able to return to England. But Paris, and I, of course, will be ample compensation."

Felicia could only stare at him. She could think of nothing to say that wouldn't anger him, so kept her thoughts to herself.

His smile appeared again and, this time, she shivered. "What? No effusive thanks for saving you? I would have thought you'd be suitably grateful. Perhaps I have forgotten something."

He glanced around the room for a moment, his wandering eye finally falling on the small table between the chairs, and the item he had put down earlier.

"Of course." He snapped his fingers. "I almost forgot. I brought you a present." He indicated the small box on the table. When she didn't reach for it immediately, he pressed her. "Go on, open it."

"No, thank you." She remained in her chair, but looked up at him. The look in his eyes chilled her to the bone. A deep foreboding rose in her chest as she watched his eyes harden.

"Open it!" His voice lashed her, and she flinched.

Her hand trembled as she reached for the box. His smile deepened as she picked it up, but the look in his eyes fed her fear. Trying to still her shaking hands, she lifted the lid on the box and looked inside.

The blood drained from her face, the box falling from nerveless fingers as she choked back a scream. The box hit the floor, its contents spilling out and landing at her feet.

"Poor Edna." His voice was terrifyingly soft. "She was such a soft-hearted soul."

Felicia barely heard him. She was still staring in horror at the severed hand that lay on the floor, its fingers partially closed around a crumpled piece of paper. Tears sprang to her eyes, blurring the terrible sight. Her stomach pitched and she bolted from the chair for the screen in the corner.

She did not hear the door open and close again. Her stomach empty, she curled up on the floor against the wall, wrapped in her own misery.

That poor frightened maid. What had she done? No wonder the new one looked at her in terror. She had all but murdered the first one herself. How could she live with herself? What had he said? Poor Edna. The name repeated itself in her head with nearly every breath.

A touch on her shoulder caused her to lift her head, then shrink back from him in terror. Crouched in front of her, his eyes roved over her with hungry intent and she shuddered.

He shook his head and a malicious smile appeared. "There's no need to be afraid of me. I would never harm you, but you must realize I could not let anyone find you." He got to his feet. "Come." He returned to the chair in front of the fireplace.

She didn't move. She had been afraid of many things in her life but had learned to school herself to hide the fear. Now, however, she couldn't mask the terror that enveloped her.

"Don't make me come get you." His voice, low and dangerous, reached her. It's very mildness, chilling.

Forcing her limbs to move, she rose on shaky legs and returned to collapse into the chair she had vacated no more than five minutes ago. Turning her face into the padding of the chair back, she refused to look at him.

"Now," he began as if they were chatting over tea, "Mamie tells me you have a nervous stomach. She has prepared something for you which will eliminate the problem. I must return to London, but will return in a week, then we will leave." When she did not respond, his voice became hard, gloating. "I will enjoy taming you. With your husband dead, you are now mine. You must learn to call me Jeffrey."

"Never!" She couldn't help the adamant explosion. "I will never be yours."

"Ah, good. Your courage hasn't deserted you completely yet. It will hold you in good stead—for a while."

He picked up a glass containing a liquid and held it out to her. "Drink."

She shook her head, keeping her face averted.

She heard him sigh and rise to his feet. "Why must you be so difficult?"

Crossing the room, he opened the door and she heard another person enter the room. The next moment she was dragged from the chair and held in an iron grip while the glass was forced against her mouth. Clamping her lips and teeth together, she tried to move her head away from the foul-smelling brew, but to no avail. Her nose was pinched closed and when she gasped for air, the bitter-tasting concoction was summarily poured down her throat.

When she was released, she collapsed, coughing, on the floor in a small heap. Above her she heard Lord Caverdown's voice.

"When I return in a week, I expect her stomach problems will be solved and she will be ready to travel." The matron, Mamie, nodded, and after one last look at Felicia on the floor, he turned and left the room.

The woman helped her to her feet and on to the bed, loosening her dress and removing her stockings and slippers. Then she, too, left the room, locking the door behind her.

Two hours later, a sharp pain lanced through Felicia's abdomen. Gasping in shock, she slipped off the bed and removed her dress, then crawled back between the sheets. When Mamie entered the room a short time later, she found Felicia curled into a ball in the bed, whimpering in pain. Looking down into wide, frightened eyes, she said, "It's for the best. You'll be fine by this time tomorrow, and your belly will no longer trouble you."

Not realizing the significance of the statement, Felicia nodded as another pain tore through her. Gritting her teeth, she looked up into Mamie's cold eyes and shuddered at what she saw there. Another pain wracked her, this one sharper than the other two and a short scream escaped. Clutching her stomach, a memory flashed through her head—of her sister, Tina, curled up on her bed much the same way, crying out in pain as the doctor informed Jay she was going to lose their baby. The comparison was not lost on her and she was suddenly horrified.

"No!" she screamed. "Oh, God, no!"

Mamie was beside her, wiping her brow with a cool cloth. "It's for the best. The master wouldn't want someone else's babe."

Felicia looked up at the woman through her tears. "Why?"

"Because the master wished it," was the simple reply.

A knock on the library door interrupted Jay Collings, Marquis of Thanet, as he worked steadily through the stack of correspondence which had accumulated while he was away.

"Come!"

Keyes, the butler, entered. "A Lord Caverdown to see you, my lord."

"Show him in."

Jay rose to his feet as a young man entered a few moments later. Elegantly dressed in the latest fashion, dark brown hair over golden eyes, and a figure that must be the pride of his tailor, Lord Jeffrey Caverdown was, indeed, a fine-looking young buck. He wondered why Felicia hadn't been interested. But that was neither here nor there now.

Hand outstretched, Jay greeted the young lord. "Thank you for coming to see me so soon. I wasn't sure you had remained in the city."

Offering him a chair and a drink, both of which were accepted, Jay then returned to his own chair behind the desk, and got right to the point.

"I asked to see you because I understand you were a friend of my sister's and you happened to be among the few still in Town. I was hoping you could help me."

"Indeed," Lord Caverdown agreed smoothly. "In fact, I offered for her, but was turned down. So, how may I be of assistance now?"

"The Duke and Duchess of Warringham are missing," Jay said bluntly. "I arrived in London two days ago from Italy. Upon contacting my shipping offices, I was informed by the manager, Mr. Percival, that my partner, the Duke of Warringham, failed to keep an appointment nearly a week before and inquiries into his whereabouts have proved fruitless.

"I am aware of the hostile feelings between His Grace and his stepmother over his disappearance and reappearance. It is only due to correspondence with my sister that I am aware you are also acquainted with, and distantly related to, the dowager duchess. I am therefore, clutching at all possible straws in my efforts to find not only my partner, but also his wife, who is also my sister."

"I see. And what can I do for you?"

"The man my manager sent to The Downs returned yesterday with the news that the duke and duchess left nearly three weeks ago. When he ventured to the Dower House to speak with the dowager duchess, he learned she, too, had left. My question is—do you have any idea where she might be?"

The question took Lord Caverdown by surprise and Jay noted a flicker of apprehension in his eyes before he masked them.

"Not that I can think of."

"Have you heard from her lately?"

Lord Caverdown shook his head. "I assumed she was still living at The Downs, under the watchful eye of her stepson."

"I see." The marquis leaned back in the chair. "With the duke and duchess both missing, I think from what I understand, she probably feels she is the one with the most to gain. And yet, now she is missing, too."

"I suppose that's true. But, why would I know her whereabouts?"

The marquis shrugged. "I wasn't sure, really. But, as I said, I am clutching at the proverbial straw here. Leaving no stone unturned, as it were. Does she have any other acquaintances she might have gone to visit?"

"Not that I'm aware of. But that doesn't signify as I don't know her very well. We are only related through my grandmother, so the connection is distant at best."

A passing carriage in the street broke the silence that fell, but neither man spoke. A dog barked. Lord Caverdown watched the marquis uneasily. Having been in France for the last five years, he'd never met the marquis before and he had the feeling that between the marquis and earl, this one might be the more dangerous of the two.

He'd been surprised to receive the request for an interview, and even more surprised when he arrived. The marquis was not what he expected. He was still exceptionally trim and fit with chestnut hair carefully groomed back from a square forehead over dark brows, one lock having carelessly fallen forward. Piercing dark eyes over a sharp nose, full-lipped mouth and cheekbones that could have been carved from granite reminded him somewhat of a predator. This brother was no green youth, nor was he an aging gentleman. "I see." The marquis's brows drew together in a frown.

"Is there anything else I can do to help you find Her Grace?"

The marquis shook his head. "I have already alerted the Metropolitan Police, hired a number of private detectives, and contacted her cousins. I only contacted you because my sister wrote fondly of you to my wife, and your connection to the dowager duchess."

"Cousins?" Lord Caverdown's surprise was obvious. As far as he knew, the marquis, his wife and the earl were Felicia's only living relations.

"The gypsies," the marquis responded casually. "They are all over England and their lines of communication are quite strong. I would suspect every gypsy in England knows by now she's missing. And, of course, I have sent for Lord Wynton. He should be arriving soon."

Lord Caverdown shifted nervously in his seat. "I see." Although he'd heard the gossip concerning Felicia's great-grandmother, he'd never seriously considered the possible implications. He was well aware of the pervasiveness of the *Rom*. In France they were everywhere too.

"I have also contacted the Warringham solicitor and he will be sending for Lord Derrick."

"Lord Derrick?" Flustered, he put his now empty glass down on the desk.

"Of course. If Brand has met with foul play, which is suspected until I speak to the dowager duchess, Lord Derrick would be the new duke."

"But, but, Edward...?" He could not hide his shock.

The marquis shook his head. "I'm afraid his father disinherited him. Of course, the solicitor told me this in confidence, but I'm sure you will carry it no further. I merely told you to help you understand the urgency with which I must find the dowager duchess. She may be the key to finding my sister and brother-in-law."

"I—I see." He was at a loss for words.

The marquis rose. "Thank you for your time. I'm glad I caught you before you left town."

Rising as well, he held out his hand. "Yes, I'm glad you did. I'm sorry to hear of Her Grace's disappearance, but I will keep my eyes and ears open."

The two men shook hands and Lord Caverdown left. Watching from the window in the library, the marquis waited until the carriage was nearly out of sight before turning back to the room. A figure emerged from behind a screen, crossed the room and dropped into the chair Lord Caverdown had just vacated.

"He knows something," Brand said. "But what?"

"My guess is he knows where Felicia is, but not your stepmother."

"Then let's hope Pymm, or one of his men, can keep up with him."

"And he didn't see through the pack of lies I told him."

Brand ran a hand over his face. It had been two weeks since he and Felicia had disappeared. He'd kept his word to Charlie and Tick—the two men now being five hundred pounds richer, but neither knew where their friends had been told to take Felicia. They only knew their friends were to be paid handsomely by a "toff" to bring her to him. Unknowingly, however, they had put him on to Lord Caverdown when they described the scene when they had been hired.

His stepmother had sent Caverdown out to hire the men. She originally wanted both he and Felicia killed, but Caverdown wanted Felicia. He promised to take her away from England in return for two of the men delivering her to him at a specific location. Unfortunately, Charlie and Tick had been given instructions by his stepmother, while the other two were given specific instructions by Lord Caverdown, and neither pair had discussed their instructions with the other.

Their only hope now was to follow Lord Caverdown. The servants at his town house kept pretty mum, but Pymm had still managed to learn they had been ordered to close up the house for an extended length of time. His coachman had been ordered to be prepared to travel two days hence, but the destination had not been revealed.

Brand looked up at his partner and brother-in-law. "I used some of the same lies when I convinced Charlie and Tick not to shoot me," he confessed. "Our wives might worry about everyone's reaction to their gypsy blood, but the masses still have a healthy fear of gypsies."

Brand and Jay would have been interested to know Lord Caverdown had found at least part of the conversation amusing. It was so amusing, in fact, he could not seem to stop laughing as his coach carried him back to his town house.

"All for nothing," he hooted. "She did all the work, is the one they will pin it all on, and all for nothing. Her precious Edward *still* will not become the Duke of Warringham." His peals of laughter caused his coachman no little amusement as well, even without knowing what it was all about. "While I," he boasted to the interior of the coach, "I will have everything!"

The lady lay on the bed, curled tightly in a ball. Mamie stood beside it, her forehead creased in a frown. This wasn't good, and she knew it. The master would be back either today or tomorrow, and he would not be happy with the way things had turned out. And when the master was angry, well, one did not dwell on that. One tried to avoid that possibility at all costs.

It had been three days since the lady lost her baby. Since then she hadn't moved, eaten, or slept. She had merely curled herself into a tight little ball and stared out of vacant eyes. Mamie had tried coaxing her into a bath, to no avail. When coaxing hadn't worked, she'd tried to bully her. Nothing had worked. She and several maids had finally managed to move her by pulling the sheet off the bed and bathed her on the floor before the fire. It had taken all morning to change and clean the mess, and then lift her back. And still she hadn't moved.

Feeding her had been useless as well. She didn't fight when Mamie had tried to spoon some broth into her mouth, but neither did she swallow. The result was that most of the broth ended up running down her chin and soaking into the sheet.

Shaking her head, Mamie turned and left the room, locking the door behind her. The master was not going to be pleased at this latest development.

Felicia heard the door close as if from a long distance away. Locked tightly within herself, she had given up on life. With Brand possibly gone, and her child as well, there was no reason to go on living. Her only regret was that she'd never told Brand she loved him.

She refused to allow Lord Caverdown to spirit her away—even to Paris—and expect her to act as if nothing had happened. He was mad to think she might do so and she shuddered at the thought. Would he force her if she didn't submit? Visions of Aaron and Ella rose to terrorize her, and she knew she could not allow that to happen to her. So she waited.

She wasn't waiting alone, however. The day after they had managed to bathe and change her, leaving her on clean sheets, she had moved—once. Retrieving her pistols, they now kept her company. She was only waiting for him to return. Once she was gone, she didn't care what anyone thought. Her child would be avenged. She had enough strength left for that, then she would welcome oblivion.

Darkness fell. Night passed. Mamie came back and looked in on her again. The woman had given up trying to feed her, but Felicia heard the soft sigh of disappointment.

The door opened again. Felicia sensed the difference in demeanor of the person entering the room.

"Well?" She recognized Lord Caverdown's voice.

"She's been like that for nigh on four days now," Mamie's voice answered. "Tain't moved an inch."

"She hasn't moved?" His voice was incredulous. "I told you to make sure she was ready to travel when I returned."

"One can't force a body to live that don't want to," Mamie stated bluntly. "She's dyin'."

Caverdown moved around to the side of the bed and looked down into her nearly lifeless eyes. She looked straight through him. When he passed a hand over her face, she didn't blink. So still and white, if he couldn't see the rise and fall of her chest, he would have thought she was dead already.

"Get out!" he snarled. The housekeeper merely glared at him before she turned and left.

Removing his jacket, he went to the washstand and wet a washcloth. Coming back, he ran it over her face. No response. Throwing it back in the basin, he stood over her, his eyes boring into her, willing her to respond.

"You are not going to escape me this easily," he snapped. He reached down, grasped her shoulders and shook her. She may as well have been a rag doll. Her eyes closed, but otherwise, there was still no response. "I paid a bloody fortune for you and you are not going to deprive me of my due. Remember poor Edna?" he taunted. "Well, the new one's next. She's not any older than Edna was."

His threats fell on deaf ears. He had expected some reaction—any reaction—to the reference to Edna. Especially after her response to his little "gift" the last time. But there was none. For the first time since embarking on this scheme with the dowager duchess, he wondered if they might just both lose.

There was no doubt his dear cousin was the prime suspect in the duke's disappearance. If she ever showed her face in public again, she would be arrested and probably hung without so much as a "by your leave". He might get away with no one ever knowing he was involved, but his prize was slipping away right before his very eyes.

"Damn you!" he growled in frustration. Then he turned and stalked from the room, slamming the door behind him.

And on the bed, Felicia blinked. Not just once. Not twice. But many times, as tears gathered for the first time in days.

Not much longer, she told herself. He would come back and she would be ready.

Uncurling herself took time. She was stiff, her belly still tender from the trauma it had suffered. Her back and legs hurt, but she forced herself to continue to move. As she finally straightened her legs, she wondered if she had the strength to sit up. It didn't matter. She would do it anyway. She had to.

The door opened again as she attempted to push herself into a sitting position. The young maid entered, eyes wide with terror, a bruise already beginning to form on the side of her face. Stunned, she stared at Felicia for a moment, before rushing to her side.

"Help me," Felicia croaked, her voice barely audible from disuse.

The maid helped her to sit up and swing her legs over the side of the bed. When she was sure Felicia was balanced, she went to the armoire and began pulling clothes out.

Felicia did not attempt to stop her. The maid, however, was near panic. Guessing that the master had threatened severe consequences if she didn't make Felicia presentable, Felicia watched her scurry around the room, gathering articles for her toilette.

When the maid approached her again, Felicia shook her head, but stopped abruptly as the room spun. She grimaced—no food will make a person lightheaded.

"No," she rasped through a painfully dry throat. "No."

Through a series of gestures and one word commands, she managed to convey to the maid she wanted Lord Caverdown to return. The maid looked at her as if she had grown two heads, and tried to explain the master insisted she be dressed when he came back to collect her.

Felicia, however, was adamant, and the maid was helpless in the face of her stubbornness. Once the maid left, Felicia retrieved her pistols from beneath the pillow.

"For you, little one," she whispered, placing her hand over her belly. "He will never harm another."

When Lord Caverdown entered a few moments later, he was not surprised to find her sitting up on the edge of the bed, but his anger surfaced when he realized she was not dressed. Stepping into the room, he stared down at her suspiciously as she raised defiant eyes to his.

"Why aren't you dressed?" he demanded. "That little slut told me you were ready."

"I am," she rasped and, raising her pistol, fired.

His eyes widened momentarily, red blossomed on the front of his shirt, then he slumped to the floor.

Felicia fell back on the bed, uncaring that she had just killed a man in cold blood. She began to shake and, raising her legs, curled them back onto the bed. There was the sound of running footsteps on the stairs, then someone rushed into the room. She closed her eyes and welcomed the darkness.

She didn't care what happened to her now. She had avenged her child and Brand. It was enough.

"My God! Felicia!"

The voice was vaguely familiar. It warmed her, despite the fear underlying it. But the abyss called. Warmth surrounded her and suddenly she was floating. A void waited—it beckoned and she went toward it. From within it, she thought she heard Brand's voice, then she tumbled in and oblivion claimed her.

Chapter Seventeen

"I hope this is the right place," Brand remarked, surveying the three-story red and brown brick manor before them.

"It's well enough hidden," Jay agreed as he dismounted. "Just the place to hide someone."

"Should we just walk in the front door?"

Jay grinned. "I don't see why not. If they have nothing to hide, they won't mind a couple of unexpected visitors."

The door opened as they climbed the steps. An obviously frightened maid, a dark bruise marring the side of her face, flew out the door and down the steps, running down the drive as if she were pursued by the very devil.

Only momentarily disconcerted, Brand took advantage of the open door and stepped inside. Jay followed. The interior was dark, but surprisingly well kept. The floor was polished to a shine as was the staircase. A large, but unlit chandelier hung from the painted ceiling. He was about to call out when a shot rang out from somewhere above them.

Glancing at each other, they both bolted for the staircase. The second floor was completely dark, so they continued on up. Brand reached the top floor first. The hall was dark, all the doors along the hall closed tightly—except one. Light shone from that one, yet there was no one around.

Cautiously, Brand and Jay approached. No sound came from the room, but now they could hear someone coming up the stairs. Whoever it was wasn't moving very fast, but the footfalls were solid and heavy. Entering the room, they were both brought up short.

Sunlight spilled through an open window framed by blue

lace curtains. White walls, white furniture, and light blue and white lace. It looked like a young girl's room, complete with a four-poster bed in the middle. It was the occupant of the bed who garnered Brand's immediate attention and he rushed to her side. Jay bent down to check the person on the floor.

"My God!" The exclamation was torn from Brand. "Felicia!"

Curled up into a ball, she was shivering violently, despite the warmth in the room. Dressed only in a nightgown, her face white, her hair tangled and matted, she didn't react to the sound of his voice at all. Jay came to his side and neither of them noticed Mamie peek into the room, note Lord Caverdown on the floor, then retreat back down the way she came.

"Caverdown's dead," Jay said flatly. "She must have a pistol somewhere, maybe even two of them."

Brand reached down and wrapped the coverlet around Felicia's shaking figure, and lifted her in his arms. He was reminded of their wedding night, when he had done the same thing to a traumatized young girl. That young girl no longer existed, but he wondered what the young woman she had become had been through.

"Good," he said now. "Saves me the trouble."

Something hitting the floor caught Jay's attention and he bent to retrieve one of Felicia's pistols. "This one's been fired," he said matter-of-factly. Brand was leaving the room with his precious burden when Jay finally found and pocketed the second one.

Brand didn't care about the pistols and couldn't understand Jay's preoccupation with them. He just wanted to get Felicia out of this place and home.

Jay urged him to get Felicia seen by a doctor as soon as possible. He would remain to question anyone he could find, and tie up the loose ends.

Brand was thankful for the foresight which prompted him to bring a coach along and leave it just out of sight of the manor. Mounting his own horse with Felicia in his arms was difficult, but it would have been worse if he'd had to ride all the way back to London with her. As it was, the manor was over an hour's hard ride from London on horseback. It would take longer in a coach, but at least they would be comfortable.

The coach was waiting just as they had left it, Pymm and two detectives with it. Pymm and one detective were dispatched to the house to help the marquis, the second man dispatched on horseback to London with specific instructions. By the time Brand reached Waring House, he expected to have the doctor waiting to examine Felicia and a hot bath ready in the Royal Suite's bathing chamber.

Once the coach was on its way, Brand was able to take the time to look down at the unconscious form of his wife. Her face was whiter than the lace on the coverlet he had wrapped her in, her chest barely rising and falling with the shallow breaths she took.

"Stay with me, love," Brand spoke to her. He wasn't sure she could hear him, but he continued to talk to her all the way back to London. He didn't know whether she was in shock, or just unconscious from whatever she had suffered. She had grown so thin she hardly weighed anything at all.

He couldn't lose her now. Why hadn't he told her he loved her? That she was his reason for living? Even avenging Michael had become less important than finding her and bringing her home.

Her lips were dry and cracked, and her hair, matted and tangled, smelled of sour sweat and something else he couldn't identify. As far as he could tell, there were no marks on her, but he would have to wait until they reached home and he undressed her to find out for sure.

Caverdown was dead. He felt deprived of his target of retribution—she had accomplished it for him. But at what cost?

Had she gone into shock at what she'd done? He still believed women were too emotionally unstable to deliberately kill. Something had to drive her to it. Had Caverdown tried to assault her and she fended him off? The idea that Caverdown might have forced himself on her caused his stomach to clench into a knot. The questions swirled around in his head until his frustration knew no bounds. He knew he'd learn nothing until she awakened, yet the speculation was driving him crazy.

They arrived at Waring House during the middle of the afternoon. If it had been built like most other town houses, it might have been possible for anyone on the street to see him carry her inside. But it was not. Set back within its own extensive parkland, there was also a private, covered entrance. Lily met them as he entered, wringing her hands with worry, but having followed his instructions.

Brand carried Felicia upstairs and into the suite. Laying her on the bed, still wrapped in the coverlet, he sent Lily for more towels and went to check on the temperature of the water in the bathing chamber.

The bathing chamber in the Royal Suite was the only one in the house like it. The room was completely decorated with glazed Italian tile in a purple and white checkerboard pattern. The large Roman-style bath was filled with warm water. Lily had returned by the time he reentered the bedroom, her arms loaded with towels. Relieving her of them, he told her to lay out a nightgown for Felicia and leave. He would ring when he needed her again.

Taking the towels into the bathing chamber, he created a bed of them in the corner of the room near the brazier. Returning to the bedroom, he stripped out of his own clothes, lifted Felicia again and carried her into the bathing room. Laying her gently on the floor, he stripped her, checking her skin for wounds, marks or bruises as he did so. He found none. Lifting her again in his arms, he stepped into the warm water.

Felicia never stirred the entire time he bathed her, his hands moving gently and lovingly over her skin. Checking her more thoroughly for injuries and bruises, he found nothing unusual except some dried blood on the top of her thighs. Sitting on the ledge in the water, he laid her across his lap, keeping her face above water, and washed her hair.

When he was finished, he carried her to the bed of towels he had created, laying her down and covering her with more. Leaving her only long enough to dry himself and don a dressing gown, he returned to dry her off and carry her into the bedroom. Ringing for Lily, he toweled her hair dry as best he could, and put her into the nightgown the maid had left.

Lily appeared and told him the doctor was waiting downstairs. Instructing her to do something with Felicia's hair, then summon the doctor, he strode into the dressing room where Hardwicke had laid out his clothes.

When he returned to the room, Lily was ushering the

doctor in. Brand noted the maid had braided Felicia's hair into two long ropes, making her look even more like a young girl. Lily was asked to stay while the doctor examined Felicia, speaking to Brand as he did so.

"I'm afraid I can find nothing physically wrong with her," he told Brand. "No marks, no bruises. She's apparently healthy, if a little thin."

"That's what I thought as well," Brand said. "When I bathed her, the only thing I found was a small amount of dried blood on her thighs."

"Hmmm," the doctor intoned. "Possibly from her monthly time."

"Oh, no, sir. It couldn't have been." Lily's voice had the two men turning to look at her. She colored, but remained firm. "Her Grace couldn't have had her time while she was missing."

"The wrong time?" the doctor asked.

"No, sir. She was, that is, I don't think she knew, but I'm sure my lady was carrying."

Brand was stunned. Felicia, pregnant? He hadn't known— hadn't guessed. But, according to the maid, neither had she. The doctor's next words extinguished his budding joy.

"Well, she isn't now. Are you sure?"

Lily nodded. "She hasn't had her time since before the old duke's death."

The doctor turned back to Brand. "I could be wrong, if it's early days, but I don't think she is."

A knock on the door revealed Wharton informing Brand that the Marquis and Marchioness of Thanet were downstairs.

"Show them up," he ordered tersely, the turned back to the doctor. "Could she have lost it as the result of an assault,?"

"It's possible," the doctor surmised. "But, if she were pregnant and it was still early enough, she would have healed easily enough from the loss and appear physically healthy. Whether we're talking about an assault or a miscarriage, however, both might cause the kind of deep shock she appears to be in."

The doctor was giving Brand suggestions for feeding his unconscious wife when the door opened to admit Jay and his wife. Ignoring Brand, the marchioness rushed to the bedside to stand looking down at her sister.

Jay moved to Brand's side. "Sorry for the intrusion, but I couldn't keep her away."

"No harm done," Brand admitted. "Perhaps even some good."

The three men moved into the sitting room, leaving Lady Thanet sitting beside her sister as Lily went to straighten the bathing chamber and dressing room.

"He forced her to lose the child," Jay told him after being apprised of the doctor's findings. "After you left, I questioned everyone I could find. The housekeeper has disappeared, but one of the other maids told me Felicia tried to get a message out of the house, but the maid who attempted to deliver it was caught and murdered. The housekeeper was the one who figured out Felicia was pregnant and, when she told Caverdown, he ordered her to get rid of the baby. They apparently forced her to drink an herbal concoction that caused the abortion."

Brand nearly exploded with frustration and rage. Another life to be laid at his stepmother's door. Scandal or no, he would hand her over to the authorities when he found her. And find her he would.

After the doctor left, Jay filled him in on the rest of what he had uncovered.

"Caverdown planned to marry her," he said. "He had a special license in his pocket."

"Why?"

"I would guess he thought it was the only way he could have kept her. He had to know neither Jon nor I would allow him to keep her if we found her. Marrying her would have been the only way to try and keep us from taking her back, assuming she consented to the marriage. He had no way of knowing Jon and I would not have been daunted by something as inconsequential as a marriage if we determined she had been forced into it."

Brand chuckled. Close-knit was too tame a term for the bond between Felicia and her brothers and sister. He didn't know all of Caverdown's plans, but he did know they never had a chance of coming to fruition.

"I sent a message to St. Ayers," Brand informed Jay the next day. "I'm thinking she might go there."

"If she thought her plan had worked, isn't it likely she might come here to London?"

"What for?"

"To wait. She may have sent for Edward."

"Possibly, but she'd have a long wait. My father had a letter sent to Edward upon his death instructing him not to return to England unless I, or the solicitor, summoned him. I don't know the complete contents of the letter, but in my father's last instructions to me, he indicated he had informed Edward he should especially not heed any letters received from his mother instructing him to return."

"And you think Edward will follow his instructions?"

"I'm reasonably sure he will. I'm not sure exactly how much Edward was aware of, but he couldn't have missed some of the implications. And he knew his mother was obsessed with him inheriting. I'm not sure he would have thought she might go this far, but the suspicions couldn't help but be there."

Jay glanced around the spacious interior of the library at Waring House, where he and Brand retreated to talk after being summarily dismissed by Tina. She had taken charge of the sickroom, much to Brand's chagrin, but knew her limits. Assuring him she would inform him immediately of any change in Felicia's condition, she had then politely, but firmly, insisted Brand take himself off to do some work.

"Has she always been such a dragon?" Brand asked on their way down. It was hard to believe such a small person as Jay's wife was could succinctly dismiss two such large men, but she had.

Jay laughed. "You might say that. She's overprotective when it comes to her family. In fact, she'd kill for any of them. And so, I suspect, would Felicia."

Brand was sobered by the reminder. Jay had given him Felicia's pistols last evening. He had been surprised by their size and power, but what surprised him more was what happened when Tina had entered the sitting room while he was examining them.

"Did she use them?" she asked as if it were an everyday occurrence for her sister to be armed.

"Only one," Jay answered just as calmly. "The other one is still loaded."

Turning to Brand, she asked, "Do you know where the case is?" Sheepishly, he had to admit he didn't, but Tina didn't seem to think it strange. "She probably didn't want to worry you," she consoled him.

Lily entered then to ask if His Grace needed anything else. "Tea for Lady Thanet," he responded and the maid turned to leave, only to be stopped by Tina.

"Do you know where my sister's pistol case is?"

"Yes, my lady. Would you like me to fetch it?"

"Yes."

After the maid produced the case for Tina and left the room, he had watched in amazement as Tina, unloaded, checked, and cleaned each of the small weapons, then placed them back in their case.

Now he was restless. Worrying about Felicia, wondering where his stepmother was and whether she would try again, was wearing on him. The pain he'd survived in the past was nothing compared to the pain he knew he'd live with the rest of his life if Felicia died. He had thought losing his father so soon after being reunited had hurt, but losing Felicia would destroy him.

"Why St. Ayers?" Jay's question brought him out of his thoughts.

"Because she's familiar with it."

Among the things Pymm discovered was his stepmother had been the daughter of the last Earl St. Ayers.

"Until Pymm returned with his report, I didn't understand why my father instructed me not to allow her to take up residence at St. Ayers. But, I can only assume he thought the people in the surrounding area might still be loyal to the family."

"What family?"

"Hers." Rising from his chair, he went to the desk and searched through the papers, coming up with one. "According to Pymm, her father was the last Earl St. Ayers. The estate in Cornwall was the family seat."

"Earl who? I've never heard of anyone by that name."

"The title's tainted. It ceased to exist before either you or I were born." Returning to his chair, he rested his head back against the padding.

"Why?"

"Apparently the Earl was charged and convicted of treason for aiding a plot to help Napoleon escape from St. Helena. Parliament passed a bill of attainder, and the Crown stripped him of his title. He was due to hang, but someone smuggled a pistol in to him and he blew his brains out in his cell the night before his scheduled execution."

"I assume the family seat becoming part of the dukedom is the reason she is intent on Edward inheriting?"

"Partially. But, also according to Pymm, my father was a principal witness against her father, having intercepted a number of dispatches between the earl and St. Helena. And, knowing my father was a close friend of the king—I'm sure that's how we acquired it."

"A close friend?"

Brand nodded. "According to my housekeeper and butler, my mother decorated the suite Felicia is currently in specifically for the Prince Regent, later king, and ordered it always be kept in readiness for him. I have not asked for details, but the hints I have heard of the parties and general revelry that went on...well, you know what the early part of this century was like."

Jay chuckled. "I don't doubt the time period that George was regent for his father, and during his reign, will be looked back on scandalously. And your parents were in the thick of it, hmmm?"

"Apparently so."

Tina appeared and joined them for lunch, reporting she and Lily had managed to get some beef broth into Felicia, but there was otherwise no change.

"Where's Jon when you need him?" she demanded in frustration, her aquamarine eyes glittering.

"Jon?" Brand didn't understand what he could add to the situation. "Why?"

"He has studied enough herbs, healing, and medicine to be a doctor three times over," she told him. "But where is he when someone is sick enough to need him? Off gallivanting around the continent."

Her tone of mild disgust would have been amusing, if Brand wasn't so worried.

Brand entered the room where Felicia still lay unconscious. Dressed for bed in his purple velvet robe and black silk trousers, he dismissed Lily, discarded his robe and climbed into the bed beside her. Tina and Lily had spent most of the day watching over her, he and Jay giving Tina some time to stroll in the garden for a short while in the afternoon. When Jay had gone to join his wife, Brand sat beside Felicia, stroking her hand and reading to her from a book of sonnets.

Holding her unconscious form close, he now understood, and knew beyond a doubt that if he could, he'd trade places with her in an instant. The pain he felt when he thought of what she must have suffered losing their babe tormented him. It gave rise to visions of her in excruciating pain with no relief in sight.

"Soon, love," he spoke to her in the darkness. "Soon you'll return to me—and there will be others." He'd tell her then.

He'd known when he married her that her great-grandmother had considered them soul mates. They were each other's destiny. And, while he had felt an initial attraction to her, he wasn't sure he'd ever love her. But he had fallen hard not long after they married. Why hadn't he told her? He couldn't say, but now he regretted he hadn't.

And, what of her? She seemed to give all of herself, but was it merely gratitude? He'd never been this off balance with any woman before, he admitted to himself. Yet, he knew that losing Felicia would mean the loss of his soul. Michael's death. His father's death. Nothing came close to the devastation he'd feel if he lost Felicia.

The movement was nearly imperceptible, but he felt it. A hand against the arm encircling her. He went completely still, barely daring to breathe, wondering if he had caused the movement by his own shifting. Then her head moved and she let out a deep breath. It was just a small movement, but it was enough to make his hopes soar.

Felicia surfaced through layer upon layer of consciousness.

She didn't know where she was, yet the feeling of being safe enveloped her. Warmth surrounded her. Opening her eyes became a monumental effort, but she forced the lids up. It was dark and she could make out nothing of her surroundings. Waiting for her eyes to adjust seemed to take forever, but she was aware of the presence behind her—of the arm draped across her waist.

She tried to speak, but couldn't. She was too weak. She wanted to move, but her body wouldn't obey her. Breathing in deeply, she let out the breath in a whoosh. The presence behind her moved, leaving her. She wanted to cry out at the loss of warmth. Moments later, a light flared beside her, and she found herself looking into Brand's eyes, level on the bed with her own.

Brand knelt on the floor beside the bed, looking into her eyes. Reaching up, he stroked her cheek with one long finger.

"Welcome back, sweetheart," he said in a choked voice. "I've missed you."

"I need my pistols," Felicia said to Tina a week later. Sitting on the window seat in the sitting room, bathed in sunshine, she was still recovering, but at least she was able to leave the bed on her own—when Brand wasn't present.

Aquamarine eyes met hers. "Why?"

"Because I do," she answered. "I can't explain it, but I know I need them. It's almost as if they are calling to me."

"They must have enjoyed the last outing," Tina teased.

"Tina, please," she wailed. The tone of her voice had Tina looking at her closely.

"You're serious!" she exclaimed in astonishment.

Frustration made Felicia snap, "Of course!"

Jon might have understood better the feeling that urged her to, once again, keep her weapons close, but he wasn't here. Tina was.

She was glad to have come out of her senseless state to discover Tina and Jay had returned early. This last week would have been interminable without Tina's presence, she acknowledged. Brand might not have let her out of his sight otherwise. That he refused to let her move under her own power was still a source of amusement for Tina.

"I know where they are. Just a minute." Tina rose and hurried into the bedroom, leaving Felicia to relive the past week.

Regaining consciousness in Brand's arms had been only the start. The doctor had been summoned and she had been too weak to protest his examination. Then Brand had helped her to sip some broth. That had been enough. She had fallen asleep in his arms, waking the next morning to find him lying beside her, head propped on one hand, watching her sleep.

When Jay and Tina arrived later that same morning, she had been ecstatic to see them. Tina shooed Brand from the room and helped Lily to bathe and dress her in a clean nightgown. Tina, however, had not been able to keep Brand away. He checked on Felicia at least every half hour—to Tina's undisguised amusement.

Tina seemed to understand, however, and when Jay insisted they go home and leave Felicia and Brand alone, she had not protested too strongly. Once Jay and Tina were gone, Brand never left her side. She wondered if he wanted to ask her about what had happened to her, but she wasn't ready to talk about it yet, so was relieved with his reticence.

Tina re-entered the room carrying her case. "I unloaded the one you hadn't used when I put them back. "Do you want me to reload it?"

Felicia accepted the flat wooden box. "No, I'll do it."

Tina watched her open the box and take one of the pistols from its place. Opening the small drawer on the bottom, she extracted the ammunition and loaded it. Closing the box, she handed it back. "I only need one."

Tina's brows rose at the statement, but she said nothing.

"I can't explain it." Felicia tried to answer the question in her sister's eyes. "I just have this feeling something is going to happen and I will need it."

"A premonition?"

A frown creased her brow. "Perhaps. I've never had a feeling like this before. It's so strong, I just can't ignore it."

"Then you shouldn't. Nona would say you should always follow your heart."

Felicia smiled. "She would, wouldn't she?"

Tina nodded, returning her smile. "And she would have approved of Brand."

Felicia huffed. "She ought to. She chose him—years before I was even born."

"She chose right, though, didn't she?" Tina's question was in earnest.

"Was there ever any doubt?"

Tina cocked her head to one side, considering Felicia's question for a moment. "I don't know. Why don't you tell me?"

Felicia sighed, drawing her knees up and resting her chin on them. "Jon had to force me to marry him," she confessed. "I wouldn't have otherwise."

"Yet you love him—and he obviously loves you."

"Do you think so?" she asked. Worry caused her to chew her bottom lip. "He's never said so."

Tina sat beside her. "Perhaps he's waiting to find out how you feel. But I can tell you, as an observer, there's no doubt he loves you. It's not just the way he looks at you, it's also the way he treats you."

"I...I don't know what to say. Or when to say it. The time never seems right."

Tina patted her hand reassuringly, then gave her a gentle hug.

"You'll know when it's right. And it will be easy then."

Felicia was silent while Tina relaxed against the cushions at the opposite end of the window seat.

"I don't suppose it would be nice to gloat," Tina grinned, "but I'll just say I'm glad everything worked out just the way Nona said it would. And you even got your duke," she added mischievously.

Felicia groaned. "And you will probably never let me forget it, either."

Tina laughed. "Of course not. But I'll tell you a secret."

Neither heard the door open as Tina continued. "When you made that statement when you were sixteen, and Jay said he knew of an unmarried heir." She nodded as Felicia's eyes grew wide in understanding. "He was already thinking of Brand."

"Whether he'll ever forgive me is still to be determined," came a voice from the door. Both women looked up to find Jay standing there.

Felicia was surprised Brand wasn't with him as he closed the door, then crossed the room.

He seated himself in a chair near them. "How are you today, minx?"

She smiled. "Better. Where's Brand?"

"Downstairs reviewing some paperwork with his solicitor. He informed me that he was about to put a specific piece of property in trust for a nine-year-old boy. When I asked him why, he said I should ask you why he was about to give Journey's End to our Cook's grandson."

Felicia suddenly felt uncomfortably warm. Heat rose in her cheeks and she looked down at her hands. On the one hand, she was glad Brand was doing what she wanted, but she wished he hadn't told Jay.

"Davey?" Tina asked.

Felicia nodded. Tina said nothing more and silence fell in the room. The moment seemed to stretch and she was afraid to look at either of them. What could she tell them besides the truth? At least she no longer worried for his safety. Knowing he was with Jon and on a grand adventure gave her a measure of peace.

"Felicia?" Jay's voice was insistent and she raised her eyes to his.

"He's our responsibility," she said slowly. "Aaron would have never accepted him, but that doesn't make him any less my nephew or yours."

Jay's astonishment was clear. "Aaron?"

"He—he raped Ella."

"And, how do you know this?"

Her chest tightened painfully. Taking a deep breath, she tried to loosen it. "I—I saw him," she forced out.

Tina gasped, her hand going to her mouth.

Jay put his head in his hands and his shoulders slumped. Discouragement blanketed him momentarily, causing tears to well. She blinked them back as he raised his head. Their eyes met and, for a moment, Tina was forgotten as she and Jay remembered their older brother. Their memories were not fond ones.

"Oh, Felicia." Tina broke the spell. "I didn't realize..."

"I didn't tell you on purpose," she comforted her sister. "I was so ashamed. And I felt guilty. As if it was all my fault."

"Why?" Jay had regained his voice.

"Because when he asked me which way she'd gone, I told him. I never thought he'd...he'd attack her."

Tina reached over and hugged her. "Of course you wouldn't have thought that. You were only nine. You couldn't have possibly known."

"I didn't realize until Mira told me where babies came from that—" she blushed as Tina released her and she looked at Jay again, "—that meant he was Davey's father."

She needn't tell either of them that Jon had used Davey to force her to marry Brand.

"So, where is he now?" Jay asked. "Brand told me that he escorted the two of you to the Abbey."

"He's with Jon somewhere on the continent." She relaxed again. "I don't know why he took Davey with him. He could have easily left him at the Abbey." She reached out to take Jay's hand. "I'm sorry. I didn't want to create more bad memories."

He squeezed her hand and looked at her solemnly. "I think we all know that Aaron tainted nearly everything and everyone he came in contact with. I don't think any of us truly mourn him."

She had nothing to say to that because it was true. Aaron had wreaked havoc while he was alive and they were still cleaning up the mess ten years after his death.

Chapter Eighteen

The sound of the door closing woke Felicia. Comfortable and snug under the mound of covers, it was a few minutes before she realized she was alone. It was full dark; moonlight streamed through the window near the bed. Another noise commanded her attention and she noticed a sliver of light under the now closed door to the sitting room. She was sure it had been left open when they retired.

Slipping from the bed, she moved slowly to the door. It had been almost two weeks since she regained consciousness, and she was almost completely recovered. After a week of thin soups, broth, and the occasional piece of toast, she began to demand more, heavier, food. She needed to regain her strength, she tried to explain, but Brand continued to follow the doctor's orders to keep her diet light.

Exasperated, she and Tina thwarted him by the simple expedient of taking lunch together in the sitting room. The cook, knowing Lady Thanet was increasing, always sent up more than Tina could possibly eat. The tray always returned empty.

She frowned as she approached the door, hearing voices on the other side. Who could Brand be talking to at this time of night? Pressing her ear to the panel, she could make out only the sharp voice of a woman, and Brand's soft, controlled, one. A sudden shiver coursed through her body and, instinctively she moved back to the bed, reaching under the pillow to retrieve her pistol.

Slowly, so as not to make a sound, she cracked the door and put her eye to the opening. And had to swallow a scream. She could not see Brand, but she could see a woman, her black dress stained and muddy, gray-streaked dark brown hair streaming down her back. She was holding a pistol, and Felicia was sure it was pointed at Brand.

"You have been nothing but trouble," the woman was saying. "Why couldn't you have stayed missing—or dead?"

There was no response and the woman, who Felicia recognized as the dowager duchess, continued. "Edward will make a fine duke—and the St. Ayers line won't die out."

Felicia heard Brand's voice then. "Edward will never be duke," he said patiently. "My father took steps to ensure he never would."

"What do you mean?" The dowager's voice was unsure. "What steps?"

"Edward has been disinherited in favor of Derrick."

"Derrick? That wastrel," she spat. "He's worthless."

"True, but nevertheless, upon my death without an heir, he becomes the next Duke of Warringham."

"How? Edward is John's son. He's next in line."

Felicia could hear the sadness in Brand's voice as he answered the dowager. "I'm sure it pained my father to do so, but he disavowed Edward. Upon my death without an heir, my father left letters and documentation to be sent to the Crown. I have no idea what the contents are, but he was confident that as a result of them Edward would be stripped of everything—his title, his commission, even his name."

"Nooooooo!" the dowager wailed. "It's not true. You're making it up. John would have never done such a thing to his own son. He loved him too much." Her agitation was visible, the gun wavered. Felicia worried she would shoot Brand regardless.

"You're right, he did. My father loved his sons—all of them. And I have no doubt that it nearly crushed him to have to destroy one in favor of another. Had he another choice, he wouldn't have done so."

Felicia couldn't credit the calm in Brand's voice. Although she couldn't see him, she could almost picture him standing near the window seat, maybe even sitting on the cushions, casually discussing Edward while his stepmother held a gun on him.

"But you gave him no choice," Brand continued. "You were

too obsessed with revenge for your father, to see you had been given a second chance. Your father made his own choices and they cost him dearly."

"My father was innocent," she snarled. "He would never have done what they said he did. Never! It was all lies made up by John and his friends." The gun swung wildly now, but never far enough from Brand to allow him to disarm her.

Felicia crouched down and inched closer, widening the crack until she could just see Brand. He was sitting on the window seat. He hadn't taken the time to put his dressing gown on so he was wearing only the black silk trousers he had been sleeping in. He looked completely unconcerned, arms crossed over his golden chest, eyes hooded. Yet, she sensed he was alert and waiting for the dowager to make a wrong move.

"But they all paid. I made sure." Her voice turned gloating. "Wolston was first. The old sot. It was easy to make it look like he fell down the stairs when he was drunk. Then Barrington. At least the men I hired to kill him didn't bungle the job."

Felicia put her hand to her mouth to smother a gasp of horror as she listened to the dowager recount the men she had either dispatched herself or had murdered over the years. Six of them in all.

"I took special pleasure watching Rearden die. I even told him who I was and why before he did. He was the worst. If it hadn't been for him, none of it would have ever happened." Her agitation increased and she began to pace, never taking her eyes or the gun off Brand. "But John was the Prince Regent's favorite—his darling boy. He could have stopped it—he could have convinced Parliament not to pass the bill, but he didn't. His honor wouldn't allow it—and my father refused to speak in his own defense."

"And my father?" Brand's voice was soft.

She stopped. "John? He was the last." Her voice softened with regret for a moment, then hardened again. "If you hadn't miraculously appeared he would still be alive," she snapped. "Edward needed a few more years—but I couldn't take the chance. Especially after you married that half-gypsy slut."

Felicia saw Brand tense. Even from across the room, she could feel all his energy focus on the dowager. She knew he was about to lunge for her, but Felicia couldn't let it happen. The dowager would shoot him before he reached her.

Unaware of the change in the atmosphere in the room, the dowager continued her tirade. "But, I will make sure Edward inherits—even if I have to kill every Waring in England. When he is the last one left, no one will question his right to the title."

Brand rose to his feet. "No," he said in a low, dangerous voice. "No more. It all stops here. The lies, the killing, the manipulations. It all stops here." Then he moved, and pandemonium erupted.

The dowager raised the gun, her finger tightening around the trigger. Felicia screamed. Startled, the dowager turned toward her and Felicia raised her own pistol and fired.

In slow motion, she watched as the dowager's gun went off, the shot going into the ceiling as she was knocked backward by the force of Felicia's shot. Then she fell, hitting the carpet with a sickening thud Felicia heard from across the room.

Brand turned at Felicia's scream, stopping in his tracks as he watched her raise and fire the weapon. He was still standing, frozen in place when she dropped her pistol, scrambled to her feet, and launched herself at him.

Brand caught her shaking form, crushing her against him. For a long moment they stood in each other's arms, relief pouring through them. As her terror slowly abated and her trembling lessened, Felicia tightened her arms around him. He was hers! No one would take him away. She'd kill anyone who tried.

"She would have killed you," she hiccupped. "How could you do something so idiotic?" she demanded, outrage in her voice.

The door burst open before he had a chance to reply, Wharton and two footmen standing in the opening, all in their nightshirts. Felicia had to suppress a giggle at the picture they made.

Wharton checked the dowager. "She's dead, Your Grace," he said to Brand, who nodded in acknowledgment.

"Summon the watch—and a policeman," Brand said to one of the footmen, who moved quickly to follow his orders.

Felicia slipped into the library where she knew Brand was working. Surprised not to find him sitting behind the desk, she scanned the book-lined room. Moving further into the spacious chamber, she checked the alcove at the far end of the room. It was empty. Perhaps she had been wrong.

"Brand?"

"Here, love." She turned to find him rising from a chair near the fireplace.

Approaching, she noted the lines in his face, the haggard look in his eyes. He didn't mourn his stepmother, but wrestled with the dilemma of what to do with her body.

"I refuse to bury her beside my father," he'd declared yesterday. "She murdered him." His voice had been so full of hurt and despair. "He should not have to rest beside his murderer."

Stepping into his arms, she buried her face against his solid warmth. "Have you come to a decision?"

He held her close, breathing deeply as she fit neatly against him. Her curves conformed easily to the hollows and planes of his body. They were two halves of a whole, made especially for each other. She would have it no other way. She just hoped he felt the same way.

"I hadn't until a half hour ago."

His voice was tired, and she leaned back to look up into his face. Dare she put a name to the emotion she saw in his eyes? The fire was firmly banked. In deference to her recovery, she knew, but now she was completely recovered and she needed more than gentleness from her lion.

"What happened a half hour ago?"

"I finished reading the last letter my father left for me."

"Another letter?" She ran her hands up the front of his shirt, one hand stopping over his heart, feeling the steady rhythm pounding beneath. "Your father was quite prolific in the weeks leading up to his death."

He smiled sadly. "He wanted to make sure he tied up every possible loose end, it's true, but this letter was written three years ago."

"Three years? But, ..."

Brand led her over to the chair he had recently vacated. On

the table beside it sat an empty glass and a number of closely written sheets of paper. Dropping into the chair, he pulled her down with him and settled her against him. Then, picking up the sheets of paper, he handed them to her.

She looked up into his face, but saw nothing there but tiredness. Putting his head back, he closed his eyes as she looked down at the paper and began to read.

Waring Castle
October 1861
My son:

This is difficult to write, but I must attempt to right a dreadful wrong which was perpetrated with my help, but not knowledge, many years ago. It is a tragic story, but it is time for it to be told.

In the celebrations and revelry surrounding the final defeat of Bonaparte at Waterloo, few paid attention to the activities of a select group of young men whose job it had been to gather the intelligence necessary to bring the emperor down. And so it was that Lords Rearden, Barrington, Traynor, Jeffries, Wolston, and myself found ourselves at loose ends. I returned to The Downs; Traynor, Jeffries, and Wolston, being married men, returned to their families; but Rearden and Barrington were at loose ends—whoring, drinking, gambling, and indulging in those vices young men sometimes are wont to sample, but soon grow bored with. I lost touch with all of them, although I did hear later that Barrington married, leaving Rearden at loose ends. My father, your grandfather, died in '16 and I was busy learning to run a dukedom.

In '18, Rearden came to me. He had heard rumors about a plot being hatched to assist Bonaparte in escaping from St. Helena to return to France. He came to me because I was a friend of the Prince Regent and he wanted Prinny's blessing to pursue the rumors. He showed me several dispatches he claimed to have intercepted, but with no knowledge of who was to ultimately receive them.

I could go into much more detail, revealing how the six of us eventually re-grouped to ferret out this new threat, but it is of little importance in the outcome.

Eventually, the Earl St. Ayers came to our attention. While in

London, I had made the earl's acquaintance. His countess, Emilie, was French, a member of the Villiers family who had lost nearly everything in the Revolution, but supported the emperor steadfastly. The earl adored his wife—which eventually lead to his downfall.

By the end of '19, we had enough evidence to bring before the Prince Regent. Most of it had been obtained one way or another by Rearden, but I, too, had uncovered evidence I believed pointed to St. Ayers' guilt.

One of the Prince Regent's first acts as king after the death of his father was to act on our evidence. Parliament, although in turmoil, was outraged and a Bill of Attainder was passed against St. Ayers. At his trial for treason, he refused to speak in his defense. He was convicted and sentenced to hang. The night before his sentence was due to be carried out, a pistol was smuggled in to him and he took his own life. His lands and properties were distributed among we six. Those are the facts. Now to the rest of the story.

After your disappearance, I did some checking into Emily's background and discovered she was St. Ayers's daughter. After her father's trial and death, she and her mother fled to France and were taken in by her mother's family, where they remained. Shortly after her mother's death, she was forced into a marriage with one of her cousins—a cripple. I do not expect you to sympathize with her actions, and I will not go into detail, but she suffered greatly at the hands of her French cousins. After her husband's death, she returned to England bent on revenge.

I make no excuse for my actions in taking Emily as my mistress after your mother's death. Nor will I attempt to discount my own culpability in her eventual obsession with Edward inheriting the dukedom. I will tell you this. In the course of my investigation into Emily's background, I discovered I had unwittingly been an accomplice to a horrible crime.

Her father had, indeed, been innocent. The evidence against him was quite real, however, as it had been his countess who was orchestrating the campaign, through her family in France. The earl, I believe, said nothing, in order to protect her. Rearden, I discovered, knew the truth all along, but also said nothing. It was Rearden, I believe, who eventually helped Emily and her mother to France. To this day, I have not been able fathom Rearden's motive in all of this.

Since your disappearance, Traynor, Jeffries, Wolston, Barrington, and Rearden have all met with untimely deaths. I believe that I, too, would have by now if Edward wasn't still yet so young. With yours and Michael's disappearance, Edward has become my heir—at least in Emily's eyes. I have refused to allow it and now, with the arrival of your letter, I feel vindicated in my intractability. Your letter, however, I believe has had the effect of signing my own death warrant.

The letter ended abruptly—no signature, no ending. Felicia looked up at Brand. His eyes still closed, he might have been asleep.

"He knew all along," she whispered.

"Yes." His lids lifted and he watched her from under gold-tipped lashes. "All these years, he knew she was the one, but did nothing."

"So, what now?" she asked. "How does this solve your problem?"

"There was another letter which accompanied this one. This one was delivered to the solicitor with the instructions that I was to receive it upon my stepmother's death. The second letter, explains what he wants done with her body—and what to do about Edward."

"Oh. And?"

"She is to be buried at St. Ayers." He took a deep breath and expelled it. "He would not allow her to live there once he discovered her background, but he says he wants her to rest there —hopefully in peace."

She nodded. "You realize we cannot tell Eliza any of this."

"I know." His voice was quiet. "I wonder if that was the reason her dowry was so large. My father may have felt he was compensating Trent for the loss of his father."

"Eliza wouldn't have cared, but who knows how Trent would have reacted had he known."

"I wonder if our stepmother tried to prevent the marriage."

"I don't suppose it matters now. She didn't." She put the letter down on the side table and looked up at him again. "And what of Edward?"

"He wants me to persuade Parliament to repeal the Bill of

Attainder and restore the title of Earl St. Ayers—to him. He would have done so if Michael and I hadn't disappeared. In addition, regardless of whether Parliament and the Crown agree to restore the title, he asked that St. Ayers be the estate I give to Edward."

She was silent, mulling over all the information. It had all been for naught. The deaths, the darkness, the pain. If his stepmother hadn't tried to kill him and his brother all those years ago, Edward might, even now, be the Earl St. Ayers. Would it have satisfied her? Would she still have wanted to exact revenge for her father's death? And how would she have reconciled her mother's part in the whole plot? So many questions, never to be answered.

"Will you?" she asked now.

"Yes."

Turning, she straddled his lap and looped her arms around his neck. "Then the suffering stops here," she said softly. "Forty years is more than long enough to hold a grudge. It's time to put the past behind us, mourn its passing, and look to the future." Then she kissed him.

She was tentative at first, out of practice, as it were, but the passion that erupted between them felt as if they had never been apart. They kissed hungrily, devouring each other in their attempt to wipe away the unhappy memories. Brand took control, slanting his mouth over hers, sinking into her, immersing himself in her softness.

She was breathing heavily when he raised his head. "I love you," he said thickly. "When those thugs took you away, I was afraid I'd never see you again. Never be able to tell you."

She stared at him in wonder. "I—I..." Tears spilled from her eyes. "I never thought..."

Brand reached up and brushed the tears from her cheek. "Why not? Didn't you trust your great-grandmother?"

She smiled weakly. "I was sure you regretted our marriage." When he started to protest, she stopped him. "If I hadn't been so selfish and you hadn't tried to save me from myself, we might not have had to marry," she explained. "And, your father wouldn't have traveled to London and your stepmother might not have killed him, and you would have had more time..."

Brand shushed her by the simple gesture of two fingers

against her lips. "And, if I had returned three years ago instead of running away, I might have had more time." He sighed. "We all make choices. Some good and some bad. In retrospect, I wish I had stayed in London three years ago, but I didn't. I can't change that and dwelling on it won't change it."

She leaned against his chest, hearing the steady drum of his heartbeat. "I love you so much it hurts," she confessed. His arms tightened around her, giving her the courage to continue. "I never thought it was possible to love someone as much as I love you," she said in a low, shaky voice. "I have always thought people in love were always happy, always smiling, always content. Look at my examples—my parents, Jay and Tina, Geri and Gerald, Eliza and Trent, even Gerald's parents, the duke and duchess. I have never seen any of them anything other than completely content, comfortable and blissfully happy with each other. But with you, it hurts so much to think of what you must have suffered as a child, then to lose your father after such a brief time together. It shouldn't hurt this much," she whispered, agony in every word. "Love isn't supposed to hurt."

Brand was stunned by her revelation. He thought he knew how she felt. Was sure she loved him as much as he loved her. But he was unprepared for the depth of feelings she revealed. He understood his own feelings and knew how to deal with them, but he did not know how to assuage her pain—or if it was even possible to do so.

He knew she sympathized with him, first for his past and then for the loss of his father, but the realization she felt so deeply the pain and anguish he felt as well, shook him. No one had ever attempted to share his hurt. His own feelings seemed shallow in comparison.

He tipped her face up to his. "Then we will no longer allow it to," he said. "My stepmother can no longer intrude in our lives. We will see that old wrongs are righted as best we can, then, as you said before, the suffering and hurt stop here."

Her smile brought sunshine into the library. "I shouldn't have doubted Nona." Her voice softened as she looked at him. "I've always thought of Edward in the same way I think of my brothers. I don't know what I would have done if he'd recognized my ring before you returned."

Brand chuckled. "I've thought of the same thing myself. But, I suspect somehow your great-grandmother knew what she was doing."

Felicia nodded. "Although I'm glad she was right, I wish she'd told me more." One long finger came up and stroked softly over her cheek. She leaned into the gentle caress.

"I'm glad she was right too," he murmured as he leaned closer. He kissed her again, this time allowing his passion to wash over them. His hand speared into her carefully arranged curls, spilling them down her back, scattering the pins, and threading his fingers through the spun silk. "I missed you."

"I missed you too," she gasped when she could speak again.

As Felicia gazed up at him, her eyes glowing with her love, Brand no longer doubted the forces that had brought them together. Their destiny had been nearly fifty years in the crafting, but now it was here—and complete. She had banished his fears just as he had banished hers. They were now free to live and to love.

Epilogue

July 1872
St. Ayers, Cornwall

"I see it!" The high-pitched squeal rent the quiet of the library where Brand was working with the steward, Mr. Boggs.

"He's coming!" A second voice, nearly as high and just as excited as the first, brought Felicia from the drawing room as he emerged from the second floor library to hurry downstairs.

"Is it him, Papa?" the first voice asked.

"Of course it is, silly," the second responded in a slightly disgusted tone. "Who else would be coming here in a carriage?"

Rounding on her twin brother, Caroline Waring stomped her foot and declared, "I'm not silly. You are. And, it could be anyone."

Brand stepped between the two seven-year-olds, shooting his wife a plea for help in a glance.

"Michael," Felicia chided, reaching her son just in time to prevent him from pulling one of his sister's braids. "How many times must I tell you not to call your sister names?"

"But she *is* silly," he protested. "All girls are silly."

Brand began to chuckle, but stopped at the freezing glare he received from Felicia. Reaching down instead, he picked up his daughter and headed for the front door.

"Don't believe him," he told Caroline. "He doesn't know what he's talking about." And was rewarded with an adoring look from eyes the same color as his own. "Let's go see if it is indeed Uncle Edward returning from India."

Felicia followed, holding Michael by the hand. The children

had been awaiting this day since last week when Brand had informed them their Uncle Edward was coming home. Over the years, Edward had flourished in India, rising to the rank of Major. He and Brand corresponded regularly, but it was the twins who had become his adoring fans.

She wasn't exactly sure how it had happened, except that over the years it became obvious Brand wasn't the only Waring with a gift for storytelling and Edward's many letters had become a series of stories addressed to the children, sometimes accompanied by pictures and small carved toys. Michael and Caroline had been entranced from the beginning, impatiently waiting month after month for each new installment. When Brand informed them Edward was coming home, their excitement had known no bounds.

The carriage came to a halt in front of the steps, and the coachman scrambled down to opened the door. Michael tugged his hand free and raced down the steps before she could stop him. Glancing over at Brand, she noted he was having difficulty holding Caroline, eventually giving up and setting her down to follow her brother.

"Do you suppose we'll get a chance to talk to him at all?" he asked, sliding his arm around her waist and watching the two raven-haired imps waiting impatiently for the coachman to open the door.

"Not, I suspect, until they are in bed asleep," she answered, leaning her head against his arm.

"We've waited this long, I don't suppose another few hours will hurt."

"Will you tell him everything?"

Brand was silent for a while, watching as Edward, soberly attired in a dark coat and trousers, climbed down from the carriage to greet his niece and nephew. "I think it's for the best."

"Then what?"

"Who knows. He may not be thrilled to be an Earl. As I recall, he never wanted to be a Duke." He chuckled. "Of course, he doesn't really have a choice. As far as the Queen and Parliament are concerned, he has been the Earl St. Ayers for the past three years. He just hasn't been aware of it."

Felicia said no more, her eyes on the scene unfolding at the foot of the steps. Edward had changed. His sun-browned features relaxed into the easy smile she remembered from eight years ago, but he was leaner and his brown hair now had blond streaks in it from the sun.

It had been eight years since they had seen him last—at their wedding. So much had happened in the months following that it had been nearly Christmas before Brand had written the first of many letters, and well into the Spring before they had received an answer. Afterwards correspondence had been regular, with gifts arriving for the children frequently. Even three-year-old John was excited when a package arrived from Uncle Edward.

Edward was coming up the stairs toward them, flanked by the twins. Each one held a wrapped package.

Caroline was the first to speak. "Look Mama, Uncle Edward brought us presents. May we open them now?"

"So I see. Did you thank him properly?"

"Yes," came the chorus.

"Then I suppose you may," she replied. "You'd best go find Corrie and show her your treasures."

The children ran into the house to find their governess, leaving she, Brand, and Edward on the steps.

"Welcome home," she smiled at Edward.

"Thank you, Your Grace," he replied formally, bowing over her hand. "It is good to see you again. If possible, you've grown even more beautiful."

Brand held out his hand and Edward took it, surprised when Brand drew him into an embrace. "Eliza should be here in a few weeks," he said in greeting and laughed when Edward grimaced.

Stepping into the spacious front hall, Edward stopped and looked around with interest. "I've never been here before," he said. "Papa always came here alone."

Brand looked at Felicia, an unspoken request in his eyes. She nodded and turned to go, saying, "I'd better go make sure the twins found Corrie."

Brand turned to his brother. "Come into the library and let me tell you of St. Ayers and the family it once belonged to."

Felicia watched the two of them go, pride and joy in her heart. Everything would be fine. Edward would be fine. St.

Ayers would be fine.

Brand would ensure nothing less.

Author's Note

After the Crimean War (1854-1856), Parliament was appalled at the extent of losses suffered by the British Empire and ordered an investigation into the administration of the war effort. What they discovered was there was no uniformity in the method of supplying soldiers in the field, no accountability for supplies shipped but not received, and no real chain of command when it came to orders. The last was conspicuously apparent in the Battle of Balaklava and the horror immortalized by Tennyson in his poem, "The Charge of the Light Brigade." After years of study and reports, Parliament settled on a series of reforms, one of which was the elimination of the purchasing of certain types of commissions in 1859. A complete ban was instituted in 1871.

Despite the ban, however, it was still possible to "purchase" a commission, if you knew the right people, until the First World War. In this book, Edward's father's background alone would have given him an "in" with the War Office, and his rank would have ensured they would have refused him nothing.

About the Author

To learn more about Denise Patrick, please visit www.denisepatrickauthor.com or www.denisesden.blogspot.com. You can also send an email to denisepatrick@gmail.com.

When danger lurks, is courage alone
enough to save a country—and a heart?

To Capture a Spy
© *2008 Silvia Violet*

It's not enough Meg Wentworth has suffered kidnapping, imprisonment and torture. She kept her wits about her and escaped with her life, only to be captured by a handsome British officer—and promptly accused of spying for the French. Convincing him otherwise turns out to be easier than dealing with her next discovery: that Lucien just might be the man to help her put her life back together. If only he will let go of his rigid control long enough to let her show him they belong together.

Recovering from a near-fatal injury, British intelligence officer Lucien Archer hoped to leave the shadowy, violent world that left him scarred, body and soul. But a mysterious letter calls him back to duty, and nothing prepares him for Meg. The beautiful spy's fiery spirit threatens to break through the shell Lucien has built around his heart.

But Meg's kidnapper wasn't looking for simple ransom. He's an old enemy of Lucien's, Le Lézard, who's resurfaced with a single goal. To raise magical forces dark and powerful enough to destroy England. To do it, blood must flow. The blood of Lucien and Meg.

And the fire of passion that burns between them is the perfect lure to get them both where he wants them. On an altar of sacrifice.

Warning: This book contains wickedly delicious sex and words no Regency maiden should know.

Available now in ebook and print from Samhain Publishing.

Enjoy the following excerpt from To Capture a Spy...

Lucien Archer shifted position for what seemed like the thousandth time. The dirty blanket and lumpy sack that made up his bed weren't the problem. He'd slept in much worse conditions as an officer in Wellington's army, and he was used to staying in filthy cottages when he was out gathering information. In fact, he was lucky a safe house for British agents stood so close to where he'd found the woman. At least he had food and other necessary supplies.

The unfortunate source of his restlessness was the woman who lay across the room. He didn't know her real name. His contacts had told him that she'd introduced herself most recently as Annette Dubois, but she'd been known by many names in the last few years. She'd nearly convinced him of her innocence, but he'd been warned that she was good at what she did.

What had happened to make her run tonight? Had she quarreled with *Le Lézard*, refused to do his bidding? The rope burns on her arms, and the hint of bruises on her face, showed that someone had tried to subdue her.

He tried to calm his mind enough to allow the light, watchful sleep of a man on guard, but he kept thinking about how the woman had looked facing him across the cabin. She was stunning despite her hair twisting out from her braid in wild wisps, her skin ghostly pale from her ordeal, and her face bearing the faint traces of a beating. His contacts had been right. She was beautiful enough to make a man turn traitor. He could easily imagine a weaker man spilling his darkest secrets for a chance to be with her.

She was nothing like the woman he'd envisioned. He'd expected a cold, hardened beauty, but this woman was fresh, vibrant. Based on her history, she had to be at least thirty, but she looked ten years younger. Her body was full and curvaceous, yet she had an air of innocence and skin like fine china. Her hands were unbelievably soft and smooth. His senses had revolted at the red marks he'd seen there. He'd never used violence against women to extract information from female contacts, and he never would.

With a soft growl, he ground the heels of his hands into his eyes. What the hell was wrong with him? The information this woman had passed resulted in the deaths of hundreds of British soldiers, including most of his own regiment. Men like Geordie, who bought his commission one week before he'd died at age nineteen, and Lloyd, one of his friends from Eton, who'd been stabbed in his sleep. He shouldn't care whether her skin stayed lovely. He should want her to pay. Could he bring himself to extract information from her by any means necessary? He prayed she would give in to his demands before his ethics came into question.

How could she look so innocent and still have power over him? He'd expected her to attempt seduction, but he'd been unprepared for her subtlety. She made him want to hold her and kiss away the fear in her eyes. He was definitely going to have to keep his distance.

Across the room, the bed creaked. He jerked upright.

"No! Don't touch me!" the woman yelled as she kicked the wall. "I won't do it!"

Lucien rushed to the lantern and lit it as she screamed again. She jerked at the ropes, struggling to free her hands, but her eyes were closed. She was dreaming.

"I won't let you touch me!" she cried.

What had that monster done to her? In that moment, Lucien didn't care who she was. No one deserved to be tormented like that.

He moved to her side and saw blood seeping through the cloth around her wrist. What should he do? How could he wake her without scaring her more?

She screamed again—a high-pitched sound he felt all the way to his bones.

Placing his hand lightly on her leg, he called, "Annette, wake up. Wake up. You're dreaming." When she didn't wake, he pressed harder, shaking her gently. "Annette! Wake up!"

Her eyes fluttered open. She pulled back when she saw him.

"I won't hurt you."

Her hair was damp with sweat and her deep, brown eyes were unfocused. He wasn't sure she'd heard him. She glanced down, and the last bit of color drained from her face. His eyes followed hers, seeing her bloody wrists. "Do you remember where you are?"

She nodded.

"Don't move. I'll get a knife and cut you free." Reluctant to leave her side, Lucien backed away slowly. He pulled a knife and his medical supplies from his saddlebag. Annette watched him warily but didn't speak.

As he approached the bed, she whimpered and tried to scoot away. "I don't want to hurt you, but I need to loosen these ropes so I can bandage your wrists."

"My name isn't Annette."

"Then what should I call you?"

She stared at him for a few seconds before responding. "Meg."

"I'm Lucien." He immediately cursed himself for giving her his real name. He'd been in intelligence for years, and he was acting like a green recruit. Still it felt good to simply be himself. It had been too long since he'd shared that intimacy with anyone. "Hold your hands apart, so I can cut the ropes."

She obeyed, not letting out so much as a whimper while he cut her free. He doubted he could loosen the cloth as easily. "This will probably hurt." He began to pull the fabric from her wrists. It stuck to the wounds in several places, but she didn't make a sound.

He finished and stepped back. Her teeth were sunk into her lower lip, and she was trembling. He feared she might faint at any moment. "Lie down. I'm going outside to get some water to clean your wounds. Will you give me your word that you will stay here?"

A simple nod was all the answer he got, but he decided to risk it. In her weakened state, she wouldn't get far if she tried to escape.

When he returned, she was lying down with her eyes closed. They opened at the noise of his approach, and he saw a flash of fear before recognition set in.

"I can bandage myself. I don't need your help." She reached for the bowl he'd filled with water.

He held it firmly. "I'll do it. Your arms are shaking. When was your last meal?"

"I don't know, but I can take care of myself."

"No you can't. You're too damn weak. I've always treated prisoners better than the French apparently treat their spies."

"Why are you concerned about me if you believe I'm working for *Le Lézard*?"

He was wondering the same damn thing. Hardly aware of his actions, he reached out and traced the faint remainder of a bruise on her face. "I don't like to see women brutalized. If you tell me what I need to know, I'll see that you aren't hurt anymore."

She relinquished her hold on the bowl. He wet a rag and washed her wrists, working as gently as he could, but when he reached one of the deeper gashes, she sucked in her breath.

He looked up. That was a mistake.

As she'd struggled in the throes of her nightmare, her dress had worked its way down, and her full breasts threatened to spill out. He forced himself to look at her face, but he couldn't stop his response.

The blush on her cheeks told him she knew what he'd been looking at, but she didn't say anything as he finished his ministrations, applying some salve to soothe the wounds and wrapping her wrists with bandages. Her color had yet to return. He ordered her to lie down before she passed out.

He walked to the window and stood, pondering his predicament. He couldn't bring himself to tie her wrists again, but he couldn't trust her not to run if he left her unrestrained. He found himself wanting to believe her, wanting her to be anyone but the woman he sought.

GET IT NOW

MyBookStoreAndMore.com

GREAT EBOOKS, GREAT DEALS . . . AND MORE!

Don't wait to run to the bookstore down the street, or waste time shopping online at one of the "big boys." Now, all your favorite Samhain authors are all in one place—at MyBookStoreAndMore.com. Stop by today and discover great deals on Samhain—and a whole lot more!

Samhain publishing ltd

WWW.SAMHAINPUBLISHING.COM

GREAT CHEAP FUN

Discover eBooks!

THE FASTEST WAY TO GET THE HOTTEST NAMES

Get your favorite authors on your favorite reader, long before they're out in print! Ebooks from Samhain go wherever you go, and work with whatever you carry—Palm, PDF, Mobi, and more.

Samhain
publishing ltd

WWW.SAMHAINPUBLISHING.COM

Printed in the United States
217046BV00001B/29/P